Emily e̶ [̶ closed the door behind her, then padded down the dimly lit hallway.

She stopped. What if Jared no longer wanted her after her rejection?

She knocked on his door, but entered before he answered.

The room was dark, except for the glowing ash on the tip of his cigar. He had to be sitting in a chair, in the corner. She couldn't see him, but her fingers itched to measure his broad shoulders, count the ribs under firm pectorals, knit into his silky hair and never let go.

"Do you know," he asked flatly, "the light from the hall seeps right through your nightgown?"

Stung by a decided lack of emotion in his voice, Emily realized he was angry.

"It was very unfair of me to compare you to Ben. I'm sorry."

"Okay, so you've apologized. Now go back to bed."

Emily almost turned to obey the command. But she'd come too far to retreat. Slowly, she reached behind her and closed the door....

Dear Reader,

Every year at this time, the editors at Harlequin Historicals have the unique opportunity of introducing our readers to four brand-new authors in our annual March Madness Promotion. These titles were chosen from among hundreds of manuscripts from unpublished authors, and we would like to take this time to thank all of the talented authors who made the effort to submit their projects to Harlequin Historicals for review.

The hero of *Emily's Captain* by Shari Anton, Jared Hunter, has been sent to Georgia, posing as a Confederate soldier, to rescue the daughter of his commanding officer, but the dashing captain soon discovers that deceiving Emily Gardner is the most difficult assignment of his career. In *The Phoenix of Love* by Susan Schonberg, a Regency novel about an unusual marriage of convenience, a reformed rake and a society ice princess must overcome tortured pasts and present enemies before they are free to love. *The Wicked Truth* by Lyn Stone, about a woman with a ruined reputation and a straitlaced physician who join forces to discover a murderer in Victorian England, was a second-place finisher in the 1995 Maggie Awards.

Heart of the Dragon by Sharon Schulze, the medieval tale of a young woman searching for her identity with the help of a fierce warrior, completes this month's lineup of terrific titles.

Whatever your taste in reading, we hope you'll find a story written just for you between the covers of a Harlequin Historical.

Sincerely,

Tracy Farrell
Senior Editor

Please address questions and book requests to:
Harlequin Reader Service
U.S.: 3010 Walden Ave., P.O. Box 1325, Buffalo, NY 14269
Canadian: P.O. Box 609, Fort Erie, Ont. L2A 5X3

SHARI ANTON

Emily's Captain

Harlequin Books

TORONTO • NEW YORK • LONDON
AMSTERDAM • PARIS • SYDNEY • HAMBURG
STOCKHOLM • ATHENS • TOKYO • MILAN
MADRID • WARSAW • BUDAPEST • AUCKLAND

ISBN 0-373-28957-X

EMILY'S CAPTAIN

Copyright © 1997 by Sharon Antoniewicz

Printed in U.S.A.

SHARI ANTON's

fascination with history has led to several interesting vacations—to Civil War reenactments, medieval fairs and pioneer cemeteries, to name a few. Oddly enough, she never lacks for company on these trips, because her husband of twenty-five years doesn't mind where they go, especially if they can ride their Harleys to get there. The mother of two grown children, Shari lives in southeastern Wisconsin. She enjoys reading and needlepoint, and shamelessly spoils her golden retriever. She is also an active and proud member of WisRWA.

To the loves of my life:
Jim
Denise and Ron
Thank you for believing

Chapter One

Adairsville, Georgia
May 16, 1864

"**W**here the hell is she?" Captain Jared Randall Hunter grumbled to the descending dusk. He snapped shut his gold pocket watch and slid the keepsake into his trousers pocket. From habit, he reached beneath the ill-fitting gray uniform coat for a cigar, then decided to abstain. The glow of a burning cheroot might alert someone to his surveillance site.

He glanced north, distracted by a distant burst of cannon fire that bounced through the Appalachian Mountains of northwest Georgia. Fighting had eased within the past hour, as the Union army prepared to bivouac for the night, holding its elevated position. If the Confederates kept to recent tactics, they would use the cover of darkness to retreat south a few miles and dig in again. The Rebs might slow the Yankee advance, but—lacking men and firepower—they hadn't a prayer of stopping the Union army from capturing Adairsville.

The townspeople had either sensed or been warned of the impending defeat. From this wooded knoll on the edge of town, where he could observe Miss Gardner's house, he'd spent the afternoon watching a trickle of refugees leave town. Many walked, carrying carpetbags. Others rode in wagons burdened with baggage and furniture. Those who had nowhere else to go, would stay in their homes and pray for Yankee benevolence.

Emily Gardner's house seemed abandoned, but feminine clothing fluttered from a rope strung between the house and a small oak. Confident that the sign of everyday routine ensured her return, Jared waited, though he couldn't wait much longer. He wanted to be as far from town as possible before the battle ignited in the morning. Problem was, the object of tonight's mission wasn't cooperating. She wasn't home.

At the sound of a galloping horse, Jared shifted to see around a stand of pines. He came to full alert when a man rode up, dismounted and led the horse through the side gate, near a shelter behind Miss Gardner's house. A few minutes later, the man sprinted back across the yard, yanked the clothes off the line, then entered the house through a side door.

Mentally flipping through possibilities, Jared accounted for the known males in Miss Gardner's life. Her brother and a former fiancé were both reportedly in North Carolina with their Confederate cavalry unit. Neither should be visiting Emily. Her father, Colonel John Gardner, was definitely in Washington, the Union capital, anxiously awaiting word from Jared.

Had Emily Gardner recently married? Or taken a lover?

Jared ran a hand through his shoulder-length brown hair, wondering if he should wire her father for instructions. But Colonel Gardner's guilt-laden worry had prompted this unofficial mission. Having learned from coincidental information in an intelligence report that Emily was alone in Adairsville, in the path of a Union invasion, the colonel had asked Jared Hunter to fetch his daughter—actually, to kidnap his daughter—and bring her north. No, a message to the colonel about this complication would only burden an already distraught father.

Flickering light now danced from a downstairs window, probably from a hearth in the parlor. A few minutes later, someone lit a lamp on the second floor. As he watched the upper window, to Jared Hunter's amazement, a woman appeared.

She had to be Emily Gardner.

From this distance, he couldn't see her face, could only see a female in a prim white nightgown, her dark hair flowing down over her shoulders. She turned her head right, then left, as though watching for someone on the road. The ethereal quality of the vision enchanted him, and the strong protective rush he felt surprised him, until he realized he *should* feel protective. She was his mission. He would guard Emily with his life, if necessary, until he delivered her to the colonel.

Strange, though, that Emily was in the house. The house had appeared unoccupied.

She closed the curtains. The jolt of her disappearance allowed him to refocus on how to accomplish his mission— if he still had a mission.

Jared searched his saddlebags for Emily's picture and a piece of jerky. He again studied the picture he'd pulled out often on the trip south. The picture dated back three years, taken before the war. Sausage curls framed Emily's pixie face. Dark eyes sparked with impending mischief. The jut of her chin suggested a stubborn nature.

Colonel Gardner had reluctantly relinquished the picture to Jared during a late-night planning session in the colonel's office.

"Are you sure she won't come with me willingly, if I explain who I am and that you've sent me to fetch her?" Jared had asked his worried commander.

Colonel Gardner had run a hand through graying hair. The silver strands were a result of a Southern heart in conflict with a Northern conscience. Jared empathized. His own decision to remain in the Union army hadn't been easy.

"I'm sure Emily blames me for her predicament," the colonel had said. "I was the first to abandon her, though I didn't know it at the time. I thought she would marry Lewis Roth and spend the duration of the war at Twin Pines, the Roths' mansion. I'm afraid you'll have to force her to come north, to her Yankee father."

Jared bit off a chunk of jerky and discarded his plans for a late-night kidnapping. He hated abrupt changes of strategy, knowing from experience that the practice was unwise. However, his victim had company, male company, and that made revision necessary.

He glanced at the upstairs window. The light had gone out. Emily must be in bed, with that man, whoever he was—husband or lover.

Would passion flare in the upstairs bedroom? Would the man's hand slide under the prim nightgown, stroke her breasts and between her thighs until Emily begged for release? Would the man take her to her zenith? Would she cry out?

A tightening in his groin shook Jared from his musings. Shoving the ignoble thoughts aside, he buried Emily's picture deep in his bag. At daybreak, he decided, he would scout the house, and on some pretext, talk to Emily Gardner. Any further course of action would depend on her answers.

If Emily Gardner had married, Jared wouldn't remove her from Adairsville. With a clear conscience, he could leave her in a husband's care, return to Washington and ease Colonel Gardner's guilt over his daughter's well-being.

Jared spread his bedroll, the thought of abandoning this mission becoming more and more appealing.

* * *

Rising with the sun, Emily slipped into her dressing gown and pushed aside the bedroom window curtain. In vain, she scanned the road for a lanky Negro driving a cart.

She briefly considered remaining in Adairsville another day to wait for Sam, but she might have waited too long already. If not for Rusty, a treasured Thoroughbred mare, she might consider waiting still longer for her brother's slave, who'd been scheduled to arrive two days ago with supplies. But the mare was a prize the Yanks couldn't have, and from what she'd seen yesterday, the Yanks would soon overrun the town.

She should have left yesterday. Instead, she'd ridden into the mountains to gather personal items from the abandoned shack that had served as a refuge from the glares of the townspeople, who'd unjustly labeled her a spy. At first she'd fought their suspicion that she spied for the Union, that she sent messages to her Yankee father. Unable to sway opinion, she'd stopped proclaiming her innocence and sought escape.

Yesterday she'd seen the Yanks she'd been accused of aiding swarming through the mountains like ants over an open picnic hamper. Only by sheer luck and a thorough knowledge of her surroundings had she avoided Yankee patrols.

If she didn't leave today, some enterprising Union officer would seize Rusty as a battle trophy.

Emily ran a quick brush through her hair before going downstairs. In the parlor, she checked the clothing she'd left drying over a chair in front of the now cool hearth. The trousers' waistband was moist, and the shirt's cuffs were damp, but both garments had dried enough to wear.

A light breakfast helped calm a stomach quivering with anticipation. Nibbling on a heel of bread, she inspected the saddlebags lying on the kitchen table. Ammunition for her shotgun filled one bag, and in the other she would pack food.

She was going home! How ironic that the Yankees had provided an excuse to leave Adairsville that even her brother couldn't criticize. Two years ago, when forming his cavalry unit, Terrance had thought it prudent for her to leave the family's country estate, Rosewood, and live in town. His reasoning had sounded wise at the time. Of course, neither of them had suspected that she would be accused of spying for the Union, that friends would shun her for fear of suffering the taint of the traitor.

At a knock on the front door, Emily smiled, thinking Sam had finally arrived. Then her smile faded. Sam never used the front door. He always drove the wagon into the side yard and used the kitchen door.

Puzzled, Emily moved to the parlor window and pushed aside the drape. A Confederate officer stood on the stoop.

She let the drape fall. The knock came again, more insistent. Could the officer be from Terrance's cavalry unit? If so, she didn't want to open the door. As much as she'd grown to dislike her brother, she didn't want to hear that he'd been wounded, or worse.

Coward. Emily squared her shoulders and opened the door. The officer, his hand poised to knock again, was clearly annoyed by the delayed answer to his summons. Emily watched his arresting features smooth as irritation melted into appraisal, his gaze skimming over her in flagrant assessment. He clearly liked what he saw.

Even as caution sprouted at his insolence, she felt the thrill of his boldness, and for just a moment, Emily basked in the hypnotic lure of the officer's dark-as-midnight eyes. Over six feet tall, from the top of his rakishly angled hat to the tips of his dusty boots he exuded masculinity.

His face and hands glowed with the deep tan of a man who spent his life outdoors. Broad shoulders strained the seams of his uniform coat, whose sleeves barely covered his wrists. Deep brown, almost black, hair wanted trimming, a lock of which rested on a high, noble forehead.

Then artillery roared from the mountainside, warning of a new day's battle. But instead of yesterday's far-off turbulence, today each burst from the cannons jabbed sharp, distinct. The Yankees were closer to town. She must flee.

Emily glanced at his collar. One stripe slashed through the yellow background that labeled him cavalry. "Is there something I can do for you, Lieutenant?"

Jared knew the genteel greeting wasn't an invitation, but then, he wasn't feeling gentlemanly. In fact, it took an inordinate amount of willpower for him not to say yes, she could take him up to her bedroom and do with him as she pleased.

The reaction, undoubtedly, stemmed from last night's wayward thoughts and subsequent dreams. His musings on her exploits in bed hadn't ended upon his falling asleep. When he woke this morning, he'd told himself that reality never measured up to fantasy. He'd been wrong. She looked utterly regal, and damn enticing, despite the frayed green wrapper, with her prim, buttoned-to-the-neck white nightgown peeking from beneath.

In his dreams, Emily had worn the pixie face from the picture. The woman before him bore only the faintest resemblance to a pixie. Shiny brown hair flecked with red highlights framed her face. Her skin was a creamy white across her smooth brow, over high cheekbones and around a delicate yet firm chin. Doe-soft brown eyes peered from under velvety lashes. No mischief sparked those eyes. A shame, that. Three years had etched maturity into her face and added fullness to her figure. Emily's stunning beauty could bring a man to his knees.

"The name's Randall, ma'am, Jared Randall," he said, removing his slouch hat. "I was on my way out of town when I noticed the fine piece of horseflesh you have in back. I was hoping to speak with the owner, find out if she's for sale."

Her body stiffened. "The mare is not for sale. Rusty belongs to my brother. He is cavalry, like yourself. I keep the mare in reserve, should he lose his stallion."

Jared silently congratulated himself. He'd guessed right

about the horse, at least. The mare was indeed a fine animal, one of Colonel Gardner's prize Thoroughbreds, a
horse the colonel would be delighted to see again.

"My loss, but understandable," Jared said, then glanced
north. "Others, however, might not be so understanding.
As I'm sure you are aware, Mrs.—?"

"Miss," she said. "Miss Emily Gardner."

No husband. That meant the man he'd seen enter Emily's
house last night was only a lover, and probably no longer
in the house, having left before daylight to protect the lady's reputation.

Jared smiled. "Pretty name—Emily."

Emily couldn't help but return the officer's charming
smile. "Thank you."

A cart rumbled by, loaded with furniture, crates and people. Emily flushed with embarrassment at the disgust evi-
dent on Mrs. Potter's face. Naturally, the county's biggest
gossip *would* pass her door. The news would spread that
Emily Gardner had entertained a man at her front door, in
her nightclothes. Never mind that Mrs. Potter was leaving
town, or that the Yankees were poised to overrun Adairsville. Mrs. Potter would efficiently transmit the tale.

"It seems I'm the unwitting cause of a dent in your reputation," the soldier commented.

Emily almost laughed. Most people in town already
thought her a spy, and would now label her a harlot. To
her surprise, Emily found that the injustice of their condemnation no longer mattered. She was going home. To
hell with them all.

"My reputation, Lieutenant, is the least of my worries.
If you will excuse me, I have preparations to make."

"That is precisely what I want to talk to you about. It
might be prudent if we finish this conversation inside."

Another wagon rolled into view. Emily stepped back,
into the shadows of the doorway. The soldier took a step
forward.

"We have nothing to discuss, Lieutenant. My horse is not for sale," she said with growing nervousness.

"So you said."

"Really, sir, this is most improper. I'm not dressed."

"I noticed. I will, of course, have to insist that you not try to seduce me."

"Of all the outrageous, insulting..." she sputtered.

"Are we to have our first quarrel on the stoop, for the whole town to hear?"

Emily stepped back, intending to slam the door in the persistent officer's face. The door wouldn't budge, blocked by his muscular leg, encased in a calf-hugging black boot.

She glared. He smiled knowingly and shrugged.

Outraged, Emily pursed her lips and drew a deep breath. His arm shot out, wrapping around her waist. Air drawn to hurl scathing words blew out as she collided with his unyielding frame. The door slammed shut.

Fear flashed. She pushed against his chest, but he didn't move, not an inch.

"Let...me...go!"

"Only if you promise not to scream or go running into the street," he declared, in such a reasonable tone that her fear ebbed.

She looked up. He was smiling, the cad.

"I promise you nothing, Lieutenant."

His smile widened. "Then what if I make a promise first? I won't hurt you. In my entire life, I've never knowingly hurt a woman, and I don't intend to start now."

"And I'm supposed to believe that?"

"Yes, ma'am."

From the soft, slow drawl of his *ma'am,* she guessed at his birthplace. Southwest. A Texan? If so, he belonged to one of several companies the generals ordered forth when a battle seemed hopelessly lost. Newspaper reporters had described the Texans as deadly shots, bold, tenacious, fearless and strong.

Lieutenant Randall fit the description. He was certainly

strong. With one arm in a viselike hold around her waist, he held her so tightly she couldn't move, could barely breathe, much less scream. A firm hold, indeed, but not painful. And though his methods of getting his way were anything but gentlemanly, she sensed no threat of physical harm. She believed his promise.

She'd never been this close to a man before—close enough to catch a whiff of tobacco mingled with leather, the earthy aromas blending with the tang of a fresh spring breeze. She could feel his chest rise and fall, and with each breath a wisp of air teased her ear. She could see the faint shadow of a dark beard, though he'd recently shaved. The warmth flowing through her limbs, clear down to her bare toes, had nothing to do with her now vanished fear, or her waning anger, or the mounting heat of the day.

Agreeing to his terms might be the quickest path to freedom. Besides, even if she screamed, she doubted anyone would rush off Adairsville's streets to her aid.

Her voice thready, she said, "Ladies don't scream. Ladies heap indignities on gentlemen's heads to remind them of their manners. And you, sir, definitely need a lesson in how to treat a lady."

He loosened his hold, tilting his head. "You were about to call me several vile names?" he asked, humor coloring his words.

"Not vulgar, sir, merely pointed."

"You can now, if you still want to," he offered.

This time, when she pushed against his chest, he let her go. Emily tried to recall one of the several warranted slurs, but without the anger to sustain them, none survived. Maybe he *could* be a gentleman.

"A futile effort at this point, I would think. Nor do I have the time." She waved toward the door. "I would be obliged, Lieutenant, if you would take your leave now. Surely you have something more urgent to do than pester me."

"If you will remember, Miss Gardner, we were discussing your horse. I was about to point out that others, especially the Yankees, may have an interest in her,'' he said.

"I was aware of that, sir, before you knocked on my door. No Yank will ever touch Rusty. As soon as I finish packing, I'm leaving.''

He smiled widely. "Are you nearly finished?''

"Yes.''

"Good. I'll saddle Rusty and meet you out back.''

Lieutenant Randall sped out the door before she could protest. She reached for the doorknob, then stopped. She would *not* run into the yard in her nightclothes!

Then she smiled. Let Lieutenant Randall *attempt* to saddle the mare. If Rusty reacted true to form, the mare would give that brash lieutenant another lesson in how to treat a lady.

Chapter Two

"You know what, Rusty? I'd be willing to give odds she's headed for Rosewood," Jared said in a mellow voice. Though attuned to the sounds of the approaching battle, he purposely moved slowly and spoke softly to calm the mare.

Soothing a skittish mount revived memories of his parents' ranch in the Arizona Territory. Often during the war, especially lately, he'd considered resigning his commission and going home. He longed for the brilliance of southwestern sunshine, for the peace and dry heat of parched desert near the rugged canyon homeland of the Navajo.

But then some interesting or vital assignment would come his way. Using the code name Cougar, he'd accepted the challenge of blowing up railroad trestles and ammunition depots. He'd braved the danger of skulking into Southern cities to gather information from other Union operatives. Several times he'd served as a scout before a big battle. Often, easier assignments balanced out the difficult ones. Like serving as bodyguard to President or Mrs. Lincoln, or going to fetch Emily Gardner.

"I'm not averse to seeing Rosewood. John might like to know how the place fares," he continued, tossing the blanket over the mare. "The detour will add a few days to our trip. Not that you can't handle it. You're in great shape."

He ran an appreciative hand over the mare's flank. Firm

muscle flexed under his palm. The roan's hide glimmered
from recent grooming. The stall was clean and the tack in
good repair. Did the burden of Rusty's care fall to Emily,
or was labor the price her lover paid to use the horse?

Jared removed the bridle from a wood peg, then patted
Rusty's neck and rubbed her velvet nose. "Behave yourself, and I'll treat you to a rubdown later. That's it, easy
now."

Rusty tossed her head and pawed at the ground, but
eventually accepted the bridle.

"Object to a stranger handling you, do you? Can't say
as I blame you. If I had a mistress as pretty as Emily, I
wouldn't want anyone else handling me, either."

The innuendo gave him pause. He shook it off.

Jared heaved the saddle onto the mare's back. "I wish
you could talk. I have a dozen questions I'm sure you could
answer, like why doesn't Emily own a sidesaddle? And
who was the guy riding you last night? He can't be taller
than Emily. There's only one worn hole in this strap, so he
doesn't adjust the stirrups."

*Why is Emily here, alone? Why had a very proper South-
ern miss taken a lover?* And why the hell should that bother
him?

Jared inspected the girth strap, noting another wear mark.
"No, you don't," he scolded. He put his knee into Rusty's
side, forced her to exhale, then tightened the strap.
"Wouldn't want the saddle to slide, now, would we?
Wouldn't want Emily's lovely backside to hit the ground."

His flexing hands itched to assess the firmness of Emily's
lovely backside. His fingers had already surveyed the curve
of her spine and the circle of her waist.

Cougar often used outrageous, sometimes vile, tactics to
complete missions. Hailed as hero or lowlife scum, depending upon which army made the observation, Cougar
deceived, stole, manipulated, even killed when left no
choice.

Cougar had decided to step into Emily's house, to silence

her impending scream with an effective maneuver. Jared
Hunter, however, had held on to Emily longer than necessary. He'd known the exact second when her fear eased
and she decided not to physically fight, when her body
relaxed against his, becoming soft and pliant.

The mare shifted, pawing. Rusty's agitation stemmed
from more than having a stranger in her stall. The cannon
fire roared, getting closer. While Rusty might wear the trap-
pings of a cavalry mount, she wasn't battle-trained.

He ran a hand down the mare's neck. "Maybe after Emily sees Rosewood, she'll listen to other options. I'll just
have to suggest them until she wants to go where I want
her to go."

While he was at it, he'd best remember to keep his distance, remember that Emily Gardner was the daughter of
his commanding officer. The colonel would roast Cougar's
ass if Jared Hunter got out of line with Emily.

Over a double layer of petticoats, Emily put on the black
riding outfit she hadn't worn in months. The bodice was
tight, and the seat of the skirt had faded to gray. Hopefully,
the seat of the skirt wouldn't split open before she had a
chance to change, later, when out of town, far from enemy
guns and the unsettling presence of Lieutenant Randall.

At the bottom of her satchel she placed a peach jacket
bodice and skirt, the only decent ensemble that remained
of a once vast wardrobe. On top of it she tossed Terrance's
old trousers and shirt, and a nightgown. She shoved in her
hairbrush, then a cake of lilac-scented soap wrapped in a
towel. From the toe of an old boot in the corner of the
wardrobe, she retrieved a leather pouch. The gold coins
within jingled. She debated whether to carry the pouch or
pack it. Deciding she didn't want to jingle as she walked,
or rode, she buried the pouch in the satchel.

She quickly braided her hair and pinned the thick coil
into a tight coronet atop her head. Ready.

Downstairs, heavy boots struck the wood floor in the

kitchen. Lieutenant Randall. She shivered. The episode this morning had been disconcerting. Her whole body still tingled—with revulsion or delight, she wasn't sure—from being held so intimately. Not even Lewis Roth, to whom she'd been engaged, had held her quite so close, so close she could barely breathe, so close she tingled from the current sparked by his touch.

Half an hour in the saddle should cure the strange sensation. Emily grabbed her satchel and headed downstairs.

Meager pickings, Jared judged the supplies on the kitchen table. A slab of bacon. A sack of flour. A round tin of, what? Jared opened the tin and beamed at the contents. He snatched up two of the molasses cookies.

He picked up the double-barreled shotgun and snapped it open. Loaded. He removed the shells, put the shotgun back on the table and inspected the packs. One empty—the other bulged with shells. He tossed in the shells from the shotgun and closed the flap.

As he bit into the second cookie, Emily appeared in the doorway. Never one to notice a woman's clothing beyond what a low neckline exposed, Jared hated the black outfit on sight. And her hair! Much too severe, he judged, for a girl of nineteen.

"You bake a mean molasses cookie, Miss Gardner."

"Take more, if you like. I only made them to use up the molasses."

"Is this all the food you're taking?"

"This will last until I get home." She stuffed the food into the pack and buckled it shut. "I guess this is goodbye, Lieutenant. I hope you understand why I can't let you buy Rusty."

"I understand completely, ma'am. She sure is a beauty, though a bit high-strung."

She smiled, smugly. "Rusty's gentle, in the right hands."

"This gunfire isn't helping her disposition any. I'll take

these," Jared offered, beating her reach for the shotgun and saddlebags.

Emily picked up her satchel and followed. Halfway across the yard she stopped, dropped the satchel, and ran back toward the house.

"Where are you going?" Jared shouted from the horse shed.

"The portrait," she called over her shoulder.

Jared bit back a curse and arranged the saddlebags and shotgun on Rusty before returning to the house. He found Emily in the parlor, standing precariously on a wooden chair. With both hands on the frame, she could tilt the portrait that hung above the fireplace but not lift it off the hanger. Jared grabbed Emily around the waist. Startled, she twisted and put her hand on his shoulder.

"You'll break your fool neck," he chastised.

"I must take it down," she insisted.

"And do what with it?"

"There's a cellar under the kitchen. Please—" her voice broke "—this is the only piece in this house I value. They can have everything else, but not the portrait."

Jared softened his voice. "If someone searches the house for valuables, they won't overlook the cellar."

Emily looked up at her parents. Hiding the portrait might be a waste of time, but leaving it out in the open was unthinkable. If the town's residents saw the portrait, they might destroy the only image she possessed of her late mother to spite Papa.

"Emily?"

Those dark-as-midnight eyes of his had turned soft, and she liked the way he said her name, just above a whisper.

"I'll take it down," he said. "Get out of my way."

In her haste to comply, she moved quickly, forgetting her unstable perch. The chair wobbled. She lost her balance and instinctively threw her arms around the officer's neck. The chair crashed to the floor, but her body stayed afloat, encircled by strong arms.

Oh, dear, not again! She hadn't stopped tingling from the last time she abruptly found herself in his arms. Until she could regain her poise, she hid her face against his shoulder.

"A blanket," she muttered.

"What?" He sounded confused.

"A blanket," she repeated, louder. "I'll get a blanket to wrap around the portrait."

He lowered her to her feet. Emily broke away and scrambled up the stairs.

Jared shook his head. Keeping his distance from Emily might not prove easy. He drew a resolve-setting breath and glanced about the parlor, grimacing at the contrast of wealth amid poverty.

A gold damask chair and sofa clashed painfully with a threadbare carpet. Bookcases of oak stuffed with leather-bound volumes flanked a fireplace in need of repair. A crystal vase brimming with daisies graced a mahogany table, the spindle legs of which straddled a dark stain.

Of the rich furnishings, likely hauled from Rosewood, Emily cherished the portrait above the mantel. Jared easily deduced her reasoning. Within a gilt frame sat a serene John Gardner. Had the image of John been older, Jared would have sworn the woman hovering near John's shoulder was Emily. But the woman must be Emily's mother, Mary Beth, John's late wife. No wonder John hadn't remarried. What woman could compete with that stunning beauty— except her daughter, Emily?

Jared removed the portrait from the place of honor and took it into the kitchen.

Moments later, Emily dashed into the kitchen, out of breath, clutching blankets to her midriff. She looked down at the portrait with love in her eyes.

"My parents," she said softly.

Jared glanced at her, then looked back at the portrait. "You look very much like your mother."

She didn't acknowledge the compliment.

Lowering the painting into the cellar took twisting and turning—and sweat on Jared's part. The portrait safely tucked into a corner, he asked from the hole in the ground, "What about the books?"

"No," she said with regret. "There isn't time. If Sam were here, I might consider taking some with me. But without the cart…"

Sam. So that was her lover's name. *Too bad, pal. She's mine now.* Well, she was his, to care for until they reached Washington and John Gardner.

A blast shook the house, rattling the windows. Emily covered her ears as Jared climbed the ladder.

"What *is* that gun?" Emily shouted.

"It's called a mortar," he told her, then closed the cellar door and dusted off his hands. "The beast is so big they haul it around on rails, on a flatcar."

"Ours?" Emily asked, lowering her hands.

"Yankee. Let's get out of here before they fire it again." He cupped her elbow and pushed her toward the door.

Emily scooped up her satchel as they dashed through the yard. She entered the shelter and gaped at Rusty.

"I have a way with females," Jared said, grinning.

"I'll just bet you do," Emily wryly acknowledged. She should be grateful the mare was ready to ride. Instead, she felt betrayed—by a horse.

He held the cheek strap while she mounted.

"I'll open the gate," he said. "Hold on tight, in case that cannon goes off again."

"Lieutenant Randall? Thank you for helping me with the portrait."

"You're welcome, ma'am. Ready?"

He didn't wait for a reply. He ran for the gate as Emily guided the mare out of the shelter. Pushing the gate open, he put two fingers in his mouth and whistled. As she approached him, so did a chestnut gelding, loaded down with saddlebags, a large bedroll, and a rifle in a saddle scabbard.

"You have a horse!" Emily exclaimed.

"What made you think I didn't?" he asked, swinging into the saddle.

"When you asked to buy Rusty, I assumed you needed a mount to rejoin your unit."

Jared shook his head, explaining, "I have a long ride ahead of me. I saw Rusty and thought it a good idea to buy her, to spell my own."

"You're not going back, then, to the fighting?"

"No."

The mortar bellowed, and Rusty reared. Emily held her seat, but just barely.

"Which way?" he yelled through the deafening echo.

Emily pointed at the road east.

"Good choice of direction, but take the path through the woods. We'll make better time if we avoid crowded roads."

Oh, no, not we! That wasn't her plan, at all!

"Lieutenant, I know you mean well, and I don't wish to be rude, but—"

"Move!"

Emily wheeled Rusty and shot down the path, berating herself for obeying the command. Lieutenant Randall possessed the annoying male trait of barking orders; an asset in an officer commanding troops, but she wasn't one of his underlings!

She nudged Rusty into a gallop, and for a couple of miles raced through the woods, hoping Lieutenant Randall would take the hint and back off. He didn't. Over the thud of Rusty's hooves, she could hear the gelding at her heels.

Finally conceding that she couldn't shake Randall, and in deference to the horses, Emily slowed to a canter until she reached a brook. Since she planned to cover over thirty miles today, she stopped to let Rusty rest.

Jared blew out a relieved breath. If they'd ridden at this pace much longer, his heart would have found permanent lodging in his throat. He'd cringed every time she took a sharp curve, sure she would slam into a tree. He'd held his breath when she jumped a log blocking the path, praying Rusty wouldn't balk and throw her rider.

Why so fast? Was she trying to put distance between Rusty and the mortar? Or was she trying to lose him? She'd never looked back, not once, to see if he still followed. Of course, if she had, he probably would have succumbed to heart failure.

"We can slow down now," he stated. "We're far enough away from the guns."

She nodded, though she glanced back over her shoulder at the mountains. She obviously didn't agree.

"How far does this path follow the road?" he asked.

Her eyes narrowed, and her brow furrowed in thought. "I haven't taken this path in years." At his raised eyebrow, she shrugged. "I prefer riding in the mountains. If I remember correctly, the path comes out not too far from Canton."

Jared closed his eyes for a moment, holding back a stern lecture on her reckless behavior in taking an unfamiliar path at breakneck speed. Emily needed a lesson on caution.

She added brightly, "Just think, Lieutenant. Within a few hours you should be able to take the road, be well on your way to wherever you're going."

Without her. He tacked on her unspoken thought. *Not likely, lady.*

"Back in Adairsville, you said you were going home. To Canton?" he asked.

Emily's eyes fairly sparkled for a moment, but then wariness dulled them. "No."

"Beyond Canton, then."

"A bit."

"Your answers are very vague, Miss Gardner. One would think you don't trust me."

She stiffened. "I don't know you, Lieutenant. Why should I trust you?"

"Some people think I'm reliable. You could at least allow me the benefit of the doubt—you know, as in innocent until proven guilty? Let me tell you what I've assumed, and you tell me if I'm right or wrong."

As an answer, she crossed her arms and eyed him with suspicion. *Smart girl.*

Jared stroked the mare's neck. "Now take this horse. Thoroughbred—suggests money. The house in Adairsville—a hovel with expensive furnishings. You—educated and well versed in the manners of the highborn."

The last observation prompted a flattering rosiness to creep up her neck and settle in dainty blooms on her cheeks.

He continued, "And the nobility of the South live on plantations or country estates, where young ladies learn to put insolent men in their places, blush prettily and bake mean molasses cookies. Correct?"

The corner of her mouth lifted into a smile. "Correct."

"So your home is a big house on several hundred acres of land, either east or perhaps southeast of Canton."

"My word, Lieutenant. Your powers of observation are overwhelming."

Well, he'd known her history, but the clues were there for anyone to read. He moved his hand to Rusty's nose, stroking. "Are there more horses like her at home?"

Emily's smile faded. "I wish there were, but my brother used the herd to help outfit his cavalry unit. He took two dozen of the finest Thoroughbreds in the state to war."

"Didn't your parents object?" Jared pushed.

"My mother died when I was a little girl."

"And your father?"

After a long pause, she said, "My father left Rosewood when the war started. He wasn't home to object."

Jared noted the careful wording, giving no hint of the side John had taken or of how she felt about John's decision.

She suggested, "Wouldn't it be wise to continue now?"

Jared silently agreed and pulled his gelding onto the path,

intending to take the lead. "The farther east we go, the less chance we'll run into a patrol."

"You said that before, that east was a wise choice."

"I wouldn't want to be on my way south." Jared waved his hand toward the mountains. "That's General William Tecumseh Sherman out there. He led one hundred thousand men out of Tennessee with enough provisions and fire-power to turn a Confederate quartermaster green as a lizard. If you were Sherman, where would you lead your army?"

"Isn't he after the arsenal at Adairsville?"

Jared scoffed. "The arsenal is a bonus. He's after a richer prize. And remember the mortar? He'll follow the rail line."

"Richer," Emily echoed, then her eyes widened. "Atlanta!"

"And beyond, if no one sticks a sizable force in the way to stop him."

She tilted her head. "Our army has beaten him back before. Surely they can do so again." Her eyes narrowed. "And surely they could use your help. Shouldn't you be with your company?"

She'd come very close to suggesting that he'd deserted. The insult hurt.

"I assure you, Miss Gardner, that I am on my way to report to my commander. Now, how much farther to Canton?"

If she believed him, she gave no indication.

"Depending on how quickly we get out of the woods, I would say three, maybe four hours."

Chapter Three

Emily shifted the reins from right hand to left. She peered up through the overhead canopy of leaves. The sun's position confirmed her stomach's grumble.

On the narrow path in front of her rode Lieutenant Randall, plodding along at a walk, seemingly equally unconcerned about the Yankees behind them and her home ahead of them.

"Lieutenant? Do you think we might ride a bit faster?"

His answer drifted back. "No."

She waited for an explanation. None came. "When I said three or four hours to Canton, sir, I meant at a faster pace."

"Then it'll take us a little longer."

Emily fought her temper. "You may not be in a hurry, but I would like to reach Rosewood before dark."

"The path is too narrow and the brush too thick to push the horses any faster. Besides, if we ride at a prudent pace, Miss Gardner, you *might* get home in one piece."

The reprimand stung. Admittedly, she'd spurted from Adairsville a *little* fast, but Emily knew her limits and Rusty's abilities.

She countered, "If you will recall, you ordered me to *move*. So I moved."

"Move? Yes. Bolt down an unfamiliar path as if the devil were at your heels? No."

"He was," she mumbled. "You were right behind me the whole time."

"What was that, Miss Gardner?"

Her stomach growled again. A bodily function nagged for relief. If she could convince him to stop, maybe she could find a way to get ahead of the devil and leave him behind.

"I said, I'm hungry. Could we stop for a bite to eat?"

He turned in the saddle. Emily forced a cheerful smile. He smiled back, with that knowing expression she'd seen before. He couldn't have read her thoughts, could he?

He halted, positioning his gelding to block their path. As she slid from Rusty's back, she looked for a way to pull Rusty through the brush to get around the gelding. Impossible.

She took the piece of jerky Randall offered, tore off a piece and chewed furiously to soften the tough beef. She accepted water from his canteen, though she cleaned the spout on her sleeve before drinking.

"Ready to leave?" he asked.

"Not yet." A blush warmed her cheeks. "I need to... I need privacy."

"Go ahead. Just don't go far."

Chin elevated, Emily turned on her heel and marched into the woods. She attended to necessities, then scouted the area. There had to be a way to get around that insufferable soldier.

As she rounded a tree, she looked down, and stopped, horrified at the carnage. She heard herself scream. A boy, not more than fifteen, lay at her feet—a mound of shredded clothing, ripped-open belly, and blood. So much blood! His chest rose, slightly. Still alive!

"Emily!"

In a quivering squeak, she managed to call, "Over here, Lieutenant. Please hurry!"

"What the hell—"

Startled by his voice just behind her, she spun. A Colt revolver in his hand, Randall was staring down at the boy.

"He needs a doctor," she said. "There's one in Canton. I'll fetch him."

Jared grabbed her arm as she started to dart past. "Forget it. The kid will probably die before you can get back with a doctor."

"Only if I ride at a pace you think prudent," she snorted, jerking her arm away.

"At the reckless pace you ride, you won't make it into town! I've got one grave to dig already. Would you like a grave of your own, or should I throw you in on top of the kid?"

Emily blanched. "You're depraved!"

"I've been called worse."

Her bottom lip quivered. "We have to do something," she said hoarsely. "We can't just let him lay there and…"

She flinched when Randall put his hand on her shoulder, but his touch was gentle, comforting.

On a sigh, he said, "The word is *die*, Emily. We can't prevent it, but we can make him comfortable, stay with him till the end." He nodded southward. "If my hearing doesn't deceive me, there's a stream close. Let's take the horses down there and then we'll see what we can do for the kid."

As they walked toward the horses, she accepted the inevitable. Randall was right. The boy had lost too much blood from a ghastly gunshot wound. Being a soldier, Randall would know about deadly wounds.

She asked quietly, "You've seen wounds like this before, haven't you?"

"Yes, ma'am," he answered, shoving the Colt into his pack. "Too many times, in too many places. And stomach wounds…well, they're probably the worst. Men die slow."

Randall picked a path though the woods to the stream. After they removed saddles and packs, he handed over his canteen and a towel.

"Why don't you clean the kid up a bit? Just don't touch the wound, or he'll start bleeding again."

Emily hurried back to the boy. Kneeling beside him, averting her eyes from the gaping hole in his belly, she washed his face. From under the dirt and splattered blood, she uncovered a smattering of freckles across his nose. She finger-combed sandy-brown hair, then unbuttoned the top button of his flannel shirt.

Only then did she wonder how he'd been wounded.

She glanced furtively around her, but only saw Randall coming toward her, carrying a blanket and a white tin.

"Lieutenant, could the Yankees have passed though here? Whoever shot this boy could still be in the area."

Randall put down the tin before tossing a thin wool blanket over the victim. He pointed to an old flintlock lying in the brush. "I'd bet the wound is self-inflicted."

"Self-inflicted? A hunting accident perhaps? Then maybe someone will come looking for him. If he was out hunting, he can't be far from home."

"Maybe," he said, but she heard his doubt. "More likely he heard about the fighting and was on his way to enlist."

"He's too young."

Randall nodded. "They're all the South has left to recruit, the young ones. Call me if he starts to wake up."

She almost asked him where he was going, until she saw him pick up the camp shovel. An hour later, he returned, sweating, bits of red clay clinging to his white shirt and gray trousers.

"The kid stirred at all?" he asked.

She shook her head.

"Probably best if he doesn't wake up. If he dies while he's unconscious, he won't feel the pain."

Randall had voiced her own thoughts, but if the boy didn't wake, they wouldn't learn his name or find out how to notify his family.

"Must we bury him?" she blurted. "Couldn't we take him into Canton?"

He stared at her, then said, "Depends." He tilted his head. "Looks like you need a break, too. Why don't you gather firewood, in case we have to camp here tonight?"

For the rest of the afternoon, they took turns keeping vigil over the boy and going about their separate chores. Near dusk, as she feared would happen, the boy stirred while she kept watch. Emily grasped his hand, knowing his pain would be unbearable. The boy groaned, loud and long.

Randall suddenly appeared, flipped open the tin and pulled out a small packet of white powder.

"What is that?" she asked.

"Morphine," he said, sprinkling it over the boy's wound.

Morphine! Morphine was dear in the South. Several people, mostly women, were serving prison sentences in the North for trying to smuggle the precious drug across the border.

Thoughts of questioning his possession of the drug faded as the boy thrashed in pain. Emily pressed on his shoulders while Randall gripped his legs, holding the boy still until the drug took effect.

As the pain subsided, his pale blue eyes opened. He blinked at Randall, then rasped, "I'm gonna die, ain't I, sir?"

Randall nodded. "You do this yourself?"

"Stupid... Tripped, gun flew into a bush."

Jared rested a hand on the boy's shoulder and finished, "You pulled it out of the bush from the wrong end of the barrel. The hammer snagged and the gun fired."

"Like I said, stupid. Ma's gonna be...mighty upset," he said, his features twisting into a pain-filled grimace.

"What's your name, son?"

"Walters, sir, Scott Walters."

Scott cried out. Emily squeezed his hand, her knuckles turning white under the combined pressure.

"Easy, Scott," Emily soothed. "Please relax. It won't hurt so much."

His grip slackened as he studied her face. For a long time, he simply stared, his eyes glazed. Then a corner of his mouth lifted in a half smile.

"You know, Ma always said...when a person dies...an angel comes down from heaven...to fetch yer soul. You must be my angel."

"Oh, no, Scott," Emily protested, but Scott didn't hear. His face smoothed into peaceful repose. His grip went limp.

Shaking, Emily placed Scott's hand on his chest.

"Emily? You okay?"

She felt faint, and sick, but refused to succumb. Her voice shook when she asked, "Can we take him into Canton?"

"Too late for that, I'm afraid. We can't make it into town before dark, and we can't leave him out in the open overnight."

She knew why. Scavengers... Oh, God.

Emily gagged on the bile rising from her stomach. Cursing her weakness, she fled to the stream.

Jared followed her as far as the horses, then, realizing what was happening, gave her privacy. From his pack he gathered pencil and paper and went back to Scott.

Never having commanded a unit of his own, he'd never written one of these detestable letters, never tried to comfort a mother or wife. What did one say?

What would he want someone to tell his own mother if the worst happened? The truth.

Scott had died in pain, but not as painfully as he might have without the morphine. In the face of death, he'd accepted his fate with quiet dignity, thinking of his mother at the end. And mistaken Emily for an angel—a mistake easily made and easily forgiven.

The letter almost wrote itself, until he started to sign it. Though the possibility was remote, if Mrs. Walters ever learned that he'd falsified the signature, she might doubt the contents. He signed his full name and rank. He tucked the letter into Scott's shirt pocket, and wrapped the body and the flintlock in the blanket.

Jared buried Scott in a grave too shallow for permanent interment but too deep to attract animals. Tomorrow, in Canton, he'd find some way to get word to the Walters family.

Now he had to contend with Emily. A veteran of three years, Jared knew how to work through the aftermath of death. But Emily was like a raw recruit, blooded in a first battle.

He tossed the shovel down near his packs and glanced about the campsite. Emily sat near the remains of the fire, her arms wrapped around herself and her forehead resting on upraised knees. He threw a log into the embers. Her body uncurled, slowly stretching tension-tightened muscles.

"I need to get cleaned up," he said. "Think you could make me a pot of coffee?"

"You have coffee? *Real* coffee?" Her eyes widened when he nodded. "I'll make some. Are you hungry?"

"Famished," Jared replied, removing his boots. "I'm going for a swim," he announced, and dug through his pack for clean clothing. He tossed her the pot and a sack of ground coffee, then strode toward the stream.

Emily studied the bottom of the coffeepot. She could go down to the stream and risk disturbing Lieutenant Randall's swim, or she could forget the coffee. No, it had been far too long since she'd tasted real coffee. Heaven was sniffing the grounds.

After a glance in both directions, she decided he must have sought privacy downstream. Before she could dunk the pot into the water, she heard bushes rustle and looked toward the sound. Then she wished she'd stifled her curiosity.

Down on both knees at the edge of the stream, he wrung the water from his cotton shirt. He snapped it open, then tossed the shirt onto a bush that already held his trousers. Clad only in underdrawers, he stood and stretched full length, flexing the muscles across his wide back. Broad shoulders pivoted backward, compressing the bulge of muscle.

Then his hands lowered to rest for an instant on lean hips. Emily clamped her eyes closed when his hands moved forward to unloose his last piece of clothing. She opened her eyes only after she heard a loud splash.

She filled the pot and scrambled back to the campsite, squelching her female curiosity. Ladies did not stare at a naked male body, even if that body was trim, muscled, and most wonderfully molded.

The coffee brewing, she sliced strips from the bacon and set them to sizzling in the frying pan. An odd sense of awareness soon told her that Lieutenant Randall stood behind her, though she hadn't heard him approach.

Emily turned, and stared. He wore a pair of soft buckskin pants. A white shirt was draped carelessly over one shoulder. Dark hair sprinkled his bare chest, then arrowed down to disappear beneath his waistband. She tightened her fists to keep her fingers from brushing away water droplets glistening among the springy curls.

"I thought for a moment you were going to join me."

The accusation startled her, and she looked up into glittering obsidian eyes. She saw amusement, knew he was teasing her. But, chagrined, she answered haughtily, "Hardly, sir. The cold water must have addled your wits. I don't know of a way to make coffee without water, Lieutenant."

His throaty chuckle accompanied a widening grin. "I hope you make better coffee than bacon."

Emily spun. Seeing the smoking meat, she reached down and seized the pan's handle. She released it instantly, but not quickly enough to prevent the burn. Her eyes misted as an angry welt formed across her palm.

As her good hand tightened around her wrist in a futile effort to contain the pain, Lieutenant Randall's arm shot around her waist and held her upright. He guided her to the stream, then left her kneeling with her hand immersed in cold water.

"Better?" he asked when he returned with the white tin.

Emily nodded and started to rise. Her hand trembled. She pursed her lips, willing the pain to subside. But the tears had started to flow. She couldn't hold them back. With dizzying speed the sting of the burn collided with her anguish over Scott. Emily reeled from the torment, yielding to wrenching sobs.

She didn't resist when muscular arms lifted her from the grassy bank. Briefly she fought the looming darkness, but she soon lost the desire to struggle. Wrapped in a cocoon of warmth and strength so solid that nothing could penetrate to cause more pain, Emily surrendered to the security of Lieutenant Randall's embrace.

Jared leaned against a tree. Emily's cheek rested warmly against his chest, and her body was cradled between his raised knees. She slept, but occasionally a sniffle jerked her body.

Shifting to bandage her hand hadn't awakened her, nor had the long reach to grab a blanket. Nor, he suspected, would she rouse if he moved her to a bedroll spread by the fire. But since she was comfortable, Jared couldn't think of a good reason to further risk disturbing Emily's healing slumber.

Jared hated admitting that continuing to hold Emily had nothing whatever to do with practicality. Emily molded perfectly into the shelter he created with his body. So much for his vow to keep his distance, he thought wryly.

The scent of lilac drifted up as he dismantled the coiled crown of her hair, tossing hairpins into the night, loosening the braid. He tamped down the desire twitching his loins, resisted the urge to stroke soft skin or kiss pouting lips. At least he could keep his body under control—not an easy task, considering the way she pressed against sensitive areas.

Jared wondered at his tranquillity. Women's tears usually made him angry. He considered tears an offensive weapon, used by conniving females to force a male to relent. But Emily's tears didn't shame, or deceive, or entreat. They were real, born of pain and grief. Those beautiful brown eyes would be red, swollen, and would itch when she woke—no longer the soft, caring eyes of Scott's angel.

Too soon, Emily's eyelashes fluttered. Jared gently grasped her rising hand. "Don't rub your eyes. Stay still for a minute and get your bearings."

Confused, Emily swiveled her head against the pillow of a masculine chest. She squinted against the brightness of the campfire, then stared at her hand, wrapped in cotton strips. The burn still stung, but the sensation of her whole hand being aflame had vanished.

She tried to piece together what had happened after she took her hand out of the water. Segments refused to combine. Her only certainty was this feeling of safety, of belonging. She knew she should move, but hazily reasoned that if she stayed nestled against Lieutenant Randall a while longer, she could absorb some of his abundant vigor.

His voice broke the spell. "What do you remember?"

"Burning my hand, walking down to the stream, but after that... Oh, dear, I started crying, didn't I?"

He shrugged. "Shock. You couldn't help collapsing."

Emily didn't like the idea of an uncontrolled outburst. She felt like a child who'd thrown a tantrum.

"I would like to believe that, because I feel so foolish," she admitted, and sat up. "Please accept my apologies, Lieutenant Randall. I will endeavor to control my emotions more carefully."

"An apology isn't necessary, but I'll accept it on the condition you stop calling me Lieutenant Randall. I prefer Jared."

Emily wanted to protest. To use his first name conceded a relationship beyond mere acquaintance. But after the trial they'd shared today, formality seemed senseless.

"Jared," she said, acquiescing.

"Much better," he declared, then smiled. "Do you think you could find those cookies?"

Reminded of the burned dinner, Emily smiled sheepishly. "What, no bacon?"

"Maybe I'll let you try to cook again tomorrow. For now, the cookies and coffee will suffice."

Emily got up and set about fulfilling his request.

After eating more cookies than his hunger justified, Jared snapped the lid into place. He brushed crumbs from his shirt front, then poured the last of the coffee into his cup.

He rested his back against the log upon which Emily sat. She wore a frown of deep concentration.

"Want to talk about it?" he suggested.

She hesitated, then said, "I was trying to determine the best method of locating Scott's mother."

Jared had no intention of lingering in Canton longer than necessary to notify the authorities of Scott's death. "We'll ask around tomorrow, find out if someone knows the family and can get word to them."

"He was so young, and he wasn't even cold yet when—"

"Dwelling on the niceties will drive you crazy. Dead is dead. My grandfather would have been proud of me."

He knew the statement was harsh, and it was too late to take back the reference to his grandfather. Well, answering the questions her expression asked might take her mind off Scott.

The answers also might send her screaming into the woods.

Women typically reacted to the revelation of his heritage by either backing off in revulsion or jumping into his bed to experience sex with a savage. Since he couldn't picture Emily throwing herself from her perch into his arms, revulsion was inevitable.

"The Indians of the Southwest fear death. When someone dies, burial is swift, involving as few people as possible. Personal possessions are either left at the grave site or destroyed, so the spirit doesn't return among the people for his belongings. Even the hogan is burned if the person died in his home.''

"Dead is dead." She repeated his earlier words. "Your grandfather is an Indian."

"A Navajo chieftain."

He tensed, waiting for recoil.

"I know this is forward..." Emily began.

Jared looked up at the pause. She was chewing on her bottom lip. "Go on."

"You don't look Indian. Well, maybe a little—your eyes." She tilted her head, studying his face. "I thought you were a Texan, perhaps with Spanish blood in your family."

"One-quarter Navajo. Home is Arizona," Jared explained, astonished by her accepting attitude. "I may not have strong Indian features, but I spent a lot of time with the tribe as a boy. I've never regretted my mixed blood."

She mulled that over for a moment, then said, "It must be very hard for you to be here while Kit Carson is burning the Navajo off their land."

Jared picked up a twig and snapped it into small pieces. "Carson." He sneered, tossing a chunk into the fire. "Now there's a man even I could scalp. Most Navajo are simple farmers, eking sustenance out of an arid desert."

"But they do raid."

"They're fighting for their land, their way of life."

Another long pause. Then she asked, "Do you know where your family is?"

"My mother they can't touch, because she's half-white and married to a white rancher. The others were herded like cattle from Canyon de Chelly to Fort Sumner." He hurled the last piece of twig and stood. "Dwelling on their plight doesn't do any good, either, since there's nothing I can do to help them until this war is over. Maybe not even then.''

Emily took the hand he offered to help her stand. "You could always shoot that Yankee Carson," she suggested.

"Tempting, but not a solution." Now wasn't the time to tell her what solution he considered acceptable. It was late. Emily needed sleep.

With a finger, he lifted her chin. The swelling around her eyes had eased. In a light tone, he said, "Besides, if I go gunning for Colonel Carson, they'll brand me a savage."

Emily's fingertips skimmed the whisker-rough line of his jaw. "A little harsh along the edges, perhaps, but not savage. Good night, Jared."

Chapter Four

Canton hadn't changed in the two years since Emily last saw the town. Memories flooded back, of peaceful times and happier people. She concentrated on the road, avoiding eye contact with the people going in and out of the shops.

They tied the horses in front of the mercantile.

"I have to send a telegram," Jared stated, handing over several Confederate bills. "Would you go in the mercantile and see if they have any recent newspapers?"

Emily didn't object. Their going separate ways meant that if anyone verbally protested her presence in Canton, Jared wouldn't witness the scene. After they found Mrs. Walters, she and Jared would go in different directions, and Emily preferred to part without his learning of this silly spy business.

"While I'm in the store, I'll ask Mr. Carlyle if he knows Mrs. Walters. She might have an account there."

"Good idea. Then we'll meet back here."

Emily entered Carlyle Mercantile with a sense of coming home tinged with the dread of rebuff. A bell above the door announced her arrival, just as it had before she moved away. Bolts of fabric still occupied a table to her left. On the counter, near the cash register, lay stacks of newspapers. However, she didn't know the young lady behind the counter, who said with a sweet smile, "Good morning. Can I help you?"

Emily returned the smile. "Are the newspapers recent?"

"All but the *New York Tribune*. It's a week old."

Recent enough, Emily decided, purchasing it along with the *Atlanta Journal*.

"Are you new in town?" Emily asked.

"I came shortly before last Christmas, to help my aunt after my uncle died."

Emily slowly rolled the newspapers, feeling a pang of loss. She'd known the Carlyles for what seemed forever. "The war?" she asked softly.

"Battle of Chattanooga. He was taking supplies up to the lines, and somehow got too close to the fighting."

"Please tell your aunt... No, perhaps not. I doubt she'd appreciate condolences from me." Ignoring the girl's puzzled look, Emily asked, "Do you happen to know a family in the area named Walters?"

"The twins, Scott and Eric, come in occasionally."

"Would you know where they live?"

The young lady shrugged. "On a farm south of here, I think. You might ask Captain Morgan. He's in charge of the home guard, and the boys belong to it, so he'd know."

"And where can I find Captain Morgan?"

"He set himself up a desk in the jail."

Murmuring a thank-you, Emily hurried out of the store.

Jared hadn't returned to the horses. She tucked the remaining bills into the newspapers and jammed them under the bedroll on his gelding.

Emily cursed her conscience. She wished she could jump on Rusty and leave Canton as fast as the horse could fly. But she couldn't, not while Scott lay in a shallow grave in the woods.

She glanced up the street. No Jared. Why wait for him? The faster she found Mrs. Walters, the faster she could get to Rosewood. Emily crossed the street to the jail.

The door squealed as she entered the gloomy office. A

sense of foreboding settled in her bones as she glanced about the shabby room. Sun-rotted curtains hung from broken rods over grimy windows. A chair, sitting in front of an ancient desk, looked ready to collapse at the slightest nudge.

Behind the desk, partially obscured by haphazardly stacked towers of paper, sat the only man in the room. The Confederate officer—portly, balding, and obviously upset—scowled at the paper he was reading. Emily glanced at the placard on the desk.

Captain Gilbert Morgan.

Her luck was holding. She didn't know Gilbert Morgan—and he wouldn't know Emily Gardner.

"Captain Morgan?"

His head snapped up. He stared, his eyes widening with recognition. Emily hadn't the vaguest notion of how that could be. Then he smiled brightly, as if truly glad to see her. The combination increased her wariness.

"What brings you to Canton, Miss Gardner?" he asked, his voice as smooth as a snake's slither over mud.

Emily fought the impulse to bolt, forcing herself to stand her ground. "The young lady in Carlyle's informs me that you know the Walters boys. I would like directions to the farm."

Morgan motioned to the chair. "Please, ma'am, won't you sit down?"

Emily crossed her arms. "This isn't a social call, Captain. I haven't the time or desire to chat."

All affability disappeared from Morgan's expression and tone. He said haughtily, "It is my duty to protect the good citizens in the area from threats from the enemy, whether that enemy openly wears Union blue or not." Morgan rose and slowly walked around his desk, limping badly. "Until I know *why* you wish to impose on the Walters', you'll get no information from me."

Anger at his implication eclipsed her good intentions. If Morgan didn't want her to *impose* on the Walters', then she would give Morgan the responsibility of informing the family.

"I came upon Scott Walters yesterday. Unfortunately, he'd had an accident, and didn't live long enough to tell me where to find his family."

Morgan's eyebrows shot up. "Scott's dead?"

"Gut-shot with his own flintlock." Her blunt words rang in her ears. How callous they sounded. Anger faded as she remembered Scott's last words. "Captain, I would like to be the one to tell his mother. Scott said some things before he died that might be of comfort to her."

Morgan perched on the edge of his desk, rubbing his chin. A myriad of emotions flickered across his face as he grappled with the news. Then he got up, walked around the desk and pulled a revolver from a drawer.

"No, Miss Gardner, you aren't going anywhere," he said. "I am placing you under arrest for the murder of Scott Walters, and for treason committed against the Confederacy. You will hang, Miss Gardner, for one or the other. And then I'll receive a well-deserved transfer out of this miserable little town."

Jared stood outside the barbershop and took a deep breath to calm down. From first the telegraph operator, then the barber, he'd heard the preposterous accusation leveled at Emily Gardner. Knowing that Colonel Gardner and Emily hadn't communicated during the entire war, Jared had listened without being able to defend either father or daughter.

The men had also made assumptions about why a Confederate officer was traveling with a spy—that Jared was involved in the investigation begun by Captain Gilbert Morgan, who had spent the better part of the past year trailing Emily, trying to gather evidence. Jared left the barbershop without disabusing them of the notion.

Did Emily know what these people believed? Probably. It would certainly explain her stiff spine and downcast look as they'd ridden into Canton. He'd thought her apprehensive about finding Mrs. Walters. Now he suspected that her unease sprang from the possibility of being recognized and reviled.

Did she know about Morgan's efforts to bring her to trial? Maybe. The man had spent enough time in her shadow, following her to some shack in the mountains, hoping to catch her in the act of meeting a contact. He never had, of course, but Jared could understand Morgan's determination. The capture of a spy would make an outstanding mark on any man's military record.

Jared highly doubted, however, that Emily had any inkling that nearly a year ago a group of hotheads had burned her home, Rosewood, to ashes.

He glanced at the horses, hoping to see Emily waiting for him. She wasn't. Instead, a lanky adolescent in a corporal's uniform was warily approaching Rusty, his gaze darting between Rusty's bared teeth and the reins wrapped around the rail.

Foolishly, the corporal lunged for the bridle, apparently unaware of the muscles tightening in, and the backward shift of, the mare's sleek neck. Soundly thumped onto his butt by the mare's solid hit, the stunned corporal scrambled in reverse on hands and feet to avoid threatening hooves.

"You seem to have a problem," Jared commented, offering his hand to help the corporal stand.

"She don't like me none—sir," he amended, facing gold strips on gray.

Jared directed his words at the corporal, but focused on the agitated mare. "The ladies like a gentle touch, right, girl?" Jared spoke soothingly during his approach, watching the mare's eyes for hints of rebellion. She flinched when he touched her mane, but she didn't draw back. "No lady likes being grabbed and dragged around. You have to coax them into going where you want them to go."

Jared stroked the expanse of shiny coat, feeling the tension ease. Was the horse's resistance to strangers inborn, or had Emily trained the mare to spurn an assailant? Where was Emily, anyway? She should have completed her errand long ago.

"Gosh, that was great!" the awed corporal blurted.

"I had an advantage, because the horse knows my voice. Now, Corporal, would you care to explain why you were trying to steal the mare?"

"I weren't trying to steal her, honest, sir. Captain Morgan said to get the mare and bring her round to the jail."

An uneasy prickling crept along the back of Jared's neck. "Why did Captain Morgan send you for this horse?"

"Must belong to the lady, about so high?" The corporal gestured with a flattened hand to his nose. "She's got mighty pretty brown hair."

Jared nodded at the description of Emily.

"Well, he's got her locked up. Captain said she murdered Scott Walters."

"Murder!" Jared shouted, sending the corporal back three steps. "Morgan arrested her for murdering Scott Walters?"

"Y-yes, sir."

"Tell me," Jared growled.

"Well, sir, I was out back when she came in, but I heard them arguing, 'cause they were so loud. When Captain Morgan called me in, he was shoving her into a cell. Told me to get the mare, saying the miss killed Scott and she was going to be with us for a spell."

"What did the lady say?"

"Couldn't rightly hear the exact words after the captain shut the door, but she was putting up an awful fuss, hollering and shaking the bars like she was meaning to tear them apart."

Jared turned, making deep tracks as he strode toward the jail. What should have been a simple mission was getting complicated, and complications he didn't want. He needed to maintain a low profile to protect his identity. If the Rebs somehow learned that Cougar was in the area, with a suspected spy in tow— He refused to consider the consequences. The risk of getting caught would lessen when he got Emily out of Canton.

He kept a firm hold on his temper as he opened the door.

"Captain Morgan," Jared said to the man behind the desk, forgoing the salute it would irk him to give. Morgan wasn't looking, anyway. He was furiously writing, probably a report on the events of the morning.

"Yeah, what is it?" Morgan asked, not looking up.

"I understand you are holding Miss Gardner."

The pen stilled in place as Morgan raised his balding head. "What's it to you?"

The heady flush of conquest shone on Morgan's face, the gleam of victory flashing in his eyes. Jared felt no qualms about bursting Morgan's balloon of triumph.

"I'm Lieutenant Randall, sir, and I was with Miss Gardner when she found Scott Walters. The boy's death was an accident, sir. Miss Gardner didn't kill him."

Morgan let out an aggravated huff, but didn't deflate as completely as Jared had hoped. "You must be the witness she's been babbling about. Damn. I hoped she was lying."

Jared gave Morgan a brief account of Scott's death and a detailed description of where to find the grave. Morgan's mounting frustration satisfied Jared that the man believed the report.

After a moment's silence, Morgan rallied and began writing again. "No matter," he said. "There are other charges I hope to prove. You can be on your way, Lieutenant."

Jared sighed inwardly as he sat down. Morgan's *other charges* no doubt stemmed from his effort to prove Emily a spy.

"Now, I'm not one to question a superior officer's decisions, and I'm sure you have good reason for caging Miss Gardner, but I just sent a wire to Richmond. The people who sent me down here think I have her in custody and am bringing her in. The brass gets nasty when orders aren't followed."

The pen's scratching stopped. Morgan squirmed.

"The way I see it," Jared continued, "there will be hell to pay when I show up without Miss Gardner. When I tell them you have her, they'll want an explanation."

"Why are you taking her to Richmond?" Morgan asked calmly, though beads of sweat were forming on his upper lip.

"Seems she's been poking her nose where it doesn't belong, and they want to know why."

Morgan took out a handkerchief and dabbed at the sweat. "They want to ask her about the spying she's been doing?"

"Your reports must have caught someone's interest."

"But I didn't send any reports! How could they know?"

"Oh, come now, Captain, surely you let some higher authority know you've been investigating. I've heard about the excellent job you've done, following her around."

"I can't prove she's guilty!" Morgan's shoulders slumped. "If I can't prove anything, how can they?"

Jared wondered if Morgan would ever ask who *they* were.

"What's to prove?" Jared pushed. "Morale among the troops is low. The masses are clamoring for victories. A pretty girl on trial for spying would give the people something to chew on besides generals' behinds. Doesn't matter if she's guilty or not, as long as everyone gets a promotion and they get the populace off their backs."

"But they can't do this to me. I'm the one who spent hours on horseback, tramping through brush and up and down mountains. They can't just whisk her off and claim all the glory. She's mine, I tell you!"

From the back of the building rose an uproar with spectral qualities. A banshee wailed her evil portent, shrieking Morgan's name while rattling the chains that bound her to the world beyond. Emily's timing was perfect.

Morgan closed his eyes, a chagrined look on his face.

"Captain Morgan," Jared said as the howling ceased,

"maybe we can come to an arrangement that would suit us both."

Captain Morgan looked hopeful.

Emily gave the bars a last shake, finally admitting that the action was useless. Her caterwauling had resulted in a sore throat and an aggravated burned hand. Morgan had to come in sometime, if only to bring food and water. It was small comfort knowing that all she had to do was wait him out.

Scooting back on the cot until her spine rested against the wall, Emily wondered where Jared was. Her arms wrapped around her as she remembered cuddling in Jared's arms, drawing on his warmth and strength. She could feel the vitality that coursed through his body as if he were holding her now.

Jared could be overbearing and arrogant, firing her anger to boiling. But his gentleness could soothe her wounded spirit.

Had someone seen fit to inform him that he was keeping company with a spy? Had he then jumped on his gelding and left town? She hoped not. She needed him. Jared was the only person who could clear her of the murder charge.

For the charge of treason, she needed legal counsel. And to engage a lawyer's services, she could use Jared's help. He was an outsider, perhaps the one person who might listen to her side of the story without prejudice. For the right price, he might be willing to find and hire a good lawyer.

"Please be in town," she pleaded as she grasped the bars. "Don't leave until I can talk to you."

As Emily prepared to screech for Morgan, the outer door opened and Jared stepped into the room. Emily clutched the bars, the only obstacle preventing her from running into his arms, from disgracing herself, again. He closed the door.

"Well, hello, Miss Gardner," he said dryly. "You know,

for one little girl, you sure can get into a mountain of trouble.''

Was that how he saw her, as a little girl? Emily stifled the urge to correct his impression. His image of her didn't matter, as long as he helped her out of this predicament.

''I assume Captain Morgan told you why I'm in here.''

''Yes, ma'am.''

He sauntered toward the cell, folded his arms over the bar's crosspiece. The sleeve of his uniform brushed against her fingertips as he leaned forward. His eyes sparkled with teasing humor. ''The notorious Miss Emily Gardner. Murderess. Union spy. And champion nag. Lord, but you can holler.''

''I was screeching to get Morgan's attention.''

''You succeeded. In fact, I'll wager you got the attention of half the town.''

His comments begged for a scathing set-down, the smirk on his clean-shaven face invited a slap. Through narrowing eyes, she noted the change in his appearance. While she stewed in this jail cell, the odious man had treated himself to a shave and a haircut. Emily struggled for patience.

''I wanted someone to find you, before you left town.'' She bit the words out. ''You are the only person who can discredit Morgan's ridiculous charge that I killed Scott.''

''Captain Morgan and I had a long talk. I don't think he really believed you killed the boy. The charge simply gave him an excuse to lock you in a convenient cell while he figured out a way to prove the spy charges. Anyway, he dispatched a corporal who knows the family to notify Mrs. Walters.''

''Thank you,'' she said, releasing her grip on the bars, backing a few steps. ''I'm no more a Union spy than I'm a murderess. Proving that, however, won't be quite so easy. I need a lawyer, preferably someone from outside the county. Since I'm not in a position to find him myself, I need someone to hire a lawyer for me. Would you be willing?''

When Jared frowned and backed away, she added quickly, "I realize this is an imposition. You'll find gold in my packs to pay the lawyer." Emily took a deep breath. "And you can have Rusty as compensation for your trouble."

Jared's eyebrows shot up in surprise. "You would give me your brother's horse?"

"I can't take care of her from in here," she said, her voice just above a whisper. "The trial could be lengthy, and I couldn't bear having her shut up in a livery, not knowing if she was all right. I know you'd treat her well."

Jared shook his head. "Lady, you really are something. You have all the details worked out, don't you?"

Emily shrugged. "I had plenty of time to think, with very little distraction. Will you help me?"

He took a key from his pocket. "Do you have any idea how annoying it is for the knight in shining armor to find the damsel *not* in distress?"

Ignoring the note of irritation in his voice, she gaped at the key sliding into the lock. "How?"

"I bribed Morgan."

"Bribed?" Emily fumed. "Morgan was willing to release me for a few measly dollars?"

"No money involved. Actually, I lied a lot, and if you give me away, we may wind up back in this cell—together."

The hinges squealed, and the door swung wide. Jared held out his hand. With a small cry of relief, Emily reached out. Trembling fingers slid across his palm, along his forearm, then scurried up to find his shoulder. Emily snuggled against him as his arms encircled her, reveling in the fierce hug.

He chuckled. "Maybe the damsel *was* in distress."

"Perhaps, a bit," she said. "I've never been behind bars, and don't care to repeat the experience."

"Then let's get out of here before Morgan sees the holes in my story and changes his mind."

Slowly, she pulled away. "You're taking quite a risk on my behalf, duping a superior officer. You don't believe I'm a Union spy?"

He put his hands on her shoulders and grew serious. "Emily, you would make the worst spy in history. Now listen, no matter what Morgan says, I want you to keep quiet. I promise I'll explain everything later."

He sounded sincere. And given the choice of staying in jail or escaping with Jared, the latter appealed. "All right."

Back in the office, Morgan stood stiffly beside his desk, tapping a leather packet on his palm. For one frightening moment, Emily was sure Morgan had changed his mind, but then he handed Jared the packet.

"You will see this delivered to the proper authorities in Richmond?" Morgan asked.

"Rest assured, sir, I will take care of the matter."

"Miss Gardner, Lieutenant Randall has explained Scott's untimely death. My apologies for detaining you. Please give my regards to your brother."

Emily glanced at Jared's expressionless face. How did Terrance get into this? Why was Morgan suddenly so polite? Jared *did* have some explaining to do, but remembering his admonishment to say nothing, she nodded acceptance.

Jared put his hand under her elbow, pushing her toward the door. They had almost made good their escape when Jared turned back to speak to Morgan.

"In all the excitement, I almost forgot to tell you. When we left Adairsville yesterday, Sherman's forces were about to overrun the town. My guess is, the Yankees could be here within a few hours. Can you muster any troops to resist him?"

"Christ Almighty, man, why didn't you tell me this before?" Morgan demanded.

Jared frowned. "Yes, well, I suppose I should have, but I had other things on my mind."

Morgan gritted his teeth.

"By the way," Jared continued brightly, "if you happen to run afoul of General Sherman, mention my name—Randall, Jared Randall. He'll take good care of you, might even give you your choice of prisons, assuming you live through the fighting, of course. Good day, Captain Morgan."

Jared slammed the door behind them.

Emily eyed him warily as they crossed the street to their mounts. Jared looked like a cat who had caught a prize mouse.

"Jared, the Yankees..."

"Don't fret about the Yankees."

"Then why did you tell Morgan to prepare for them? This town will panic unnecessarily."

Jared boosted her onto Rusty, then explained, "Sherman won't move the bulk of his army, but he will send out patrols to scout the area, maybe relieve a farmer or two of chickens and horses. While they won't look for a fight, they won't hesitate to take prisoner any man in a Confederate uniform."

"You have a very low opinion of the home guards. You simply assume they can't persevere against a Yankee patrol. Frankly, Jared, I'm appalled at your lack of respect."

"My lack of respect isn't for the guards, but for this particular captain. I'd wager a month's pay that he won't call out the guard. Morgan doesn't have the stomach for a fight—he panics much too easily. He started sweating the moment I caught him in a breach of simple military procedure. And did you notice his limp? Foot wound. Most foot wounds are self-inflicted, and not by accident. That man is a coward, and he'll bolt."

Emily didn't want to believe that any man fighting for the South would desert his duty so easily. But lately the newspapers had been rife with condemnation of the hundreds of men who'd left their units before their enlistment was up, to go home.

Yesterday, she'd wondered if Jared could be a deserter.

He'd taken offense at her suggestive question saying he was on his way to join his commander. Nor would a deserter have deliberately walked into Morgan's jail. And would a coward condemn another man for cowardice? She didn't think so.

"How does a man like that become captain of a home guard?"

"Darned if I know. There's an interesting story there, but I'm not willing to hang around to find out what it is."

Neither was Emily. "So you're hoping he runs into a Yankee patrol."

"He won't go west, 'cause Sherman's there. North is Tennessee—Union territory. He can't follow us east, because we could expose his cowardice—so likely he'll head south. And if there's any justice in this world, he'll get captured."

"And spend the rest of the war in a Federal prison," Emily concluded. Then she tilted her head and asked, "Why did you tell Morgan to mention your name to General Sherman?"

"Because I know William T., and if Morgan tries to invoke privileges using my name, Sherman will put him in the darkest hellhole he can find."

"You *know* General Sherman?"

"Any officer, Federal or Confederate, who attended West Point within the last decade or so knows Sherman. Not that I consider Sherman a friend, but I know him pretty well."

"Is he as mean as the newspapers say?"

Jared looked back at Morgan's office. "He can be a nasty old cuss, depending on circumstances. Which reminds me—did you get the newspapers?"

"Under your bedroll."

He nodded his approval. "Look, there are still a few things we need to talk about, but I'd like to get out of town before something else happens. You know this country better than I do. Is there a place, maybe a few miles out of town, where we can pull up and have a private discussion?''

Home tugged hard. But she needed answers, especially about what Jared had told Morgan.

"I know a spot, about four miles out."

"Then lead on." He reached out and squeezed her ankle, smiling. "But not too fast, okay?"

As they passed the jail, Emily glanced at the window to see the curtain rise, then fall.

Chapter Five

Emily had no more than pulled up and dismounted when Jared handed over the leather packet.

"This is undoubtedly amusing fiction," he said, "but I think you should read what's in here."

"What is it?"

"Morgan's case against you."

Emily sat on a boulder and removed the sheaf of papers. The report was damning, labeling her a dangerous Yankee spy who aided the Union at the behest of her father. Citing the house's proximity to the state arsenal, believing she watched troop movements at the rail depot, Captain Morgan had set out to detect how she relayed information. His notes contained a map showing the mountain shack, a list of dates on which he'd stalked her, and an inventory of items in the shack.

Morgan admitted he'd never seen information passed during these jaunts, or found documents for an accomplice to collect. In his summary, Morgan recommended forcing a confession from her and then hanging her for treason.

The report was absurd, yet terrifying.

"Hungry?" Jared asked, squatting down to hand over a hard, square piece of a breadlike substance.

Emily turned it over, then back. "This is edible?"

"Armies live on hardtack. Granted, the stuff isn't tasty, but most soldiers aren't fussy when they're hungry."

Emily appreciated Jared's attempt to distract her from the report, but she needed to dispel any doubts Jared might harbor about her innocence.

"Have you read this?" Emily asked softly.

"No. I have a pretty good idea of what's in there, though. My conversations with the barber and Morgan were enlightening."

Emily was silent for a long interval, remembering long-ago trips into Canton, sitting beside her father, who had handled his team of magnificent bays with ease. Terrance had usually shunned the carriage, preferring to ride along-side on his horse.

Dressed in their finest, they would spend the day shopping and visiting, always ending the day at Fisk's barbershop, sucking on a piece of peppermint produced to keep her and Terrance quiet during Papa's haircut. Mr. Fisk had been one of Papa's closest friends, and one of the first to condemn Papa.

She tucked the papers back into the pouch. "My father took an unpopular stance when Georgia seceded from the Union. He felt a unified nation provided the states with better defense and trade opportunities. Papa was never comfortable with slavery, either, though we owned several Negroes. Many people felt that way, but Papa was one of the few who acted on his convictions and chose to serve the Union.

"Some people were enraged, regarding Papa's decision as a personal betrayal." She added bitterly, "They couldn't understand why I stayed in Georgia. The prevailing gossip said that I voluntarily stayed to be Papa's connection with the South. Nothing I said could change their minds. But I never dreamed the falsehoods would go beyond suspicion, that someone would try to prove the lies. Apparently, I was wrong."

"Why didn't you go with your father?"

"I was engaged to be married. Lewis Roth, however, decided that his inheritance meant more to him than I did. When his father threatened to disown him, Lewis broke the engagement. I haven't seen him since."

Jared glanced at the packet. "May I?"

Since he knew most of the story, there wasn't any reason he shouldn't know the rest. She gave him the packet.

Emily paced and fumbled with the bandage on her hand, trying to stay calm while Jared flipped through the pages. He mumbled under his breath, called Morgan a vulgar name, then shoved the papers into the case. He walked over to his gelding, exchanged the leather packet for his medical kit, then pointed to the boulder. Emily sat, wary of the thin set of his mouth and his deeply furrowed brow.

He squatted down. "Let me see your hand."

He made quick work of the knot, unwound the bandage and tossed the cotton strip into her lap. A flip of the kit's lid uncovered the salve. Why did he seem so angry?

"The salve you use works very well," she said, trying to divert his hostility.

"That's why I carry it. Hold this," he commanded, and plunked the tin into her good hand.

He dipped into the tin with a forefinger, then gently spread the green, sticky salve over her palm. The measured, hovering stroke caused a chill to snake up her arm and down through her torso, melting in a deep pool of flustering female heat. She snatched her fingers from the nest of his hand.

"Why are you snapping at me?" she demanded.

"Do you have any idea how lucky you are that Morgan was obsessed with this spy idiocy?" Jared growled as he grabbed the tin, replacing the lid. "What if, just once, he'd bothered to notice how pretty you are and decided to take advantage of the seclusion of that mountain shack?"

Pretty? Jared thinks I'm pretty?

"You certainly gave him enough opportunity," he continued to scold. "Morgan has been sniffing around your skirts for over a year. What if he'd decided to have a look at what was underneath?''

On that ominous note, he stalked off.

Emily hurriedly wrapped the bandage around her hand, scrambled to her feet and followed in his wake. She caught a handful of his uniform sleeve, forcing him to turn.

"I know how to take care of myself! I wouldn't have let Morgan get that close!"

"Well, he got pretty damned close without you knowing he was there, didn't he?" Jared taunted. "Several times, too. He could have ravished your delectable little body on any number of occasions, and you wouldn't have been able to stop him."

"I am not as helpless as you insist on believing! I do know how to use a shotgun."

Jared reached out and grabbed her wrist, pulling her stumbling in front of him. With his other hand on her backside, he pressed her firmly against his body.

"To use a weapon effectively, one must be prepared. Where is your gun now, Emily? How will you stop me from throwing you on the ground and using you any way I please?"

Emily responded instantly to the brazen caress, her belly pressed against the hardening proof of his lust. Twisting, trying to break his hold, she ground against him. Mesmerized by his smoldering midnight eyes, she stilled. Her memory flooded with the image of Jared's lean, naked body, proud and virile in his pose before the stream. And his mouth, so angry and tempting, was only a breath away.

Then he kissed her.

Emily felt lost, adrift in a strange land of heady sensations. But she had a guide, a soldier to lead the way. And lead he did, away from the first crush of lips, in a gentler direction. Her arms sought mooring, reaching upward, along the expanse of his chest, to curl around his neck.

Vague warnings of danger surfaced, but enticed by his warm, moist mouth, she paid no heed. Her lips moved in response, returning the kiss. Pressed along the hard length of him, her woman's place churned with long-buried yearnings. Emily trembled, and as though the soft tremor were a signal, he broke the kiss. Ever so slowly, the swirling in her head settled, to let reason return.

Captain Morgan might have taken her body, used her in unspeakable ways, but she wouldn't have let Morgan touch her without a fight. From Jared, she sensed no malice. Felt no fear. Only desire. If Jared chose to touch her, she wasn't sure she could muster any resistance.

"You wouldn't take me—against my will," she said faintly, firm in her belief.

His hold softened. "No, I wouldn't," he said quietly. "If you and I ever came together, it would be as lovers."

"Never!" her pride declared.

Jared released Emily, awed by his body's reaction. Why did he crave Emily, a woman he shouldn't want at all? She was barely more than a child! John Gardner's child!

Lovers! What a stupid remark to have made. But he had seen the desire in her eyes, felt her melt in his arms and revel in the kiss. Bedding Emily would be total joy, the pleasure far exceeding the mere slaking of lust.

There had been other women. He'd taken his pleasure when it was offered, giving it back. Always the liaisons had been light and brief, neither party wanting more than a physical diversion. Somehow, though, Emily had squirmed under his skin. He cared. For the first time in his life, he actually cared about a woman, and therein lay the danger.

Emily backed away on unsteady legs. "It's time we parted company, Lieutenant Randall. Circumstances may have put us on the same path, and kept us together for longer than I would have wished. But no longer. I don't need your help, Lieutenant, I never did. I can easily find my home from here, and would prefer that you not come with me."

"And let you starve to death?" Jared pointed at the hand she cradled. "Your hand will be useless for a few days."

"I will manage."

"Maybe," he acknowledged. Emily had survived on her own for two years, with only the help of her lover, this Sam person. He knew why, now, she'd taken a lover. Sam had likely been the one person to show her any affection, even if that affection had come at the price of her body. A price he wouldn't extract, no matter how much he wanted her.

"By the way, how *did* you bribe Captain Morgan?" she asked.

Rather pleased with his quick thinking earlier, he smugly explained, "Morgan was willing to believe you were my prisoner, that I was taking you to Richmond for questioning. I let him think his hide would be worthless if he didn't turn you over to me. He gave me his notes because I promised to deliver them to the authorities so he would receive his share of the glory."

Emily's eyes widened. "I wasn't tied to the saddle! Did he think I would go willingly?"

Jared shrugged. "You're supposed to think your brother sent me to fetch you and the horse."

Emily threw her hands in the air. "If everyone thinks I'm headed to Richmond to face a trial for spying, what will they do when they discover I've only moved back to Rosewood? Do you realize, Lieutenant, that you've just turned my home into another jail, with me as the only prisoner?"

She didn't wait for an answer. Emily stomped toward Rusty. With furious grace, she swung into the saddle. Her scowl was so eloquent that Jared could feel the flames of hell licking at his legs.

The mare surged. Jared leaped out of the path of flying hooves. "So much for gratitude," he grumbled, brushing the dust from his sleeves.

Jared looked up the road. Emily was riding too fast,

again, but at least she was on the road. Damn, she could be reckless.

And, damn, she was heading for Rosewood.

Jared fastened his packs and mounted, knowing he couldn't catch her in time to save her from the horror. Her mare could run rings around his gelding.

Lord, how much more could Emily suffer before she broke? In the past two days she'd fled a home and a lover, watched a young man die and been arrested for murder and treason, and now she was speeding toward Rosewood, a home no longer standing.

And his own actions toward Emily weren't above reproach. Since almost the moment they'd met, Emily had been trying to get rid of him. She'd finally found the opening to run from him, and taken it without hesitation.

He kicked the gelding into a gallop.

Emily bent low over the saddle, her braid flipping in rhythm with Rusty's gait. Eyes aimed at the road, she sped past fields that lay beyond split-rail fencing, past landmarks she'd used to find her way home since first learning to ride.

Consumed by the obsession to reach Rosewood, she gave Rusty her head, until she felt the mare's labored breathing. As Emily reined in, her concentration on the road lessened and the horror of Jared's betrayal returned.

Idiot! She berated her foolishness in believing Jared a savior. Relief had overshadowed common sense. She should have pressed Jared for details before leaving the jail. If she had realized, then, that she would be exchanging one jail for a prison of sorts, she would have stayed and fought her battle through the courts. Now, she must sustain Jared's lies.

She hadn't planned to announce her return to Rosewood, but neither had she planned to keep her presence a secret. She'd anticipated a rebuff from neighbors, but they wouldn't have questioned her right to live in her home—until today.

Word of the arrest and the reason for her release would spread. Anyone who saw her at Rosewood would wonder why she hadn't accompanied the lieutenant to Richmond. Due to his meddling, she had to hide in the house, keep Rusty from sight, until she discovered a way to prove her innocence.

Unwarranted calm washed through her as she spotted a barren field. Waist-high cotton had once blanketed this plot—Papa's reluctant surrender to the necessity of a cash crop to support his greatest love, the Thoroughbreds.

Emily clung to the belief that her father would return when the war ended. Though principles had compelled him to leave Georgia, John Gardner's love of Rosewood would bring him back. Determination sprouted as she thought of preparing for Papa's return. Restoring the estate would take months of hard work. Merely cleaning the house would require days of scrubbing and polishing.

She hoped Sam would think to look for her at Rosewood when he found the house in Adairsville empty. Sam would enjoy putting the small stable in order. The long, low barns, designed to shelter dozens of horses for breeding and sale, could remain closed until Papa restocked his herd.

From beyond the next hill, obscured by lush foliage, a stately white mansion beckoned. Anticipation heightened as she approached the tree-lined drive that led to the front portico. Emily's smile widened. Home! At last she was home!

Emily turned up the drive, her smile fading at the first glimpse of her beloved home. As though she had stepped into a living nightmare, Emily blinked, doubting her eyesight, but the scene didn't change.

Rosewood lay in blackened ruins, and with it her refuge, her heritage, her last hope for security.

Jared wished he could turn back time and revise his plans, if only to spare Emily this anguish. He found her at the back of the house, near the charred heap that had once been a gazebo. Emily stood very still.

"Emily, I'm sorry," he said, hearing the inadequacy of his words.

She didn't look at him, only waved a hand at a distant pile of rubble. "The barns were full when Papa left," she said, in a voice that was too quiet, too steady. "Some of the horses were spoken for, and most of the buyers came to claim them. A few men broke their contracts."

Jared listened to her ramble as she pointed out various piles of ash and explained their significance. Of the dozen or so buildings that had once served the Gardners, only one remained standing in skeletal defiance—the mansion.

The south wing had collapsed in on itself, the timbers sticking up at odd angles. Though the other outer walls stood, Jared knew it was only a matter of time before they succumbed and crumbled.

Emily pointed to a second-story window. "That was my bedroom. I could sit at my window for hours and watch the river and the training ring. Papa would tease that I could oversee the entire estate from that window."

A wink of light flashed at his feet. Jared bent and picked up the heat-formed glass. He rolled the smooth, perfectly shaped teardrop of melted window in his fingers, then let it fall back among its fellows.

Emily whirled to face him. "Why did you follow me?"

"We were on the same road, remember? When I saw the destruction, I thought you might need help."

"Your kind of help I don't need." Emily brushed past him, crossed to the pump and grasped the handle. "You're like the plague, Lieutenant. You showed up at my door, and I've been miserable ever since. I would be particularly grateful if you would just go away!"

Jared watched her force the handle against its will. The squeal of metal on metal echoed through the eerie silence until she gave a frustrated push and let go. She stomped over to his horse and grabbed the canteen.

Sensing her need for some small victory, Jared held his ground as Emily primed and pumped. He almost cheered when a trickle of water rewarded her persistence.

"Be reasonable, Emily. I didn't plan to stumble on to the Walters boy, or get involved with Morgan. All right," he admitted when she glared at him, "I got a bit careless in what I told Morgan. I simply thought it the easiest way to spring you."

"Apology accepted. Have a pleasant journey, sir."

"Emily, we have to talk."

"*We* have nothing further to discuss," Emily said, grabbing the shotgun.

"Ah, what do you intend to do with that?"

"Hunt. In case you hadn't noticed, there has been a fire, which means that the food I counted on being in the pantry isn't there. As much as I would dearly love to hunt down the…the bastards who…" She glanced at the mansion, then shook her head. "But since I don't know who, I'll settle for shooting a rabbit or two for dinner."

Jared held out his hand for the gun. "You'll blow it to pieces, in the mood you're in. Why don't you let me hunt?"

"Think I can't bring down a rabbit? Well, just watch me, mister."

Jared hesitated to tell her he'd unloaded the shotgun, but she would find out soon enough. "Your gun isn't loaded."

She stared, disbelieving, then spat out, "You? Why?"

"Seemed a good idea, at the time."

She growled—a most unladylike, furious growl. Jared tensed as she efficiently snapped the shells into place. She was, with justifiable cause, ready to do murder. Or at least use the weapon to make him leave. But she only glared at him before turning toward a wooded area.

Emily brushed away the tears blurring her vision. Raw hate pierced her soul and quickened her heartbeat. The urge to scream tightened her hand on the shotgun.

She tried to blame the Yankees for Rosewood's destruction, knowing it was impossible. The Yanks hadn't invaded this area of Georgia. The Yanks hadn't torched her home.

Her hands trembled, and her common sense told her to put the gun down. Gently she eased her shaking body to the ground and laid the gun aside.

Instinct had guided her feet to this spot by the river. Emily hugged her knees and called up memories of quiet moments and impromptu picnics spent in this girlhood retreat. An ancient willow stood guard, casting branches out over the water where she and Terrance had once swum.

Did Terrance know? Did Papa? Terrance would have sent word if he'd learned of it, and Papa—well, no one knew where Papa was.

Emily had little choice but to admit that men who had once valued John Gardner's opinion and respected his position in the community, once called Papa a friend, had ravaged Rosewood. They were punishing a man whose sin had been to follow his conscience. Papa was the enemy, conveniently absent, unable to defend his beliefs or his property.

Men loyal to the Confederacy had torched Rosewood, not only because they despised John Gardner, but to warn anyone who shared his opinions to beware.

Revenge. She longed for it, but realized the futility of brandishing an avenging sword. No one would rally to her cause for fear of losing their own homes.

Emily put her fingertips to her temples and rubbed at the pulse of her headache. Only now did she realize the futility of her earlier plan to deny and fight Captain Morgan's charges. A local jury would convict her, on the flimsiest of evidence, to protect their own homes and families. If Jared hadn't rescued her from Morgan, she might well have hanged.

And she'd berated Jared, almost run him down on the road, likened him to a plague, told him to go away. She owed him an apology. She'd thank him, somehow, though not in the manner he obviously thought appropriate.

Lovers, he'd said. His arrogance was insufferable, if he believed she would yield out of gratitude. True, he aroused blissful sensations whenever he smiled at her or touched her gently. She squelched the awareness of how easily she could fly into his arms, let him kiss her senseless, obliterate the ache in her heart and head. But as much as she wanted to, she couldn't lean on Jared for support or comfort. If he hadn't already left, he would, soon.

With gun in hand, Emily rose and brushed the grass from her skirt. Resolved to be practical, she studied the ground. The least she could do, if he was still here, was feed him a decent dinner.

Hearing a muffled shot, Jared had nearly raced into the woods. He'd envisioned Scott's bloody body, substituted Emily's, and drove himself crazy with morbid visions. Hearing a second shot, he'd relaxed, but his relief hadn't been complete until Emily returned with two gray rabbits dangling from her hand. Dry-eyed, shoulders squared, she'd apologized for her rudeness and asked formally if he cared to share her meal.

Not only could Emily shoot, but she could skin and cook her prey, too. Now here she sat, with her back to the ruins of the mansion, making polite dinner conversation over roasted rabbit. The contradiction between prim Southern belle and earthy frontierswoman had never been so apparent—or so bothersome.

"I'm sorry," she said.

"For what?"

"I'm jabbering away, and you haven't heard a word I've said in the last ten minutes. I'll clean up, if you care to turn in. You've lost a full day's travel because of me, and you'll want to leave early tomorrow."

"Emily," he said slowly, "we don't have to leave tomorrow. We could stay another day, if you feel the need."

"I'm not leaving. I must stay, for a few days, anyway,

to wait for Sam,'' she stated, then became thoughtful. ''Would the Yankees stop him from leaving Adairsville?''

If Emily's arrangement with her lover had been to meet at Rosewood, Jared sincerely hoped the Yankees would keep Sam in Adairsville. ''That depends. Is there some reason why the Yanks might detain him?''

''He's traveling in a cart loaded with hay and grain.''

Jared mulled over the implications, then asked, ''Is Sam supposed to bring feed to Rosewood for Rusty?''

''I'm hoping he'll guess that I came to Rosewood.''

Guessing? No previous arrangement. Good. ''The Yanks would certainly confiscate the feed, and probably the horse and cart. I'd say the odds are against Sam showing up.''

''I suppose you're right,'' she said, resigned. ''Poor Sam, he'll be so confused.''

The more Jared heard about Sam, the more he disliked him. Emily needed a dependable partner, someone strong enough to control her recklessness and take care of her.

''I'll have to go to Terrance, I suppose,'' she said.

''Do you know where he is?''

''Last I heard, somewhere in the Carolinas. Sam will know exactly where Terrance is.''

''Didn't we just agree that Sam wasn't coming?''

''Sam might not find me, so I have to find Sam.''

''By going back to Adairsville?''

''If I must.''

''And risk losing Rusty to the Yankees? Emily, there has to be another solution. Forget Sam, and Terrance, too. I doubt your brother would appreciate your showing up in the midst of a skirmish.''

''What you don't seem to understand is that I don't have any choice!'' Emily rose, and paced. ''I can't imagine any of our former friends extending hospitality. I haven't enough money, food or clothing to survive for very long. And I can't abandon Sam.''

''Sam is a man. He can take care of himself. Concentrate

on you. Emily, there has to be somewhere you can stay, some friend or relative willing to shelter you.''

"The only relative I have is an aunt in Petersburg."

Finally, she'd voiced an option. Colonel Gardner's sister lived in Virginia. If bringing Emily to Washington proved too hazardous, John had advised, Amelia Richards would be willing to shelter Emily. "It's right on my way."

Emily stopped pacing. "On your way to where?"

"Richmond. I have…a package to deliver, to my commander."

Her eyes narrowed. "Captain Morgan's report?"

Jared smiled. "No. I'm afraid I can't discuss the details, but as for Morgan's report, I never intended to let anyone but you see the contents."

He wished he could tell Emily of her final destination, of how John Gardner anxiously awaited her arrival in Washington. But they were still too deep in Rebel territory to risk exposure. If she agreed to go as far as Virginia, he could choose the right place and time to tell her about John.

"You're offering escort to Petersburg?"

"Yes."

She studied his face. Jared hid his duplicity behind a mask of indifference. She resumed pacing, glancing at him occasionally. Jared kept his peace, giving her time to decide to do exactly what he wanted her to do.

Emily halted, facing him with her chin uptilted. In her best Southern-belle tone she said, "I accept, with conditions. I shall hire you as my guide and pay our expenses. Also, there will be no further mention of a…personal relationship. You will, at all times, conduct yourself as a gentleman."

Surprised, and offended, he growled, "Would you like me to sign a statement to the effect?"

"I'm willing to accept your word."

The renowned Cougar reduced to being a paid lady's escort, with an admonition to behave himself, no less.

Humbling. But if his agreement satisfied Emily's sense of propriety, what the hell, why not?

"Agreed." He nearly choked on the word.

Emily shivered and pulled the blanket tight around her neck. Bedding down near the fire would have been warmer, but she'd chosen a spot as far away from Jared as practical. Jared was asleep, hadn't stirred for over an hour.

Silently Emily gathered her blankets and crept toward the narrow strip of grass between Jared and the fire. With a minimum of movement, she spread her bedroll and eased between the blankets. But in her search for warmth, she'd forgotten her bandaged hand. The only comfortable position for both her body and hand forced her to face Jared.

Not that he was hard to look upon—far from it. Even in slumber there was an aura about him, refined yet primitive. She knew she wouldn't feel quite so safe, moving within two feet of his sleeping form, if he hadn't agreed to her terms.

He had accepted her stipulations, hadn't argued at all, so Emily wondered what had bothered him for the rest of the evening. He'd been unfailingly polite, but sullen. Maybe he regretted his rash offer.

The fee for his escort hadn't been decided. Jared said he would keep track of expenses, because he didn't want her spending her gold and drawing attention. They would settle accounts when they reached Petersburg.

She felt bad about leaving Sam on his own, but Jared was right—Sam could fend for himself, would find his way back to Terrance. Or maybe he wouldn't. Emily knew she was the only reason Sam tolerated Terrance. With her gone, the Negro might take advantage and seek his own freedom.

Jared didn't stir, but his dark-as-midnight eyes opened and questioned her new sleeping arrangement.

"I was cold," she explained.

He grasped her hand, lightly kissed the fingertips, then closed his eyes. The expanding warmth couldn't be blamed on the fire. She looked at her hand, cradled firmly in long fingers. If she pulled away, she'd dislodge the bandage covering the burn. Within minutes, she slept.

Bound at wrist and ankle, weary and splattered with mud, Captain Gilbert Morgan pushed a slat from the shattered wagon off his legs. It had taken an hour to extricate himself from the tangle of bodies and wooden planks strewn over the road. The man next to him groaned, but Morgan ignored his fellow prisoner and crawled away from the wreckage.

He glanced around him, searching for the horses. They were gone, but then so was the bear that had panicked the horses on this badly rutted road.

He cursed, sawing at the rope with a jagged piece of iron. His mission of mercy, to comfort the widow Walters, had ended in disaster. He'd wandered too far west, galloping into a Yankee patrol. He'd surrendered his weapon, upon demand, to a young private bearing a Henry rifle. After all, one must live to fight another day.

They'd tried to put him in with the common prisoners, two of whom were men from his home guard unit. Officers deserved better treatment. And so he'd taken Lieutenant Randall's advice and demanded an audience with General Sherman.

The officer in charge had laughed at the demand, until, in a clear and loud voice, Morgan claimed to have a personal message for the general from Jared Randall. A small but effective lie. Within the hour he had been taken to the general's tent, and that had been when he made his error.

He'd mentioned *her* name when relating the events of the day. He'd caught the glances, one officer to the other, when he mentioned Emily Gardner. She must be of more value than he'd realized!

Sherman's scorn had grated on Morgan's sensibilities. How dare the pompous invader call him a fool? How dare he treat an officer and hero of the South no better than scum?

The rope snapped, freeing his hands to work on the bindings at his ankles, his wrists bleeding from the chafing.

An accident had saved him from prison. Though he wished for a horse, he could endure the pain of walking a few miles until he found a mount. Then he would ride to Richmond to collect the deserved reward and accolades.

He would be careful to travel slowly, so as not to arrive before Lieutenant Randall. Randall would give the report to those who would hand out the promotions. The South would then know of Gilbert Morgan's dedication to the cause. Then he would watch Emily Gardner hang for her crimes.

Free of restraints, Captain Gilbert Morgan limped southward, beginning the long trek back toward the edge of the Yankee encampment, where the horses were staked.

Chapter Six

Emily stood near the blaze incinerating the gazebo, feeling the heat of the flames, unable to move, unable to cross the yard and get into the house to raise an alarm.

Men on horseback surrounded the mansion, torches raised.

"Burn the traitor out!" they chanted, and began circling, thundering past her, throwing torch after flaming torch at the mansion.

Smoke stung her eyes, scorched her lungs.

"Papa!" she shouted, but she knew he wouldn't hear. Nor would Terrance or the house servants. They would all die if she didn't warn them.

She struggled to move. Her feet wouldn't budge.

"Emily, wake up. You're dreaming."

Jared. Oh, thank God.

She grabbed the lapels of his uniform coat. "Make them stop, Jared!" she pleaded. "Please, make them stop!"

He shook his head sadly.

A wall of fire roared up, consuming her home. High into the night the flames ascended, into the heavens, killing everyone she had ever cared for.

She screamed.

"Emily!"

With a gasp she woke, half sitting, half lying against

Jared. He held her tightly, running a hand along her spine, his cheek pressed against her forehead.

"It's only a nightmare, Emily. Let it go. I won't let anyone hurt you, I swear."

Safe within his embrace, she believed. Her heart thudded against her ribs. She was sweating and trembling, but not crying, thank goodness.

Only a nightmare. Only a dream. It had seemed so real, so terrifyingly real.

And she'd felt so powerless.

"Awake?" he asked.

She nodded against his chest, not wishing to move. She would sit right here until the flames in her lingering vision died down, until the men stopped chanting, until she could truly believe that no one had died in the fire.

The night air smelled sweet, not smoky. No flames soared to the stars. The sound of thundering horses gave way to the chirping of birds rousing to greet the day.

"I'm sorry I woke you," she whispered, not sorry at all.

"I was already awake. Look, the sunrise."

She swiveled her head. Low on the horizon, a brightening sky glowed, but all she could see was the rubble of the charred remains of the horse barns.

"My grandfather says there's powerful medicine in the sunrise," Jared said. "He gets up every morning before dawn, goes out into the desert to pray and greet the sun."

"Even in the rain?" she asked sardonically.

"He says on some days one has to look a bit harder for the sun, but it's always there."

"If you're about to spout some drivel about new days and new beginnings, save your breath."

"I wouldn't dream of it. There are days all I want to do is stay in bed, cover my head with a pillow and hope nobody comes looking for me. You also have to remember that where my grandfather lives, it doesn't rain much."

She'd stopped trembling. The dream had faded, some

An image of an old, wizened Indian displaced the

She pictured him sitting amid cactus and sagebrush, silent, thoughtful, awaiting sunrise. She tried picturing Jared doing the same, but somehow the vision wouldn't come.

Jared claimed Navajo blood flowed in his veins. Emily saw a hint of it in his features, but saw not a trace of it in his manner. He didn't strike her as being either savage or heathen, capable of committing atrocities against innocents.

She glanced at the mansion. This raid had been carried out by men who considered themselves civilized.

"Sun's up. Time to get moving," he said.

Emily took a deep breath, not ready to face the day, much less the journey ahead. But she had little choice. "How far do you plan to go today?"

"Hadn't given it too much thought. How about if you make some coffee, and I'll get out a map?"

He helped her to stand. While she started the fire and set the coffee brewing, he fetched a tube from his saddlebags, from which he pulled several sheets of paper. He unrolled them and studied the top sheet.

"Well, this doesn't look too complicated," he declared. He turned the map slightly for her to see. "We head east until we hit the Chattahoochee River. Not easy terrain, but passable. Should reach Gainesville in a couple of days. From there we follow the railroad tracks northeast."

It seemed a reasonable route, Emily thought, with one exception. "There aren't many towns that way. I had hoped to find a dressmaker's shop relatively soon."

Jared rolled the maps. "Leave it to a woman. She sets out on a journey and she wants a new wardrobe to do it in."

Emily spread her arms akimbo. "This outfit will not hold up all the way to Petersburg. I'm fortunate the seams haven't burst or the skirt worn through before now."

"Isn't there something in your satchel you can wear?"

A nightgown. A peach silk bodice and skirt, the only decent ensemble she had left to her name. Terrance's old ⸱⸱⸱ and trousers, which she refused to wear around Jared.

"Nothing suitable."

And, frankly, she would rather not arrive at her aunt's looking like a pauper. Though she didn't voice the thought, as she looked into Jared's softening eyes, she knew he'd somehow heard and understood. She wasn't sure she liked that.

"We need to stop somewhere for supplies anyway," he said, relenting. "We'll see what we can do."

Fog rolled off the Potomac, blanketing Washington in a cloud of thick spring mist. Colonel John Gardner bent before the hearth in his library, took a chunk of wood from the box and tossed the fuel into an already roaring fire.

He flicked ash from his blue wool uniform. Even dressed warmly, standing by the fire, he shivered at a chill. *Getting old*, he admitted, feeling every one of his fifty-five years.

John ran his fingers through silver-threaded black hair and ambled over to the window. Outside, the marigolds lining the front walk disappeared behind a white curtain of fog near the street. He watched for movement, wishing Hunter would suddenly appear through that white curtain.

If the information John had gleaned from the telegrams he'd received was accurate, Captain Jared Hunter could be in a lot of trouble.

And he has my daughter with him.

A sharp rap on the library door heralded Captain Frank West, a blue-eyed Kansas farm boy—tall, broad in the shoulder, and solid as an oak. His code name, Viking, suited Frank's size and coloring perfectly.

"You sent for me, Colonel?" Frank asked, closing the door.

John waved at a chair in front of his mahogany desk. "I did." As Frank sat, John slid two sheets of paper across the desk. Frank picked them up.

"I received both telegrams this morning," John said. "The one from General Sherman is dated yesterday. The one from Hunter is from three days ago, written in code, of course, and sent through an operative in Richmond.''

Frank nodded, understanding. ''Takes a while to pass coded messages through operatives. Says here he has your daughter. That's good news.''

''That's why I sent for you. I'm not at all sure the news is good.''

Before Frank could question or John explain, the library door opened and Hanna, John's Negro housekeeper, entered. Her hands gripping a large tray, she closed the door with a nudge of her ample backside, then waddled across the room.

She set the tray, laden with coffee fixings and pastry, on the desk between the two men. Gnarled fingers dipped into a deep apron pocket for a silver flask, which she set in front of a smiling Frank.

John scowled. ''Hanna, just because Captain West hands you his flask every time he comes over, doesn't mean you should feel obliged to fill it with my best bourbon.''

''But I do,'' she said, ''just like I give Captain Hunter sweets when he comes nosin' around the kitchen. Those boys are fightin' a war and deserve a bit of spoilin'.''

Arguing was pointless. No matter what he said, Hanna would continue to pamper Jared and Frank, her favorites from among his men.

From his library office, Colonel John Gardner commanded an élite force of operatives, most Southern-born but serving the Union. Their mission—swift and efficient covert operations. Countless times they had nullified an objective, making full-scale battle unnecessary, saving soldier's lives, civilian casualties and private property loss. His men were fighting a secret war, a dangerous war, one that demanded superior physical and mental abilities. Hanna was right. When not on assignment, they deserved a bit of spoiling.

Suspecting her real purpose for interrupting, John told Hanna, ''One of the telegrams that arrived this morning was from Captain Hunter. He has Emily. You might want to ready a room for her.''

''Already done,'' she told him. ''You want me to bring your dinner in here?''

''No. I'll eat in the dining room as usual.''

Wagging a finger at Frank, she ordered, ''Don't you keep him too long. His food will get cold.'' Her tone scolded, but the gentle pat on Frank's shoulder belied any sting.

John stared at the door that closed behind Hanna. ''There are times when I wonder who's in charge in this household.''

Frank set the telegrams on the desk and laced his coffee with the bourbon. ''I don't wonder. That's why I hand Hanna the flask, not you. I suspect she ran Rosewood with the same efficiency as she runs this house. I've got news for you, Colonel. She may have once been a slave, may still be a servant, but she has you figured out, dead to rights.''

John nodded. ''I've never regretted the day I let Mary Beth talk me into buying Hanna and her husband. She and Zeke are free now, and yet they stay with me. I'm not sure who needs who more, them or me.''

After a long silence, Frank asked, ''What is it you want me to do, sir?''

John indicated the telegram from General Sherman. ''See what you can find on Gilbert Morgan. Maybe army intelligence or the Pinkerton Agency has a record on him.''

''You think this Morgan is a threat to Jared?''

John stood up and paced. ''I don't know! According to Sherman's wire, one Confederate Captain Gilbert Morgan stated that a Lieutenant Jared Randall had told Morgan to mention his name to Sherman should the occasion arise. That tells me two things. First, Jared isn't using the false name we agreed he should use. Second, goading Morgan to seek out Sherman means Jared wants Morgan out of his way, permanently. Sherman tried to oblige, but Morgan escaped.''

John stopped pacing long enough to pick up the second telegram. "The agent in Richmond said Hunter's message originated in a town east of Adairsville. He was supposed to travel north, through Tennessee. He's improvising, changing strategy in midmission. I don't like the idea of Cougar roaming around northern Georgia."

"Have you seen the Southern newspapers lately?" Frank asked. "An article in the Atlanta paper says Cougar is doing dastardly deeds in Savannah. The Richmond paper puts him in Mississippi, of all places. I always did admire Cougar's ability to be hundreds of miles apart on the same day. The Rebs may know his code name, but that's all they know. They don't know Jared Hunter is Cougar."

"My concern is someday the Rebs will connect the two. I would rather that not happen, ever, but especially not while Emily is with him."

"Colonel," Frank said gently, "he won't let anything happen to Emily. Jared's the best there is, slippery as a greased pig when he sets his mind to it. He'll be careful."

"He might be *too* careful. Having Emily in tow will weigh heavily in any decision Jared makes if he gets into trouble. He might hesitate to act if he thinks Emily might get hurt." John sighed. "I wish he would get over his aversion to using the rail system. The journey would be so much faster by train than on horseback."

"I can understand his reluctance, sir. We've tampered with too many rails and locomotives to feel comfortable traveling by train."

John smiled, remembering a rather spectacular trestle collapse engineered by Cougar and Viking. During that operation, the Rebs had learned Jared's code name. From then on, the Southern newspapers had blamed Cougar for every explosion, break-in or wayward communication the Confederacy couldn't otherwise explain. John shrugged a shoulder. "I guess it's Emily's father who wishes this trip were shorter."

"This is the mighty Cougar we're talking about here, sir.

I know Jared. If they run into trouble, he'll tell your little girl what to do and when to do it, and not take any nonsense just because she's your daughter.''

"The little girl I left in Georgia didn't much like taking orders,'' John mused.

Frank guffawed. "What woman does?''

Ready for a change of subject, John sat down in the leather chair behind his desk. "How is Kate these days?''

"Kate is…Kate. She's all sunshine and bubbles, unless she perceives suffering. Then she turns tigress. Her latest crusade is to improve the conditions in the field hospitals. I doubt there's much she can do, but I intend to stay out of her way.''

"How are you getting along with her father?''

"Major Drew? All right, I guess. I gotta tell you, Colonel. It's not easy courting the daughter of the head of army intelligence. Major Drew seems to know what I've been doing before I've had the chance to do it. He's never said so, but I'm not sure he approves of me, at least not as a prospective husband for his daughter.''

"Maybe that's good,'' John said wearily. "This way you'll have to prove your love for Kate over and over. I wish I'd mistrusted Lewis Roth when he asked for Emily's hand. As it turned out, when I left Georgia, he broke the engagement.''

Frank rose from his chair, tucking the telegram from General Sherman in his pocket. "I'll see what I can find out about this Morgan character, but I don't think you should worry too much. Hunter will be fine, and he'll take care of Emily.''

John tried to smile. "I'm sure you're right.''

Emily entered the dressmaker's shop and inhaled deeply of the scent of lavender. The aroma emanated from a small bouquet of dried flowers attached to the white-ribbon band on a wide-brimmed straw bonnet displayed in the window. Though she longed to try it on, she resisted. A riding outfit—if the dressmaker had one made up—would be an expensive but necessary purchase. Not so a bonnet.

As Jared closed the door behind them, a matronly woman appeared from behind a curtain that doubtless led to the shop's fitting rooms and work area. Emily wasn't surprised at the look of near horror that flashed on the woman's face.

Knowing she looked an absolute fright, Emily held her arms out and appealed to the woman's sense of fashion and propriety. "As you can see, I desperately need to replace this habit. Can you help me?"

The woman exclaimed, "Oh, my dear, I certainly hope so!" She looked Emily up and down, in the way of dressmakers everywhere, to discern her size before verifying it with a tape measure. Emily assisted by turning around, slowly.

The woman's eyes fairly sparked with glee. "Yes. Oh, yes. I believe I have the perfect solution." Gloating, she disappeared into the back room.

"What about this one?" Jared said.

Emily turned to where Jared had wandered—beside a dress on a form in the corner of the shop. The costume was pink, festooned with bows and lace. It was pretty—for someone of about fifteen, who would wear such an outfit for a trot in the park, just to show off the dress.

"I don't think it would do."

"Why not? I think you would look rather fetching in it."

She would look ridiculous in it. "That dress isn't made for heavy wear, Jared. Likely, I would leave a trail of bows from here to Petersburg."

"Your wife is quite correct, sir," the dressmaker stated, coming from behind the curtain. "Besides, that dress would not fit her."

Wife? Emily thought to refute the relationship, but refrained. She'd addressed Jared by his given name. Naturally the dressmaker would assume they were husband and wife. Oh, dear, if Jared corrected that assumption, the woman would jump to another conclusion and order them out of her shop. But how could she warn Jared without exposing…?

Jared suddenly turned a charming smile on the dressmaker. His stance shifted subtly, in a way that showed off his buckskin trousers and calf-high boots to best advantage. He crossed his arms, slightly straining the seams of his white shirt, presenting a very virile image. Like a pirate. The man was utterly shameless.

"No?" he asked. "I thought the waist and shoulders seemed near her size."

The dressmaker wasn't immune to Jared's magnetism. She fairly preened under his regard. "I will allow that her waist is tiny, but, sir, your wife is too richly endowed in the bosom for that particular dress."

Emily blushed furiously, thankful that the dressmaker was too intent on Jared to notice. Jared, however, noticed far too well. His smile widened.

"Yes, of course she is." He pointed at the dress draped across the woman's arm. "You think this one will better accommodate her, ah…attributes?"

Emily forgot her embarrassment as the woman held up the dress. It had a bodice of royal blue brocade, and a collar and cuffs trimmed in black velvet, sporting a dozen jet buttons. It was, without doubt, the most gorgeous dress Emily had seen since the beginning of the war.

"This will suit her much better, don't you think?" the woman asked.

"Possibly," Jared said.

She heard his doubt, and her heart sank, because she knew he was right. The brocade was almost as unsuitable for a long, hard ride as the pink.

Emily fingered the brocade. "How much?"

"Fifty dollars."

She swallowed, and let go. She couldn't afford to spend that much money on one dress. "I'm afraid that's beyond my means."

Jared came up to her side, put a hand on her shoulder. "Emily, if you really want it, we'll work something out."

Spoken like a true husband wishing to indulge his wife. He need not carry the farce this far. But as she looked at him, she realized he was serious. If she truly wanted the dress, she could have it. And, somehow, passing it by suddenly didn't hurt so much.

She put her hand over his. "Thank you, but no." She turned to the dressmaker. "The outfit really is beautiful, and the workmanship is exquisite, but it is beyond me."

Emily turned to leave.

"Wait," the woman said. "I have one more. It isn't fancy, and it isn't quite finished."

Emily turned back. "Another? I was amazed you had one. How do you happen to have three?"

The dressmaker fingered the brocade. "All three were commissioned by a friend of mine, for herself and her daughter. The family has since fallen on hard times, and as much as I hate to sell them to others, I must eat, too."

Once more, the woman disappeared into her workshop. When she returned, she held up a bodice of sturdy brown cotton, its only decoration a lace-trimmed white collar.

"As you can see," she said, "it wants for buttons and the skirt needs hemming, but if you're willing to finish it, I can let you have it for twenty."

"Try it on," Jared urged, with a little push.

Emily snapped up the bodice and skirt. In the fitting room, she quickly changed. Perfect. Carefully she folded the habit to avoid further creasing, then struggled into her old clothes and returned to the shop.

Jared was standing at the counter, handing the dressmaker a stack of Confederate scrip. On the counter sat the straw bonnet with the lavender sprig tucked into the white band.

The woman stuffed the bills into a box behind the counter, then produced brown buttons and a spool of brown thread.

"Here you are," she said, dumping buttons and thread into Emily's hand. "Your husband says he has a needle, so I needn't sell you one." She then picked up the bonnet, put it on Emily's head and tied the bow. "There you are, my dear. Have a nice journey."

"Thank you," Emily managed, before Jared ushered her out of the shop. As they walked toward the horses, however, her astonishment vanished and anger at Jared's presumption surfaced.

"How much did the bonnet cost me?" she asked.

"Nothing," he claimed.

"Surely she didn't give it to you."

"No, but you needn't reimburse me for the hat, only the dress."

Emily carefully placed the new outfit in her satchel. "I can't accept such a personal item as a gift. It isn't proper."

An exasperated look on his face, he stated, "I noticed you admiring the hat when you entered the shop, so when you went into the fitting room, I went over to look at it. That woman suggested that if I was forcing you to ride all the way to Petersburg, the least I could do was buy you a hat to protect your skin from the sun." He tossed his hands in the air. "What's a husband to do in the face of such logic?"

He looked so put-upon that Emily couldn't help but smile in sympathy.

"But we're not married."

"Did you want me to tell her that?"

"Well, no, but—"

"Lady, either you wear that hat, or I'll cut a couple of holes in the brim and let Rusty wear it!"

What was a woman to do in the face of such an absurd suggestion?

"The hat is beautiful, Jared. Thank you."

Chapter Seven

Emily rubbed the palm of her hand against her hip. The healing burn itched, as did her whole body. She looked longingly at the Chattahoochee River, then finished arranging the few pieces of firewood needed to boil water. Jared wanted coffee, even in this awful heat. At least he'd agreed to a cold supper.

She wiped her forehead with her sleeve and wrinkled her nose at the stench. Washing hurriedly in streams did not replace a bath. Using Jared's detailed maps, each night they'd been able to camp near water. Jared would grab his towel, head for the water and plunge in. But ever since seeing him nearly naked on that first night, Emily had hesitated to go near the water while he swam.

At the moment, Jared was off making his routine tour of the campsite. Determined to have a thorough wash during the hour he would spend scouting the area, Emily fetched soap and a washcloth and quickly shucked boots, stockings and dress, but couldn't find the courage to remove her chemise and petticoats. She pulled the petticoats up between her legs, tucked the hems into the waistband and gingerly stepped into the river. With both hands she scooped water and splashed it over her face. Cold water trickled down her arms, raising goose bumps.

With the soapy cloth, she wiped away sweaty grime from

face and arms. This washing would use up the cake of lilac soap. She mourned the loss of the fragrance. Sweetly aromatic, the scent had lifted her spirits on days when she desperately needed to feel feminine.

Now that she was refreshed, her daring increased. She slid the thin white chemise straps down over her shoulders. Modesty, however, prevented her letting the garment slip down over her breasts. She merely plucked the chemise away from her chest, sliding the soapy cloth between her breasts and then over them.

Emily tugged the straps back into place, then dunked her head into the water to wash her hair. She longed for hot water, vinegar rinse and a fluffy towel. Lacking those luxuries, lilac soap and brush-drying would suffice. She wrung the water from her hair and reluctantly splashed back to the bank. She put on her new clothing, which she'd managed to finish during their various stops to either eat or rest the horses.

The bodice and skirt fit so well and looked so nice that for the first time since leaving Adairsville she felt truly feminine. The new hat, too, had boosted her spirits.

Remembering Jared's chagrin at having been manipulated into buying the hat by the dressmaker, Emily had to smile. She shook her head, trying to banish other thoughts she'd struggled with all day. Ever since he'd slid, quite easily and with such virile charm, into playacting as her husband, Emily had wondered if Jared was married, or promised to a woman. He hadn't mentioned anyone special, nor did he wear a wedding band, but then, soldiers normally didn't wear jewelry or carry valuables, though Jared did carry a gold pocket watch.

Emily hadn't thought it possible, but Jared had become the very model of the hired guide. He showed her his maps and explained his planned route. He rode at moderate speed, pacing the horses. He chose private areas, off the road to camp in. When he paid for supplies, or this morning's purchase of a riding outfit, he recorded the amount spent in a notebook.

Except for that brief touch of reassurance on her shoulder in the dressmaker's shop, Jared hadn't touched her since holding her through her nightmare at Rosewood. He was behaving exactly as she'd demanded.

Obviously, she'd overreacted to his comment about their coming together as lovers. Jared impressed her as a man who found ways to obtain what he wanted, which meant he didn't want her very badly. Or else he'd buried the desire so deeply she couldn't see it. Jared could do that, hide whatever he was thinking behind an emotionless mask.

His divided personality disturbed her at times, and frankly, the man who'd threatened to toss her into a grave could be cold, harsh, and more than a little dangerous. He was the man who scouted the camp every night, whose eyes darted from building to building and person to person whenever they entered a town, as if he expected a threat or confrontation.

Maybe it was the soldier in Jared, or maybe the Navajo blood, that stiffened his spine to rigid alertness if someone looked at them too long, or a twig snapped unexpectedly. In that persona he could move with such precision, and such stealth, that she rarely knew he'd returned to their campsite until she sensed his nearness.

Oddly enough, it was that man with whom she felt safe, protected from any physical harm.

The other Jared, the gentleman with the charming manners and the gentle touch, was tying knots in her stomach and tugging at her heart.

The physical attraction had become stronger. His full, warm mouth would tempt any woman. Emily wet her lips in acute awareness of how persuasively his mouth could evoke unchaste responses.

Her common sense warned her to beware. She need only remember Lewis's perfidy to know how easily a man could discard a woman. And Jared would eventually leave her.

After escorting her to Petersburg, he would go on with his life as if she didn't exist.

Emily grabbed her brush and sat on the ground, wondering how the devil she could erect a barricade against the pain of that parting, and fearing it was already too late.

Jared's head came out of the water with a backward jerk, the spray from his shaking mane settling back into the river. With his skin cooled, he willed the turmoil of his inner self to yield to the calming effect of the water.

As an imaginative lad, he remembered wishing himself other than human, as a cougar or a wild stallion. Never in his flights into fantasy had he imagined being transformed into a square of cotton lathered with lilac-scented soap.

Returning early to the campsite, he'd watched as Emily slipped out of her garments. He should have left then, given Emily the privacy she thought she enjoyed. But, seeing those bared shoulders and that enticing, graceful neck, how could any man have torn his eyes from the vision? Instead, his feet had refused to move, and a lump had formed in his throat when the straps of her chemise drifted down her arms.

Unknowingly, she'd enticed his heightened senses, driving him wild with curiosity and desire when, instead of exposing her firm, high breasts, she slid the washcloth down to caress hidden flesh.

Unwilling to let his lust gain control, he'd sought the only relief available, lest he pounce upon Emily. The shock of cold water helped, but the inner inferno still raged.

Emily had made it clear that she didn't want to take up with him where she'd left off with her lover. Hell, maybe she loved Sam and intended to find him after the war.

His bodily urges at a precarious level, Jared knew he needed a woman. Tomorrow, instead of a private camp, he would find an inn to spend the night. Any innkeeper who could run a business in this stifled economy would know of a woman willing to earn money between the sheets.

And the inn would stock whiskey, either smuggled from over the border or from an illegal home still. A couple of shots of potent brew would bring on drowsiness, aiding a good night's sleep.

His decision firm, Jared shrugged into his white shirt and his buckskins. This time he announced his return to the campsite, making enough noise to alert the deaf.

She glanced up as he strode into the clearing, then returned to her chore. With deft fingers and brush, Emily yanked, then separated, then plied the brush again to her drying mahogany hair.

She'd changed into the outfit she'd worked furiously to finish. It lent sophistication to her slender but nicely rounded figure, hugging her curves without binding. She looked all woman, her posture erect and expression slightly guarded, but she sat like a little girl, with legs tucked beneath her, tailor-fashion.

"Shoot," she complained when the brush stuck.

Jared took the brush from Emily's hand. She looked up, surprised, then turned her head and closed her eyes.

He located the stubborn twist of hair and gently urged its surrender. Emily's hair was so soft. He marveled at the glistening highlights that sprang to life as her hair dried.

Each stroke of the brush released a puff of scent. He'd never noticed how fragrant lilacs smelled until meeting Emily.

Emily sighed, snapping Jared back to reality. He gave her the brush and took the hair ribbon from where it rested across her thigh, resisting the urge to linger.

"If we ride hard tomorrow, we should reach Gainesville," he said, gathering her hair into his hand and tying the ribbon. "I thought we might stay at an inn there, if you agree."

Emily brightened. "Oh, it would be lovely to sleep in a bed."

"And we could eat supper at a table. I might even treat you to a glass of wine, if they have some."

Her smile widened. "I might skip supper. If they can provide one, I intend to call for a bath and spend hours soaking and washing my hair. And then I'm going to crawl into a warm, soft bed and drift into peaceful slumber."

Jared forcibly pushed away thoughts of their sharing a bath, a bed, or both. He walked away, to give his good intentions a fighting chance. "Maybe this isn't such a good idea. You'll get spoiled and start complaining about having to sleep on the hard ground again."

Wide-eyed, Emily scrambled to her feet. "No! Please don't change your mind," she pleaded. "I promise I won't complain. I haven't so far, have I?"

Not once had she complained, Jared mused. Emily had endured the journey without uttering a word of protest about the lack of conveniences or privacy. Asking for help only when she needed it, Emily never played the frail female.

"Well, not so far. But if I start pampering you, I may eventually regret it."

"Pampering? One night at an inn is not pampering. Doesn't a bed sound good to you, too? How long has it been since you've slept on a mattress, with a pillow under your head, instead of a rolled blanket or a saddle?"

Jared knew he shouldn't bait her, but Emily responded so winsomely whenever he teased that the temptation proved irresistible.

"Once asleep, it's hard to tell the difference between bed and bedroll."

Jared opened his pack to look for a snack. Hardtack and jerky were filling, but hardly satisfying.

"Supper!" Emily exclaimed, reading his mind. "Hot, juicy meat and steamed vegetables... Warm, flaky biscuits, with butter melting down the sides..."

"More likely they'll serve thin stew and corn bread."

"A card game, then. I'll even stake you. You could sit up half the night and drink beer and smoke your cigars and not lose any of your own money."

Jared smiled to himself, thinking of the many nights he had played poker with her father. Emily was desperately reaching for some argument he would find impossible to turn aside. Would she offer what he really wanted, if he held out long enough? Did he want her to?

He shook his head. "I'd lose every penny in about ten minutes."

She crossed her arms, vexed. "If you didn't mean to stop at an inn, then why did you suggest it? Really, Jared, your...shifts in mood can be very annoying."

He couldn't tell her the truth. He couldn't tell her that he was losing his edge, that Cougar was berating Jared Hunter for the slips in his attention to duty, for changing his route and slowing his speed to accommodate Emily. Nor could he tell her, having gained her trust, that she was endangered, not by an enemy, but by him.

If he didn't regain his perspective, this mission could blow up in his face. To regain control, he needed a night away from this siren who lured him toward the rocks of destruction.

And he needed to find out if this attraction to Emily was purely physical, if a romp with another woman would diminish the nagging hunger. If not, if he was permanently afflicted with a craving for Emily Gardner, he had to decide what to do about it, and when.

"We'll stop," he finally said. "The horses haven't had any feed but grass for several days. They need grain, and could use a good rubdown."

She tilted her head. "That's the only reason?"

"It's the best one. If they're going to carry us all the way to Petersburg, we'd best take care of them, right?"

"We could take a train out of Gainesville."

Jared inwardly shuddered, hoping Emily didn't perceive his coiling innards and pounding heart at the mere suggestion.

"No trains."

"I suppose it would be horribly expensive, for passage for us and to transport the horses."

Expensive, but not beyond the hefty allowance John Gardner had provided. Still, Jared didn't correct her assumption.

True to Jared's estimate, two days after they'd left Rosewood they entered Gainesville, Emily tried not to notice the boarded-up windows of abandoned buildings, or the bare feet of the children scampering along the street. Small towns throughout the South were strangling in the grip of poverty. Larger cities along the coast were doing better because of the success of the blockade runners—or so the newspapers claimed.

Jared pulled up in front of a building of whitewashed brick trimmed with black shutters. Marigolds bloomed in a planter under the window facing the street. Grundy's Inn, the sign read. Emily stayed with the horses while Jared went into the inn. A minute later, he came out smiling.

"There's room at the inn," he quipped. "Let's get the horses settled."

As Jared unsaddled his gelding, he watched Emily charm the stable boy, a Negro youngster named Horace. A once yellow shirt dwarfed Horace's small shoulders. Brown suspenders, clasped to the waistband of baggy pants, held them up to an area approximating his waist. Barefoot and agile, he pranced about Rusty, giving Emily a knowledgeable commentary on the mare's qualities.

Horace told Emily, "You and your man done picked the best inn on the road. Why, Grundy's place is always full of rich and important folk!"

If Emily gave any thought to denying the boy's assumption about their relationship, or the state of their finances, she let it pass.

"I'm sure that if the rest of the staff is as efficient as the stable boy, we'll enjoy our stay," Emily said.

The boy's chest puffed. "Even Marse Robert Lee beds

down here when passin' through. See that stall?'' Horace pointed, Emily dutifully looked. "Traveller done used that stall.''

Jared kept his skepticism to himself. Traveller was a well-known mount. There were almost as many stories told about the horse as about General Lee.

"Horace,'' Emily was saying, "if your skill is such that General Lee would trust you with Traveller, then I can do no less than trust you with Rusty. You will take very good care of her, I'm sure.''

The stable boy beamed, his face awash with obvious adoration. "I'm the best stable boy in these parts, ma'am,'' Horace declared.

"Good, then I'm sure you'll notice that Rusty can be temperamental.'' With a wry smile and an emphatic glance at Jared, Emily added, "Of late, she's shown a tolerance for strangers. However, I want you to be careful.''

"Heck, I ain't gotten kicked at in a whole month.''

Her smile widened as she picked up her saddlebags and satchel.

Jared picked up his bags and headed for the inn. Emily followed, glancing back, once, at Horace.

"Do you think Rusty will give him trouble?'' she asked.

"I'll go out and check later, but you heard him, he's unequaled.''

As they stepped up to the bar in the common room, a thin, harried-looking little man greeted them. "Welcome to Grundy's Inn. Something I can get you? We've got some mighty fine stew cooking.''

"Two rooms,'' Jared said.

Mr. Grundy's eyes flickered between Jared and Emily. Then he said, "Sorry, we're near full up. Only got one room left, number seven, top of the stairs on the right.''

Jared rested an elbow on the bar and leaned casually toward the little man. "Are you Mr. Grundy?''

"Yes, sir.''

"Mr. Grundy, I believe there's been a mistake. When I

was in here, not five minutes ago, the young lady standing behind this very counter assured me *two* rooms were available."

Mr. Grundy pondered for a moment, then ran a finger down the register. "Oh, of course, you must be Randall. When Tess ran though the kitchen and said we had only one room left, I assumed... Well, my apologies, sir."

Jared heard Emily exhale.

The innkeeper fetched two keys from beneath the counter. "Tess put you in number six, Miss Gardner. I'm sure you'll find it satisfactory."

"Does the room have a bed?" Emily asked wistfully.

"Big and comfortable."

"May I have a bath sent up—immediately?"

"It'll cost a bit extra, but yes, of course."

Emily held out her hand for the key. "Thank you. Now, if you gentlemen will excuse me?"

Jared chuckled at the glee on Emily's face as she scampered up the stairs.

"Pretty little miss," Grundy commented, and gave Jared the second key. "Are you sure you want number eight?"

"Something wrong with number eight?"

"Well, no, but... Ah, I guess Tess assigned the room without explaining." Grundy's eyes twinkled. "Number eight is near the back stairs. We use the room for gentlemen who request, shall we say, certain amenities?"

Intrigued, Jared slanted closer to Grundy. "Would the amenity happen to be blond and full-busted?"

"That's our Tess."

Jared flipped the key and caught it, remembering his plans for a frustration-relieving romp. He wasn't sure, however, if he liked the idea that Tess had claimed him for the night. "May I take the room and decide later about amenities?"

Grundy chuckled. "As you wish, sir."

Chapter Eight

Alone in her room, Emily stared at the forlorn waif who stared back from the full-length mirror. Her hair was dry and frizzy, and her poor nose had turned rose-red with sunburn.

Emily opened the door to a light rap, admitting a buxom blond whose strong perfume preceded her.

"My name is Tess, ma'am," the woman announced, dumping two towels and a cake of soap onto the bed. "I'm to supervise your bath and get you spruced up for supper. I daresay this could take a while."

Emily bristled under Tess's slow perusal, which openly tallied flaws. True, she looked a mess, but to have Tess so blatantly agree was not to be tolerated. Emily summoned her pride and faced Tess squarely.

"Have you training, or are you the only maid available?"

Tess's eyes narrowed before retorting haughtily, "I've served guests as lady's maid before. I'm sure my talents are far beyond any you might require."

Emily couldn't help but notice that Tess's "talents" fairly spilled out of her low-cut blouse.

"Yes, I'm sure they are," she cattily agreed. Ignoring the thin set of Tess's mouth, Emily crossed the room and pulled her peach outfit from the bottom of her satchel. She deposited the clothing into Tess's outstretched arms. "I'm assuming you count laundering as one of your talents. Take care not to scorch or melt it during pressing."

Tess mockingly curtsied. "Yes, Miss Gardner. Will there be anything else, ma'am?"

Emily picked up the cake of coarse soap. "Can you supply scented soap, preferably lilac?"

"It'll cost you extra," Tess warned.

Emily touched her nose. "Lotion and powder?"

"There's a store down the street that might—"

"And vinegar rinse," Emily went on, interrupting. "Can you get those items for me?"

"Miss Gardner, all those items are luxuries! Do you know what the powder alone will cost?"

Emily hesitated for only a moment before digging into the satchel for the leather pouch and one precious gold coin. She handed it to Tess.

"This should cover any expenses you may incur, and if you hurry, you can keep the change for your services."

Tess ogled the coin. "It's gold," she said reverently.

"Which I'm sure the shopkeeper will be happy to accept. Be sure to get the best bargain you can for it."

Tess smiled widely. "Ben is going to take one look at this and think he's died and gone to heaven." Then she sighed. "Except he won't hang on to it. He'll be down in the taproom later, spending it on liquor."

Emily crossed her arms. "I don't much care how Ben spends it. Just make sure you get the items I want."

"Yes, ma'am. Lilac soap, lotion, face powder, vinegar rinse. Anything else?"

Emily marveled at the change in Tess's demeanor, from rudely flippant to almost respectful. Amazing what money could buy. "Nothing else. Just be quick."

Jared shifted in his chair and took a sip of homemade wine. Why did women always take so long to bathe and dress?

Set apart from the taproom, the dining area held several round tables, each covered with a white cloth. Kerosene lamps glowed from wall sconces. Silver and crystal table settings sparkled in the flickering light. The other diners, civilians in business suits, conversed over venison stew and hot bread.

He raised his wineglass again. An appreciative moan emitted from a man at the table behind him. Only a woman could cause such sweet suffering. Expecting to see Tess, Jared glanced at the doorway.

Emily had entered the dining room. He felt the now familiar tug on his insides, snared on the line she cast out and yanked to set the hook.

Her hair flowed in soft waves over her shoulders. Her lace-trimmed peach blouse enhanced the fresh color in her cheeks. Puffed short sleeves exposed the delicate structure of her arms. The matching skirt hung in gentle folds over shapely hips to the instep of her boots.

Emily looked fragile and vulnerable as her gaze traveled the room. Entranced, Jared rose and strode to her side. In gentlemanly fashion, he guided her to their table. As he held the chair for Emily, with a slow turn of his head, Jared challenged every bold male's stare. When all had looked away, he returned to his seat.

"Wine?" Jared asked, pouring the burgundy into her glass.

"It's been a very long time since I last drank wine." She took a sip. "Mmm...this is almost as good as Zeke's."

"Zeke?" Jared asked, sensing an opportunity to learn something of Emily's upbringing, and her current feelings toward her father.

"Zeke is...was our butler. He was a field hand before Papa bought him and his wife, Hanna, and brought them both into the house as butler and housekeeper." A sad smile graced her lips. "Zeke didn't know how to greet guests properly, but Mama patiently taught him. What Zeke could do well, however, was make excellent wine. So every year at harvest, Papa would buy all the grapes he could manage and Zeke would make our wine.''

Emily reminisced about the old slave's brew, of sunlit days spent training horses, of dances held on the veranda under Chinese lanterns. She described a world of privilege and ease—a world far removed from his own childhood experience.

Jared responded with tales of painted deserts and cactus in bloom, of caves carved into plunging ravines in the canyons near his home, and wild mustangs.

"You caught your first horse?" she asked, incredulous.

He nodded, smiling. "Just me and a rope, and a whole lot of luck. That paint gave me fits. Got away from me twice. But he was the one I wanted, so I kept at it. Eventually, I got him trapped in a ravine."

"Did you have to break him yourself?"

"And had the bruises to prove it, too."

Emily giggled. "On your head or…posterior?"

"Both."

Emily's giddy laughter made Jared glance at the wine bottle. Empty. He looked about the dining room. Only the two of them remained. He took out his pocket watch.

"Almost midnight."

Emily's softly glazed eyes studied the watch. "Your watch is very beautiful. May I see?"

Jared handed Emily the timepiece. "A present from my parents, when I graduated from West Point. I consider it my good-luck charm."

"Most men put a picture of a sweetheart or wife inside. You've no picture in yours."

He thought of the miniature of Emily buried in his packs. It just might fit in the watch if he trimmed the corners.

"Maybe someday." Jared took the watch from the cradle of her palm. "Come on, upstairs with you."

Her gay mood vanished. "Did I say something wrong?"

His abruptness had caused her to frown. It wasn't Emily's fault he'd envisioned her picture inside the watch.

"I just thought you should take full advantage of your bed," he said. "Who knows how many nights you'll spend in a bedroll before you see a soft mattress again?"

The lightened tone restored her smile. He walked her to the stairs. She took three steps up before she realized he wasn't following and turned to look back.

"Aren't you coming up, too?"

He wanted to, but if he escorted Emily to her room, he would be tempted to forget he had a room of his own.

"I think I'll sample Grundy's beer first. See you in the morning."

"Good night, then."

His body burned as he watched Emily sashay up the stairs. He didn't move until he heard her door open, then close.

Jared glanced around the taproom. No Grundy. Two men sat at the far corner table, conversing over mugs of beer.

At another table, a man clad in a shabby waistcoat held on to the neck of a whiskey bottle as if guarding it. A beaver top hat sat next to the bottle. The man was obviously drunk, but not about to stop indulging until the whiskey was gone.

Jared considered ordering the beer he'd told Emily he wanted. But he didn't want beer, he wanted Emily. He needed sleep. A shot or two of whiskey might cloud his mind enough to push Emily out of his thoughts and make sleep possible.

The drunk poured another glass of amber liquid. In a movement as smooth as the liquor, he tossed back the whiskey.

False courage.

The impression propelled Jared up the stairs. He forced himself to pass Emily's room without breaking stride. As he reached the door to his room, he caught a whiff of perfume.

Tess stood near the back stairway, a seductive arch to

her mouth, a suggestive tilt to her hips. She held a bottle of whiskey in one hand, two glasses in the other.

"I thought you might like some company," she said sweetly.

He'd forgotten about the amenities offered to the occupant of room number eight, and Tess might be the perfect cure for what ailed him.

"Sure, why not," he said, and opened the door.

Emily snuggled into the soft mattress, pleasant memories of the supper with Jared gliding through a wine-induced haze.

Jared could be charming, so very easy to talk to, when he made the effort. Several times she had wanted to reach across the table and touch him, let herself respond to the magnetic attraction.

At a tap on the door, Emily called out, "Who is it?"

A male voice mumbled, but she couldn't understand the words. Her visitor could only be Jared, checking on her, she supposed. Lacking a dressing gown, she draped a blanket over her shoulders to cover her nightgown before opening the door.

The man was a stranger and smelled of whiskey.

"You have the wrong room," Emily stated, moving to close the door.

His arm shot out to hold the door open. "Nah, I have the right room," he slurred. "You're Miss Gardner, ain't you? You're the miss Tess was playing lady's maid for today, right?"

"Look, mister—"

"Hummel. Ben Hummel. Owner of Hummel's Dry Goods. Tess paid for your purchases with gold today…my store."

"Mr. Hummel," she said, her patience thinning. "Either you go away, or I will scream and bring everybody in this inn running."

He removed his beaver top hat and bowed, nearly tumbling over. Emily stepped back to avoid being knocked over. Ben lurched into the room and closed the door. "No need. Come to talk business. You have gold. I need working capital. Never transacted this kind of business with a woman before, b-but desperate times call for desperate measures."

Ben Hummel wanted her gold, a coin of which he'd obviously spent downstairs in the taproom, as Tess had said he would. Maybe if she gave him a coin or two he would go away. In the morning she would report Ben Hummel's infamous behavior and send the authorities to retrieve her money.

Nervously she fumbled with the satchel and pulled out the leather pouch. Before she could fetch a coin, he grabbed the pouch and emptied the coins into his hand. He frowned, looking puzzled and not pleased. "Where's the rest?"

"That's all I have." Emily tried to keep her voice calm, though rising panic twisted her insides.

"Tess said you were rich as C-Croesus."

"Tess overstated."

"This is all?" the drunk cried, and flung the gold at his feet, his face twisting into a grotesque visage of anguish and anger. "Not enough, not nearly enough!"

Enraged, he picked up the wooden chair and smashed it against the floor. Emily cried out and stepped back. The gold lay scattered on the rug, the shiny coins glittering amid the broken chunks of the chair. The drunk swayed, wild-eyed.

"A trick!" he spat, waving the sharp point of a broken spindle like a knife. "You lying, cheating bitch!"

"I didn't lie. I don't even know what you're talking about!" Emily argued, glancing at the door as she backed another step, away from the weapon still waving in his hand.

Where is your gun now, Emily? Jared's previous taunt haunted her, but also gave her purpose. Emily dived for her shotgun, but he caught her by the arm and sent her sprawling to the floor. The blanket fell from her shoulders. Her gown twisted around her thighs.

"Ah, what lovely legs," he said with false admiration. He pulled her to her feet and pushed her toward the bed, still clenching the knifelike weapon in his white-knuckled fist.

Emily trembled violently. He was going to rape her. She could see the intent in his eyes. She tried to scream, but all that came out was a whimper.

"Now, lovely limbs, take off the nightgown, slowly," he ordered. "Show old Ben if you compare to Tess."

Emily clutched the neckline of her gown as she struggled to keep her wits and fight the nausea in her stomach. She told herself to be patient, to wait for Ben to make a mistake.

His leer followed her fingers, ogling her flesh as she unfastened the buttons. Impatient, he batted her hand away, slipped his hand under her gown to clumsily fondle her breast. Emily held her breath and stiffened, not daring to show revulsion as Ben's hand roamed. Her time would come, and when it did, she swore, she would make Ben pay dearly.

Two rooms away, Jared heard voices, one male, the other female, both loud and angry. The hair on the back of his neck itched in warning. The female sounded like Emily.

"Did anyone register after us? Take room seven?" he asked the woman curled on his lap.

"No," she whispered while nibbling on his ear.

He easily ignored the flick of her tongue, just as he hadn't responded to Tess's other practiced touches. He'd removed his boots and Tess had removed his shirt, but as yet there wasn't much reason to get out of his pants.

Tess had cured him. He'd lost all carnal appetite, unable to summon a whimper of arousal. He pushed Tess to her feet and headed for the door.

"Where you going, love?" Tess asked breathlessly.

"I think those voices are coming from Emily's room."

A loud crash. Breaking wood. Emily—he was sure it was

Emily—cried out. Jared grabbed his Colt from the night-stand and crept down the hall to her room. Silence. Too quiet.

"Emily," Jared called, rapping on her door. "It's Jared. Are you all right?"

Emily tried to answer, but Ben's hand flew to her throat, holding her jaw in a strangling clamp.

"Send him away," Ben demanded through clenched teeth.

Emily's thoughts raced, cutting through her fear. Jared was on the other side of the door. *Scream.* The sharp spindle against her throat changed her mind. Emily nodded slightly, and Ben's hold loosened, allowing her to speak.

"I'm fine, Captain *Morgan*," Emily called through the door, praying Jared understood the inference that, once more, she was in dire need of rescue and she hoped he would hurry.

The pause was eternal before he said, "Make sure you lock your door."

Jared wanted to know if her door was locked, she was sure of it.

"I will," she said in answer.

Emily winced as she heard Jared's footsteps retreat down the hallway.

Ben chuckled. "There now, sweet thing, we're all alone again. He's gone back to Tess. She'll keep him humming for the rest of the night."

Jared with Tess? Ben's revelation hurt, but the weapon against her throat demanded immediate concentration.

"Please, don't do this," she begged.

Swaying above her, Ben unbuttoned his pants, exposing his swollen organ. "See what I have for you, lovely limbs? Bet I can poke you good as he does."

Ben froze at the deadly click of a revolver hammer behind his left ear.

"Too bad we'll never have the opportunity to compare,"

said a low, derisive male voice. "Button up and back off, or you'll never use it again."

The drunk misbuttoned his pants as he obeyed Jared's orders. Emily scrambled off the bed and eagerly tucked herself under Jared's outstretched arm. Her eyes closed, she pressed against his bare chest and used the steady thump of his heart to regulate her breath.

Jared's voice was soothing. "Are you calm enough to hold this gun on him while I tie him up?"

Emily turned in Jared's arms, took the gun and faced her attacker. Her fury flashed as she recalled her resolve to punish the drunk. "What will the law do with him?"

"Oh, probably lock him up for a few days, let him sober up." Jared used Ben's belt to bind the drunk's wrists, then pointed to a spot on the floor. Ben immediately sat. "Since he didn't actually complete the act, the judge will most likely charge a fine and let him go."

"That's all?" Emily squealed. "Well, that doesn't hardly seem fair, does it? I mean, the man comes barging in here, threatens to..." Emily swayed, feeling her blood drain from her face. She refused to faint.

"Why don't you let me guard him now, while you summon the innkeeper?" Jared suggested.

Emily saw though Jared's ploy to get her out of the room, away from her attacker. Denied revenge for the burning of Rosewood, denied exoneration from Morgan's unjust accusations, Emily's pride demanded justice. She wasn't going anywhere.

She shifted her aim and pulled the trigger. The bullet slammed into the wall, mere inches from the drunk's head. A deafening echo bounced around the room and, Emily hoped, throughout the quiet inn.

Jared grabbed his gun. Ben looked totally sober.

Deprived of the gun, Emily searched for another way to torment the drunk. At her feet lay the spindle with the knifelike edge. An idea swirled and formed.

She asked, "How do Indians punish a rapist?"

When Jared's mouth twitched, Emily knew she'd remembered the penalty correctly.

"Depends on the tribe and the social standing of the lady. If you were the daughter or wife of a chief, the punishment would certainly involve castration."

The drunk watched her every move as she picked up the spindle and ran her thumb along the edge. Ben let out a moan and drew his knees to his chest.

"What do they do with the…pieces?"

Jared coughed back a laugh. "There's one tribe that forces the man to swallow them."

Emily glared at her victim. "Raw or cooked?"

Jared roared as Ben's eyes rolled back and his limp body slumped to the floor.

From the hallway, someone shouted, "Miss Gardner?"

"I believe that's Mr. Grundy," Jared said, quelling his laughter. He picked up the blanket from the floor, folded it into a triangle and draped the makeshift shawl over Emily's shoulders. "Let's straighten you out before I let him in."

"I don't much care what I look like," Emily muttered, and tossed the spindle at Ben's feet.

Jared swept her hair from beneath the blanket. Emily might be unaware of her state of undress, but Jared was very much aware of it. The unbuttoned nightgown allowed a tantalizing view of the delving valley between her breasts.

"At least button your nightgown."

Emily gasped and quickly closed the fastenings.

"Miss Gardner!"

After Emily was decently covered, Jared opened the door. The male population of the inn, having responded to the gunshot, were now milling about outside the door. Jared admitted only the innkeeper.

"Oh, my word!" Grundy exclaimed, viewing the damage. "Why, that's Ben! What in blazes happened?"

"It seems your drunken friend decided to torment Miss Gardner. Have him removed. We'll talk about charges later."

"Y-yes, yes, of course." Grundy went back into the hallway, then returned with two burly guests he'd recruited.

"Miss Gardner, I can't tell you how sorry I am about this incident," Grundy said apologetically. He hooked his thumbs around the suspenders striping his red long johns. "I've never known Ben to turn violent."

Emily's gaze followed Ben's shoes as the men dragged him from the room. "He certainly wasn't rational. He smells like a still."

Grundy had enough conscience to look embarrassed.

To speed the innkeeper's departure, Jared said, "Miss Gardner is upset and exhausted. Can we leave further discussion until later?"

"Yes, I'm sorry. Miss Gardner, this is most distressing. I hope you'll accept my apology. I'll have Ben locked up. He won't bother you again."

"Till daylight, Mr. Grundy," Jared urged.

Grundy shook his head, mumbling as he walked out of the room, "Most distressing business... Terribly sorry..."

Jared closed and locked the door.

Ensconced on the bed, Emily watched Jared circle the room, picking up coins and tossing pieces of the broken chair into the corner. He had ordered her onto the bed because her bare feet might pick up a sliver. He'd ignored her argument that his uncovered feet were just as susceptible. She'd relented when he threatened to throw her onto the bed.

The leather pouch landed in her lap.

"Why did you have this out? Count," he ordered.

"There are twelve pieces. I counted as you picked them up." Emily threw the pouch back, annoyed by the reprimand. "Ben came up here looking for gold. I thought if I gave him some, he would leave. But apparently I didn't have enough gold to suit him."

Jared was quiet as he put the pouch into her pack, then asked, "He came for the gold?"

Emily haltingly related a condensed version of the confrontation, omitting Ben's more vulgar comments.

"I was afraid for a moment you wouldn't understand why I called you Captain Morgan. What would you have done if the door had been locked?"

Jared shrugged. "Kicked the door down, or maybe come through the window. What would you have done if I hadn't understood?"

"I was going to give you thirty seconds before I clawed his eyes out."

"Not a lot of time to allow for a rescue. Since he can still see, I must have accomplished it with record speed. How did I do?"

"You entered the room at fifteen. The hammer on your gun clicked at twenty-three."

"Did you see me come into the room?"

Emily thought for a moment before answering. "No," she said slowly, "but I knew you were there. I didn't see or hear you, but I felt you in the room. Does that make sense?"

More sense than Jared wanted to admit. They were becoming attuned, sensing one another's presence. He and Frank West shared a similar awareness, each man knowing from years of working together how the other would think and react. Jared had never expected to share that intangible bond with a woman.

A knock on the door interrupted. "If that's Mr. Grundy making more profuse apologies, I may tie and gag him." Jared opened the door, and Tess swept into the room.

"You were gone so long, I thought Miss Gardner might have been badly hurt," she said, in a scolding tone.

Jared felt a twinge of remorse as Emily's eyes widened with complete understanding of what he and Tess had been doing when events intruded.

"My goodness, Ben did make quite a mess," Tess fluttered. "He's usually a docile person, even when drunk.

Poor dear, he must have been absolutely *desperate* for company—to try to proposition a stranger, I mean.''

Tess made a show of thoughtfulness by plumping the pillows and checking the water in the pitcher on the nightstand.

"You look a bit peaked, Miss Gardner," she continued. "Such an ordeal you've been through! Well, if there's nothing else you need, we should leave you to your beauty sleep. Shall I put out the lamp?''

Emily paled. "No! I... I'll do so later.''

Tess turned to Jared. "I'll wait for you in your room," she said brightly, laying a possessive hand on his forearm before leaving.

"I'll be right back," Jared muttered.

Dark, sharp pain pierced Emily's heart, so overpowering she held her breath. Desperately she fought the unwarranted bitterness. She had no right to be jealous, to feel betrayed because Jared had made love to Tess.

"Don't bother, Lieutenant," she said. "Tess would be sorely disappointed if you left her again.''

Jared closed the door. "Tess was already disappointed. Nothing happened, Emily.''

"Obviously something was about to happen. Not that whatever you intend to do with Tess is any of my concern, sir. I apologize if I spoiled your evening.''

Jared walked over to the bed. Though he loomed above her, she felt no fear, not the least hint of a threat—even though he looked a bit angry. When Ben stood in almost the identical spot, she'd been terrified. But Jared wasn't Ben. Jared would never harm her.

"Oh, you spoiled my evening, all right," he said. "It's your fault I have no desire to touch her.''

"*My* fault?''

"I don't want her, I want you. I've wanted you from almost the moment we met. I can't get you out of my head, though Lord knows I've tried. I decided to settle for Tess because *you* pushed me away, damn near said outright to keep my hands to myself. Well, I'm trying, Emily, and let me tell you, it's one hell of a fight.''

Jared's voice swirled around her, wrapping her in a befuddling mist. She remembered what he'd said about them coming together as lovers, remembered the desire in his eyes that she'd told him to forget—and later regretted.

He reached out to touch her cheek. Emily recoiled, backing away from the scent of Tess's perfume on his hand. He claimed he hadn't touched Tess. How could she believe that, when he reeked of the woman?

Jared's hand fell back to his side. He took a long, deep breath. "Stopping here was a mistake. We'll leave in the morning. Make sure you lock your door."

Emily's hand trembled on the key as the lock clicked into place. She turned—to see Ben's beaver top hat sitting on the table. The room shrank. Emily suddenly wished for a bedroll and a starlit sky overhead.

She walked over to her satchel and took out the leather pouch containing the lifesaving and troublesome gold coins. Of the bagful Papa had given her, only twelve remained.

Papa had called her into his study on the bright spring day on which her engagement to Lewis Roth was announced to a throng of party guests. Placing the heavy pouch in her palms, he'd wrapped his hands around hers. "I want you to hide this. You needn't tell Lewis or your brother about the money."

"But Papa, if this is an engagement present, of course I must tell Lewis. He'll want to thank you for your generosity."

"This isn't an engagement present. This money is for you, to use as you see fit. There may be very hard times ahead."

"Oh, pooh," she'd said with a pout. "I think it dreadful that the men insist on talking about nothing but the possibility of war. Why, one would think they were looking forward to marching off and getting themselves shot!''

Emily put the coin pouch back into the satchel. Had she paid closer attention to her father's mood, to the pained expression on his face, she might have guessed sooner how the heated debate among the men had solidified his decision to leave Rosewood.

A mere week after the engagement party, Papa had left for Washington, to enlist in the Union army.

In stunning succession, Lewis Roth had broken the engagement and the neighbors had begun to shun Rosewood. Terrance had turned bitter. A long year later, he had formed his cavalry company and moved Emily and Rusty to the house in Adairsville. The waiting had begun.

Waiting for Papa to come home to make everything all right again. Waiting for Terrance to remember she was alive. Waiting for the war to end, for the Yanks to go home and leave the South in peace.

Then Jared had wandered into her life, with the subtlety of a hurricane.

Emily closed her eyes and took a deep breath. She'd grown used to having Jared near when she slept. And he was so good at exorcising her demons. He'd held her through the torment of Scott's death. At Rosewood he'd hushed her frightened cries, soothed away the nightmare. Only Jared's voice could silence Ben's vulgar words. His smile could erase the ugly vision of the drunk's aroused flesh. His touch could clean the imprint of Ben's crude hand from her breast.

And Jared had never been dishonest with her, or taken advantage, even when he wanted to. If he said he hadn't made love to Tess, then likely he hadn't.

Emily's heart thumped as she realized she was about to offer her body, her heart, her very soul, to the man she loved. She loved Jared. The startling admission heightened her fears.

Lovers. Could she settle for the relationship without

commitment on Jared's part, knowing that once they reached Petersburg, Jared would leave and she might never see him again? Damn her scruples. She'd had commitment once, from Lewis, and where had it left her? Rejected, alone.

Emily extinguished the lamp, closed the door behind her, then padded down the dimly lit hallway. She stopped. What if Jared no longer wanted her, after she'd recoiled from his touch? What if Tess was still in his room?

She knocked on his door. No answer. She tried the doorknob. It wasn't locked. She opened the door.

Jared's room was dark, except for the glowing ash on the tip of his cigar. She watched the spot of light glow brighter, then make a long arc of orange between his mouth and knee. He had to be sitting in a chair, in the corner.

"Do you know," he asked flatly, "the light from the hall seeps right through your nightgown?"

Stung by the lack of emotion in his voice, Emily realized Jared was angry, probably hurt by her rejection. Heavens, she'd come to his room for the express purpose of *being* seduced, not of seducing Jared. Where did a lady begin?

"I'm sorry."

"Go back to bed, Emily."

Emily almost turned to obey the command. But she'd come too far to retreat. She closed the door.

"I'd like to stay."

He took another drag from the cigar. With a sigh, he said, "You can't sleep in your bed, so you want to use mine."

Emily resisted the childish urge to stamp her foot. Usually so astute, Jared had chosen this awkward moment to be blindly imperceptive.

"I am trying to say I am willing to share yours."

Chapter Nine

There could be no other possible explanation, Jared reasoned. He'd finally cracked under the strain, and he was enjoying an enchanting hallucination. The whiskey, provided by Tess, was combining with the wine from dinner and fogging his brain. Upon returning to his room, he'd opened the bottle and guzzled several healthy swigs. He'd never been able to get stinking drunk on whiskey. Something in strong spirits always put him to sleep, and he was quickly approaching oblivion.

The trigger for this fantasy had to be the memory of Emily, barely covered by her white nightgown—a garment he considered sexier than any filmy, revealing gown he'd ever removed from a woman's body. Prim and proper, of white cotton and a tiny bit of lace, the gown had teased his imagination. Burned into his brain was an alluring glimpse of the cleavage he'd made her cover after Ben's attack. And now, adding to his misery, he was envisioning the shadowy spread of her long legs under a white veil.

Emily wasn't in his room asking to share his bed. Not *his* Emily, his lady who pulled away when desire sparked between them. Not his sweet, beautiful Emily, who had scorned his touch. No, not his adorable love, who didn't trust him, and with reason.

But Emily *was* in his room. He could hear her breathing,

hear the hardwood floor groan as she shifted her weight from one foot to the other. Seeking comfort? She'd narrowly escaped rape, and she couldn't bear staying in the room where she'd been attacked. He could understand her fear. Since he was the only person in the inn she could turn to, she'd decided sleeping with him was preferable to being alone.

He'd be a fool to let her stay.

Jared crushed out the cigar. "Come here, Em," he said softly, and held out his hand. Like an arrow shot to the center of a target, she found him and promptly curled in his lap.

Emily's arms manacled his neck. She clung like a second skin in her search for security. "Jared, help me," she breathed into his neck.

Jared tightened his arms. "Relax, sweetheart. I'm here."

He closed his heavy eyelids and rested his cheek against her hair—soft, so soft, and scented with spring lilacs. With firm, long strokes, he massaged her rigid spine, damning Ben for causing Emily's terror.

Slowly he kneaded away the tenseness, his palm warming from the friction. She relaxed in gradual stages, becoming pliant under his skilled massage.

"Do you want to talk about it?" he whispered.

"Is it necessary to talk?"

"No, not if you don't want to. I thought talking might help make you feel better."

Emily had no idea how she could possibly feel better than she did right now. Her back was heating from the circles he was drawing, his flattened hand circling lower, and wider, until the downstroke cupped her buttocks and the upstroke brushed the side of her breast.

She inwardly cursed her inexperience, but didn't think she was doing too badly. Jared had let her stay, taken her onto his lap, called her sweetheart. He seemed content, however, to massage her back, had sounded even a bit...bored?

Maybe a man needed encouragement, some word of praise to let him know his partner liked his touch. And she *did* like his touch. The steady, comforting stroke melted her insides.

"You do have a way with females. If you petted Rusty like this, I don't blame her for letting you saddle her." She gave a nervous laugh, thinking of her headstrong mare.

Jared's hand stopped. She didn't want him to stop.

"I do feel better, much better," she added quickly. A gentle pat on her fanny was her reward for the compliment.

"Then why don't you crawl into bed?"

Always a fast learner, Emily vowed to praise and encourage at every opportunity. Her fingertips lingered on his sinewy shoulders a little longer than necessary for balance as she slid from his lap.

On her way to the bed, she wondered if she should remove her nightgown, but even engulfed in total darkness, knowing he couldn't see, she wasn't quite that brave.

Thankfully, the furniture in the inn's rooms was similarly arranged. She stepped carefully as she neared the bed, but still managed to bruise her shin. Chagrined at the sound reporting her clumsiness, she wiggled under the blanket she didn't need for warmth. She waited quietly between the cool sheets, but Jared didn't move from the chair.

"Jared? Aren't you coming to bed? I mean…I like having you hold me."

Jared grabbed the whiskey bottle for a last, numbing drink. If he had to hold Emily through the night, in a bed, he needed to pass out to keep from going crazy. Emily didn't want to make love. She wanted a warm body to snuggle against.

His hearing was still sharp enough for him to know she'd claimed the right side of the bed. He'd get in on the left and lie atop the blanket, to put an extra layer between them.

The floor creaked as he cautiously ambled toward the bed. When he plopped down on the mattress, he discovered that Emily had pulled the covers back, out of his reach.

Rather than start a tug-of-war, he submitted to getting between the sheets. He stretched out on his back and extended his arm along the lower edge of the pillows. Emily pulled the covers up and nestled against his side, settling her arm across his chest. Her head resting on his shoulder, she sighed.

The most natural place for his hand seemed to be the curve of her waist. Almost. He pulled her in a little closer. Emily responded to the tug by sliding a slender limb into the space between his legs. Jared's loins twitched.

"Comfortable?" he asked hoarsely.

"Oh, this is very nice," she whispered. "You make a wonderful pillow, but I'm afraid my hand will fall asleep."

Emily wiggled the fingers of the hand pressed between their rib cages. Her knuckles bumped over his ribs as she squeezed her hand between their bodies until it rested against his hip.

"That's better," she said.

Jared prayed she would keep her hand still. If she wiggled her fingers, she would discover his swelling sex. He fought to squelch his growing passion, twisting his hips slightly to avoid accidental contact.

"Are you comfortable?" she inquired.

He was damned uncomfortable, but resolute. "Yes."

Emily giggled. "That tickles."

"Sorry." Jared stilled his fingers, which of their own volition had been swirling around the soft curve of her waist.

Then Emily moved her hand from his shoulder, fingers skimming across his collarbone, to the hollow of his throat. The cool touch raised goose bumps on his hot skin, and sweat broke out on his upper lip.

"Are you ticklish, too?" she wondered aloud.

If she discovered that a light stroke in the area around his navel set him to quivering, he would never survive. He grasped her wrist and rolled Emily onto her back. He heard her breath quicken, felt the rise and fall of her chest. His lips hovered inches from her mouth.

"Emily, this isn't going to work. I'm going to take my noble self back to the chair. You can have the bed."

Emily's long silence ended with a single word: "Stay."

Jared hazily heard Emily's long-awaited invitation. He released her wrist to cup her chin, wishing he could see her eyes, read the expression on her face. She turned her lips into his palm.

"Are you *sure*, Em?" he whispered.

"Love me, Jared."

Jared kissed her waiting mouth, surrendering to the desire his lady ignited. He'd loved her so often in his dreams that a well-planned campaign of titillating touches sprang into his head. Problem was, he wouldn't last very long. Very soon now, no matter how much he fought it, he would fall asleep.

Emily's words and actions since entering the room took on new meaning. The whiskey had dulled his wits. If she was half as ready as he was, their joining would be fast and furious. A slow, lingering coupling could come later, maybe in the morning, when he was awake enough to really appreciate her, with the sun streaming though the window so that he could see her eyes glaze when she climaxed.

He kissed her eyes, feeling her lashes flutter. "All this time you've been trying to tell me you want me. I'm usually not so slow."

"It's not all your fault," she told him, excusing his delayed understanding. "I'm not much of a temptress."

"Don't sell yourself short, love. You're bewitching. Any time you feel the urge to practice seduction techniques, I most humbly offer myself as your victim."

The uncertainties she'd struggled with retreated as Jared collected kiss after kiss. Emily wrapped her arms around his torso, clung to his solid mass, returned his kisses with matching fervor. Jared groaned and ran his tongue over her bottom lip. She opened her mouth to the gentle foil's thrust and parry.

"Whiskey," she said, identifying the taste.

"I'm not drunk, sweetheart."

"I know."

The nightgown was no barrier. Heat flowed though the thin garment as he explored. With a slow sweep he measured the distances between face, bosom, hip and knee. As if assured that each sensitized area was within easy reach, he reversed his survey for a detailed inspection. His hands were large, his fingers long, and Emily flexed into his touch.

Then he confined his attention to her breast, puckering the nub with a nudge of his thumb. Nimble fingers unbuttoned the nightgown and pushed the fabric aside. She moaned when his mouth clamped on the tip of her breast and suckled.

Her bosom swelled to gentle kneading. Then he pushed the spheres upward and played until the points stood proud. He kissed both nipples, then buried his face in her cleavage.

He nuzzled for a long time, and Emily took advantage of his stillness to trace the ridge of muscle across his back and upper arms. She had only a moment to wonder about the jagged scar on his right biceps when she felt his muscles ripple and bunch. He pushed himself upward, shook his head vigorously.

Concerned, Emily asked, "Jared, are you all right?"

"Not by a long shot. I want you, Em—now."

Jared rolled to the side and tugged at the hem of her gown. She lifted her hips and raised her arms. As he stretched over to toss the garment onto the floor, she reached up and raked through his chest hair with her nails.

"I've been wanting to comb your chest since I first saw you with your shirt off. I didn't know a man could be so hairy."

"Do you like hairy men?"

Sensing uncertainty in his voice, she teased, "I could develop a definite preference."

Through the haze of fatigue, Jared heard a comparison. Was Sam's chest hairless?

The comment plagued him as he aroused her. Emily writhed under his sensuous stroking, responded with flaming ardor. She gave herself so freely that it shook his confidence. Sam must have been a good lover. Emily would expect at least equal performance.

His fingertips moved lower, seeking her moist center. She arched as his finger slid through the liquid. Swollen, his touch told him, hot and flowing with juices to ease his way into her passage.

He grappled with exhaustion and buttons. Emily pushed him onto his back. "Let me," she pleaded.

He should be thankful she was eager and ready, but a small part of him wished she was ignorant of sex. How he would have loved to be her first, to introduce her to pleasure.

Inflated to the point of pain, his member rose as each button came undone. His stomach muscles tightened when Emily ran a finger along the sensitive underside of his unleashed and fully extended sex.

"Oh, Jared, you're...huge. Will it fit?"

Her hand trembled as her fingers wrapped around him. Unable to endure further handling without exploding, he rolled Emily over and nudged her legs apart. She opened, wide, and he crawled between her thighs. With the marble-hard tip of his aching need, he probed for her entrance.

"I'll fill you, love," he promised, sliding just the head into her warmth. "Are you ready for me?"

She arched at his slight encroachment into her body. He plunged to the hilt. Emily bucked and contracted. His need to possess Emily, to be one with her as he had been with no other, obliterated all awareness except the part of his body buried deep inside his woman. He'd make her forget

Sam, drive away her need for any man but himself. Emily belonged to him now.

Emily swallowed an outcry as he burst through her maidenhead. Jared penetrated deep, filled her as a sword would a sheath. She'd known about first-time pain, and she tried to relax until the sharpness subsided, but Jared didn't allow a rest.

"Who am I, Emily?" he whispered hoarsely.

She managed to moan, "Jared."

"Remember," he told her, then withdrew, and plunged again.

Lava flowed through her veins. Sparks ignited in her head as the pressure inside her increased.

Jared cried out and throbbed in completion. Within moments, his ragged breathing smoothed. His weight became oppressive. Then he snored.

The pain went away for Emily, but not the emptiness. Into the void slipped a doubt about the wisdom of having come to Jared's room, seeking solace. She might love him, but did that excuse initiating intimacy with a man she'd known for less than a week? A man who didn't love her?

Jared's soft rumbles quieted as she wiggled from beneath him, but he didn't wake up. He wouldn't know she was no longer beside him until morning. Emily shuddered. Morning. What would she say to him in the morning? Worse, in the stark light of day, what would he think of her?

The bolt of lightning missed the building, but the accompanying crack of thunder shook the inn and snapped Jared's eyes open. His head felt stuffed with wet sand, too heavy for his stiff neck to lift. Raw, uncleaned Georgia cotton filled his mouth, and there was no saliva to help him spit it out. Rain drummed against the window. He and Emily weren't going anywhere today.

He rolled over. Emily wasn't in the bed.

Uneasy, he ran his fingers through hair as tossed and disheveled as the bed. He eased out from under the blanket and frowned. He was still wearing his buckskins. Lord, he'd been so eager to possess Emily that he hadn't taken his pants off!

As he tugged them down over his hips, Jared noticed the fresh dark stain. It looked like— No, it was impossible. He found his uniform pants and pulled them on, ignoring the niggling suspicion that had to be wrong.

He'd sworn off virgins after one experience. The constant reassurance, the time, the crying, hadn't been worth the effort. He'd have gone through it again for Emily. But she'd fired under his touch, eagerly touched him in return. She'd recently had a lover, Sam.

He looked at the bed, growing colder. Impossible, he told himself again, but the thought nagged at him until he reached over and drew back the blanket. He growled a curse and dropped the blanket to cover the proof of his unforgivable mistake.

Whatever her reason for coming last night—loneliness, fright?—she had offered him beauty and fulfillment beyond his most vivid hopes. He'd taken her priceless gift, ripped open the package and violated the contents.

Dear God, how I must have hurt her!

The pounding on the door assailed his melon-size head. "It's Mr. Grundy, sir. Are you awake?"

Jared winced and considered ignoring the summons.

Tess's singsong voice rang out. "There's coffee."

Jared opened the door. Tess was holding a pot and a mug. The beverage probably wasn't coffee, but one of the many roasted-grain substitutes prevalent in the South. Anything hot and liquid would clean his mouth.

Mr. Grundy puffed out his chest, assuming an officious manner. "I must offer again, sir, my most sincere apologies. I run a respectable establishment, and have never had a guest assaulted before. Most distressing business. The authorities would like to speak with you regarding the incident."

Jared drained the first cup of the bitter but hot brew, then held out the mug for Tess to refill. She looked smug.

"This is of no small matter to me," Grundy went on, "for my reputation and honor are involved."

"Mr. Grundy, I appreciate your concern. But this can surely wait until later, after I've had a chance to speak to Miss Gardner."

Grundy frowned at Tess, no doubt noticing her smirk. "Tess, you have other duties."

"Yes, Mr. Grundy," she answered, but her eyes remained on Jared. "I'll be cleaning Miss Gardner's room, if you need me."

"Wait," Jared said as she turned toward the door. "Let her sleep, if she isn't up yet."

Tess's laugh was low and nettling. "But Miss Gardner has been up and about for some time now."

"Tess!" Grundy barked, then cleared his throat as the maid sashayed from the room. "My apologies, again," he said. "Tess is correct, however. Miss Gardner was up rather early, and most distressed when she came down. Poor lady must have tossed all night, from the look of her. Before she left, she said you would handle the situation with Ben."

The cup paused just short of Jared's mouth. His muddled head cleared instantly. "You let her leave—in this storm?"

"The storm came up suddenly, only an hour ago. The sun was out when she left. Miss Gardner was most insistent about leaving. I had no reason to stop her. She refused to let someone come for you, said it was unnecessary."

Jared took another sip from the cup and turned toward the window, watching the pelting water bead on the glass. "Did she say where she was going?"

"No, sir."

"Have someone saddle my horse."

"Yes, sir, right away. Ah, about Ben…"

Jared spared Grundy a quick glance over his shoulder. "I trust you will no longer let him drink himself senseless in your taproom, so the incident won't be repeated."

Grundy shook his head.

"Then let him go, with a severe lecture, of course."

Grundy promised to deliver the tongue-lashing himself.

Jared hurriedly dressed and splashed water over his face to remove the last traces of his stupor. Where would Emily go? Would she continue, try to reach Virginia alone? Or would she turn back toward Rosewood?

Assessing her strategy was a welcome mental exercise. He couldn't bear to dwell on the reason she'd left. He would deal with that later, after he found her, unharmed.

He reached the stables as Horace led the saddled gelding from the stall. Jared almost smiled as the boy tried not to meet his eyes.

Scrunched down so that the child wouldn't feel too intimidated, Jared asked gently, "Which road did she take?"

"She told me not to tell," Horace blurted. "She don't want you to find her."

"No, I don't imagine she does. But Miss Gardner is out there in that storm, and before long will be wet and hungry, with nobody to take care of her. She's a very special lady, Horace, and we don't want her to get sick or hurt, do we?"

"No, sir."

"Then I have to find her. I need your help, boy."

Horace looked up at the sky, the dark clouds, the pouring rain. "You promise to take good care of her?"

"If she'll let me," Jared assured him.

Horace pointed north, and then scurried off.

Adjusting his slicker, Jared wondered if Emily had rain gear stashed in her packs. He didn't think she did, so she would have to seek shelter.

The sky showed no sign of clearing as he urged the reluctant gelding forward, creating new pools, rearranging others as the horse plodded through the red clay.

Emily had run from him before, leaving him standing in the road when she bolted for Rosewood. But then he'd known where she was going. And she hadn't made any effort to cover her tracks.

Jared tilted his slouch hat forward, keeping the rain from stinging his eyes. Somehow, he'd find her. He had to find Emily. She carried his heart.

Chapter Ten

Several miles and an hour later, Jared spotted Rusty as she grazed, unsaddled, between a house and dilapidated barn. But for the Thoroughbred, the place appeared deserted. He hobbled his gelding near Rusty and took his saddle and packs into the barn.

The rain had stopped, so only wind rushed through a gaping hole in the west wall, scattering dirt and bits of hay before whistling through the slats on the opposite side. Sparrows flitted among the beams on the far end, selecting pieces of hay from a mound in the sagging loft.

On the ladder leading to the loft hung Emily's brown riding outfit, her petticoats and her chemise. Water-soaked boots stood nearby. In a dry corner, Emily had curled into a blanket, using her saddle as a pillow, her unbound hair fanned over a face paler than flour. Her eyes opened as he dropped his belongings.

Emily's heart beat a little faster as Jared removed his hat and slicker and tossed them in a heap near his packs.

His voice echoed through the empty barn. "You got farther than I thought you would." He took a few steps, until he stood over her, arms crossed, feet spread like an omniscient, powerful genie. Onyx eyes glistened with irritation. "This is getting to be a bad habit, running away."

Emily pulled back the blanket and sat up, revealing the

male clothing she wore. His eyes narrowed, though, considering other recent transgressions, wearing a shirt and trousers seemed the least of her sins.

"I didn't run away, Lieutenant. I merely decided to continue on alone." Even to her own ears, her voice sounded rough, her tone flat.

"I thought we agreed to travel together to Virginia, or did I imagine your offer to pay me as escort? How did you plan to get to Petersburg without knowing where you were going?"

"I saw your map often enough to have an idea of which roads to take. If I got lost, I'd simply do what Sam does—ask for directions."

She expected him to scoff. Instead, he sat down beside her and asked, "Just who the hell is Sam?"

"Sam belongs to my brother." When he continued to look puzzled, she explained. "Terrance's slave. When Terrance formed his cavalry company, he took Sam along. Sam delivers whatever grain and hay Terrance can buy or confiscate for Rusty."

"So Sam's been acting as messenger between you and your brother."

There were never any letters, only hay and grain, but Jared needn't know that.

"I was expecting Sam when the Yanks attacked Adairsville."

"And you were hoping he'd know you'd gone to Rosewood."

Jared was sitting far too close for her peace of mind. Emily rose and walked over to check her drying garments.

"Where did you get those clothes?"

She knew he didn't mean the brown outfit. "When Terrance outgrew them, I took them from the pile of discards meant for the slaves." She shrugged a shoulder. "They're comfortable for riding."

"Why didn't you wear them before this, then?"

"I only wear them when I'm alone."

"Like when you rode into the mountains?"

She nodded.

As the last piece of the puzzle snapped into place, Jared remembered standing on a knoll, watching a *man* ride into Emily Gardner's yard, snatch clothing from a line and enter her house. The man hadn't been a man at all, but Emily, returning from a ride in the mountains—with a third of the Union army swarming over the terrain.

Good God, if a Union patrol had found her...

With a great deal of effort, Jared bit back a lecture. He couldn't comment on her recklessness without giving away that he'd staked out her house. Not yet.

As Jared's mouth thinned, Emily turned back to her chore. She jerked the chemise and petticoats from the ladder rung.

What had she expected? That Jared would overlook all her faults, could love her despite how low she had sunk?

Once, a long time ago, she might have been worthy of a handsome West Point graduate, a man of integrity, a gentleman, no matter that he protested the latter appellation. He had a temper, certainly, and an arrogance that sometimes grated. But always, though some of his methods might be questioned, his concern for her welfare had directed his actions.

Even last night, he'd tried to sway her from disgrace. He'd offered to leave the bed, sleep in the chair.

Emily stuffed the undergarments into her satchel, wishing she owned a pair of pantaloons. Her wool trousers scraped against inner thighs chafed from Jared's lovemaking, roughened further from this morning's ride.

Her hand bumped the coin pouch. Of course, she finally realized, Jared might have followed her only because she owed him money for supplies, her riding outfit, the fee for escort. In her haste to leave the inn, to escape her shame, she'd forgotten.

She pulled out the pouch, tossed it to Jared. "I apologize for the oversight. You may take what you feel fair. I'm releasing you from your obligation as escort. I no longer need your services, Lieutenant.''

"Funny. Last night I could have sworn you needed me."

Heat rose to her cheeks. Emily bit her bottom lip and turned away. She heard Jared get up, toss the coin pouch into her pack. She tensed as he put his hands on her shoulders—those long-fingered, gentle hands. Her nipples hardened and her core tightened as she remembered how his hands had stroked and caressed. She stepped away.

"I know you must be angry, and hurt," he said.

"I am utterly *mortified,* Lieutenant! Last night was a horrible mistake. Please let it be!"

Jared's gut tightened as her revulsion rang clear. Through clenched teeth, he said, "So that's why you left my bed. You couldn't stand the thought of waking up next to a savage."

She spun to face him, eyes wide. "That's not— I never thought—"

"Why deny it? What gently bred lady wouldn't be *mortified* that she'd given her virginity to a half-breed?"

After a moment of silence, she said quietly, "I do deny it. Who am I to cast stones? I swear to you, I never gave your heritage a second thought."

Had she shouted a denial, he might not have believed her. "Then why, Em?"

She hesitated, then ordered, "Look at my nose."

"Adorable. What of it?"

"It's peeling."

He looked closer. "I hadn't noticed you'd burned. We'll put some salve—"

"Jared, it's *peeling!* No lady of sensibility would allow her nose to become sun-browned or burned, let alone peel! For this indiscretion alone, I should not appear in decent company. And look at these clothes. What gently bred lady would don male clothing? And when was the last time you saw a *lady* ride astride, or grab a shotgun to hunt for dinner?"

"Granted, you're a bit unconventional. But, Emily, you've only adapted to circumstances, done what you felt you must to survive."

"That's what I kept telling myself. Every time someone looked at me with scorn or turned away at my greeting, I told myself I could rise above the nastiness." She put a fist to her chest, above her heart. "Inside, I was still a lady, Emily Gardner, daughter of a wealthy man, peerless in a town full of small-minded and common people." Her voice turned thready. "But I can't lie to myself anymore."

"Not a lady? Who was kindness itself to a black stable boy? Who was that stunning, gracious creature who dined with me last night?"

"Sometime between supper and dawn, she disappeared!" Emily took a deep breath. "After I…left your room, I looked into the mirror. I didn't know the person looking back at me. I looked for the lady, and saw a…fallen woman."

"A whore? You?"

She crossed her arms. "Well, you needn't be *vulgar.*"

"Emily, whores go to bed with anyone who can pay their price. Call yourself a whore again for what happened between us, and I'll tan that firm little backside of yours. Don't you dare turn away from me again! Now listen, little Miss Prim. You looked in that mirror for Emily Gardner, the girl. Who you found was the woman. *That's* what scared the hell out of you."

"Nonsense."

"Is it? You can't go back, Emily. The life you knew as a girl is over. Your home is gone. The South is damn near destroyed. No one and nothing here will ever be the same, no matter who wins the war—not the land, the way of life or the people. If you wish to mourn, fine. If you want to wallow in self-pity for a time, be my guest. But don't berate the woman you've become. I won't allow it."

"Maybe I don't like her."

"Too bad. I do. You've got more steel in your backbone

than any woman I've ever known. Hell, a man's got to respect a woman who would threaten to boil a man's balls.''

Emily buried her furiously flushed face in her hands. ''I still can't believe I could say such things.''

''Now don't go missish on me again. You were magnificent. Ben will never forget your fury or your threat. He'll never approach another woman with violent intent, believe me.''

Her hands came down. She nodded slightly. ''I hope you're right,'' she said. ''No woman should suffer what he intended. I was terrified....''

The silence lengthened, deepened. Then she shook her head. ''But my fright does not excuse my later behavior. I don't deserve your respect. I should have dealt with my feelings by myself, not come to you.''

''I'm honored that you did.''

''Gallantly stated, sir.''

Jared knew he was treading on rough terrain. The pitfalls were endless. ''You'll never convince me that our making love was a mistake. I'm only sorry I botched it so badly.'' He braced for her reaction. ''I didn't realize until this morning how much I must have hurt you. If I'd suspected last night that you were a virgin—''

Emily's eyes snapped wide. ''Whatever made you think otherwise?''

''I misunderstood your concern and obvious affection for Sam. I thought you and he were...keeping company.''

''Keeping company?''

''Lovers.''

''Oh, my God!''

Jared forged ahead. ''In my ignorance, I caused you a lot of pain. Had I been more awake, I might have realized at the end and eased it a bit.''

Emily lifted a shoulder, ever so slightly. ''The pain went away shortly after you fell asleep.''

Jared couldn't ignore the implication. Not only had he

taken her virginity, she hadn't climaxed. He'd left her to battle not only her lowered self-esteem, but also an aroused, pained body. He had no right to forgiveness, none at all.

"I fell asleep because of the whiskey. If I drink anything stronger than beer, I fall asleep. Whiskey, rum, brandy— all have the same effect. Last night I drank a quarter of a bottle of whiskey on top of the wine we had at supper. I'm lucky I stayed awake as long as I did."

"Are you telling me you passed out?"

"Not quite, but close. If I'd known you were coming into my room, I wouldn't have taken a sip."

She'd never heard of strong spirits acting as a sleeping potion, but she supposed alcohol could work as such. She'd seen somber people turn giddy after a few drinks, and others turn mean.

Emily stepped back from his upraised hands, but Jared's stride was longer. His palms cupped her cheeks and tilted her head, forcing her to see the sincerity in his eyes.

"You're no whore, Emily. You wouldn't give yourself to a man you didn't care for, and yes, I'm more honored than I can tell you. I think we've found something special, you and I. Please give us a chance to find out."

Then he kissed her, a lingering, knee-melting kiss that curled her bare toes. A faint voice in her head wondered if she was making the biggest mistake of her life, but the joyful choir of heart and body drowned out the apprehension.

Emily uncrossed her arms and wrapped them around his solid torso. Jared broke the kiss and enfolded her into his embrace, squeezing so hard she could barely breathe. But she didn't complain. Breathing wasn't as important as prolonging the rapture of his secure hold.

"Am I forgiven?" he asked softly.

"Oh, Jared, I'm so afraid."

"So am I, love. So am I."

Jared suddenly pushed her away. Startled, Emily looked up. He stared at the doorway, his head tilted.

"Riders," he quietly explained.

Three riders slowly approached the farm. Their style of dress was bizarre. Heavy fringe trimmed the side seams of buckskin trousers, as well as the yoke and sleeves of their shirts. Furry hats, a dead animal's bushy tail dangling down the side, completed the outrageous uniform. As though the clothing weren't enough to identify the mountain men by, they cradled long-barreled rifles in their arms.

"Kentuckians," Jared confirmed. "Looks like a scouting patrol. You stay here while I find out what they want."

Emily grabbed his sleeve. "They could be Yankees."

"I doubt it. At least I hope not." He dropped a kiss on her forehead and removed her hand. "Stay out of sight."

Then he strode out the doorway.

Oh, Jared, I'm so afraid.

So am I, love.

Emily moved to the corner and peered between a gap in the boards, watching intently as Jared approached the Kentuckians. She shook her head. Lieutenant Jared Randall didn't know the meaning of the word *fear*.

Jared longed for his buckskins. His bogus uniform declared him a Reb, and the Kentuckians *could* be Yanks. Kentucky had remained Union, but nearly a third of the men who'd enlisted in an army had joined the Confederacy.

He wasn't worried about explaining his mission to a Union commander. His story could be verified. But the thought of having Emily learn that he was a Yankee, before he was ready to tell her, bothered him immensely.

The patrol's casual approach was somewhat reassuring, though Jared didn't mistake poise for slackness. Any sudden move would bring three rifles to immediate, deadly aim.

Armed with bravado and bluff, he approached the riders with a steady stride. One man, bearded and steel-eyed, dismounted. Hands clasped behind his back, Jared assumed an authoritative pose and waited.

"This place yours?" the grizzled Kentuckian asked. Jared didn't move or answer. With a wry smile, the soldier touched fingertips to forehead and added, "Sir."

Jared relaxed at the salute. A confederate patrol posed little threat.

"No, just getting out of the rain for a spell," Jared said. "You are…?"

"Sergeant Smith."

"Lieutenant Randall. Where you boys headed?"

Sergeant Smith's gaze darted around the abandoned farm, and Jared knew the instant when Smith spotted Rusty and the gelding, where they grazed near the barn.

"Ain't quite sure," Smith intoned. The signal was almost imperceptible, but one of the Kentuckians dismounted, the other shifted his rifle. "The colonel, now, he just didn't ask me to okay his plans."

"Cigar, Sergeant?"

"Don't mind if I do. Go easy, Lieutenant," Smith warned when Jared reached into his inner pocket.

Jared pulled out two smokes and handed one to Smith. The cigars lit, Smith reached for his canteen and stated, "You're not alone."

Jared had to admire Smith's cool acceptance that, just maybe, someone in the barn had a rifle pointed at his forehead. Resigned to the soldier's need to identify the person in the barn, Jared cocked his head.

"Sergeant, your timing is pathetic. It's taken me several days and the assistance of a storm to get the lady out of her clothes."

"A woman?"

"How do you spend your leave time, Sergeant?"

Smith took a long drink, wiped his mouth with his sleeve. "Hell, it's been so long since I've had leave, I don't rightly remember."

Jared took the canteen from the sergeant's outstretched hand. The pungent smell of bourbon wafted to his nostrils. Jared inwardly sighed and drank.

"I was about to refresh *my* memory when you and your men showed up," he growled and returned the lightened canteen.

"Sorry for the interruption, sir," Smith stated, but his wide grin said he wasn't the least bit sorry. "You understand we have to check."

Jared had hoped Sergeant Smith would accept the story and forgo the inspection. Arguing would arouse suspicion. He could only hope Emily wouldn't feel she had to talk to the investigating soldier.

"Of course. All I ask is that your man stay out of the barn. I don't want the lady frightened."

"Hank," Smith said with a nod to his underling.

Jared watched Hank stroll toward the barn and cautiously approach the door. He sidled up to the frame, then spun into the opening, rifle at the ready.

"Well! Ah *nevah!*" came an outraged female cry.

Hank stood frozen for a moment, then shook his head. He took a piece of charcoal from his pocket and drew an X on the side of the barn. The mounted trooper repositioned his rifle.

"Where you headed?" Smith asked.

"Virginia."

"Last I heard, Virginy's a real hornet's nest. You been south of here?"

"West. I hear Johnson's backing up to Atlanta. Is that where you think you're going?"

"That's the rumor."

Hank stopped beside his sergeant and shot Jared an envious glance. "Next time, Sarge, you check. I'm gonna dream about long legs for a week."

Long legs? What the hell?

Knowing grins brightening their faces, Sergeant Smith and Hank mounted. Smith lingered as his companions rode ahead. "Better get your pecker up and in quick. The column's a couple miles behind us. Hank's mark on the barn tells them the place has been checked, but if they hear moanin'..."

With a chuckle, Smith wheeled and rode off.

Jared rushed toward the barn. As he rounded the door, his mouth went dry. Emily was lounging between blankets, propped on an elbow, blatantly nude. Rich brown hair caressed creamy-white shoulders. A dainty hand clutched the blanket to her bosom. A long, silky leg lay erotically exposed from above her knee to her bare toes.

Desire inflamed his loins as he gazed at the enchanting temptress. He quickly calculated how long it took for a column of men to move two miles. Damn.

Besides, the next time they made love, he planned a slow, lingering seduction, with Emily's pleasure his goal. She'd been cheated last night, and he wasn't about to change that plan, not for a quick romp in a barn.

Emily must have seen the heat in his gaze, or his pants grow tighter in the crotch, because she blushed.

"I can explain," she stated, pulling the blanket higher, slipping the slender exposed leg beneath the cover. "I hope I did the right thing. You told them you had a woman waiting, so I gave you one."

"So I see."

Emily sat up, reached under the blanket and pulled out her flannel shirt. With much shifting of hands, and help from her chin to hold the blanket in place, she struggled to button the shirt. He kept a hopeful watch on the blanket, but it never slipped.

He held his breath when she flung the cover aside. She'd left the trousers on, merely scrunched a pant leg up to her thigh. The fabric fell as she stood.

Jared tucked his lust away. A Rebel company would pass by within the hour. "Emily, why didn't you go into the house?"

"I felt like an intruder, I suppose."

"The sergeant said there's a column due to pass here shortly. I'd feel better if you were inside."

"Can't we just stay in the barn? I'd feel awkward breaking into someone's home."

"Emily, if some weary traveler had sheltered from a storm at Rosewood, would you object?"

"Well, no," Emily said, then smiled. "You don't think the owner would object if we use the house? Southern hospitality *can* be generous in time of need."

"At its most gracious and heartily welcomed." Jared executed a gentlemanly bow, then held out his hand. "Madame, shall we look at what our hosts have provided for our comfort?"

With Emily safely in the house, Jared fetched the horses and tied them in the barn.

A short while later, from behind the obscurity of a dark window, Emily watched the column of soldiers tramp south. The men were quiet, their faces grim, as they concentrated on putting one foot in front of the other.

Here and there a piece of uniform appeared, mostly low-brimmed, billed caps. Supply wagons rumbled past, bouncing over ruts from lack of ballast.

Emily couldn't help remembering past parades. Decked out in their finest, people had lined the streets to cheer and wave flags at newly outfitted companies. Proud and confident, the men had marched away from home and family. The contrast was disheartening.

"Where are they bound?" she asked Jared, who stood stiffly behind her.

"Probably Atlanta."

Jared's hand came up to rest protectively on her shoulder when a soldier left the road and took a few steps toward the house. But the man only sat in the mud and tightened the twine that bound the sole to the toeless top of his boot. Then the soldier rose and rejoined the column. Jared's hand didn't move until the last straggler had trudged past.

She heard him plop into a high-backed upholstered chair.

"There are a few pieces of wood in the box," Emily said. "Shall we see if the stove works?"

Jared didn't answer. Emily turned, and then smiled. He'd been close enough during their vigil over the column that she could smell the spirits on his breath. He must have taken a healthy swallow of whatever liquor the Kentuckian carried in his canteen. Jared was sound asleep.

Chapter Eleven

Proud of how the rooms glistened after a frenzied cleaning spree, Emily felt less guilty about breaking into the house. She'd found both cleaning supplies and linens in the cupboards. There was no food, of course. But yesterday, while she took her bath at the inn, Jared had replenished their foodstuffs. Among those supplies were the ingredients for molasses cookies.

Her decision to clean and bake had driven Jared from the house. She gleefully measured and mixed. Rich aroma soon permeated the kitchen with the tangy sweetness of molasses. As she removed a hot pan full of treats from the oven, she felt the sensation of being observed. Without turning to look, she knew Jared had returned and stood in the doorway, watching.

"Are you coming in, or do you intend to stand there all day ogling the cookies?" she asked. The door's hinges squealed. "Please leave your muddy boots outside," she ordered, scraping the cookies onto the counter.

"They're on the porch, next to yours," he said, and reached around her to snatch a cookie. "You've been busy."

"It seemed proper, under the circumstances. I didn't want the owners to think we abused their hospitality." She laughed as he juggled a hot cookie. "You could have taken a cool one."

"I like cookies the way I prefer women—warm and soft, sweet yet spicy."

Emily blushed profusely at the comparison and moved away. "While I was cleaning, I couldn't help wondering why the owners left their home."

"I doubt this house has been a home for years. My guess is the house is an old Cherokee cabin, converted to some rich gent's hunting lodge."

The Cherokee removal had happened before Emily's birth, opening much of the Carolinas and Georgia to white settlement. She'd heard stories of the evacuation of the Indians and their long march to Oklahoma. So many of the Cherokee had died that the removal came to be known as the Trail of Tears. The Navajo were currently enduring a similar forced trek, crossing the New Mexico Territory at the point of Union guns.

At certain times, when he slipped into quiet contemplation or became hard-as-rock stubborn, she could see his mixed blood. Not that it mattered to her, though she wondered if others could pinpoint his heritage more easily. Had the facial features she thought of as handsome somehow hampered his life in ways she knew nothing about?

And why, of all professions, would an Indian choose to become a soldier? Her curiosity piqued, she asked, "Jared, why did you join the army?"

He looked a little taken back, but answered, "For the education, mostly. Few Indians are granted admission to universities. By going to West Point, I avoided rejection based on prejudice. Not that anyone at the Point welcomed me with open arms, but they didn't toss me out."

"Isn't there some sponsorship requirement for West Point?"

He smiled. "That's why they didn't toss me out. My recommendation for admittance came from Franklin Pierce."

"President Pierce?"

Jared nodded. "My father wasn't always a rancher. He'd tried his hand at trapping, and surveying, and during the Mexican War he served in the army, under then General Pierce. During one particular battle, my father saved Pierce's life. Pierce repaid the debt of honor when my father requested a letter of recommendation for me."

"What would you have done if the army had sent you West, with someone like Kit Carson?"

He shrugged. "I never had to face the choice. The war interfered." He grabbed another cookie. "There's a duck pond on the property. If I bring one down, think you can cook it up for supper?"

Emily wasn't surprised at the change of subject. She knew nothing of his life since the war had begun, because each time conversation veered close to the topic, he evaded further discussion, as if the war were too painful to talk about.

Had it been as painful for Jared to join the Confederacy as for her father to join the Union? Possibly. But she was glad he'd made that choice. Otherwise, he wouldn't be standing before her now, resplendent in his Rebel uniform, chomping down cookies. They never would have met.

And she never would have fallen in love with him or conjured up fantasies of marriage and children and home. Jared wanted a lover. Might he also want a wife? Emily reined in her racing hopes. Dashed dreams hurt too much.

"I've never roasted a duck before," she stated with a frown, trying to remember how Hanna prepared the fowl.

Jared hid a smile as Emily pushed the inedible scraps to the center of her plate. He picked at the carcass to find a morsel not burned or raw. The poor bird had been victimized twice, the gunshot that killed it more merciful.

"It's not *that* bad," he said to her downcast expression, wiping the grease from his hands.

"Don't patronize me," she snapped. "It's awful."

Jared leaned back in his chair and savored his coffee, as well as the sight of Emily battering the dishes. The duck made a final flight when Emily picked up the pan, stomped outside and heaved the carcass into a clump of bushes. The pan clanged into the sink. She scrubbed with enough vigor to shave metal.

"Remind me never to let you scrub my back when you're in a *foul* mood," he quipped, then dodged a wet towel.

Emily huffed and went out onto the porch.

Jared knew he shouldn't tease about the ruined dinner, but Lord, she was beautiful when piqued. Her eyes flashed and her mouth formed a tempting, kissable pout.

Her face was so expressive. She'd worked hard all day turning an abandoned house into a cozy haven—and she'd enjoyed every minute. He'd heard her humming as she dusted, seen the bright smile when she shook the rugs.

While Emily indulged her domesticity, he had pondered how to tell Emily the truth about his mission. If there was any hope of a future with her, he had to tell her soon.

Was there hope? Could a daughter of the South love a son of the West? She'd reacted unexpectedly to his Indian ancestry, but his heritage wasn't personally threatening. Learning he was a Yankee, the enemy, the infamous Cougar—well, that was different.

When he came into the cabin, half-decided to tell all, he hadn't been able to find the words to destroy her obvious contentment.

He wanted it all: the barefoot cookie-baker, the furious pot-scrubber, the tender nurse, the skilled rider, and even the haughty belle. And they all came bundled in a package of sleek legs, creamy shoulders and doelike brown eyes.

Jared walked over to the door. Emily sat on the edge of the porch, her legs dangling, swinging.

"Would you like some company?" he asked.

"Only if you can refrain from making any more fowl jokes."

"You're taking this much too seriously." He sat down behind her and scooted forward to wrap himself around Emily, his thighs flanking her derriere. "I remember some bacon you were able to laugh about afterward, and this time you didn't burn your hand in the process."

"A gentleman would not remind a lady of past errors, especially when he's likely to get an elbow in the ribs for his comments."

"Warning heeded, but then, I never claimed to be a gentleman, did I?"

Goose bumps rippled along Emily's arms where he stroked. Jared entwined their fingers, then folded their arms under her breasts. Her heartbeat quickened.

"I wanted so badly for dinner to be perfect. I think I put too much wood in the stove."

"It's been my experience that very little is perfect the first time," he breathed into her hair. "Anything worth doing well usually takes practice—" he kissed her neck "—and patience—" he nibbled on her ear "—and refining."

Emily closed her eyes, engulfed in riotous desire sweeping through her as he nuzzled. "Shall I roast another duck?"

"There's another kind of hunger between us that needs satisfying. Unless we get back into the house, I swear, I'm going to have dessert right here on the porch."

His erotic allusion set her heart palpitating. She tightened their mutual grip to relieve the emphatic pounding. "I distinctly remember hearing the word *patience*."

"You still have your clothes on, don't you? I'm going to count to five, and then they're coming off. Your choice, Emily— the porch or the bed. One." He tugged her shirttail from the waistband and slipped his hands beneath the shirt.

"It's still daylight!"

"There's no law against making love during the day. I want to see, as well as taste and touch, every inch of you. Two," he continued, cupping her breasts.

"Jared, this is insane," she said censoriously, reveling in his bold, sensuous caresses.

"My sanity is certainly doubtful, and I can think of only one way to restore my wits. I'm going to have you under me shortly, and I don't give a damn where. Three."

Emily's breath turned ragged. Her body ached for the feel of his, for his touch to roam her skin once more. But the underlying fear burst forth. The pain and horrible emptiness she'd endured hovered like a threatening storm cloud.

"Then promise me it won't hurt this time," she begged.

Burly arms lifted and spun her around until she knelt before him, staring into passion-filled eyes.

"I wish I could, but I don't know how long it takes for a woman to be able to have a man without pain. All I can promise is to do whatever I can to lessen the pain, to pleasure you so thoroughly that maybe it won't matter. I want to make love to you this time, not take you. Three and a half."

Emily's love for him swelled at the half-count, his delay meaning more than no number at all. How could she say no, to him, to herself? "I think I would prefer the bed. Four."

"I'll be damned," he muttered, before swinging her around to pick her up.

Emily marveled at his strength. As though she were a cloth doll, limp and light, he carried her into the bedroom. He kissed her before setting her on her feet. Dazed by the power and need in that kiss, the next thing she sensed was the flannel shirt sliding off her shoulders. She flushed as Jared admired her exposed bosom.

"Lovely," he said, then bent to taste.

Emily suffered the sweet torture until her legs threatened to dissolve. She tugged at his hair, pulling his head up for another kiss. His lips never left hers as he unbuttoned her trousers and pushed them from her hips. He picked her up and laid her on the bed.

With mesmerized fascination, she watched Jared undress.

Muscle rippled under bronzed skin—all-over bronze, even skin never exposed to sun. Firm and corded along every inch of his frame, Jared's acute masculinity took her breath away. Molded contours and rugged angles merged into a heart-stopping blend of brawn and grace. Dark hair covered him from the springy coils on his chest to the tiny strands across his toes.

Jutting from a nest of curly hair, his swollen male organ begged her to touch. Her hand rose but, unsure of what he expected, she curled her fingers into her palm and lowered them.

Seeing her hesitancy, Jared clasped Emily's hand and pressed her fingers against his heat. The cool touch on his arousal sent a tremor of anticipation through his veins.

"You like that, when I touch you," she whispered. "I thought so last night, but I couldn't see your reaction."

"So now you know."

With a small smile, she said, "Now I know."

Jared endured the stroke of curious fingers, allowed Emily to fondle until she became bold, pressing and squeezing with budding understanding. He joined her on the bed. A small sigh escaped her lips when their bodies melded along their full length.

Then he rolled her onto her back and searched for signs of fear. Greeted by a shy smile on her gently curved lips, a glow of trust and expectation in her eyes, Jared lowered his lips to her velvet sweetness.

His mouth took hers in a searing kiss, demanding her response. He probed until she parted her kiss-bruised lips. Tenderly he drew Emily ever closer to the precipice.

Drugged by wanton sensations, Emily struggled to stay alert. She wanted to cherish each breathtaking moment and lock it away in her heart. Jared made good his oath to touch every inch of her. Kissing and caressing, he wandered from forehead to eyelids, to cheeks and chin. The lower he blazed his trail, the harder Emily struggled to concentrate. By the time he reached her throat, Emily's thoughts had scattered.

He moved over her then, blanketing her body. With both hands, he sought, then gently kneaded, the silken mounds of her breasts. The long, slow pull of his mouth, combined with the soft grazing of his thumbs, drove her wild.

Needing to move, to touch, Emily's hands roved over each area of male skin within her reach. Down his back and up again, over his shoulders and into his hair, she repeated the pattern until she knew intimately each knot of hard muscle, each bump of backbone.

Jared turned onto his side, his hand on her buttocks to press her soft curves against his stiffened shaft. With deft, gentle strokes, he flirted with her inner thighs until she parted her legs to his questing hand. He claimed the treasure she offered. Emily trembled and arched sharply. Her breath labored, she moaned his name as Jared slipped a finger into her woman's heat.

Beads of moisture burst forth across Jared's upper lip as he fought for control, caressing her until she moaned from deep in her throat. Every ounce of willpower he could summon kept him from piercing her too soon. Near bursting with need, he roused Emily to fevered heights.

Craving, so intense it brought tears to her eyes, built urgently around his delving fingers. Just when she thought her body would shatter, he withdrew his hand and covered her with his lean, hard frame.

"Relax, love. Open for me," he whispered, and without hesitation she widened the pathway.

His hands on her hips, Jared slowly eased his hardness into her softness. So tight, and yet the silken walls yielded to accommodate his size. He groaned with the strain of stopping his hips from rocking forward.

Emily opened her eyes and gazed into smoky, questioning onyx. Why did he hesitate now, when she wanted him so much? And then she knew, and smiled her happiness and lack of pain. "You feel so good," she whispered, and then gasped as he lunged.

"This makes you mine," Jared declared, and strummed chords of passion, in a rhythm older than time, newer than spring.

Her hips rose and fell, arched and receded, as he plunged and withdrew. From deep in the nether reaches of her body, the pressure spread and enveloped her until she couldn't tell where Emily ended and Jared began. As they fused together in love's perfect bonding, her raw nerves sparked until a bright light exploded.

Jared caressed Emily's mouth with kisses as she cried her pleasure. Wanting to feel each pulse that signaled the richness of her fulfillment, he stayed deep and motionless until, awed by the intensity of it, he felt his control snap. He came, hard, adding his pounding pleasure to her soft ripples.

Bodies locked in shared consummation, they lay quietly until their breathing neared normal, kissing and nuzzling until the last waves of love's domination calmed.

Jared rolled to his side, relieving her of his weight, but brought her with him. Unwilling to separate their union, he kept their hips snug, preserving their joining. Emily settled into his embrace and soon fell asleep, content. Stroking her hair, appeased beyond his wildest imaginings, he maintained their union until it was physically impossible for him to stay within.

Emily was everything he wanted in a woman. His body knew its true mate. Somehow, he had to bind her to him. He had no plan yet, no idea how he would overcome all the deceit his mission had necessitated.

Placing a soft kiss on the top of her head, he knew beyond doubt that he would find a way to keep Emily. He couldn't let her go. *She's mine,* he thought ruthlessly, and tightened his hold.

* * *

Emily cuddled the pillow, still warm and damply scented with musky, male aroma. Eyes closed, she could hear rain pattering on the window and noises coming from the kitchen.

After the wondrous loving following supper, they'd slept. It had been dark when she first woke, and reached out to touch Jared, make sure she wasn't dreaming.

Jared slept like a stoked boiler, hot to the touch. Emily thought of the cold winter nights in Adairsville, when she'd huddled under every blanket she owned to stay warm. With Jared beside her, heating the bed, she would never be cold.

He'd stirred and pulled her close. His kisses had ignited her newly discovered sensuality. Like a sculptor shaping clay to its finished form, Jared had molded her body and prodded her senses toward the final firing. And he had taught her of his body.

An apt, curious pupil, she'd learned, and reveled in her power. Over the slate of his hard, lean body, she'd sketched her brand of ownership. Each moan elicited, each sharp intake of his breath, had made her bolder. Emily blushed, remembering where her hands and mouth had lavished intimate attention.

Together they'd spiraled in reeling, dizzying fulfillment.

Emily unfurled, stretched, and opened her eyes. The room looked the same, Spartan but cozy. Yet within this tiny room, in an abandoned farmhouse far from home, the earth had tilted on its axis. For the first time in years, Emily felt whole.

Foolishly or not, she had fallen deeply in love with Jared. He held her heart as surely as he'd claimed her body. Jared hadn't promised more than a physical relationship. He was honest, at least, in not offering permanent ties to lure her into his bed. *Something special* was all he wanted to explore. Calmly, knowing full well what the hazards were, Emily accepted her fate as Jared's partner in a grand adventure.

Emily heard a floorboard squeak, and looked up. Jared stood in the doorway, leaning against the frame, holding a cup of the steaming coffee he drank by the potful. Clad only in the buckskin britches he preferred to his uniform, he emanated virility so robust it caught her breath.

His slow, lazy smile was infectious, and Emily couldn't resist returning the grin. Jared was the devil incarnate, and at the same time an angel of mercy, an enigma packaged as a raw male animal. A man that rare was worth loving.

Jared stood in awe of the tempting siren sprawled between the sheets. It was hard to believe Emily had shared his bed last night, impossible to believe her complete abandon.

He shouldn't have given in to the urge to show Emily how to please a man, telling himself he was dissolving her fear of his extended shaft. Emily had learned quickly and greedily snatched control. This sorceress of white magic had reached his soul, leaving him seared and bound in her spell.

Emily sat up, clutching the sheet to her chest to hide her nakedness, but Jared remembered vividly what she strove to keep from view. A radiant glow surrounded her like a halo. Kiss swollen lips smiled, beckoning him into the room.

Their eyes locked as he walked toward the bed, offering the cup. He sat, trapping her legs between his thigh and hand and watched her take a sip.

"The service here is exceptional." Emily raised the cup in a salute. "I'm sorry we must leave. I could grow accustomed to such comforts."

"The bed is lumpy," Jared argued.

Emily raised her eyebrows in mock surprise. "Really? I hadn't noticed."

"You must have noticed that the food in this place leaves a great deal to be desired. Supper was a disastrous affair."

Emily waved a hand of dismissal. "Release the cook."

"I kind of like the cook. She's attractive, and witty—"

he ran a finger along her chin "—and very, very tempting."

"Tempting enough to get a good-morning kiss?"

Jared honored her request with enthusiasm.

Some minutes later, she said breathlessly, "You're a cruel man, Jared Randall."

"I'm cruel because I kissed you?"

Emily shook her head. "You're going to tell me that I have to get out of this bed and get on a horse. After that kiss, I'm not sure I can do so without help."

"Are you telling me you're too weak to get out of bed?"

Emily answered with a dazzling smile.

"Good Lord, woman, you'll wear me out."

"Is that possible?"

Jared set the cup on the floor and crawled into the bed, pulling her on top of him.

"I'd like nothing better than to spend a *week* in bed with you and test my limitations." He felt her light laughter at the thinly veiled boast. A week wouldn't be long enough, nor would a month or a year. He wanted a lifetime of making love to Emily.

Jared stroked her hair. "We don't have a week, but we do have today. It's still raining, and I think we both had our fill of rain and mud yesterday."

Emily nuzzled into the hair on his chest. "Rainy days are for curling up in a comfortable chair with a good book."

"Among other pursuits." Jared chuckled and pressed Emily into the feather mattress.

Jared wilted under Emily's hopeful expression. "I can't, love, really I can't."

"You didn't like it?"

"I've never had better, but a man has limits." Jared fingered the thigh he'd been nibbling. "How many did you have?"

"Two."

"Do you want more?"

Emily shook her head. "No, I'm satisfied."

"I had four. That should prove how much I enjoyed it."

Emily's slumped shoulders rose a bit. "I suppose so. I just wanted to make sure you'd had enough."

"I'm so satisfied I may burst." Jared picked up the towel and wiped his hands and mouth. "Emily, the duck was delicious, but I just can't eat another bite. Leave the dishes for a while, and let's take a walk."

Hand in hand, they strolled across the grassy clearing, toward the surrounding woods. Emily closed her eyes and tilted her face upward. The world smelled freshly washed, cleansed by four days of rain. The warm breeze tugging at her hair would dry the stalks wetting her skirt hem—and the roads.

Emily opened her eyes and glanced at Jared. For the past two days, Jared had been as restless as a caged cat. He delayed leaving the farm because of her, she knew, but Emily refused to feel guilty for praying for more rain.

"Have you spent much time in Virginia?" she asked.

"Some, mostly along the coast. Why?"

"Curious about Petersburg. Have you been there?"

Jared shook his head. "Are you anxious to leave?"

"No, but I know we must. The horses will be glad for the exercise, at least."

Jared looked over his shoulder at the barn, then stopped walking. "We have company."

Emily turned in time to see the back of a wagon entering the barn. "The owner?"

"I doubt it." Jared put his hand in the small of her back and pushed her toward the tree line. "I'll circle back through the woods. Listen, if something happens—you see that path?"

"Yes, but—"

"If there's any shooting, you hightail it out of here, fast. That path leads down past the duck pond. You can hide there until it's safe to come out."

Emily swallowed the lump threatening to choke her. If something happened to Jared— Emily refused to complete the thought. It was too horrible to contemplate.

"I'm not staying here. I'm coming with you."

"Emily, I don't have time to argue."

"That's what I'm counting on."

He sighed. "Will you at least stay in hiding in the brush until I can find out what we're up against?"

"Yes."

Jared wound his way through the woods. Emily followed, cringing every time a twig broke under her boot. Compared to Jared's silence, each snap she made sounded like a clap of thunder.

Emily stole a glance at Jared while they huddled behind a bush and he surveyed the back of the barn. She felt no fear, only heightened anticipation. Jared knew what he was doing, carefully planning each step and action. The game of stalk and capture seemed as natural to him as breathing.

If Jared's plans went awry and he told her to run, would she obey? He would be furious if he realized she had no intention of obeying any such command. Somehow, she would get into the house, get her shotgun.

Quick motions of his hands told her to be quiet and stay put. Emily reached up and grabbed his sleeve.

"Be careful," she pleaded.

Jared bent down and kissed her nose. "Always."

Emily held her breath while Jared soundlessly sprinted toward the barn, then hunkered near a slit between the boards. After watching for a moment, he smiled and motioned for her to join him.

She left her hiding place and ran to his side. Emily peeked through the narrow crack and giggled. Shuffling his feet in a crazy little dance, his eyes crinkled with delight, a gawky Negro was celebrating.

Emily beamed at Jared. "Sam."

"How the hell did he find us?"

"Let's find out. Come meet your rival," she teased.

Sam's grin stretched from ear to ear when Emily approached him. "Hey there, Missy Emily. You sure gave me a fright, that you did. But I found you, for sure I found you."

His elation quickly faded when he spotted Jared.

"This is the owner of the other horse, Sam. Lieutenant Randall," Emily said.

"Heard you was travelin' with a soldier. Much obliged, L'tenant, you lookin' after Missy Emily."

Jared nodded amiably, but something in Sam's eyes caught Emily's attention. He looked wary.

"Sam, what's the matter?" Emily asked.

He rallied, but his weary smile didn't reach his eyes. "Nothin' a good sleep and a good meal won't fix," he said. "Been traipsin' all over God's creation looking for you."

"I can't believe you found me."

"Weren't all that hard, Missy. If folks didn't remember you, they remembered Rusty. Horse like that, folks tend to notice. Got a bit of grain in the wagon for her. Got a surprise for you, too. A letter, from L'tenant Roth."

Emily assumed the very worst, sure that Lewis Roth would write for only one reason. She gripped Sam's arm and haltingly asked, "Is Terrance all right?"

"Yes, ma'am. Leastwise, he was when I left him."

Emily drew back, puzzled. "Then why would Lewis write?"

"Don't know, Missy, seein' as how he ain't never done the like of that before."

"C'mon, Sam," Jared said, interrupting. "Let's get your horse out of harness. Emily, why don't you heat the rest of the duck for Sam? He can tell us about his trip over a hot meal."

"How thoughtless of me. Of course, Sam is hungry. Come into the house when you've finished."

Emily hurried off toward the house.

Jared swore to himself as he slapped the nag's rump, urging her to follow Sam.

NO COST! NO OBLIGATION TO BUY!
NO PURCHASE NECESSARY!

PLAY "LUCKY 7" AND GET FIVE FREE GIFTS

HOW TO PLAY:

1. With a coin, carefully scratch off the silver box at the right. Then check the claim chart to see what we have for you—FREE BOOKS and a gift—ALL YOURS! ALL FREE!

2. Send back this card and you'll receive brand-new Harlequin Historical™ novels. These books have a cover price of $4.99 each, but they are yours to keep absolutely free.

3. There's no catch. You're under no obligation to buy anything. We charge nothing—ZERO—for your first shipment. And you don't have to make any minimum number of purchases—not even one!

4. The fact is thousands of readers enjoy receiving books by mail from the Harlequin Reader Service®. They like the convenience of home delivery...they like getting the best new novels BEFORE they're available in stores...and they love our discount prices!

5. We hope that after receiving your free books you'll want to remain a subscriber. But the choice is yours—to continue or cancel, anytime at all! So why not take us up on our invitation, with no risk of any kind. You'll be glad you did!

You'll love this plush, cuddly Teddy Bear, an adorable accessory for your dressing table, bookcase or desk. Measuring 5½" tall, he's soft and brown and has a bright red ribbon around his neck—he's completely captivating! And he's yours absolutely free, when you accept this no-risk offer!

PLAY "LUCKY 7"

**Just scratch off the silver box with a coin.
Then check below to see the gifts you get.**

YES! I have scratched off the silver box. Please send me all the gifts for which I qualify. I understand I am under no obligation to purchase any books, as explained on the back and on the opposite page.

247 CIH A7C9
(U-H-H-03/97)

NAME

ADDRESS   APT.

CITY   STATE   ZIP

DETACH AND MAIL CARD TODAY

THE HARLEQUIN READER SERVICE®: HERE'S HOW IT WORKS

Accepting free books places you under no obligation to buy anything. You may keep the books and gift and return the shipping statement marked "cancel". If you do not cancel, about a month later we'll send you 4 additional novels, and bill you just $3.69 each plus 25¢ delivery per book and applicable sales tax, if any.* That's the complete price—and compared to cover prices of $4.99 each—quite a bargain! You may cancel at any time, but if you choose to continue, every month we'll send you 4 more books, which you may either purchase at the discount price...or return to us and cancel your subscription.

*Terms and prices subject to change without notice. Sales tax applicable in N.Y.

BUSINESS REPLY MAIL
FIRST-CLASS MAIL   PERMIT NO. 717   BUFFALO, NY

POSTAGE WILL BE PAID BY ADDRESSEE

HARLEQUIN READER SERVICE
3010 WALDEN AVE
PO BOX 1867
BUFFALO NY 14240-9952

NO POSTAGE
NECESSARY
IF MAILED
IN THE
UNITED STATES

Why would Lewis Roth write a letter to Emily? Why now? Why, after three years of silence, had Roth suddenly had the urge to write to the lady he'd callously deserted?

Jared glanced at Sam, who was coaxing his nag to eat while getting reacquainted with Rusty. Satisfied with Sam's distraction, Jared untied the wagon's tarp and flung it back. A battered jacket lay tucked between two bales of hay. Jared quickly searched the pockets.

Wrapped in a piece of oilcloth was a map, Sam's travel pass, and the letter. He glanced over the first two, but read the letter, twice.

Jared considered disposing of the letter, but destroying it would only get Sam into trouble. Besides, Lewis Roth was too late. No way in hell…

But how would Emily feel? Did she still have feelings for Roth, enough to resume their engagement?

Only one way to find out. Jared wrapped up the papers and shoved them back into Sam's jacket pocket.

Chapter Twelve

Jared leaned against the sink, arms crossed, fighting impatience. Emily sat at the table, conversing with Sam, watching him eat—ignoring the packet on the table that contained Lewis Roth's letter.

"In all my days, I ain't never seen so many blue coats in one place before," Sam said, between bites of duck, of his arrival in Adairsville.

"What about the house?" Emily inquired.

"Officers stayin' there. They told me the place was empty when they took it over. Figured you'd skedaddled. Asked around a bit. Heard you'd left town with a soldier, a Reb officer. So I walked back to where I hid the rig and lit out for Rosewood."

"Did you stop in Canton?"

"Didn't see no need."

Emily slumped in her chair. "You went to Rosewood?"

Sam said on a sigh, "Cap'n Terrance—he'll slip a cog when he hears. Anyway, I saw where you'd made a cook fire, bedded down for the night. Next mornin', I headed east. Like I said, if folks didn't remember seein' you, they remembered seein' Rusty."

There could only be one reason for Sam to follow Emily's trail so doggedly, Jared reasoned. That damn letter. Why didn't Emily open the packet? His patience snapped.

"Sam," he said, drawing the Negro's attention, "why follow Emily? Why didn't you just return to Captain Gardner?"

"Rusty." Sam shot an apologetic glance at Emily. "Your brother, he wants me to bring the mare."

"He lost Titan," Emily said flatly.

"Titan ain't dead, Missy, leastwise not yet. But he's worn to the quick. That stallion's got heart. He'll keep goin' till he drops."

"This war has been hard on horses."

"Sure has."

Jared heard a touch of anger in Sam's voice. There was something about the situation that Sam wasn't telling Emily.

"Where are you supposed to take Rusty?" Emily asked.

"Charlotte."

"Terrance is in Charlotte?"

"Should be, by now. That's where they was headed when I left for Adairsville."

Emily rose from her chair and turned toward Jared, with that look on her face that always turned his resolve to mush. He knew what she would ask, and knew what he would answer, despite Cougar's dire warnings, echoing in his head. Lord, he was such a sucker for the soft plea in those doelike eyes. Though he was prepared, the request still hit him in the heart.

"I know it's out of our way, but can we take Sam and Rusty to Charlotte?"

"Why?"

"Maybe I can trade Rusty for Titan. I haven't seen my brother for some time."

"I doubt your brother will be happy to see you. I think we should take Rusty and Sam and head for Petersburg."

Emily hesitated, then said quietly, "If I don't take the stallion, they might put him down. I have to go, Jared, whether you come or not."

He didn't doubt Emily would try to go without him. He

could stop her, but not without harming their fragile relationship. She wanted to trade horses and see Terrance. The letter from Roth, yet unread, hadn't influenced her decision.

Whatever transpired between Emily and Roth, Jared's mission remained unchanged. Emily wasn't staying anywhere in the South. He would take her to Washington if he had to tie and gag her and throw her over his saddle.

Besides, some perverse part of him argued for a face-to-face meeting with Lewis Roth. He wanted to meet the man Emily had loved enough, at one time, to agree to marry.

"All right." Jared pushed himself erect. "We'll go to Charlotte, but we don't have time for a long family reunion. We'll exchange horses with Terrance and leave. Clear?"

He didn't wait for an answer, but left the house with brisk strides.

"I didn't mean to cause trouble, Missy Emily."

"You didn't, Sam. I'm afraid I did, though."

Emily picked up the oilcloth containing Lewis's letter. It was cowardly to have put the letter aside, but for some reason she hadn't wanted to read it in front of Jared.

She scoffed at the salutation. *"My dearest Emily,"* indeed. Emily read the brief account of Lewis Roth's change in status and of his desire to revive their engagement.

Blond, blue-eyed Lewis Roth was easy to picture. Wealthy and sophisticated, handsome and charming, Lewis had been courted by every northern Georgia matron with a marriageable daughter. It had been no surprise to anyone, however, when he proposed to Emily Gardner, his best friend's sister.

To a young Emily Gardner, Lewis Roth possessed the finest qualities of a suitable husband. He was her social equal and would eventually inherit Twin Pines. She'd believed his aloof manner the mark of a gentleman.

For one glorious month, she'd basked in the romanticism of her engagement and planned a lavish wedding ceremony and party. Then, with one swift stroke, her dreams had crumbled. John Gardner announced he couldn't support secession and would join the Federal army. Emily had neither seen nor spoken to Lewis Roth after the day Papa left.

A year later, Lewis received permission to join the cavalry unit Terrance had formed to regain his standing among his peers. But Mr. Roth stood firm against his son's marriage to a traitor's daughter. Now Mr. Roth had died, freeing Lewis to make his own choices.

Lewis wanted marriage. But Lewis's kiss had never evoked a tingle. His cool gaze had never sparked desire. His touch had never melted her insides.

"I hope it ain't bad news," Sam said. "I hate bringin' bad news."

"Not bad news, just unexpected," Emily said, and put the letter in her pocket.

She found Jared on the porch, staring out over the countryside, clearly not at all happy about yielding to this detour. "I'm sorry, Jared. I shouldn't have asked you to come with me. I know you have to go to Richmond. I don't want you to get into trouble with your superiors simply because I have a whim to save a horse and see my brother."

Jared brushed his knuckles across her cheek. "It really isn't a problem. Why don't you take Sam for a walk? Take him down to see the ducks. He might enjoy that."

Confused by the suggestion, she asked, "Why would Sam want to see the ducks?"

"While you're gone, I'll move my belongings into the barn. Sam and I can bed down in there tonight."

Emily could only nod. She should have realized earlier that with Sam here, Jared wouldn't share her bed, wouldn't even stay in the house. Jared sought to protect her reputation, shield a virtue she could no longer claim. The fondness she'd once mistaken for love, for Lewis, paled to insignificance when compared to the depth of her love for Jared.

No, there wouldn't be a long family reunion in Charlotte. She needed only time to trade horses with Terrance. And she had no intention of gracing Lewis's proposal with a reply.

Emily lightly touched Jared's sleeve and found enough voice to whisper, "I'll miss you." Fearing she would cry if she said more, she called out to Sam and suggested the walk.

Jared shifted, trying to get comfortable. After sleeping in a bed for several nights, he was finding the hard-packed floor of the barn an unsatisfactory substitute.

"L'tenant, you awake?" Sam's soft voice floated through the darkness.

"What's on your mind, Sam?"

"About Missy Emily, sir. I don't think her goin' to Charlotte's a good idea. She won't like what she finds, make no mistake."

Jared assumed that Sam meant Terrance's stallion. "Titan is in rough shape?"

"Yes, but that don't make no never mind. Missy Emily said you're takin' her to Virginia, to her relation. I'm thinkin' on hitchin' Rusty up to the wagon and leavin' the nag for Missy. I'm thinkin' you should take Missy and keep on goin'."

Jared closed his eyes and laid an arm across his forehead. "Have you ever tried to talk Emily out of doing something once she's set her mind to it?"

With an understanding chuckle, Sam said, "I never got anywhere, but I think you could. She might listen to you."

Sometimes. Not often enough.

"She'll need a reason, a damn good one. Why shouldn't Emily go to Charlotte?"

Jared could almost hear Sam thinking, deciding what to tell the unknown Rebel officer.

"Missy Emily, she shouldn't see what Cap'n Terrance did to Titan. She shouldn't see the cap'n neither. He's changed since she last set eyes on him. Man's got demons in his craw. The whiskey can't drown 'em. The fightin' can't chase 'em out. Now, L'tenant Roth, he's a good man. He keeps a sharp eye on the company, tries to keep Cap'n Terrance from gettin' himself killed. But someday, he's gonna ride into a hornet's nest of Yanks and not come out.''

Jared nearly cringed. He'd seen the type, understood how demons could drive a man. A commander, driven to prove himself, finding courage in a bottle, leading men into suicidal skirmishes. Luckily, most had intelligent junior officers to keep annihilation at bay. Roth, apparently, filled that role for Terrance Gardner. Jared quickly shoved aside a grudging respect for Lewis Roth.

"Captain Gardner abused Titan and isn't fit for command," Jared observed. When Sam didn't comment, Jared continued, "If Terrance abuses his horse and his men, then he likely abuses you. President Lincoln declared the slaves freed, proclaimed Jubilee. Why do you stay with Terrance?"

"Missy Emily. Weren't right, leavin' her alone. Cap'n Terrance, he moved her into that house, told her take care of Rusty, but he didn't give her the means. Oh, he finds ways to get feed for the mare, sends me with the wagon, but he don't give no thought to Missy Emily. I try. I find food, here and there. And sometimes, after a fight, there's canned milk and such layin' about. I take them and put them away for Missy.''

"That's a lot of responsibility to take on out of pity.''

"Ain't pity. I owe Missy Emily. She done dragged me away from the pearly gates, one time. Weren't for Missy Emily, I was a goner for sure.''

Jared sat up and hugged his knees. He'd heard a few stories of Emily's life, from her father and Hanna, but not this one. He also had the feeling he wasn't going to like what he would hear.

"Emily saved your life?''

"Sure did. About four years ago now, a pair of slavers came by Rosewood. I was alone out in a field. They thought

I was a runaway they was lookin' for, set the dogs on me. Missy heard. Lordy, she came flying across that field on a big stallion, screamin' and carryin' on. Took a crop to them dogs, beat them off. I swear, she woulda taken a crop to them slavers if her daddy hadn't come along.''

The picture Sam painted made Jared's blood run cold. Slavers. Reports of the methods used to capture runaway slaves had goaded moderates in the North to turn staunch abolitionists. And Emily, at what age— fourteen?...fifteen?—had ridden into their midst armed with a riding crop. Brave? Foolish?

"I hope her daddy tanned her backside for such a stunt.''

"If he did, I never heard tell of it. I only know that I woke up on the kitchen floor in the big house, and there was Missy Emily, hoverin' over me. I was pretty chewed-on, clawed up. Even Hanna, the housekeeper, thought I was done for. Not Missy Emily. She doctored and fussed, wouldn't let me die. Kept tellin' me that if I gave up she'd never forgive me. Said she'd take that crop to my dead carcass. So you see, L'tenant, I owe Missy Emily. I'll do for her like she done for me.''

A life for a life—a practice revered by many cultures, including the Indian. Sam was paying a debt he owed. Taken a step further, that meant John Gardner now owed Sam for taking care of Emily. Taken one more step, it meant Jared did, too. And Jared would settle the debt, gladly.

"What about Terrance? Do you owe him, too?''

"No, L'tenant. Don't owe him nothin'.''

Jared cautiously planted the suggestion of a hopefully workable payoff for Sam's loyalty. "Sam, you don't have to take care of Emily anymore.''

"Guess not. If she's goin' to Virginia, to live with her relation, guess they'll take care of her now.''

Both Sam and Emily would learn otherwise, later, but for now Jared decided to let Sam believe that part of the story.

"If you don't have to stay with Terrance to get supplies for Emily, then there's no reason for you to stay with Terrance any longer."

"Ain't thought that far ahead."

"Think about it, Sam."

Jared stretched out on his bedroll, already planning on how to smuggle Sam to Washington, to the home of John Gardner.

"L'tenant? We goin' to Charlotte?"

"Yes, Sam, we're going to Charlotte."

Emily tightened Rusty's girth strap as Jared asked, "Ready?"

She gave Rusty an affectionate pat. "Always."

"Always?" he repeated in a low drawl, a wry grin spreading across his face.

With a deliberately saucy smile, Emily gazed steadily into his flashing eyes. "Care to test my word, soldier?"

His grin faltered.

Laughing, Emily tied her bonnet and, with a flourish, mounted Rusty.

At midmorning, a wagon wheel caught a rut at the wrong angle. The resulting snap brought them to a halt. Sam crawled under the wagon and inspected the axle.

"She's cracked, but not broke."

"If we brace it, will the axle hold out until Charlotte?" Jared asked.

"Could be."

"Should be easy enough to find a suitable chunk of wood. Come on, Sam. Let's look."

"Is there something I can do to help?" Emily asked.

From his pack, Jared pulled out a knife—the most wicked, lethal knife Emily had ever seen.

"Cut some strips from the tarp," Jared said, placing the handle of the bowie knife in Emily's palm. "Be careful, this is sharp."

As the men headed into the woods, Emily set about her

task. The blade sliced through canvas like a duck gliding over a glassy pond. She'd cut three strips when Sam and Jared returned, a stout tree branch perched on Jared's shoulder.

"Enough?" she asked, holding up the strips.

Jared nodded. "Why don't you get out of the sun while we fix this?"

Emily gladly handed over the knife. Sitting in the shade, she watched the men work. Both men were sweating, their shirts clinging to their backs.

Then Sam removed his shirt.

Emily shot to her feet. Years ago, she'd tended Sam's wounds. She knew his body had been scarred by dogs' teeth and claws. But the scars on his back— Dear God, he'd been whipped!

"Who did this to you?" she spat.

"Missy, I..."

"Don't look away from me, Sam. Terrance whipped you, didn't he? When? What for?"

"Now, Missy, don't get riled."

"Riled? Sam, I swear, either you tell me what happened or I'll show you riled!"

Sam shuffled from foot to foot. "You got to understand—Cap'n Terrance, he weren't himself that day. He got beat back by the Yanks, bad. Got to drinkin' after. The liquor was muddlin' his head, guidin' his hand."

"Don't you dare make excuses for Terrance. What could you possibly have done to deserve whipping?"

Very quietly, Sam said, "Wanted chicken for his supper. I couldn't find him one."

"I'll kill him." Emily voiced her instant reaction aloud. "I'll strangle that...bastard. Or maybe I'll borrow Jared's knife, cut that...fiend's heart out."

She turned to Jared, who leaned against the wagon, trying to hide a smile. Hands on hips, she asked, "Is that axle fixed yet?"

"Yes, ma'am."

"About time."

As Emily stomped toward her horse, Sam said to Jared, "I didn't mean for Missy Emily to see my back. Don't hurt no more. Just forgot. L'tenant, might be best if you was with Missy Emily when she meets up with her brother."

"Think I'll guard my knife, too. One of these days, Emily just might slice some poor man to pieces."

At Sam's questioning expression, Jared chuckled. "Remind me to tell you about another drunk who riled Emily."

Jared walked over to Emily, helped her mount. "You can still change your mind," he said. "We can forget going to Charlotte, take Sam with us to Virginia."

She looked down at him, a tight smile on her face. "I'm going to Charlotte."

Cougar prowled the shadows of an upper crust neighborhood in Charlotte, his task made easier by hovering clouds that threatened rain. They also kept residents indoors, a welcome circumstance, considering his destination. The fewer people who noticed his approach to the home of a man known in Washington as Uncle, the better.

Contacting an intelligence agent was risky business, especially in daylight and without prior arrangement. But through Uncle a message could be sent to Colonel Gardner, and swift, secret passage to Washington for Sam could be arranged.

When he rounded the last corner before his destination, caution gave way to an urgent sense of trouble. A less observant man might not have noticed so quickly that the front door of the house stood slightly ajar, or that thick smoke rose from the chimney, or that the sound of male voices raised in anger emanated from within. Cougar noticed, and Jared Hunter took heed, sliding into the obscuring shade of a stately elm.

Within moments, a civilian male, flanked by two Confederate officers, came out the front door. The civilian's hands were bound behind his back. Following the trio, a private struggled with an armload of papers, some of which bore fire-browned and curled corners.

Jared inwardly shivered at the implications of both the arrest and the papers that Uncle had obviously tried to burn, without success. Names revealed. Codes broken. An intricate network of communication destroyed.

The arrest heightened the difficulty of sending a message to John and arranging transportation for Sam, but the task wasn't impossible. Options existed.

As he filtered through those options, the sight of those partially burned papers kept intruding. Hopefully, the name of Captain Jared Hunter didn't appear within the salvaged pages, or his code name of Cougar. The possibility was remote, barely worth contemplating, and certainly not worth worrying over. At least it wouldn't be if he was in Charlotte alone.

But he wasn't. He'd ensconced Emily in a hotel, sent Sam off to tell Terrance of their arrival, then set out to make his arrangements.

Jared vowed that if he made it out of Charlotte with his cover intact, this mission was going to take a decidedly professional turn. He would head for Richmond, with due haste, to collect the passes that would see him and Emily safely through both enemy and friendly lines, and into Washington—no matter what Emily said or tossed in his path.

Cougar silently applauded.

Chapter Thirteen

On the hotel's third floor, Emily stood at the window of a private sitting room, looking out over Charlotte. Under less trying circumstances, she might have succumbed to the restful decor, or even been curious about the city. But torn between dread and anticipation, she waited for Terrance with all the tranquillity of a coiled snake.

Jared was no comfort. After sending Sam to find Terrance, Jared had disappeared, returning two hours later with a stack of newspapers. He now sat on the sofa, in a white shirt and his buckskins, riffling through the papers.

She'd glanced at the headlines. They blared dismay at the relentless drive of General Sherman toward Atlanta. In the two weeks since she'd left Adairsville, Sherman had made slow but steady progress toward his goal. One of the smaller headlines blamed the notorious Cougar for much of Sherman's success. Emily was skeptical. If this Cougar was so good, why didn't the Union promote him to general and give him an army to lead?

"We could leave now, you know," Jared suggested. "All your brother wants is his horse. If we left Rusty at the livery, he would find her."

"I have to talk to Terrance."

"Nothing you can say will change his attitude."

Maybe not, but for Sam's sake, she had to try. "How

could he become so cruel? We never whipped slaves at Rosewood.''

''War tends to bring out either the best or the worst in a man. What I don't understand is why Sam stuck around and took the abuse.''

Emily turned from the window. ''Are you suggesting he run away, live in the squalor of a Negro encampment? Mr. Lincoln declared the slaves free, but he certainly didn't provide for them. On a plantation they were clothed and fed. Now they wonder where their next meal is coming from.''

Jared put the newspaper aside. ''Maybe, but few of them would return under the old system. Not everyone treated their people as well as your father did. Now that they've had a taste of freedom, they won't give it up.''

A crash in the hall ended the discussion. A man bellowed in vulgar language to be left alone. Jared got up and moved to her side. The door flew open.

Thinly held hope shattered as Emily inspected the brother she hadn't seen in two years. His disheveled uniform was filthy. He reeked from lack of a recent bath. Bits of food decorated a shaggy beard.

Emily tried to picture the dashing figure of the brother she'd idolized as a young girl. This complete change was repulsive. Terrance looked more suited to shoveling manure than to leading a company of men into battle.

Jared spared a glance at Terrance Gardner. He noted the resemblance between Terrance and John, but his interest in the son of his commander shrank beside his interest in the man who stood behind Terrance. Blond, blue-eyed, a Southern gentleman to his core, the man had to be Lewis Roth. Roth was also observant. Assessing eyes flickered over Jared, then softened when they rested on Emily.

''You've grown up, little sister,'' Terrance uttered, his tone derisive and laced with strong drink.

''One of us had to,'' she snapped, not bothering to hide her disgust.

"Just what the hell do you think you're doing here?"

"My *brother* wanted his horse, or are you too drunk to remember you sent for Rusty?"

"I can't imagine being so drunk I could mistake my *sister* for my mare! I want an explanation, Emily, and I want it now."

"We were only a few days away when Sam found us. It didn't make much sense to send Rusty and not come myself, though at the moment I wish I'd stayed away."

"Us?" Terrance finally noticed Jared. "Who are you?"

"Jared Randall, sir."

"And why are you in the company of my sister?"

Jared opened his mouth, but Emily beat him to an answer. "You can thank Lieutenant Randall for helping Rusty and me. Were it not for him, your horse might be the treasured mount of some Union officer."

Terrance's eyes narrowed. "You're not in uniform, Randall."

"It needed cleaning," Jared said.

"If Captain Gardner doesn't thank you, I will," Roth said, coming from behind Terrance to stand in front of Emily. He took her hand and lightly kissed the knuckles. "Emily is very precious, to both of us."

Emily stiffly accepted his greeting, noting the subtle changes in the man she had once adored. Lewis had matured, and was no longer boyish in look or manner. His brilliant blue eyes peered from under golden lashes. But his cold hand held hers too long. With this simple welcome, he expected to lay claim to her, as though she were still the naive girl he'd forsworn. She pulled her hand away.

"How touching," Terrance droned. "Lewis, you are a fool."

"You could at least have the decency to thank Randall here for escorting Emily out of Adairsville."

"Yes, well, I wonder what other decencies we must thank him for. I'm sure the story is fascinating. Emily?"

Emily gave Terrance a brief account of how Jared had

offered to buy Rusty and then gallantly helped her leave Adairsville. She told him about Scott Walters and explained why Captain Morgan had placed her under arrest. Terrance paled when she told him about Rosewood's destruction and the deal she and Jared had struck to see her safely to Virginia. Emily sketched her near rape by a drunk and Jared's timely rescue. She ended with Sam's finding them at the abandoned farm.

Terrance's voice dripped with mock admiration. "It seems we have a real hero in our midst."

"The South needs heroes, to make up for the *riffraff*," Emily countered.

"And who do we have to balance out the sluts?"

Emily's strangled shriek voiced her outrage.

Terrance whined, "For two years, I've fought to negate the disgrace of Father's desertion. After all I've accomplished, my sister decides to slander our name again! Not only does she get herself arrested for spying, but she decides to travel across country, unchaperoned, with a man she barely knows!"

Jared growled, "If you're suggesting that Emily has done anything to dishonor your name, you're mistaken."

"Am I? I don't think so. You look like a healthy male to me. I find it hard to believe a man would go to so much trouble for a woman merely for money. I hope the *bonus* was pleasurable. She's let you ruin her reputation. By all that is decent, sir, you should marry the chit."

Lewis was the first to recover, his words jolting the stunned silence. "No, Terrance. If you're so anxious to be rid of your obligations toward Emily, then I'll marry her. I wanted to wait until after the war, but since she's here, there's no reason to delay." He turned to Emily. "I can arrange for you to stay in Charlotte, for now. When it's possible, we can go home, to Twin Pines."

Emily reached into her skirt pocket and pulled out his letter. She ripped the paper in half and gleefully watched Lewis's eyes narrow as she shredded the letter into tiny pieces. With a flick of her wrist, she flung the scraps down to rain over his boots.

"So much for your kind offer to salvage my reputation," Emily said acidly. "Where were you three years ago, when I needed someone to believe in me? Where have you been since then? Go to hell, Lewis."

"Emily, you don't mean that," Lewis protested.

"Oh, yes, I do," Emily affirmed, and then turned on her brother. "And you can go to the devil with him. I'm going to Aunt Amelia's. She'll be happy to take me in, so you needn't concern yourself with my welfare—not that you've shown any concern for several years, either."

Terrance's expression changed from angry to vicious. "I can see I've left you on your own much too long. You seem to have forgotten that in Father's absence you must heed my wishes. You will *not* travel to Virginia in the company of a man not your husband!"

"Then what do you propose I do?"

"You can marry Lewis, who, for reasons known only to himself and God, is willing to have you. Or you can marry your hero here. Or you may stay in Charlotte, under guard, until I can figure out a way to return you to Adairsville."

Emily never doubted that Terrance would carry out his threat. Unless she married Lewis, she would become a recluse again, locked away in some dreary hotel or boardinghouse in a city she didn't know. Dreams of Petersburg and the loving home and affectionate smile of her aunt clouded and vanished.

She didn't dare look at Jared, for fear of losing her fragile grasp on her composure. He hadn't said a word after Terrance's outrageous suggestion that Jared marry her, which was out of the question. Jared wasn't the type of man who would allow another to force his hand.

If enforced confinement was her fate, then she would face it with dignity. Terrance would never have the pleasure of seeing her cower or grovel. Emily squared her shoulders and said firmly, "I will not marry Lewis."

Lewis threw his hand into the air. "Why are you being stubborn? Why condemn yourself to what amounts to imprisonment, when we could have the marriage we'd already planned?"

"I thought I loved you, once. But I was wrong. I prefer incarceration to marrying a man I neither trust nor respect."

Wishing she'd had the good sense to listen to Jared when he suggested they bypass Charlotte, hoping she could say her goodbyes without weeping, Emily turned toward Jared. He stood stoic, staring at her with those inscrutable obsidian eyes that could chill her spine or heat her flesh.

She crossed the short distance between them, longing for privacy that she knew Terrance wouldn't allow. She wanted a parting kiss, a hug, but she knew that either would release the tears she refused to shed.

"This isn't the way I meant to say goodbye," she whispered.

Jared placed a finger on her trembling lips and said quietly, "Then don't. Emily, what I'm about to suggest may seem a radical solution to this situation, but I really don't see an alternative. Would you consider exchanging temporary incarceration for a temporary marriage?"

Her heart leapt into her throat. She stared at him as if he'd lost his mind. He lowered his hand.

Emily realized that he was trying to rescue her again, as he had from Captain Morgan's jail cell, and Ben Hummel's attempted rape. Jared's offer of a temporary marriage as a solution to her current predicament meant he expected an eventual divorce or annulment. Expensive, time-consuming, demeaning, and not always possible, depending on the reasons and a judge's whim.

"Are you serious?" she finally asked.

"Would I ask if I weren't?"

She should thank him kindly, decline his offer, and send him away before her heart broke. But, given the chance of having a dream come true, one she couldn't resist clinging to, if only for a few days, she said, "Yes."

Jared smiled. "Now, can you sit demurely and let me handle negotiating with your brother?"

"I think I've forgotten how to be demure. What do you mean, negotiate?"

"Do you trust me?"

Emily nodded. Jared took her hand and led her to the sofa. She sat on the edge, prepared to calmly endure whatever came next, but a niggling uncertainty over trusting Jared so hastily kept peace at bay. Jared had negotiated for her release once before, from Captain Morgan. And what a debacle that had been!

Raising his voice, Jared asked, "Captain Gardner, are you still willing to consider Emily's third option?"

"I assume she's agreed to marry you?" Terrance slurred.

"She has, with a condition." With a wave of his hand, Jared indicated the door. "Roth, if you'll excuse us?"

Emily nearly gasped at the glare of abhorrence Lewis shot Jared's way. In Lewis's glare, Emily saw the prejudice and disdain that Jared must have had to deal with from those who judged him inferior because of his heritage.

In clipped tones, Lewis said, "Emily, I know you're angry with me, but you can't marry this man! He's obviously a—"

"A what, Lewis?" she asked furiously, cutting off whatever slur he intended.

To Lewis's credit, he understood her suggestion to revise his statement. "He's unsuitable for a woman of your station."

"Station? If you will think carefully, Lewis, you will realize I no longer have a station! You would also do well to remember that you bear some responsibility for that loss. You've been asked to leave. I suggest you do so."

After a deep breath, Lewis uttered his final appeal. "I love you, Emily. Please reconsider."

Without regret, Emily turned away in a silent, cold rebuff.

"Get out, Roth." Jared's command broke the icy silence. "The lady obviously doesn't want you."

Lewis turned on his heel and left the room.

Looking a little confused by the heated exchange, Terrance asked, "What condition?"

Jared answered, "That you sign a statement, saying you forced this marriage. Further, you'll admit that Emily's only recourse was incarceration."

"Give her the foundation on which to apply for an annulment? That, sir, is absurd!"

The statement is not for me, brother dear, but for Jared. This was his insurance that he could terminate their marriage without difficulty, turning to vapor the silly notion she'd held that Jared might actually want to marry her.

"Unusual, maybe," Jared admitted, "but entirely fair if you've made a mistake. I can vouch for Emily's recent conduct, but before that, who can say what type of mischief you allowed her to engage in?"

"Any misconduct on her part has been of her own doing," Terrance answered in an attempt to exonerate himself. "I certainly didn't allow it."

"You left an unchaperoned girl in a strange town, housed in the most convenient setup for running a discreet whorehouse I've ever seen. Some might believe her brother equipped her with a means to support herself."

Emily clenched her teeth to bite back a protest. She'd given Jared permission to negotiate, but the insult stung, even though he intended to insult Terrance.

Terrance paled. "Who would believe such rubbish?"

"Are you willing to take the chance? The people in Georgia were quite ready to label Emily a Union spy. It's amazing what people will believe. Either sign a statement or face yet another scandal."

After a long moment, Terrance nodded.

Jared turned to Emily. "Get yourself prettied up. I should be back in about an hour with a minister."

Still stunned, Emily slowly rose from the sofa. "You are sure you want to go through with this?"

"It will be all right, Emily. I promise."

His promises were as good as gold. She left to do as Jared asked.

Jared turned to Terrance. "I'll have someone bring up pen and paper. If you can manage, I'd like that statement written before the ceremony."

"I don't understand, Randall," Terrance asked in a strained voice. "What's in it for you?"

Jared knew Terrance was roaring drunk, probably wouldn't remember most of what was happening today by morning. "I'm going to do my damnedest to convince Emily not to use the statement. I happen to want this marriage."

"You'll take care of Emily?"

Jared wondered at the sudden concern. "I'll take very good care of Emily."

Terrance suddenly laughed raucously and slapped his thigh. "Get her pregnant, boy. Only way to keep women in line, so they tell me."

The very real possibility of having created a child with Emily sent a tingle down Jared's spine. They'd never taken any precautions. So, what was he going to do about it?

Not a damn thing. If Mother Nature took a notion to help his cause, he wasn't about to interfere.

Emily prettied up in her peach bodice and skirt, which could have used a pressing but would have to do, all the while weighing the consequences of proceeding with Jared's wedding plans. By the time she returned to the sitting room, where Terrance was sprawled sleeping on the sofa, she'd resolved to send Jared on his way, without her.

But when he entered the room with a pleased-with-himself smile on his face, a bouquet of daisies in one hand, a wedding band in the other and a squat, harried-looking justice of the peace by the name of Williams in tow, she couldn't find the words.

While Jared roused Terrance, Emily hailed a maid. Before God and witnesses, Emily vowed to love, honor, obey and worship Jared with her body until death should part them, knowing that a legal document would sever the ties well before either of them died.

"I now pronounce you man and wife," Justice Williams intoned, snapping shut his Bible and sealing Emily's fate. "You may kiss the bride."

Jared promptly complied with a short but tender kiss, diverting her thoughts from apprehension over the future to anticipation of a wedding night.

Williams spread a piece of paper on the table and handed Jared a pen. "Signatures, please."

Jared gave the pen to the maid, who was wiping tears from her eyes with her apron. "I'm sure you need to get back to work. Thank you for doing us the honor."

"La, sir, 'twas a pleasure," she said. "Purely brightened my whole day, it did." She signed the license and gave the pen to Jared, who promptly put it in Terrance's hand.

On impulse, Emily plucked three of the daisies from the bouquet and handed the remaining flowers to the maid. "Would you put these in water and put them in room twenty?"

"I'd be pleased to," she said, then smiled. "I hope you and your mister will be very happy together."

Emily managed to smile back. "Thank you."

As she tucked the trio of daisies behind her ear, Terrance belched and staggered toward the sofa. Would he remember, tomorrow, the mayhem he'd inflicted this afternoon? Would he even remember that she'd been in Charlotte?

"Your turn, my dear," Jared said gently.

Emily took the pen. Her hand trembled.

Jared removed the daisies from where she'd tucked them into her hair. "Let's see if I remember how to braid," he said, gathering the hair on the right side of her face. "My nother twines flowers into her hair on special occasions. I hink today qualifies as special, don't you?''

Her heart beat a little faster. Today might be the most pecial day of her life. She glanced down at the gold band n her left hand, and made a silent vow to never remove t. Jared cared for her, she knew, beyond the physical relationship they shared. Terrance had made the point earlier hat no man would endure all Jared had endured merely for noney. Nor, she was sure, had Jared stayed with her simply o see if he could get her into his bed.

He might not love her, but he cared—and that was a olid foundation on which to build a life together. Though naking him realize that their marriage was destined to be permanent, not temporary, might not be easy.

But, by God, she was going to try. He didn't know it et, but Jared Randall had just married the most ardent over, steadfast friend, dependable helpmate and ferocious lefender a man could possibly hope for.

Her hand stopped trembling as he knotted the braid. She miled up at him and put her left hand on his cheek, resting er wedding band on his jawline. ''Every day with you is pecial.'' She raised on tiptoe and leaned toward his ear. 'The nights, however, are wondrous.''

His eyes widened a fraction.

The justice of the peace cleared his throat.

Emily signed the license, then placed the pen in Jared's and for him, so that he could perform the only legality emaining.

He bent over the paper, pen poised, then glanced over at Terrance. ''While I finish with Mr. Williams, why don't ou take Terrance to the dining room? If we get some food lown him, maybe he'll sober up.''

Emily shrugged a shoulder. ''Does it matter?''

''I would rather not spend half the night escorting him ack to his encampment.''

Having her own plans on how Jared would spend the night, Emily cajoled Terrance off the couch.

With Emily and Terrance safely out of the room, Jared signed his name—his full name—making the marriage legal.

"I still don't feel right about this," Williams said, taking the license and accepting the money Jared held out. "I feel I must warn you, again, that if your young lady is unaware of your true name, she is entitled to an annulment."

Jared handed over another twenty dollars, excusing the lie he was about to restate as a deception necessary to avoid complications at this juncture. "As I told you, I only asked you to avoid using my last name in the ceremony to spare Emily the possibility of some embarrassment. Her brother isn't happy about this marriage, and I feared that any blatant reminder of why he objects might set him off. I simply didn't want him to create a scene."

"If her family objects—"

"Only her brother. Her father approves."

Jared prayed her father would approve, as he was counting on Colonel Gardner's help in explaining away the reasons for his mission and the lies he'd had to tell to get it accomplished. In less than a week, Emily would know the whole truth. How she chose to cope with the information would determine the course of his future.

He wanted this marriage to Emily, more than anything he'd wanted in his entire life. Terrance, unwittingly, had given Jared the means to bind Emily in legal shackles. Maybe, if it was presented as a fait accompli, he could persuade Emily to give the marriage a chance.

But he wouldn't trap her. If she couldn't find it in her heart to understand his actions, and forgive him, he would give her the keys to unlock the shackles—this license, and the statement from Terrance. Presented with both, no judge on earth would refuse her petition for a divorce.

She'd enjoyed the wedding dinner. But now, having sought the privacy of their room, Emily felt her confidence waning. She frowned at the butterflies fluttering in her stomach and commanded her knees to stop shaking. Stripped down to her chemise, she sat on the small stool in front of the dressing table and began to remove the daisies that Jared had entwined in her hair.

"Allow me, my lady."

Jared relieved her of the chore. In the mirror, she watched his long bronze fingers play among the flowers, his bared chest hovering in the reflection.

"What happens now?" she asked.

"Was my lovemaking so unremarkable you've forgotten?"

They hadn't made love since leaving the farm, but no, she hadn't forgotten. "Hardly. I meant, are we leaving in the morning, and is Terrance willing to trade horses? That is why we came to Charlotte, remember?"

His fingers skimmed along her shoulders. Jared's light caresses always drew the most delicious tingle from under her skin. Now was no exception.

"I remember," he said. "I'll take care of it in the morning. Right now, I'd rather make love to my lovely bride."

Jared's naked need pressed warm and hard against her spine. His possessive endearment stung her heart. All too soon, she might not be his wife.

"I'm told men take mistresses because wives are boring," she said huskily. She grasped his hands, moving them down to cover her breasts. "Let's remain lovers."

Jared almost laughed at the ridiculous notion that marriage would diminish his lust. Mesmerized, he watched in the mirror as she stood. He kicked the stool out of the way. Up and over her head the chemise soared, baring his woman and her reflected image.

"Look at you. See how beautiful you are," he breathed in her hair. "You would drive a man insane before he had a chance to become bored."

Emily watched the reflection of Jared's bronzed hands roving the milky white of her torso. Her desire blossomed under his masterful caresses, her breasts pressing into the cup of his hands. He played with agonizing tenderness, taking pleasure in her body's response. Emily reached up and entwined her fingers in his hair as swirling colors engulfed her senses.

Emily closed her eyes to the woman in the mirror and focused on the wanton in Jared's arms. She turned and hurled her arms around his neck, clinging to the naked heat she had missed terribly. He swept her from her feet and carried her to the bed.

Chapter Fourteen

Emily bit her bottom lip as she closed her satchel. Jared had let her sleep late, and now she knew why. He'd been out making arrangements, again.

"Believe me, Emily, when you see Titan, you won't have any problem saving Rusty from the same fate. Terrance doesn't deserve either horse."

Anger flashed in Jared's dark eyes. This man, trained for war, had a tender heart and unwavering honor. And he was trying to convince her to become a horse thief.

"If we leave Terrance without a mount, he'll alert the authorities and have us hunted," she argued. "Jared, they *execute* horse thieves."

"Only if they catch us."

"Terrance knows we're going to Petersburg. If they don't find us on the road, someone will be waiting to arrest us at my aunt's house."

He ran a hand through his hair, frowning. "That's something else we need to talk about. Your aunt. Does she live in Petersburg proper, or on the outskirts?"

"On the outskirts, a mile or so southwest. But I fail to see what the location of my aunt's farm has to do with our taking both Thoroughbreds."

"Nothing, but... Well, here," he said, giving her a newspaper.

She read no farther than the headline. She sat on the bed. "Grant is making an attempt to take Richmond. What does this have to do with us?"

"If Grant can't take Richmond, I'd bet my last dollar that, this time, he'll lay siege to Petersburg."

Emily couldn't keep the worry from her voice. "Amelia is nearly sixty years old, and all alone. Oh, Jared, if the Yankees are so near—"

"Knowing how sieges are conducted, and knowing something of Grant's battle tactics, I'd say that the Yankees will camp several miles out of town. Grant will concentrate on cutting communication and supply lines, not harassing old ladies."

"But if there's a battle..."

"She'll have ample warning to evacuate, just as you had advance warning that Adairsville was threatened. My point here is that she will probably seek refuge within the city. We might not be able to find her."

She knew nothing of campaign strategy or battle tactics. Jared did, and if what he believed was true, once more she could be facing the prospect of having nowhere to call home.

Emily put the newspaper aside. She felt like some rudderless ship, buffeted by the winds of events over which she had no control, with no harbor in sight. She didn't want to stay in Charlotte, but might not have a choice.

Except that Jared was planning to leave, was planning to take her with him, along with the Thoroughbreds.

"So where are we going?" she asked.

"Virginia." He picked up the newspaper and studied the front page. "We'll skirt Petersburg, see what the situation is, then make plans from there."

"And you have to somehow get into Richmond. I imagine your superior officer is wondering what happened to you."

Jared's mouth quirked into a small smile. "I've been sending the colonel telegrams right along. He has a good idea of where I am, and frankly, I'm sure he's more concerned that I arrive with…my package in good order, rather than how quickly I arrive. Though, given these developments, I'm sure he'd like me to speed up the process a bit.''

Emily got up. ''Then I suppose we should get moving. I take it you've located Titan.''

''He's in the livery, getting reacquainted with Rusty.''

''How did you manage that?''

''With a little help from Sam.''

''I guess I should be grateful that you only want to steal the horses, and not Sam, too.''

If she hadn't been looking at Jared so intently, she might have missed his brief glance at the floor, the tightening of his mouth. Her heart skipped a beat as foreboding blossomed.

''Oh, Jared. What have you done? Where's Sam?''

He hesitated, then said softly, ''Safe, Em. Sam is with trustworthy people. He'll never have to endure a whip again.''

Emily's knees went weak. She sank down on the bed and put her face in her hands. She wanted to scream at Jared for putting himself at risk by aiding a runaway slave, then hug him for saving Sam from further abuse.

Jared sat down next to her, his arm draped comfortingly over her shoulder. A single tear ran down her cheek as she threw her arms around Jared's neck.

''Sam will be fine, Em. I promise. His disappearance will look like running away was his own idea. Nobody will know I had anything to do with it. He'll be free, and cared for, just as he was at Rosewood.''

''How?'' she asked on a sob.

''You don't want to know. Safer that way.''

Emily nodded and drew back. He was right, of course. The fewer people who knew the details of Sam's disappearance, the safer for Sam, and Jared. But… ''When?''

Jared chuckled. ''Lady, you just don't know when to

quit." He wiped the wetness from her cheek. "Yesterday, about the time of our wedding. Old Sam got his freedom about the same time I lost mine."

His face darkened, but he gave her a reassuring squeeze before he rose. "Come on, we should be getting out of here."

She knew Jared wouldn't tell her further details, and she knew she wouldn't ask. She trusted Jared with her life, with Sam's. But there was still the matter of the horses.

"Jared, about Rusty—"

"We'll decide when we get to the livery. After you see Titan, if you can bring yourself to relinquish Rusty, we'll leave her for Terrance."

Captain Gilbert Morgan stared at the woman in the dark brown riding habit and wide-brimmed bonnet. He hadn't expected to see Emily Gardner again until Richmond, but here she was, riding north out of Charlotte on that magnificent mare of hers. And she was leading another horse that looked like death, plodding along on legs that moved purely from habit.

Behind them rode a man, not in uniform, but definitely Lieutenant Jared Randall. They shouldn't be here. He'd given them a good head start. Randall, obviously, hadn't taken a direct route to Richmond. One would think that, with a notorious traitor as his prisoner, Randall would have made for Richmond with all haste.

Damn. He'd planned to arrive in Richmond after Randall turned Emily over to the authorities and gave the packet of maps and reports to the officer who would prosecute the case. Now, because of Randall's dawdling, the plan to ride into Richmond to the accolades of his peers wouldn't unfold as he'd expected.

But then, very little of his journey to Richmond had gone as expected. The horse he'd borrowed from the Yankees' camp hadn't stood the test of distance. Relying on the rural populace for an occasional wagon ride and food and shelter had proved galling. And so many of them had looked at him with suspicion—a lone soldier, tramping the road like one of the common herd. One man had dared to suggest Morgan had deserted. That man would never again insult some other poor soul who found himself in dire straits, and the money scavenged from the bastard's pockets would now pay for train fare to Richmond.

Morgan watched the two riders until they disappeared from view, then headed for the depot. He had little choice but to ride the rails, and he had to do it quickly, while the trains were still running through Virginia. With the Union forces swarming around Richmond, in all likelihood, trains into that area would suffer delays soon, if they were not halted altogether.

But maybe arriving ahead of Randall wasn't at all a bad idea. Maybe presenting his case first, before Randall arrived with both prisoner and packet of evidence, would work in his favor. If he could discover the right people to talk to, maybe he could persuade them to hasten his reinstatement in the regular army.

And given the situation in Virginia, they might even give him a command. Not with his old battalion, of course, but with some company needing a valiant leader, whose men would gladly serve under a man willing to spur them into battle.

He would need a promotion to be effective.

Major Gilbert Morgan. He liked the sound of that.

General Gilbert Morgan. He liked that better.

"Titan looks better already," Jared commented, running an appraising hand over the stallion's withers.

"I wasn't sure he'd survive," Emily admitted, applying a brush to Titan's marred hide.

They'd traveled slowly, given Titan extra rations, curried and petted him until some spirit glimmered in his haunted eyes. Now, no more than twenty miles out of Petersburg, Emily wondered if all their efforts had been for naught.

What good was keeping the stallion alive if she had nowhere to take him?

Jared had already scouted the area. Between their camp and Petersburg lounged tens of thousands of Union troops, all waiting for General Grant's order to move on the city.

She feared for her aunt, surrounded by Yankees, her house possibly occupied by the enemy. Emily tried to think of a way to help Amelia without endangering herself, the horses or Jared. No, she realized after wrestling with the urge, to go anywhere near Petersburg was sheer folly. The risk of capture was too high, especially for Jared.

The Yanks would put him in one of those god-awful prisons where men died of starvation or untreated wounds. Congested, disease-infested prisons burdened both governments. A man like Captain Morgan deserved to spend his days rotting in a Yankee prison, but not Jared. Nor could she risk the Thoroughbreds' falling into Yankee hands.

"Lord, but I hate this," she complained aloud.

"What?"

"Being a...refugee. I keep looking over my shoulder for someone to come riding up to arrest me for horse theft. And one of these days a Union patrol is going to pop up in front of me and demand to know where I'm going, and I don't have an answer."

"Feeling a little sorry for ourselves, are we? Come on, Emily. It's not so bad."

"Consider, if you will. I'm a homeless, temporarily married accused spy who has stolen two horses. I'm stranded in the wilds of Virginia, with very little money, all the clothes I own either on my back or in a satchel that's wearing thin. And as if that weren't enough, the entire Union army is sitting in front of me, preventing me from going to the one place I might seek refuge."

He had the audacity to smile. "That about sums it up, except it's only one-third of the Union army, nor are you stranded. And you might want to ease up on that brush. Titan can't afford to lose any more hide."

Emily immediately stopped brushing and quickly reined in her temper. Titan didn't deserve the punishment of an anger-guided hand, nor did Jared deserve the lash of her tongue.

"I'm sorry," she said to both horse and man. "I know that getting upset isn't going to help, but my lack of control over my life is becoming quite exasperating."

Emily detected a note of uncertainty in his tone when he said, "Well, maybe we can change that."

He held out his hand, and Emily let him lead her over to a log, where he indicated she should sit. She obeyed with trepidation, looking into his troubled face, and somehow knowing he was about to reveal some plan he'd concocted to resolve her predicament. Problem was, some of Jared's solutions had proved more harrowing than the original problems.

"I've learned a lot about you in the past month," he began, seeming to choose his words carefully. "In spite of everything you've endured, you aren't bitter or callous, just wary of making another mistake."

"I've made so many," she whispered.

"Maybe," he said gently. "But your original mistake was trusting Terrance and Lewis to see to your welfare, instead of your father. I think you realize your error and regret the decision."

Putting her faith in Lewis had been a mistake, but did she truly regret her decision to remain in Georgia?

"Not completely. Oh, I suppose my life would have been easier, less lonely. As much as I love Papa, I have trouble accepting that he could leave Rosewood or Georgia. I do love my home. I love the South."

"If you could reverse your decision, would you?" he asked.

"I've often thought I would, but I'm not sure. Aren't we getting a bit far off the subject?"

He squatted in front of her, clasping her hands. "No, actually, we're right on target. You're not really homeless;

you just haven't considered all the alternatives. Emily, since we won't be able to find your aunt, I want you to come to Richmond with me. From there, if you want, we can send you to your father.''

Emily withdrew her hands from Jared's grasp. Of all the solutions Jared might have come up with, she hadn't expected this one. She would never have considered trying to find her father.

"Jared, my father is a Yankee!"

"He's also your father. You just admitted you love him, in spite of his politics.''

Her thoughts wandered wildly. Memories woven with hopes and disappointments assaulted her fragile composure.

"Papa could be anywhere," she contended, torn between the delightful prospect of seeing her father again and wishing Jared had suggested that she stay with him in Richmond.

Jared patiently waited for Emily's shock to dissipate. He needed her trust and cooperation now more than at any time during the past weeks.

"There's a strong possibility that your father is very close," Jared said. "If we can locate him, would you be willing to go to him?"

"Would I be able to?"

"Depending on his assignment, probably.''

"But what if he's somewhere in the North?"

"You go north. All you need is a pass.''

"Really? It's that easy?"

"Mary Lincoln, the president's wife, is from Kentucky. Her family is split—half Yank, half Reb. Her sister is probably the most famous border-hopper. She travels to Washington to visit Mary quite often.''

"But I'm not related to President Lincoln.''

"You're the daughter of a Union officer. The North will grant permission if the South is willing to let you leave.''

She tilted her head, her eyes questioning. "What makes you think Papa is an officer?"

Jared could have kicked himself for the blunder, but recovered easily. "From what you've told me of your father, I can't imagine him enlisting as a private. Can you?"

She thought a moment, then conceded, "I suppose not. Papa would insist on joining the Union army in some capacity where he could be of true service, or not enlist at all. But what if we can't locate him?"

"We make other arrangements."

"Like what?"

"Why don't we see what happens in Richmond first?"

He read her answer in her weary, resigned smile.

At the Spottswood Hotel, in the center of Richmond, Jared paced the floor as Nathan Wilkins, Jared's contact, sat on the edge of his cot and hurriedly pulled on his boots.

Lord, what a mess. Jared could almost feel the repercussions rippling through the intelligence network. Nathan worked in the basement of the hotel, in the Confederate post office. The Union was about to lose a set of highly placed ears and eyes, and neither the Pinkerton Agency nor Major Drew at army intelligence would be less than furious.

And Colonel Gardner must be going insane with worry.

"If the wrong people saw you coming here, sir, my butt ain't worth dust," Nathan declared. "I'm going with you."

Having unwittingly put Nathan in grave danger, Jared didn't argue against Nathan's decision to leave town. But if the Rebs now knew Cougar's identity, having the wiry Pinkerton agent join him and Emily didn't seem wise.

"You're assuming I can get the three of us out of Richmond. If my identity is known, maybe you should take another route."

Nathan gathered his few possessions and tossed them into a satchel. "If you'll have me, I'd rather take my chances with you. Cover or no, you're still Cougar. Besides, they're searching for you and the lady around Petersburg and City Point. They think you're looking for safe harbor with Grant.''

"Then if we hurry, maybe we can ride out without anyone realizing I've been here,'' Jared hoped aloud as they descended the back stairway. He stopped at the bottom. "Can you get your hands on some passes through Union lines?''

Nathan smiled and patted his satchel.

Jared headed down Main Street at a brisk pace. "How did this Colonel Bricker learn my name?''

"Seems there was a big raid on an intelligence ring down in Charlotte. Your name came up too many times to ignore. They've been pondering and analyzing ever since.''

"Must have been Uncle,'' Jared deduced, remembering his anxious moments while watching the raid take place.

"Where's the lady?'' Nathan asked.

"Eating dinner at the Columbian Hotel. Now tell me about Captain Morgan.''

"They assigned him to Commandant Turner over at Libby Prison. That Morgan is a crazy old coot. He came prancing into town, demanding a promotion, like it was his due. They decided Libby was the best place to keep an eye on him until they can decide what to do with him.''

Libby Prison was three floors of Union misery on the banks of the James River. Incarcerated in the brick warehouse were some of the finest officers in the Union. Being in prison was bad enough. Now those poor souls had to contend with Morgan.

"Did anyone believe Morgan's accusations about Emily?''

"They're pretty skeptical.''

Jared had been sure Morgan would panic and ride south. But he couldn't worry about a misjudgment now. He had to get Emily and Nathan out of Richmond.

He turned onto Twelfth Street, then slowed his pace as they neared Cary Street. He easily identified the woman in front of the Columbian, who was resisting getting into an open carriage with a Confederate officer. Jared swore under his breath.

"We left the horses at the hotel's livery," he informed Nathan. "I'll get Emily and meet you there. If I don't come in half an hour, or if you sense trouble, take the stallion and get out."

Nathan disappeared into the shadows.

The Reb officer climbed into the carriage and took the seat opposite Emily, behind the driver. Jared retraced his steps, hoping to intercept the carriage near Exchange Alley.

There wasn't a warning before the explosion.

The horses screamed and reared. Emily grasped the side of the carriage to keep her seat. She could smell smoke and hear people shrieking as they scrambled to avoid flailing hooves and the lurching carriage. A body clad in buckskins flew in a blur through the narrow space between Emily and her captor. She heard Jared's fist connect with the officer's jaw.

No sooner had Jared climbed in one side than he leaped out the other, calling her name. The Confederate officer groaned and started to push up from his prone position. Without thinking, Emily bunched her fist and aimed for his jaw. The officer's eyes rolled back as he slumped from the blow. Emily turned, balanced as best she could manage, then dived into Jared's outstretched arms.

After an impulsive squeeze, Jared set her down and grabbed her hand. They dashed away from the pandemonium, weaving through Richmond's steep streets until Emily lost all sense of direction. The stitch in her side grew painful. She tugged on Jared's hand.

Jared swung into a dark, narrow space between two buildings. Emily strained for breath as she collapsed against Jared's cushioning chest.

"What happened?" Jared asked.

"He was…in the lobby when…I asked for a room," she gasped. "Looking…for you. Wouldn't tell me why."

"Captain Gilbert Morgan regaled the Confederate hierarchy with tall tales a few days ago," Jared explained.

Emily's head lifted, her eyes wild, her sun-tinged complexion flushed with exertion.

Poor lamb, Jared thought, gently cupping her cheek, nudging her head back against his chest. "Yeah, I know," he said, so that Emily needn't state the obvious. "I sure didn't judge Morgan's actions correctly. This is the last place I expected to meet him again."

"What do we do now?"

"Retreat from the skirmish, regroup and plan our next offensive. Basic military strategy."

"Against our own army?"

Jared gave in to a short burst of laughter. "Getting a bit confusing, isn't it?"

Planting the heel of his boot on the rough brick he was leaning against, Jared pushed forward. Emily placed her hands on his chest and shoved him backward. Surprised, he looked down into her upturned, serious face.

"Why are they looking for you, then, and not me? Morgan must have told someone about his belief that I'm a spy."

"He did, and they didn't believe a word," Jared said to ease her distress. It worked for a moment, but then she frowned.

"But if you're in trouble because of something Captain Morgan said, then I'm the cause. You lied to a superior officer because of me, and you've taken a very long time to return to Richmond."

"Emily, can we discuss this after we get out of the city?"

"Let me go to them. I can explain—"

"And be accused of hiding behind a lady's skirts?" Jared teased to hide a moment of panic. "No. Thank you for the thought, but no."

Teeth gritted, Emily emitted an exasperated groan. "Be sensible. Someone has to tell them what really happened.

I'm the only person who knows the whole story. Jared, please," she begged. "I love you. Let me help."

Emily died a little when she felt Jared stiffen. Of all the times to confess her deepest feelings, this was the worst. She pressed her forehead against his chest. "I never meant to tell you. I know you don't love me, but that's not important now. We have to find a way to clear your name."

Jared's hands caressed her cheeks as he tilted her head back. She closed her eyes and savored his tender kiss.

"You have a twisted sense of what's important," Jared chided. "Tell me again. Say it, Em, please."

"I love you, Jared Randall," Emily breathed, watching his slow smile spread, his eyes light. "I think I've loved you since the day you showed up on my doorstep."

"You surely picked a strange time—" Jared stopped, listening. He spun and pinned her between his body and the building. "Soldiers," he whispered as they flattened together in the darkness.

Heavy footsteps beat a sharp cadence. Rifles rattled, and a patrol leader shouted orders.

Smothered between the building and Jared's shielding body, Emily realized that no matter what she said, Jared wouldn't listen. He would continue to protect her, as he always had, regardless of the cost to himself, to his career.

The only way she could help Jared was to tell the authorities the whole story. Once they understood why Jared had lied to Captain Morgan, understood his delay in reaching Richmond, they would drop whatever charges Jared faced.

Emily remembered the last time she'd tried to flee from Jared, and how naive she'd been about his persistence. This time would be different, because she intended to run until completely beyond his reach.

This might be her only chance to rescue Jared, to truly repay him for all he'd done for her. To prove she loved him.

The patrol moved on. Jared relaxed, easing slowly away.

Emily waited until the space between them widened, then took a last look at his beloved profile.

Emily took one slow step, and then darted from their hiding place.

Chapter Fifteen

"Thank you, Sergeant," Emily said with a grateful smile, taking the offered cup of tea to soothe her raw throat.

For nearly two hours, Colonel Bricker had listened to her story. He'd asked very few questions before being called from the room on some urgent matter. Except for the taciturn sergeant, who she assumed was her guard, Emily hadn't seen another person since arriving at Colonel Bricker's office.

The door opened. Colonel Bricker strode in and sat down behind his desk. Emily's uneasiness returned. Bricker was of an age with her father, and quite handsome in his obviously tailored uniform and neatly trimmed beard. She didn't like Bricker, but couldn't have said why. Maybe because he studied her with steel-gray eyes as though knowing she hadn't told him everything. She *had* kept a few secrets—those moments that were personal and none of Bricker's business.

"I'm inclined to believe your story," he said in his cultured voice. "The details you gave me match Captain Morgan's statement. They are also consistent with information I received from Charlotte."

Emily kept her poise, but held on to her teacup with both hands. She hadn't mentioned their marriage and, in her haste to help Jared, she'd forgotten about stealing the horses. Naturally, Terrance would have had to explain to someone why he didn't have a horse. While she thought it odd that news of the theft had traveled all the way to Richmond from Charlotte, she didn't doubt that it could.

"From Charlotte?" she asked—innocently, she hoped.

Bricker smiled knowingly. "You'll be happy to learn that your brother found another horse. He is not pressing charges."

Emily took another sip of tea, silently grateful that Terrance had chosen not to pursue the matter, though she doubted he had done so as an act of chivalry. He just didn't want the name of Gardner attached to another scandal.

"Did Lieutenant Randall tell you why he was coming to Richmond?" Bricker asked.

"Jared said he had a package to deliver. Colonel, if you are questioning Jared's integrity and sense of duty, I can assure you of both. He didn't show me the package he carried, and at all times his goal was to reach Richmond."

"If his actions are so easily explained, then why isn't he here to account for his time? Why would he let a woman endure an interrogation, when by rights he should answer for himself?"

"He merely wanted time to plan his defense without involving me. He's very protective, you see, and—"

"Do you know where he is now?"

"Somewhere in Richmond, I would imagine."

Colonel Bricker looked past her and said, "Sergeant Taylor, would you bring in the bag from the hall?"

Within moments, a satchel lay on Bricker's desk. Emily reached out and touched the familiar cloth.

"Yours?" Bricker asked. When she nodded, he continued, "My men searched it, for identification. Would you check to see if anything is missing?"

Emily's fingers trembled as she put the teacup aside and opened the satchel. "Someone removed a small leather pouch containing several gold pieces. I assume you will return my property."

"We can't return an item we don't possess. Your bag is as it was found. It seems your Lieutenant Randall took your horses and gold and left the city."

The hair on Emily's neck itched. "He'll return."

"I truly hope so, but he's very skilled at vanishing. We've been searching for this man for years, but only lately learned his identity. Madame, I am sorry I must be the one to inform you that the man you know as Jared Randall is really Captain Jared Hunter, an infamous Yankee operative."

Emily opened her mouth to deny the possibility, but suddenly remembered several observations she had meant to question and never had: the morphine in his medical kit, the large amount of cash he carried, the coffee.

What was she thinking? Jared could explain away the misidentification if given the chance. Jared wasn't a Yankee.

"Mrs. Hunter..." Colonel Bricker began.

"No," Emily said, interrupting him. "Mrs. Randall."

"I fear your marriage license says Hunter. A Lieutenant Roth discovered the deception and initiated an investigation which, combined with other information we received from another source, helped us piece together your husband's identity and status within the Union army. You are legally Mrs. Hunter. You may, of course, file for an annulment because he falsified his identity."

Emily remembered ushering Terrance out of the parlor while Jared paid the justice of the peace and signed the license. She hadn't seen his signature on the document.

No, she wanted to scream, but a growing lump in her throat blocked any response. Bricker had to be wrong. There must be some mistake. And why had Lewis bothered to verify her marriage, going so far as to look at the license? Yes, she'd treated him rather coldly, but no more coldly than he deserved. Was Lewis capable of a deed as dishonorable and cruel as altering her marriage license?

"Mrs. Hunter, from the details you've given, it appears

Captain Hunter took on the responsibility of finding you refuge. He aided your escape from Adairsville. He duped Captain Morgan into releasing you from jail, then escorted you to Rosewood. When you reached the estate and found it destroyed, he offered to take you to Petersburg, to a relative's home.''

"Yes," she whispered.

Bricker picked up a pen and twirled it in his fingers. "Why? Why would a man of his reputation, with his need to maintain a low profile, defy the odds of being captured to aid you, unless…unless he was under orders? Yes, of course," Bricker continued, thinking aloud. "If under orders, Cougar would go to extraordinary lengths to complete a mission."

"Cougar?" Emily breathed.

Colonel Bricker leaned forward, his steel-gray eyes slashing a deep wound in her soul, giving no quarter. "Mrs. Hunter, when you learned that Petersburg was under siege, he brought you to Richmond. Why, Mrs. Hunter? What was to be your next destination?"

"Jared said…he said he could send me to my father."

Bricker tossed the pen onto the table, nodding. "Could have done so, too. Getting you into Washington, to Colonel Gardner, would be child's play for Cougar."

Emily felt silent tears slide down her cheek.

You're the daughter of a Union officer.

She knew then that Colonel Bricker told the truth. Jared had claimed he could find John Gardner, had declared Papa must be an officer. Jared must know Papa. Had Papa sent the infamous Cougar to her doorstep?

Bricker said to the guard, "Sergeant Taylor, I've ordered a room prepared for Mrs. Hunter at Garson's Boarding House. Please escort her over there and see that nothing disturbs her rest. Mrs. Hunter has had enough shocks for today. We'll continue our discussion tomorrow."

Emily wiped her eyes. "I have a room at the hotel."

"The hotel isn't secure. Until we capture Captain Hunter, we'd like to keep you in a place where you'll be safe."

"You think he'd come after me?" Emily asked.

"He might. If our conjecture proves correct, he is under orders to take you to your father. And you are, after all, Cougar's wife."

Sergeant Taylor grabbed her satchel. Emily followed his straight back and courteous pace down the street and, without a word to the house's owner, up the stairway. Taylor opened a door, then stood aside as Emily entered the stark room—a bed, a small trunk, a washstand with pitcher and bowl and a straight-backed chair furnished her prison cell. Not as bad as being behind bars, but this was a prison nonetheless.

"Mrs. Hunter, there's something you oughta know," Sergeant Taylor said, placing her belongings near the chest. "You watch yourself around Colonel Bricker. He's smooth as whiskey, with the bite of an asp. He wants something from you. Could see it, I could."

Emily heard the edge of dislike in Taylor's gravely voice, and liked Taylor at once. But dare she trust him? Dare she trust any man for advice? Oh, God, she'd trusted Jared.

She sat on the bed and put her hand to her forehead, kneading at the headache that pounded behind her eyes. "I don't understand, Sergeant. What more could Colonel Bricker possibly want from me?"

"Don't know yet, but the colonel uses people. You give yourself time before you agree to whatever he's scheming. Get some rest. I'll bring your supper in a couple hours."

Emily heard the lock click behind Taylor. Locking out a man named Hunter, tagged Cougar, or locking her in?

She tried to block the flood of memories of Jared: standing on her doorstep offering to buy Rusty, teasing from the other side of iron bars while holding a key, leveling a revolver at a drunk, facing down Terrance.

...under orders...

Four days on a farm. A stuffy parlor in Charlotte. Days of sunlight and laughter, nights of starlight and ecstasy.

    ...go to extraordinary lengths to complete a mission...

Unable to hold back hot tears, Emily sobbed her misery into her pillow. She cried for her gullibility, for letting a Yankee operative dance into her life and waltz her clear across the South. She'd kept in step to his tune, followed his lead, and, mesmerized by the music, she'd fallen in love with her partner.

But mostly she cried because no matter how hard she tried to deny it, Emily longed for Jared's arms around her, his mellow voice to soothe away the nightmare.

The next morning, Colonel Bricker calmly offered her an opportunity for revenge against the redskin Yankee who had so shamefully misused a daughter of the South. He offered to send Emily to Washington, to her father. In exchange for her freedom, Emily would become a Confederate spy.

Hidden behind the brush that lined the road, Jared answered Nathan's low whistle.

After three days of narrowly avoiding both Federal and Confederate forces, Nathan had ventured to the outskirts of Richmond to contact another Union agent, seeking information on Emily's whereabouts.

"Idiots are going to try to trade her," Nathan told him.

"How are they treating Emily?"

"They're watching over her real careful-like. They took her over to a boardinghouse they use for prisoners who aren't precisely prisoners. She can't leave, but she'll get decent food and clean sheets."

Satisfied that Emily hadn't been harmed, Jared said, "Grant won't agree to an exchange. Emily isn't even a military prisoner."

"No, but she's Gardner's daughter, and your wife. They'll want something in exchange for the lady."

"The Rebs should know better. They'll have to turn her

loose after a time. They may even send her to Washington.''

''Maybe they're hoping to draw you out, capture Cougar.''

''Expecting me to try a daring rescue?'' Jared reviewed the plan that had gelled into feasibility yesterday. Except he needed Emily's cooperation to come quietly. He highly doubted that, after learning from the Rebs of his identity and of how he'd deceived her, Emily would cooperate. ''Uh-uh. But if the Rebs plan to hold Emily until Cougar appears,'' Jared reasoned aloud, ''then I should let them find him.''

''Captain Hunter, I know this lady is important to you, but surrendering to the Rebs isn't the answer.''

''The thought never crossed my mind, Nathan.''

Confused, Nathan shook his head. ''Well, whatever you decide to do, I have to hustle my bones into Washington. Got some papers to deliver.'' Nathan handed over a packet. ''Donner didn't say how he got them, but these are plans for a Reb attack on Washington.''

The urgent importance of the packet settled the issue. ''That's it then. Come on, Nathan, we're going to Washington.''

''What about Mrs. Hunter?''

''As soon as I take a stroll down Pennsylvania Avenue, the Rebs will know Cougar is beyond them again. The spies will report to Richmond, and then the Rebs will release Emily.''

Upon arriving in Washington, Jared took the time to escort Nathan Wilkins to the building that housed the War Department, riding brazenly down Pennsylvania Avenue. Nor did he make any secret of his presence as he rode to his boardinghouse to change into dress uniform. By the time he arrived at Colonel Gardner's house, Jared was satisfied that several of the swarm of spies who haunted Washington had seen him and, even now, were wiring Richmond with the news.

Zeke answered Jared's knock. The white-haired Negro smiled, at first, then shook his head sadly. "Best come in and get it over with."

Jared removed his hat as he stepped over the threshold, into the house where he'd always felt welcome, until today. "The colonel knows I'm back?"

"Yes, Cap'n."

He took off his gloves, tossed them into his hat and handed them to Zeke. "And he knows I didn't bring Emily?"

"Oh, yes, Cap'n, he sure does."

Jared ran a hand through his hair. He'd never before dreaded facing John Gardner. He didn't like the feeling. "I suppose he's waiting for me in the library."

"The colonel's been pacing a footpath in the carpet that any fool could follow. He's waitin'."

Jared stepped up to the door, sympathizing with the biblical Daniel at the entrance to the lions' den. He reached for the latch, then stopped and looked over his shoulder at Zeke. "Did Sam arrive all right?"

Zeke's smile returned in brilliant affirmation. "Sam thinks you're one of the archangels, one of the Lord's warriors sent to earth. Too bad the colonel ain't of the same opinion."

Jared wanted to ask if Sam had informed John of Terrance's cruelty, then decided not to ask. If Sam hadn't, Jared wouldn't bring it up.

And he was stalling. He opened the library door. John was right where Zeke had said he would be, wearing out the carpet in front of the fireplace.

The colonel looked old, careworn, and Jared took the blame for the new wrinkles furrowed into his commander's brow.

"About time you showed up," John growled. "You

crossed the lines three hours ago. Where the hell have you been?''

Jared saluted, to the only man it had never irked him to salute. John waved it off with an angry swipe of his hand.

Resigned to an all-out verbal lashing, which he richly deserved, Jared lowered his hand. He stood rigid, not quite at attention, but not far from it.

"Colonel, sir, if you know when I crossed the lines, then you also know I escorted an intelligence agent to the War Department and stopped to change into uniform. I reported as quickly as I could, sir.''

"Report?'' Gardner shouted. "Do you have any idea of how little you need to report?'' He strode over to his desk and picked up a stack of telegrams. "In the last three days, either Major Drew or a Pinkerton agent has been here almost hourly, showing me reports from nearly every operative in Richmond and its environs. I would hazard to say I am more fully informed of Emily's situation at present than you are.''

Jared simply nodded an acknowledgment, dying to ask what those telegrams contained, but wisely keeping his mouth shut.

"And if these weren't informative enough, you should see this!'' Gardner picked up a newspaper, easily recognizable as the *Richmond Examiner*. Jared closed his eyes, praying that the reporters had misconstrued or embellished only half the facts.

Gardner sighed. "Did the artist do her justice?''

Jared's eyes popped open. He crossed the room to the desk and looked down at the newspaper.

"He certainly did,'' Jared said. The ink sketch of Emily's beautiful face covered half the page. "You should know, sir, that Emily highly resembles your late wife. I saw the portrait of the two of you while in Georgia. She was a lovely woman.''

"The portrait survives?''

"Emily wouldn't leave Adairsville until the portrait was tucked into the cellar."

Emily's expression said she'd posed under duress, which anyone who didn't know her well would misinterpret as anger, an impression given further credence by the headline: Georgia Lady Escapes Cougar's Clutches.

"Read the article," Gardner commanded. "I want to know what's true and what they've made up."

Jared scanned the columns. "The part about leaving Adairsville is fairly accurate, and our stopping at Rosewood." Jared looked up. "It's not true that General Sherman's forces burned it to the ground, however. I'm afraid the estate was destroyed long before, probably shortly after Emily and Terrance left."

"I guessed as much," John said, sinking into his leather chair. "Go on."

Jared hesitated to mention Emily's arrest, but knew that if he didn't, Gardner would eventually find out from some other source. Briefly he described finding Scott Walters, the boy's death, and the series of events that had led to Emily's arrest for spying.

Gardner paled. "Emily and I never exchanged so much as a letter. I didn't write to her, so as to avoid some such nonsense. Who would believe it?"

"A home guard captain by the name of Gilbert Morgan."

To Jared's surprise, Gardner's eyes lit with recognition.

"So that's the connection."

"You've heard of Morgan?"

"Yes, but I'll fill you in on that later. Read on."

Jared stifled his curiosity and complied. "We did purchase a riding habit, but Emily had *not* been riding in rags. Nor was she half-starved," he added, his anger rising. "We did stop near Gainesville, at Grundy's Inn, and she was attacked." Jared looked up from the paper and smiled. "You should have seen her, John. She was absolutely magnificent. You'd have been proud of how she handled it."

"I hope she shot the bastard."

"Better. She threatened to cut off his balls."

John raised an eyebrow. "My Emily?"

No, my Emily, Jared thought, but kept it to himself.

Jared turned the page—and went livid. "If I ever get within a mile of the reporter, I swear, I'll kill him."

Humor tinged Gardner's voice when he asked, "You didn't keep Emily tied up in a barn for four days?"

"No." He'd made love to her for four days, before Sam showed up and they headed for Charlotte.

Next came details of the wedding, and Lewis Roth's portrayal as a hero for unmasking Cougar.

Jared took a long breath. "When Sam found us, he told us about Terrance needing Rusty. We went to Charlotte. While we were there, Roth proposed to Emily, and she turned him down. He took it rather hard. He must have taken her marriage to me even harder—hard enough to send him searching for the justice of the peace who married us, to see if the marriage was legal."

"Is it?" John asked softly.

"Yes. I put my full name on the license."

"And Lewis took the information to someone with enough clout to start an investigation."

"It wouldn't have taken much prodding. The Confederates had captured Uncle the day before. From what I understand, from the papers in his possession, the Rebs already had what they needed to connect my name with Cougar."

John leaned back in his chair. "So I've been informed. Why, Jared? Why the marriage?"

"Emily's reputation was at stake." Jared began the speech he'd rehearsed, knowing John would ask. But the words turned sour in his mouth. The truth poured out. "When Terrance got angry at what he saw as Emily's improper behavior, he suggested that since I'd ruined her reputation, I should marry her. That's when Roth stepped in and proposed. To my utter relief, Emily turned him away."

Jared folded the newspaper and tossed it on the desk. Emily's picture stared up at him, accusingly. "So I asked. She accepted, with the knowledge that she could dissolve the marriage. I couldn't tell her that the name on the license would give her the means to an annulment, so I asked Terrance for a statement that would be as effective."

He pulled out the statement, and Emily's gold, and gave them to John. "Keep this for her, in case she needs it," he said of the statement. "I took the money because I feared the Rebs would confiscate it. Emily's shotgun is in the scabbard on Rusty's saddle. Your horses are in your stable."

John read the words his son had written, then put the statement and the leather pouch in a desk drawer. "My son forced your hand."

"He'd had a little too much to drink, and—"

"You needn't defend Terrance. I've seen Sam's back, and he tried to soften the story, too. Thank you, by the way, for sending Sam to me. So, you married Emily in order to get her out of Charlotte."

"I married her because I love her, John. Emily is the sweetest, brightest, most courageous woman I've ever known." Jared turned away and stared into a fireplace as devoid of light and warmth as his future. "I'd hoped that, once we were here and I explained my mission, she might understand and forgive me. But after what happened in Richmond—" Jared shook his head "—I won't even ask her to now."

"What *did* happen in Richmond?"

Jared turned back and waved at the stack of telegrams. "You probably know better than I do."

"I'd rather hear your version."

Jared told him about contacting Nathan Wilkins for the passes, about learning that Cougar's identity had been flushed out, about Morgan's presence in Richmond and the rescue of Emily from a Confederate officer.

"We ran hard. Emily started panting, so I pulled her into

a space between two buildings. Naturally, she wanted to know what was going on, so I told her that Morgan was in town and making trouble. She offered to go to the authorities, to help clear me of any charges. I thanked her and implied that I would handle the situation. I misjudged the depth of her determination.'' Jared swallowed the coil of anger and despair threatening to clog his throat. ''She looked up at me, told me she loved me, then ran as fast as her legs would move, straight into the arms of a Reb patrol.''

The helplessness, the terror, came flooding back, as strongly as if he stood on that street in Richmond. ''I knew that if I went after her we would both be locked up, so I decided to bide my time and attempt rescue at a later date. But every plan I came up with depended on Emily's cooperation, and I didn't doubt that she would scream the rafters down the minute she laid eyes on me. I hung around Richmond long enough to make sure she wasn't being mistreated. Wilkins voiced the opinion, and I tend to agree, that the Rebs were using Emily as bait to catch me. Then Nathan received a packet of vital information, so we came back. I'm hoping that, when they realize I'm beyond their nets, they'll release Emily.''

John was quiet for a moment, then said, ''The patrol took Emily to Colonel Bricker, the man who put it all together and ordered your arrest. He wrote that newspaper article and gave it to an *Examiner* reporter, who used it word for word. You'll notice that he never mentioned her arrest for spying, or Morgan's involvement, or Emily's part in absconding with a couple of Thoroughbreds. Nor did Bricker reveal that her father is a Yankee colonel. For whatever reason, he's chosen to present Emily as an unblemished, abused heroine.''

''All the better to denounce me as the devil incarnate.''

John rubbed his chin. ''Possibly. Bricker's motives, however, don't concern me. Getting Emily out of Richmond, does. If the siege of Petersburg draws Lee's army out of

Richmond, as Grant hopes, then Emily is sitting in the middle of a doomed Confederate capital. I've put out, through private parties, that I'm willing to listen to whatever Bricker proposes as a suitable arrangement for her release.''

"Colonel, Grant is not going to authorize an exchange. We both know that.'' Jared was warming to the idea of redemption in the eyes of his commander, as well as that of removing Emily from Richmond. "Look, I know where Emily's being held. If Bricker doesn't release her within a few days—''

John sprung out of his chair. "Captain Hunter! If you so much as set foot on Southern soil, I'll give orders to have you shot on sight.''

Jared ignored the ludicrous threat. "Who better—''

"Anyone!'' John declared, and pointed at the newspaper. "How many of those people mentioned in that article saw you in Rebel uniform?''

"A few,'' Jared allowed.

"And if you were captured, how many would testify to that fact? Lord above, people would line up from Richmond to Savannah, willing to perjure themselves if they thought they could help get Cougar hanged. And the first person Bricker would put on the witness stand would be Emily! You had sense enough not to go after her in the first place. Don't go stupid on me now.''

Reluctantly Jared acquiesced. "Yes, sir.''

Colonel Gardner sat down heavily. "Report to General Thompson at the War Department in the morning. He seems to think you might be of some use to him on some project.''

Jared's heart sank. "I'm being reassigned?''

"No. I'm lending you to him for a couple of months, until the chaff from this debacle settles. I certainly can't send you on a mission at this point, and I don't want you hanging around here, driving me mad with crazy schemes. Dismissed.''

Jared took a step toward the door. "For what it's worth, Colonel, I'm sorry."

"Save it for Emily."

He would try, but he doubted Emily would listen.

"And double-quick march though the kitchen on your way out," John added. "Hanna's been baking all morning. No sense disappointing the woman. Frank West has been hanging out back there for the past hour, making a nuisance of himself. Get him out of here before he guzzles down all of my bourbon."

Honey cakes and a bull session with Frank. God, how he needed both. Jared reached for the doorknob.

"Hunter, my daughter threatened to cut off a man's balls?"

Jared didn't suppress a small smile. "Yes, sir."

John shook his head in disbelief and waved Jared out of the room. Jared walked toward the kitchen, wishing Emily was here to share Hanna's treats. But Emily was in Richmond.

Despite John's objections, Jared had another avenue by which to appeal for a rescue mission to Richmond. If John's efforts proved fruitless, and Bricker didn't release Emily by the end of the week, Jared intended to pursue it.

Chapter Sixteen

Emily experienced a sharp but fleeting sense of déjà vu. As she had in a room at Grundy's Inn, she noted the distance between herself and a door. But the man who blocked the exit this time wasn't a drunk named Ben. Captain Gilbert Morgan was stone sober and furious.

"Bitch!" he spat. "You've ruined my career, you and that bastard Yankee! You were supposed to hang. Instead, they're treating you like royalty. Where's my report? Did anyone bother to ask you for my report?"

Emily strove to keep a clear head. "I don't have it, Captain Morgan. Everything I own is in that chest. You may look, if you wish."

Morgan dumped the contents onto the bed and rummaged through the pile of clothing. Not finding his report, he heaved the chest across the room, missing Emily by inches.

She screamed. Sergeant Taylor burst into the room and wrestled the intruder to the floor.

"I only want to talk to her!" Morgan protested from flat on his stomach, his hands pinned behind his back, Taylor kneeling by his side.

She shook with fright, but managed to utter, "I want to see Colonel Bricker."

Taylor's head snapped up. "You sure?" At her nod, he

glowered at Morgan. "Let me show this…officer the door, then we'll go, if you're still of a mind. Did he hurt you?"

"I'm…I'm fine. He didn't touch me."

Taylor grabbed Morgan by the collar, pulled him to his feet and shoved him into the hallway. "Didn't Colonel Bricker tell you to stay away from Mrs. Hunter?"

Morgan put a hand to his bleeding nose. "I'll have you court-martialed for daring to lay hands on an officer."

"Yeah, well, you go tell Bricker why your nose is bleeding. He'd like to hear why you ignored a direct order."

As Sergeant Taylor hustled Morgan down the hallway, Emily sat on the bed, holding her stomach. Nausea roiled, as it always did from the slightest agitation. At first she'd been ill only in the morning, but now she couldn't walk quickly without bile rising to her throat.

In spite of her upset, Emily was thankful for Morgan's violent intrusion. She'd been searching for a plausible reason for changing her mind. Now she had one.

For a month she'd resisted Colonel Bricker's pressure. It hadn't been easy. Bricker couldn't understand her lack of desire for revenge against Jared Hunter—or against the Union, in general, since Terrance had been killed in a skirmish near Atlanta. She mourned her brother, but suspected his death was more his own fault than that of the Yankees.

As for Jared, she still had trouble meshing the man and the legend. Nor did she believe, at least most of the time, Bricker's assertion that everything Jared had done or said during their journey had been cleverly, insidiously calculated as a means of accomplishing his mission. In weaker moments, she wondered if she was a complete fool. Then she would remember a kind word, the tenderness in his touch, the delight in his eyes when she'd told him she loved him.

Taylor appeared in the doorway. "Ready?"

"My bonnet," she said, rising slowly.

"I'll get it." Sergeant Taylor hurried over to the coatrack to fetch her hat. He'd been treating her like a piece of porcelain for over two weeks. If Taylor knew of her pregnancy, and Emily was almost sure he did, he hadn't said a word to Bricker. If Bricker had found out, he would have tried to use it against her somehow.

Emily took Taylor's offered arm for support. The day was a fine one for a stroll—a warm, sunny late-July day.

"You've decided to go north," Taylor stated. "Because of Morgan?"

"That's what I intend to tell Colonel Bricker. Do you think he'll believe me?"

"Might."

Emily slowed to a snail's pace. Taylor had served more as guardian than as guard. He deserved some explanation.

"I've been a 'guest' of the Confederacy far longer than I would have wished. My brother is dead, and my aunt has problems of her own. I need to be with family right now, and the only family I have is in Washington. If Colonel Bricker is willing to help me get there, I intend to let him."

Taylor stopped. "This family of yours—your father and husband—you tell them *everything*, and let them help you."

Emily smiled. Sergeant Taylor knew she was about to lie to Bricker, that she had no intention of spying for the South. Would she tell her father? Maybe, if necessary. As for her husband, she wasn't sure she had a husband. Jared had the means to annul their marriage, and he'd had the past month to do it in.

"I'll keep your advice in mind, Sergeant."

Emily took a deep breath as the pressure gathered in her midsection, then subsided. Worry and conjecture vanished under the onslaught of her greatest fear. Far more than wishing to see her father, more than yearning to know where she stood with Jared, more than wanting out of Richmond and away from both Bricker and Morgan, Emily needed Hanna.

Hanna would know how to cure the horrible sickness and

the strange aches. Hanna would know how to save the baby.

Feet spread, arms crossed, Jared Hunter stood statue-still in the shadow of the dockside tavern, his gaze scouring the deck of the *Arabelle*.

"Nothing yet?" Frank West asked.

Jared shook his head and took the pewter mug from Frank's hand. Frank's answer to the boredom of waiting was to sample the tavern's beer. The mug sweated—cold beer embraced by August heat.

"What the hell's going on? They should have disembarked long ago," Jared complained. He took a long pull from the mug, barely aware of the taste of the brew.

"Want me to find out?"

"No," Jared said reluctantly. "If Colonel Gardner sees you, he'll suspect I'm here, too."

"We shouldn't have come in the first place. Gardner will throw a tantrum if he knows you're within a mile of Emily."

Colonel Gardner had already thrown several tantrums.

The worst had been on the day Jared's request to General Grant for a Richmond mission to rescue Emily came back, via Colonel Gardner, marked Denied—with instructions to Gardner to bring the pup to heel or put him in a kennel.

Bricker had proposed an exchange. The Union had refused. Then had come the weeks of discreet inquiries through private parties, with John's burden magnified by grief over Terrance's death. And then, suddenly, Bricker had relented, but at a price. Jared still thought the two-thousand-dollar bill for Emily's food, lodging and transportation was a bit steep. He also suspected that most of the money would find its way into Bricker's pocket.

Jared had paid the bill, wiping out his savings. It was worth every penny, and more, to get Emily out of Richmond.

The colonel had thrown his last tantrum several days ago, when he refused Jared's request to go along to fetch Emily.

"If Kate was about to walk down that plank, could you stay away?" Jared asked.

"Probably not, but I'm not sure that seeing Emily is going to help you rest easier."

Jared gave the empty mug back to Frank. "It may be my only chance to make sure she's all right."

"I'd bet my new pair of boots Colonel Gardner will tell you right quick if she's not."

Jared heard him move off to return the empty mugs.

From bow to stern, the steamer swarmed with sailors, rigging the ship for an overnight berth. Heads capped with cloth berets popped in and out of the hatch.

Jared marveled at the precise coordination between the dockworkers and the sailors as cargo was transferred from wharf to ship and disappeared below decks. The teamwork rivaled that of a gunnery unit, firing the cannons of artillery batteries.

Among the freight on the dock were boxes waiting to be loaded on the *Anabelle,* a Sanitary Commission steamer. Though destined for prisoners at Libby, most of those boxes wouldn't get inside the prison. Supplies were so scarce it was commonplace for guards to confiscate food and clothing.

The families of the prisoners complained, the Union protested, the prison officials denied tampering. Libby Prison was bad, and Andersonville in Georgia was a nightmare, but the Union prisons weren't much better—too many men crammed into too little space. And soon winter would take a heavy toll.

What caught Jared's eye was the wave of quiet, immobile sailors along the rail, allowing the civilian passengers to make their way along the deck. Clinging to her father's arm, Emily walked slowly, her head bent as she listened to something John was saying. Jared's heart lurched when she paused at the top of the plank, her head pivoting as she scanned the docks.

"Don't do anything rash, partner," Frank said as he returned to Jared's side.

"Who? Me?" Jared said absently.

For the briefest moment, Emily's perusal lighted on the tavern. Jared squashed the urge to step out of the shadows and into the sunlight. Beyond all reason, he envisioned Emily scampering down the plank, crying out with glee as she ran into his open arms. God, how he wanted to hold her, just hold her.

But the moment passed, and Jared exhaled a breath he hadn't realized he was holding. His eyes narrowed as John's arm went around Emily's waist. John appeared to be coaxing her to step onto the plank.

"Something's wrong," Jared said softly.

Halfway down the plank, Emily clutched her midsection and her knees buckled.

Jared didn't think—he ran.

"I've got her." Jared's look dared anyone to protest as he swept Emily from her father's tenuous hold. To Jared's surprise, John looked grateful.

John led the way to the coach, plowing a path through the milling workers. Zeke opened the door and held it as Jared climbed in with Emily held tightly in his grasp.

"Take the smoothest route home," John told Zeke. "After we get Emily to the house, I want you to fetch Doc Ellis."

"Yes, sir," Zeke answered quietly.

Frank strode up to John. "I'll follow with our horses. Should I stop and get Kate?"

"Hanna might appreciate the help," John agreed.

Within the confines of the coach, Jared heard but ignored the conversation. He held Emily across his lap, her head resting against his shoulder. His fingers gently roamed her face, pushing a stray lock of hair into place.

"She's lost weight," Jared observed.

John took the opposite seat and ran his hands over weary eyes. "I've never seen anyone so seasick in my entire life. She was horribly ill the entire voyage. Whatever she tried to eat came right back up, even water. The doctor on the steamer finally gave her laudanum to put her out. She's still groggy from the last dose."

"No wonder she collapsed," Jared said. "Did she tell you anything about Richmond?"

John settled back against the seat. "Not very much. I met a Sergeant Taylor. He was her guard the whole time. His protectiveness convinces me she wasn't mistreated."

He took a deep breath before continuing, "Emily knows about Terrance. It seemed to be the one thing she felt she had to tell me. After she was sure I knew about his death, she relaxed and accepted the doctor's care." John paused before admitting, "I'm sorry I didn't let you come with me. She asked for you. It might have helped her to have you there."

Emily groaned. Her knees jabbed into Jared's side. Jared tightened his hold and whispered against her cheek, "Easy, love. Just a few more blocks and you'll be home."

Her eyes opened, staring, glazed. She tried to smile, but failed. The pain in her expression shot a bolt of anguish straight to Jared's heart.

"Hurts," Emily whispered.

"You've been sick, sweetheart. Go back to sleep and—"

"Baby...hurts," she forced out, then closed her eyes.

Jared fought to swallow the acidic lump that formed in his throat. Unable to speak for several long seconds, he cast accusing eyes at Colonel Gardner, but one look at Emily's father told him that Gardner shared his surprise.

"Tell Zeke to hurry," Jared ordered his commander.

John nodded, then yelled up at Zeke to use the whip.

Hearing footsteps coming down the stairs, Jared pushed away from the mantel in the parlor, where he and John Gardner had been waiting for news. He reached the doorway in time to see Frank West engulf Katherine Drew in an embrace. Short, plump, with tawny hair, Kate had no pretensions to beauty, until one looked into her startling emerald eyes. Within them shone her vitality, her compassion, and the ability to love without reserve that had drawn Frank to her flame and held him fast.

Frank offered a handkerchief; Kate dabbed at her eyes as she turned toward the parlor.

"I'm sorry about the baby, Jared," Kate said softly. "Dr. Ellis did all he could, but…"

Jared had expected the miscarriage, and he felt he should mourn. But he couldn't, not yet. "How's Emily?"

"Weak and sleeping," Kate said. "The doctor and Hanna are still upstairs. It will be a while yet before he comes down."

Impatient, but resigned to a longer wait, Jared shrugged out of his blue uniform jacket, tossed it over the back of the sofa, then sagged into the cushions. Across the short expanse of a braided rug, John sat in a high-backed leather chair, staring into the cold fireplace.

"The day Emily was born…" John's voice came out a rasp, and he cleared his throat. "The day Emily was born, one of our mares decided to foal. I spent the day running between the house and the barn. It was a painful day, for both mothers—and me, who had to watch them struggle to bring forth their babies. Emily came out pink and beautiful, squalling. The foal wasn't so lucky. We couldn't save it."

Jared said sarcastically, "Thanks, John, I really needed to hear that."

"My point is, the mare survived. She gave birth to three healthy foals over the years. She was Titan's dame."

The silence deepened, the tension rose. About to jump out of his skin, Jared sprang from the couch. "Damn it all, John, why didn't the Confederates tell us Emily was pregnant?"

"Maybe they didn't know."

"What the hell did they think was wrong with her, a long bout of influenza?"

"She was seasick!"

Jared had noticed the changes in Emily as he carried her to the coach. Her cheekbones were pronounced, her neck was thinner. A familiar bosom that had once filled out the peach blouse had shrunk. He'd felt bone where he once caressed padded, rounded hips.

"The day we were married, she wore the peach outfit she had on today. It fit her perfectly. Now it hangs on her. She lost more weight than her seasickness can account for."

"You could be right, but we'll have to wait for Emily to explain. It doesn't really matter now. There wasn't a thing we could have done differently, even if we'd known."

"Like hell!"

John ran a hand over his weary eyes. "This is old ground, Jared. General Grant refused your request to return to Richmond, and his word was final."

Frank interrupted them. "Doc's coming down."

Dr. Ellis barely stepped into the parlor before Jared asked, "Can I see her now?"

The doctor put his black bag on the floor next to the sofa. He accepted a glass of spirits from John, then sat down.

"In a minute. You the husband?"

Jared nodded.

Dr. Ellis swirled the liquor in his glass, seeming to consider the wisdom of Jared's request. "I won't mince words with you. She's very weak, mostly from the loss of blood. She'll probably develop a fever. If it's not severe, and of short duration, your wife has a chance of surviving. I've given Hanna and Miss Drew instructions for her care. I'll be back tomorrow to check her progress."

Jared felt the blood drain from his face, his gut tighten. "And the odds of her surviving?"

The doctor looked at Colonel Gardner and then Frank before he faced Jared squarely. "Slim," he said quietly, and tossed back his whiskey.

Jared took the stairs two at a time. He paused outside the bedroom, took a deep breath, then pushed the door open.

Emily lay still, barely breathing, wraithlike in the bed.

Jared pulled a chair to the side of the bed. He picked up Emily's hand and brought it to his lips. He let the tears flow, tears he hadn't shed since he was a young boy.

So frail now, the hands that had controlled a willful mare, waved a broken spindle in a drunk's face, decked a Confederate officer—hands that wrought havoc with his senses when she touched his body. In the aftermath of loving, content and drained, Emily had always snuggled against his side, her head on his shoulder, an arm flung across his chest.

"I should have gone, love. I should have disobeyed orders and gone after you. I'm sorry, Emily. I'm so sorry."

Jared wiped his eyes on his shirtsleeve. Crying wouldn't help Emily get well, wouldn't bring back the baby she'd lost.

His baby. He'd failed mother and child so miserably.

Jared looked up when Frank knocked and entered.

"You staying?" Frank asked.

"Yeah."

"I'll go back to the boardinghouse and pack you a bag. Anything you want, besides a change of clothes?"

Jared thought for a moment. "Throw in the medicine box. There's a packet of herbs in there my ma swears by for fever."

An hour later, Hanna and Kate evicted him so that they could bathe and cool Emily's burning body. Jared changed into his buckskins and gave Hanna his mother's herbs. That night, Jared slept in the chair, his head resting near Emily's. He would have heard her if she woke, but she slept.

During the following morning, Hanna bustled in and out

bringing cool water, which heated quickly from the rag Jared used to wipe Emily's face. Hanna showed him how to force water and broth down her throat, then changed the bed linens while Jared held the patient.

Dr. Ellis returned. He praised Hanna's nursing skills, but offered little encouragement. He looked askance at the strange herbs Hanna added to the broth, but declared they couldn't hurt.

Near noon, Kate arrived. She breezed into the room with a smile on her face, which soon turned to a frown.

"You look terrible," she scolded. "How do you propose to help care for Emily if you don't take care of yourself?"

"I'm fine."

"Rubbish. Jared, weren't you ever sick as a child?"

"All children get sick at one time or another."

"And did your mother hover over you and moan for you not to die, or did she admonish you to get well because she had better things to do than look after a sick little boy?"

Jared took a long time to answer. "I was never this ill, nor am I moaning at her."

Kate huffed, "You aren't saying a word to her, are you? How is she to know that you're here, waiting for her to wake up, if you don't tell her? Emily needs to hear laughter, and us telling her we expect her to get better. Put a smile in your voice, man, and talk to her."

"Kate, she's unconscious. Emily can't hear me."

"Don't be so sure. If you insist on keeping a vigil, make sure Emily knows it's not a death watch. I'll fetch you something to eat. While I'm gone, see if you can't improve your attitude."

Kate flounced out of the room. Her scolding struck a nerve. Could Emily somehow hear whatever went on in the room? Would the sound of his voice comfort her, or drive her into deeper sleep?

"Hey, lovely lady, wake up," he whispered. "You've got to wake up, if only to rant at me for being an irresponsible, selfish, no-good bastard for getting you into this mess.''

Over the next two days, though Emily's fever raged, conversations on everyday events flowed over the sickbed: discussions of the upcoming election, John's plans for rebuilding Rosewood and reestablishing his herd, Hanna's amusing stories of Emily as a little girl.

Jared teased Kate about the dinner she'd ruined the night before. Kate blamed the temperamental stove that Colonel Gardner should replace. Hanna disagreed, saying she could cook on the old stove just fine.

Unable to resist, Jared told them about Emily's experience with a duck and an unfamiliar stove. During the hearty laughter that followed, Jared felt Emily's fingers squeeze his hand—the first sign that she could do anything other than breathe.

Small signs of improvement followed. Emily moved occasionally, becoming restless at times. On the fourth night, Jared's eyes snapped open when her fingers touched his face.

''Am I a bear, too?'' she questioned hoarsely.

She'd turned onto her side to face him. Her brown eyes were hazy, confused, in the dim lamplight. He wanted to whoop for joy, but didn't dare. Fever dream, he realized. He knew he was a sight, mussed and whiskered. But a bear? Why not?

''The very prettiest of bears,'' Jared said stroking her hair. ''You have beautiful brown eyes, and sleek, velvety fur.''

''I'm so warm.''

''You're supposed to be warm. Why don't you go back to sleep now? You'll feel better when it's time to wake up.''

''Will you be here?''

He wanted to be here, but Emily's health and peace of mind had to be considered before his own wishes. Though he hadn't been able to resist going to the dock to catch a glimpse of Emily, he hadn't intended to approach her. He'd decided long before then to leave the fate of their relationship in her hands.

She may have asked for him while on the boat, and tried to smile at him in the coach, but she'd been very ill and under the influence of laudanum.

Now, she'd lost their baby and damn near died. And she had the right to blame him for both. When she came to her full senses, he wouldn't be the least bit surprised if Emily never wanted to see him again.

"No. But there will be others here," he added quickly when he saw her concern. "There are others who love you and will be here when you wake. You won't be alone. I promise."

She closed her eyes. Jared couldn't go back to sleep. He watched her face until the sun rose and flooded the room with light. The pink splotches had faded from her cheeks. Jared leaned over and kissed Emily's cool forehead.

Jared packed his belongings and went down to the dining room, where John was sipping his morning coffee. John's gaze flicked to Jared's satchel.

"Emily's fever broke," Jared said. "You should probably be with her when she wakes." He poured a cup of coffee from the urn, but didn't sit at the table. "I think it best if Emily doesn't know I was here."

"Jared, I know I've been rough on you over Emily, but you are her husband."

"Technically. She can correct the situation when she feels strong enough. Lord knows I've given her enough reason to dissolve the marriage."

Emily blinked against the morning sunshine pouring through white, lacy curtains. Her head hurt and her body ached, but it seemed important that she wake. The urge to close her eyes and go back to sleep was strong, until a blue shadow blocked the rays that made her eyes water.

John Gardner asked, "Are you really awake this time, or are you faking again?"

"I'm awake, I think," Emily said, wondering why her voice sounded so strange. "How long have I been asleep?"

"For the better part of a week." John eased into the bedside chair. "You've been a very sick young lady. For a while there, we weren't sure you were going to live. You have no idea how happy I am to see those beautiful brown eyes."

"A week," she whispered, glancing about the cozy room. It felt almost as though she were back at Rosewood, in her childhood bedroom. How could she have been here for nearly a week without noticing?

"How much do you remember?" John asked gently, taking her hand, holding it tightly.

"The steamer, taking so long to get dressed in that little cabin. We were walking down the plank. I remember seeing Zeke, being relieved at getting off the ship. Did I faint?"

"Yes. Then we got into the coach and brought you here."

Bits and pieces of memory whirled in her head. Vaguely she remembered floating in strong arms that carried her to the coach, and telling Jared about the baby.

Jared.

Emily glanced quickly around the room, then up at her father. No, it must have been Papa she told. Or had she?

She thought she remembered hearing voices, muted, so she couldn't hear the words clearly. She remembered being frightened, but then a comforting presence had calmed her, urged her to get well, told her she was loved.

It must have been Papa sitting at her side, holding her hand as he was now. She rose a bit, intending to sit up. The pain hit. She winced.

"Not yet," John said, pushing her back down. "You need time to heal."

Heal?

Silent tears fell as her hand drifted down the white sheet to her abdomen.

Chapter Seventeen

Jared waited until he was out of the War Department building before voicing his frustration. "Now *that* was a waste of time," he said of the meeting he and Frank West had just attended.

Frank nodded his agreement. "It's as though the generals are postponing the war until after election day. Even Sherman is waiting it out, cooling his heels in Atlanta."

"I wish Grant would call us down. There must be something we could do in Virginia."

"Grant says mid-January, and that suits me just fine."

Jared hated the prospect of spending the rest of the autumn and part of the winter attending these meaningless sessions. Frank, of course, had a personal reason to stay.

"Is the groom getting nervous yet?" Jared asked.

"A little, I guess. The wedding is three weeks away."

"I still can't believe Katherine agreed to marry you."

"Took a lot of persuading, I'll tell you. She's scared I'm going to get my head blown off, but I think she understands my risk is low, compared to the soldiers in front-line trenches. It helped that you returned in one piece."

"Speaking of getting back in one piece, have you talked to Tom Reed?"

"Yeah, isn't that a story. He was lucky to get out of Georgia alive. Too many good people along Uncle's network weren't so fortunate. You know, once his arm is mended and out of the sling, Reed will be looking for some action. What do you think of including him on the mission we've got cooking?''

Jared considered for a moment before answering, "The accent he developed might come in handy. You'd swear the man was born and raised in Georgia.''

"His being built like an ox won't hurt, either. Along with Bob Atkins and Nathan Wilkins, that would make five of us. Do we need anyone else?''

This next mission, if Grant approved Jared's proposal, required talent, skill and a heavy dose of luck if it was to succeed. If any of the men involved made a mistake, a battalion of men wouldn't be able to save Jared—nor the entire population of Libby Prison.

"If we take too many men, we might draw attention. Better to keep the unit small but talented.''

"Five it is, then,'' Frank said, then asked, "Got plans for tonight?''

"Not really. You going to see Kate?''

"Yep. She bought fabric, *yards* of fabric, for her wedding dress. I'm supposed to help her cart it over to the Gardners' tonight. Emily is helping her make the dress.''

When Jared didn't comment, Frank continued, "Kate says Emily is much stronger. She doesn't need a nap in the afternoon any longer. John has had her out to show her around Washington, and on milder days she takes a walk in the morning.''

"I'm glad to hear Emily is getting out,'' Jared said stiffly. "Kate has been a good friend to her.''

"Emily also accepted an invitation to the wedding. It will be a small affair, Jared. You won't be able to avoid her, and I won't let you back out on being my best man.''

"I don't intend to back out. I'll just have to stay out of Emily's line of sight as much as I can.''

"It's been a month since you last saw her. Maybe it's time you went over there and talked to her.''

Jared shook his head. "If Emily wants to see me, she'll

let me know. When she does, it will be because she's ready to have our marriage dissolved."

"I know you don't want a divorce. Why are you so sure Emily does?"

Jared mentally listed all the reasons Emily would never want to see him again. There were so many, but one indisputably topped the list.

"I failed her, Frank. Because I didn't protect her the way I should have, she lost our child and damned near died. If that isn't reason enough for her to hate me, to want out of our marriage, I can give you a dozen more."

"Ouch!" Kate cried for the third time that afternoon, sticking her needle-pricked finger in her mouth. Emily stifled her impolite amusement by seeking diversion. She glanced around the parlor for an object on which to focus.

Papa had rented the house, completely furnished, upon his arrival in Washington. Though it would never feel like home, it was comfortable. The well-lit, elegantly appointed parlor had become her favorite room. Sprawled on the divan in front of the window, she could enjoy the bustle of the city without venturing into the streets. At Papa's insistence that she get some fresh air, she'd been outdoors a few times, but never alone and never for long.

Remaining inside seemed the safest way to avoid the possibility of meeting Jared. He hadn't come to see her, nor had he sent a message. His silence eloquently expressed his lack of interest.

Staying within the house also eliminated the chance of being contacted by an agent of Colonel Bricker's, a good reason for watching the world though a parlor window.

At present, the parlor served as a sewing room. Tables overflowed with strewn pieces of fabric, thread, scissors and pins. Sections of Kate's wedding dress hung over the backs of chairs, threatening to spill onto the carpet in puddles of slippery white silk and delicate blue flowers.

Kate sighed. "I'm all thumbs when I try to sew. You make such fine, neat stitches, and nary a drop of blood anywhere. Thankfully, I've become proficient in the kitchen. At least we won't starve.''

Emily admired Kate's determination to master domestic chores—not an easy task for a woman who'd always had servants to attend to her every whim, as Emily well remembered. While Emily had been forced to learn to do for herself, Kate did so voluntarily. Frank wasn't poor, but neither was he wealthy.

Emily said wryly, ''I have a feeling Frank cares more about your culinary skills than how you sew. Your talents will be sorely tested keeping that man fed.''

Laughing, Kate dismissed the concern. ''Feeding Frank will be easy. Darning his socks will be another matter.''

Hanna bustled into the room with a tray laden with a teapot, cups, and a plate heaped with biscuits.

''Ah, a reprieve at last,'' Kate said, setting aside the bodice pieces she'd been attempting to put together.

Hanna said to Kate, ''Heard you screech again, and thought your poor fingers could use a rest.''

''I swear, I could put thimbles on every finger and still manage to draw blood. I trust, however, that with practice I shall, one day, sew as nimbly as Emily.''

''I don't suppose Missy told you about the red cloth she practiced on, or the bandagin' I did on her little fingers.''

''Hanna, please,'' Emily exclaimed with a mirthful pout. ''You'll tarnish my image.''

''Taught her how to cook, too,'' Hanna reminisced. ''Oh, the stories I could tell you about smokin' stoves.''

''Hanna, please,'' Kate remonstrated, rising from the sofa. ''If we start trading stories about smoking stoves, you'll tarnish *my* image!''

Once more, a fragment of memory that she'd dismissed as fever-bred nonsense niggled at Emily. She again heard Kate and Hanna arguing over the quality of a stove. And afterward, Jared's voice, in an amused tone, describing a disastrous duck dinner. She'd tried so hard to distract him from telling the embarrassing story, but he'd ignored her plea.

But Jared hadn't told anyone the story of a burned duck, at least not the way she'd dreamed. Jared hadn't been here. No one had mentioned his name since her illness. Nor had she asked Papa about Jared. She just wasn't ready to hear that he'd obtained an annulment and had gone on with his life, which, because of his absence, she assumed must be the case.

It was Papa who'd sat by her bedside, mopped her brow, talked and laughed, said over and over again that he loved her, begged her to wake up. It couldn't have been Jared who lightly kissed her forehead and said her fever was gone, assured her she would be all right.

"Emily?" a voice above her urged softly.

Kate stood before her, concern reflected in her emerald eyes. Emily set aside the skirt piece and took the offered cup of tea. "Thank you, Kate."

"It's the least I can do. Heavens, if not for your help, I would be an old woman before I finished this dress."

Emily smiled at the exaggeration. "How is your finger?"

"On a par with a pincushion. If it's all right with you, I think we'll stop for today. Not only could my fingers use a rest, but the day is really much too fine to spend indoors. Would you feel up to an outing?"

Emily's reluctance fell victim to the sunshine streaming through the window. "Was there somewhere you wanted to go?"

Kate sat down on the chair across from Emily. "Actually, yes. You know of the work I've been doing to improve conditions in the field hospitals?"

"You told me about soliciting funds and supplies and shipping them to surgeons in the field. It must be gratifying to know your efforts are helping so many."

With an air of chagrin, Kate said, "Gratifying, but not completely satisfactory. You see, my father won't let me travel to any of the field hospitals so I can verify that my efforts are truly helpful. Unfortunately, Frank shares Father's opinion."

"I can't say that I disagree with them, Kate," Emily said

with a shiver. "I've heard the field hospitals are horrendous places. And I can tell you, from experience, that you wouldn't wish to be near a battlefield."

"So Father and Frank have told me, and though I would go if permitted, I'm not. So, I've decided to gather the information in another way, through one of the local military hospitals. Since most of the patients first pass through a field hospital, they will be able to tell me. And the surgeons here will surely know if their peers in the field are benefiting from the extra funds and supplies. Also, I've been thinking of volunteering to aid with nursing duties."

Emily raised an eyebrow. "That's where you want to go today, to a military hospital?"

"Armory Square Hospital is a few blocks from here. We could have Sam take us in Colonel Gardner's carriage. We won't be gone more than an hour or so. Please, Emily, come with me."

If ever she had to be in a hospital, Emily decided, she would like to stay in a place as pleasant as Armory Square. Gravel walks, lined with shrubs, connected a cluster of various-size white buildings.

The view from the hilltop was breathtaking. To the east, the ponderous dome of the Capitol seemed to rise above a sea of autumn-painted trees. The only evidence that a hospital occupied this peaceful place was the row of flat-boarded four-wheeled ambulances.

Kate's enthusiasm was infectious. They quickly located Major Mitchell. Somber, his fingers toying with his black mustache, the hospital's chief surgeon conducted the tour.

"Not what you expected, Miss Drew?" the surgeon asked as they entered a ward.

"I'm most pleasantly surprised," Kate admitted, voicing Emily's thoughts as they entered the dormitory-style room. Sturdy cots, most occupied, lined the walls. Scenic pictures hung between the many windows. The high ceiling added to the ward's light, airy feeling.

"You really don't need to know anything about nursing,'' Major Mitchell said. ''This is the enlisted men's ward. Some of these men can't read or write, others aren't physically able to. The medical staff doesn't always have time to help the men with letters. Just having someone to talk to, especially a pretty young woman like yourself, can do wonders to lift their spirits.''

Major Mitchell had addressed his remarks to Kate after hearing Emily's Southern accent when introduced. Emily felt the sting of the doctor's rudeness, but regarded it as only a petty annoyance. After all, Kate was offering to volunteer her time and talents to the hospital, not Emily.

She followed Kate and the doctor as they sauntered down the wide aisle. So much bandaging, she thought, wound around heads and arms exposed above green wool blankets.

At the far end of the ward, two men lay segregated from the rest. An armed corporal guarded the two patients.

The question had barely formed in Emily's mind when Kate asked, ''Why the guard?''

''You need not concern yourself with those two,'' Mitchell answered sharply. ''They're Rebs. As soon as possible, they're going back to the prison's sick ward.''

Emily couldn't drag her attention from the prisoners. And when one of them rolled over, giving her a clearer view of his face, Emily felt the blood drain from her face.

Kate put her arm around Emily's shoulders. ''Dr. Mitchell, do you have a place where my friend can rest for a bit? She's been ill, and I fear I've overtaxed her.''

''No, I'm fine Kate, really,'' Emily said, shaking off her initial shock. ''Doctor, the young man with the bandage over his eyes, do you know his name?''

''No. Ah, Mrs. Hunter, I don't think that's a good idea.'' The doctor's protest fell on inattentive ears as Emily slid out of Kate's grasp and scooted past him.

Impossible, Emily's reason told her, but she couldn't deny the resemblance. Tousled sandy-colored hair flowed over the top of the bandage covering the boy's eyes. Light freckles dotted his nose and upper cheeks. His eyes, when uncovered, would be a haunting pale blue.

"Do you know this boy?" Kate asked from behind her.

"He looks so much like a boy I met, but he can't possibly be Scott."

"This here's Eric Walters," said the Reb in the next bed. "If I remember correctly, he had a brother named Scott."

"Dear God," Emily breathed. "No wonder I thought I was seeing a ghost. Eric Walters is Scott's twin."

"Ladies, it's time to move on," Dr. Mitchell said, his voice sharp with irritation.

"He's asleep right now," the Reb said as he pushed up on an elbow, ignoring the doctor.

"How can you tell?" Emily asked.

"There's a Bible under his pillow. Soon as he wakes up he'll pull it out and hold on to it for all it's worth. Says it belonged to his ma 'fore she died. Won't let anyone touch it."

Emily turned to Kate and asked, "Do you think we could stay a while longer? I'd like to be here when Eric wakes."

"This is highly irregular," Mitchell blustered.

"We can stay," Kate said, smiling. "Let's find you a chair. I don't want you to overdo."

Kate neatly dispatched the doctor. Emily sat on a chair between the cots and stared at Eric.

Corporal Seth Jones rambled about Eric, himself, and their short army career. Seth and Eric had enlisted at the same recruitment rally and found themselves assigned together. Being the older, Seth told her, he tried to look after Eric.

"Knew he was lyin' about his age," Seth said. "But he needed the money bad, and the army was lookin' for bodies. He done himself proud right off. Then we got ourselves into a bad skirmish, got wounded. The prison hospital was full, so the Yanks sent us over here."

"How badly are you wounded?"

"My head got banged up a bit." Seth fingered the bandage covering his forehead. "The knee ain't never gonna work right, but I got me a brain that's sharp. I'll do just fine."

"And Eric?"

"He's okay, except for his eyes. Won't know about them for sure till those wrappins's come off."

Emily held her breath when Eric stirred, wondering how in heaven's name she would explain about Scott. Would Eric believe she hadn't murdered his brother?

Seth spoke first. "Hey, Eric! Get yourself awake there, boy. We got us some company. Right pretty company, at that."

"Ah, quit your funnin', Seth. Ain't no pretty little Northern gal gonna bother with the likes of us," Eric drawled.

"'Course not." Seth winked at Emily. "But this here Southern gal came waltzin' in, took one look at you sleepin' so peaceful-like, couldn't tear herself away till you woke up."

"Sure, Seth," Eric droned as he pulled a frayed book from beneath his pillow. "And they're gonna feed us corn bread and fried chicken for supper, while a fiddler plays 'Dixie.'"

Seeing her opening, Emily entered the bantering. "I might not be able to find a fiddler, but I could probably arrange the corn bread and fried chicken. Would you prefer peach pie or molasses cookies for dessert?"

Eric's jaw dropped in surprise. "Now don't that beat all! Well, how do, ma'am?"

"Very well, now that you've joined us."

"You were really waitin' for me to wake up?"

"Yes."

"Well, ain't that somethin'," Eric said, almost to himself, and then frowned. "How come? I mean, I don't know you, do I?"

"We've never met, but as soon as I saw you, I had to stop." Emily hesitated, reluctant to break the gaiety. "You look so much like Scott."

"People always did have trouble tellin' us apart," Eric said thoughtfully. "Could of swore I knew everyone Scott did."

Emily steeled her resolve and asked, "Do you recognize the name Emily Gardner?" Her heart sank as Eric's frown deepened. "I know you probably heard about my arrest for Scott's murder. It didn't happen that way, Eric. Your brother's death was an accident, a senseless accident."

"Jesus, lady," Seth swore.

"It's okay, Seth," Eric murmured. "I knew, but I never expected to meet her. Damn!" he shouted, his hands flying toward the bandage covering his eyes. "Scott's angel! You're *Scott's angel,* and I can't see you! Damn!"

"The bandage!" Seth cried, flinging an arm toward Eric's cot. "Don't let him take off the bandage!"

Emily didn't need the warning. She grappled with Eric's hands as he struggled to tear away the strips of cotton.

"Got him, Mrs. Hunter," a gown-clad soldier calmly stated, his hand gripping Eric's right wrist. On the other side of the cot, a guard grabbed Eric's left. Emily let go.

Eric fought the bonds. "I have to see her!"

Emily put her hands on Eric's shoulders. "Please, Eric, calm down. You must leave the bandage on a while longer. If you want, I'll be here when the doctor takes it off."

"You promise?"

"I promise. I'll even remove the bandage if the doctor will allow me."

The promise calmed him. Emily looked around at the crowd Eric's shouts had drawn. Kate stood at the end of the bed, flanked by several patients.

"My Bible..." Eric said.

"It's here, Eric," Kate said, and retrieved the book from the floor where it had fallen.

"Who's she?"

Emily introduced Kate Drew to Eric Walters, then asked him, "How did you know Scott mistook me for an angel?"

"From the letter in Scott's pocket for my ma." Eric nodded toward the man holding his right wrist. "He called you Mrs. Hunter. You must've married the captain."

Completely confused, Emily asked, "What letter?"

"Miss Drew, if you still have the Bible, there's a letter

stuck near the middle. Would you read it, please? You guys can let go now."

The patient and the guard looked to Emily for permission. Emily nodded, and the men slowly released Eric's wrists.

Kate cleared her throat. "This letter is dated the seventeenth of May, 1864."

"That's the day Scott died, ain't it, Mrs. Hunter?"

"Yes, Eric, it is."

"'Dear Mrs. Walters,'" Kate read. "'I am writing this note in the event we are unable to personally tell you how Scott died. We found him in the woods, not far from his grave. I fear his flintlock misfired, unfortunately wounding Scott. His wound was such that we were unable to prevent his death, but it may comfort you to know I was able to administer morphine to lessen his pain during those final hours.

"'Miss Emily Gardner and I were with your son when he died. We exchanged few words, but I can tell you that he spoke of his mother near the end. Scott was very brave through the ordeal. He never complained or lashed out to blame God or the Fates. You may grieve for him, Mrs. Walters, as every parent grieves upon losing a child, whether due to this horrible war, an accident like Scott's, or by sickness. But be proud, for your young man died with his religious beliefs firmly intact.

"'As he took his final breaths, Scott looked into the face of the lovely young woman who had nursed him, sharing her gentle strength. With his last words he thanked his mother for being right about the angels who eased one's soul into heaven.

"'He died peacefully, Mrs. Walters. We share your grief. Captain Jared Hunter, United States Army.'"

Astonished at the signature, Emily stared at Kate. Kate turned the letter. In a bold scrawl, Jared had indeed disclosed his true identity.

Eric broke the heavy silence. "Took us back a bit at first, the captain bein' Yankee. I was spittin' angry, but not Ma.

She said the captain must be a good Christian, takin' care of Scott like he did, lettin' us know how he died."

"I didn't know Jared wrote the note," Emily said hoarsely.

"When we brought Scott home, we found the letter in his shirt pocket. Ma must have read it a hundred times, found comfort in the words. When she passed on, I took her Bible and the letter with me when I enlisted."

Kate folded the letter, tucked it into the Bible and laid the book on the bed by Eric's side. "Emily, it's almost time for us to leave."

"You'll remember your promise?" Eric asked quickly.

Emily smoothed the bandage. "Of course I will."

"Mrs. Hunter, I don't know if it's possible, but seein' as how I got to meet you, could I meet the captain, too?"

The request took Emily by surprise. The look on Eric's face was so hopeful. "I can't promise, but I'll ask."

With Kate at her side, Emily left the ward in a state of wonder tinged with misgiving.

As they walked toward the carriage, Kate asked, "Did I detect a touch of hero worship in Eric's request?"

"I would diagnose a rather advanced case," Emily admitted. "I can't blame Eric, though. That letter!"

"I'm sure Jared would come to the hospital if you asked."

"Is Jared in Washington?"

"He's working at the War Department. As I understand it, Jared hasn't left Washington since his assignment involving you. Emily, are you all right? You've gone pale again."

"I need some time to think this through. If you don't mind, I'd like to walk home."

"I'll send Sam to tell Hanna we are—"

"No, Kate. Please, I'd like to walk alone."

Chapter Eighteen

Emily pulled her cloak a little tighter, a useless gesture against the chill she felt from within.

Dead is dead, Jared had once said, but his letter to Mrs. Walters negated his espoused callousness. When had he found the time to pen those comforting words?

It certainly wasn't practical to sign the letter as he had, not knowing how the family would react. Twice during his mission, Jared had risked using his full name—once to Mrs. Walters, then again on their marriage license. Though he hadn't identified himself as a Union soldier on the license, his name had aided the Confederates in discerning his identity.

Every parent grieves upon losing a child. Jared had been in Washington all this time. Surely Papa or Frank West would have told Jared of her miscarriage.

Did Jared grieve for his lost child? Did he feel the emptiness that plagued her dreams and haunted her waking hours? Did he mourn the lost chance to hold his baby, count tiny fingers and toes and see a first smile?

Why hadn't he come to see her?

He had.

Emily shivered at the realization. She could no longer discredit those dreamlike flashes of memory. Papa might have taken a turn in the chair by her bedside, but so had

Jared. Jared *had* held her hand, encouraged her to fight the fever, told that awful duck story to Hanna and Kate.

I should have gone after you, love...disobeyed orders...so sorry, Emily.

As far as she knew, Jared hadn't taken steps to have their marriage dissolved. Emily drew her hand from under her cloak and inspected the gold ring encircling her finger. Despite all that had happened, she still loved the man who'd placed the gold band on her finger. It might not be wise, but it was true.

He'd stayed only as long as the fever lasted, while her life hung on a fragile thread. Had he done so merely out of his sense of duty? Why hadn't he stayed until she was fully conscious? Why hadn't she heard a word from him afterward? And why hadn't Papa, or anyone else in the house, for that matter, spoken of Jared's presence during her illness?

Struggling with conflicting emotions, paying scant attention to her surroundings, Emily bumped into a man in her path. Dressed in a gray frock coat and matching top hat trimmed in black, the gentleman smiled as he steadied her.

"I'm terribly sorry," Emily told him.

"No harm done, Mrs. Hunter," he replied.

"I fear you have me at a disadvantage, sir. Have we met?"

"No, we haven't, and probably shall not meet again, for our mutual protection. For now, you may call me Noah."

"Protection?"

"Ah, I see you don't understand. Let me explain. We have a mutual friend named Bricker."

Noah's pencil-thin mustache twitched with amusement when she took a step backward. Emily chided herself for her small show of surprise and lack of caution. She'd been so careful, until this afternoon. However, now that contact had been made, Emily was glad to have it over with.

Emily stated firmly, "You may tell *your* friend Bricker that he erred. I don't have access to any government secrets."

Noah put his hand on her arm as she tried to scoot past. "Don't be hasty, Mrs. Hunter. You may not care for the consequences."

"How dare you!" Emily snapped, shaking off his hand.

"I would dare harsher measures if you ignore your bargain with Colonel Bricker. Consider not only your well-being, but the safety of your loved ones, your friends."

"But I told you, I—"

"You have adequate sources, Mrs. Hunter. Some of our best information comes from a careless word uttered at the dinner table, or from an accidentally overheard conversation. You have only to write down those tidbits and pass them to a courier. Walk this way again next week. You'll be contacted. Remember, Mrs. Hunter, this isn't a game. It's war."

He tipped his hat, then walked away.

Emily's anger and fear rose with each brisk step toward the house. Noah's threat of violence directed at Papa and her friends set her resolution to thwart Bricker's expectations. But, knowing little of spies and their tactics, she needed advice. Sergeant Taylor had told her to tell Papa and Jared. She probably should, but either of them would take over, try to solve the problem for her.

Her involvement with Bricker was of her own doing. Surely she could extricate herself from this mess without involving either Papa or Jared. Besides, who better to advise her than Kate, whose father worked in army intelligence?

After extracting a promise of secrecy, Emily paced the library and told Katherine Drew about the bargain she'd made with Colonel Bricker, and the meeting with Noah.

"All I wanted was a safe haven for myself and my baby. I admit I wasn't terribly rational when I agreed to Bricker's demands," Emily admitted. "I thought I would be beyond his reach, that he couldn't force me to cooperate. I'm afraid I was very naive. What can I do about Noah?"

"Emily, are you willing to meet the courier?"

"You have a plan?"

"Just the beginnings of one. I shall have to tell my father," Kate said, and held up a hand to silence Emily's objection. "We may be able to capture this Noah, but we must do so cautiously, without Noah or Bricker suspecting your involvement. Therefore, we need my father's help."

"Major Drew won't tell Papa or...anyone, will he?"

"My dear, my father's business is secrecy. He won't expose your predicament unless you agree. I'll speak to him, and we'll see what he says." Kate grasped Emily's hands and said softly, "Don't fret overmuch. My father's dealt with dozens of spies in Washington. He may even know of Noah and have already arranged a trap."

Emily hoped so.

"I'm sorry, Papa," Emily apologized. "I never thought of the cost or inconvenience. I've caused too much turmoil in your household already, and don't wish to add undue burden to Hanna or your budget."

Seeking Papa's permission for the chicken dinner had slipped her mind. For two days she'd argued politely with Dr. Mitchell about serving a dinner to the patients in the ward, all the while worrying over Kate's meeting with Major Drew.

Perched on the edge of her chair, facing her father's irritation, Emily fidgeted with her apron's hem. The fragrance of frying chicken wafted into the library. The smell mingled with the aroma of bubbling pie and pungent cookies. Thank heaven she'd shown reluctant but wise judgment by substituting apples for costly peaches.

"This is your household, too," Papa said. "Your heart is in the right place. Just remember, we're living on a soldier's pay."

He walked from behind his desk and leaned on the front edge. He peered down at Emily with a look she recognized as a prelude to a scolding or lecture. She could have kissed him, for suddenly she felt on solid ground. She felt a young girl again, and loved every minute. For the first time in years, she knew the rules and how to play the game. Thank the Lord, Papa hadn't changed.

"All I ask, my dear," he said, "is a little moderation the next time you choose a cause worthy of your regard."

"You're not truly very angry with me, are you Papa?"

Her downcast pout, combined with shy brown eyes that flicked from her hands to his face, was nearly his undoing.

"Oh, no, you don't, young lady. That ploy may have worked when you were ten, to wheedle your old father into forgiving your mischief, but no longer."

Emily sighed and sat back in the chair. "Actually, it worked until I was fourteen."

"I can't have been so gullible so long."

"I see I must find a more sophisticated method," she mused. "Would an invitation to share our feast pacify you?"

"Don't you think having an officer in their midst might put a damper on the men's spirits, make them feel ill at ease?"

"On the contrary, I would think having an officer pay some attention to them would be a great compliment."

"When is this grand party supposed to take place?"

"Dr. Mitchell is grudgingly allowing me to feed them supper tonight, about six. Can you come?"

"Grudgingly?"

"Mitchell isn't pleased with my interest in the prisoners. I think he fears I'll wrap up the boys and carry them out with the trash."

Papa crossed his arms. His eyes narrowed. "I gather the good doctor is suspicious because you are Southern?"

"He hasn't outright said so, but he hasn't bothered to hide his bias."

"Well, then," he said, "since I'm paying for this meal, it's only fair I should help eat it."

Emily smiled as she rose and kissed his cheek. "Thank you, Papa."

She'd almost made it out the door when he called, "Emily?" his tone rising.

From his expression, Emily knew he'd figured out that she'd managed to get her way.

"Yes, Papa?"

"I believe the adage is, 'Better the devil you know than the devil you don't.' If you switch your tactics, girl, I may not survive them."

"Yes, Papa."

Emily returned to the kitchen.

Hanna was chuckling, her whole body shaking with mirth. "Did it to him again, huh? Wound him right around your little finger till you got your way."

Chagrined, Emily admitted, "He's getting faster at the game. I didn't even make it out the door. All the same, he's coming to the hospital, and that's what I wanted. Would you believe he told me not to change tactics?"

"Don't surprise me none. A man gets accustomed to havin' his womenfolk act a certain way, gets comfy in the knowin'."

"The hoyden daughter is gone, Hanna. I grew up during our separation."

"He knows that in his head, but not in his heart. Your papa would do most anythin' for you, same as always. He wants his little girl to be whole and happy."

Emily sat on the stool next to Hanna's worktable, which sagged under the weight of the baked goods. *She's getting old,* Emily lamented as she watched Hanna putter. Fingers once deft moved with arthritis-cramped slowness. Though age and bulk now slowed her body, Hanna's eyes sparkled, and her mind was sharp. Very little escaped Hanna's notice.

Emily ventured, "Hanna, would you answer a question?"

"If I can."

"Why hasn't anyone in the household mentioned that Jared was here when I was ill?"

"Now there's a man used to havin' his own way," Hanna said gruffly. "Made a real nuisance of himself, sittin' in that chair by your bedside. Body couldn't move without him pryin'."

Emily noted the affection in her tone. "You're very fond of Jared."

"He's a right fine young man."

"There was a time I would have disagreed."

"Then I'm glad to see you found your good sense." Hanna rearranged a plate of cookies as she explained, "Not tellin' you he was here was Captain Hunter's idea."

"Hanna, tell me about Jared, please."

For an hour Emily listened, making few comments, as Hanna related the events during that harrowing week, beginning when Jared had carried Emily through the front door.

When Hanna finished, Emily said, "At least now I can separate reality from the dreams. I must have been on the verge of waking several times, but too weak to open my eyes."

"Were the dreams awful, child? Sometimes a fever does that to a person."

"Some were." Emily remembered a blood-chilling vision of Terrance dying on a battlefield. "Others were of home and better times, particularly one of my mother. I saw her standing at the end of my bed, but when I tried to go to her, she got very angry. I'd forgotten how Mama could scold."

"Your mama was a gentle soul, but she could get downright ornery when crossed. Made you two little ones mind your elders, and didn't take no sass."

Emily smiled. "One dream was even funny. I was staring at this huge brown bear. His fur looked so soft that I reached out and touched it. I asked him if I was a bear, too. He looked at me oddly, told me I was, and to go back to sleep."

"Maybe it weren't no dream," Hanna commented. "Captain Hunter looked mighty scruffy there at the end."

"Oh, dear," Emily uttered, at the unsettling realization that Hanna might be right. There was no fear attached to the dream; in fact, she had felt safe in the bear's den.

"Jared must have thought I'd completely lost my senses."

"Doubt he thought any such thin'. People utter the darnedest nonsense when half awake and sick."

"Why did Jared leave before I was fully conscious?"

"That's somethin' you'll have to ask him, honey. I don't rightly know for sure. He came down one mornin', told us your fever was gone and that he was leavin'. Your papa tried arguin' with him, sayin' you'd want to see him when you woke, but Captain Hunter, he was of a different mind."

Shooed from the kitchen, sent to her room for a nap by a perceptive Hanna, Emily sat at her writing table and stared at the blank sheet of white paper.

Should she merely tell Jared about Eric Walters, ask him to come to the hospital? No, that wouldn't be reason enough for Jared to come immediately. Nor would inviting him to the dinner, because he might refuse the invitation.

Asking Jared to visit Eric was simple; guaranteeing an appearance this evening was more difficult.

Emily rested her chin in her hand, tapping a pencil against the desk. Jared could masterfully convince people to behave as he wished, and all he had to do was…

The pencil stilled, poised over the paper. It was suddenly so easy—but at least she would be polite and say please.

"Something wrong, Jared?" Frank asked.

"I'm not sure. All Emily's note says is that she and Colonel Gardner are at Armory Square Hospital and to please come."

The abruptness of Emily's summons led Jared to conclude that Colonel Gardner was ill and Emily had taken him to the nearest army hospital.

"Maybe you should go now," Frank urged. "We're almost done here. Emily must have a reason for sending for you."

Jared looked around the room. A general, three colonels and several aides had gathered in the War Department office to study a map of Virginia, to debate whether Boydton

Plank Road, near Hatcher's Run, was a crucial Confederate supply route. Having decided the exercise futile without direct field information, Jared and Frank attended the meeting, but neither expected results.

"With your permission, sir, I would like to find out what this is about," Jared said to the senior officer in the room.

"Yes, yes, of course, Captain. Go."

Jared galloped through the streets of Washington. Lather was dripping from the gelding's mouth when Jared pulled up next to Zeke, who stood near the Gardners' carriage.

"I'll take care of him, sir. They're right in there," Zeke said, pointing to a ward.

In his haste to reach the building, Jared nearly ran down an orderly on the gravel path.

"Leftovers go to the officers," the orderly said as he juggled a platter. "Would you like a piece, sir?"

Jared studied the yellow corn bread and browned chicken. *Leftovers?* "No, thank you. Carry on," he said, moving aside to let the relieved private pass.

Stopped because of the near collision, Jared stood outside the doorway to the ward. He could hear laughter and the clank of dishes landing in tin tubs. Above the clatter, Hanna's voice admonished, "You done had your share of those, young man. Don't you snitch no more between here and the officers' ward."

"No, ma'am, I won't. They sure are good, though," came the wistful reply, seconds before another orderly, bearing a plate of cookies, bolted out the door.

"Whoa, Private." Jared stopped the orderly, recognizing the molasses cookies. He took one. "If I had charge of that plate, I'd hide a few cookies away for later."

The orderly glanced back over his shoulder. "Permission to return to quarters for two minutes, sir?"

"Granted, but move smartly, soldier, before Hanna catches you."

Enlisted ward, Jared realized. No self-respecting army doctor would quarter an ailing colonel here. Then why the urgency to Emily's request?

Hanna appeared in the doorway. "You gonna stand out there all night or come in for supper?"

"Emily sent for me. Do you know why?"

"Didn't know she had," Hanna said as she stepped outside. "Might be because she's been askin' questions and needs some answers. Did you really tell that poor child she was a bear?"

"She caught me off guard at three in the morning. Letting her believe her dream was easier than arguing."

"Might've been," Hanna mused, then turned to go back inside. "Well, she's down on the end with the Rebs."

"There are prisoners in the hospital?"

"Missy knows one of them. That's how she got the notion for this here supper."

Jared followed Hanna into the ward.

Emily knew the instant Jared entered the building, by nothing more than the strange sensation that crept along her spine. Having spent the past few hours cooking, carting and serving, she hadn't given much thought to what she would say to him when—if—he answered her summons. She still wasn't sure.

"Mrs. Hunter? Is that Captain Hunter?" Seth asked.

Emily glanced quickly toward the other end of the long building to confirm what she'd already sensed.

"Yes, Seth."

"Ooo-wee. So that's Cougar. Damned if he don't look like the devil's own."

His observation sent her attention back to the end of the building, this time for a longer look at her tall, broad-shouldered, thoroughly imposing husband. Her heart did a little flip-flop—part joy and part panic.

The panic, she decided, was caused by the uniform. She'd never seen Jared in Union blue, which flattered his physique and skin tone as Confederate gray couldn't. He still wore his hat at a rakish angle, tipped forward and to the side. He took it off and tossed it on a table where Papa had discarded his, bringing onyx eyes into clear view.

Hanna handed him a piece of pie, for which he exchanged a dazzling smile.

"Is he coming down here, Mrs. Hunter?" Eric asked.

"Not yet."

Jared was eating his pie, and doing a slow survey of the situation. His perusal stopped momentarily where Papa sat near one of the patients, engaged in a heated chess game, then continued down the rows of cots and men until he found her, sitting on a chair between Seth and Eric's cots.

Time to face the music. Emily got up and began the long trek to where Jared stood.

As though his hands traveled the length of her body, Emily felt a surge of desire follow the course of his examination. She blushed as her nipples hardened and her womanhood burned. Whatever else had changed between them, the strong physical attraction pulled as a magnet to iron.

She walked toward him at an unhurried pace, reminding herself that she hadn't requested Jared to come for her, but for Eric Walters. Jared took a last bite of apple pie, then put the plate on the nearby table.

"Good evening, Jared," Emily said softly.

"Looks like I almost missed the party. My invitation arrived a bit late."

Emily refused to feel guilty for having brought Jared here under false pretenses. Besides, he didn't seem angry, only a bit put out.

"I was beginning to wonder if Sam wasn't able to locate you—or if you couldn't come."

"Your note reached me about a quarter of an hour ago. I came as soon as I could excuse myself from a meeting." Again he looked her over. "You look good, Em."

"Better than when you last saw me? I should hope so."

His head tilted in an unspoken question.

"I know you carried me from the ship to the carriage. I also know you stayed with me several days after...after."

He nodded—an acknowledgment of her distress, an acceptance that he'd lived through it with her. What she failed to understand was why he'd left without a word. With all the bustle going on around them, and too many ears around to overhear, it didn't seem the appropriate time to ask.

Jared was here. Had come when she needed him. That would have to do, for now.

"Emily, why did you send for me?"

"There's someone here who wants to meet you," she said, and held out her hand.

Jared wanted to pull her into his arms. He settled for the simple pleasure of her hand in his. That Emily would one day offer any olive branch had seemed impossible during these past weeks.

"Hunter."

Jared acknowledged Colonel Gardner. "Sir?"

The colonel picked up a knight and made his move. "When I'm done here, I'd like a word with you."

Jared looked over the chess board. The patient would have the colonel's king in about three moves. "I'll be waiting."

They reached the prisoners too quickly, to Jared's way of thinking. He got his first good look at the boys, and knew why Emily had sent for him. "I'll be damned," Jared softly swore, recognizing the face around the bandage-covered eyes.

"I'll get you some supper while you get acquainted with Eric," Emily said. "He has quite a story to tell."

"She wants me to do something about those prisoners," Colonel Gardner said. "I'll be damned if I know what, but that's what Emily wants. Give me one of those."

Jared handed over a cigar. "Did Emily tell you that?"

John's face glowed in the circle of light from his match, and the smoke from the long beginning puffs drifted up into the crisp night air. He shook the match twice and tossed it onto the walk, leaving only the glowing embers of cigar tips to mark their position near the supply building.

"Not outright. I thought, at first, Emily wanted me here as a buffer against Mitchell. The man is a fine surgeon, but lacks compassion. Then I watched her fuss over those two boys." John let out a short laugh. "When I recall all the strays she's brought me over the years—rabbits, squirrels, dogs, cats. Well, now it's these boys she wants taken care of, and Papa's supposed to make it right."

"Too bad you can't just send them home."

John gave a sad smile. "Yeah, too bad. Have you figured out yet why Emily wanted you up here tonight?"

"That's easy. Eric Walters said he asked Emily to arrange a visit." Jared looked over his shoulder at the ward. "Looks like the party's over. They're dimming the lights."

A loud cheer erupted from the ward, followed by a wild Rebel yell. Cigars flew in all directions. Jared's younger legs propelled him through the doorway first.

Emily held Eric's head against her shoulder, rocking slowly on the narrow cot. The bandage had been removed from around Eric's eyes. Emily gently pushed Eric away.

"Describe him for me, if you can," she said.

Eric blinked a few times before he said, "Tall, dark hair, Yank officer—must be Captain Hunter! He's kinda fuzzy. Think I'd rather look at you," he added, turning back to Emily.

"Close 'em, soldier," Emily ordered sternly, the catch in her voice subverting the harshness of her words. "Now!" she said to enforce her command when Eric opened his mouth to protest.

"Captain Hunter, you're one lucky man," Eric stated as Emily finished tying a cotton strip around his head. "You best take care of our angel."

The admonishment was so serious, coming from a child who could barely see, that Jared couldn't contain a tight smile. Then Emily turned. Tears glistened on her cheeks.

Jared did the only thing he could do when faced with Emily's tears. He opened his arms. As though in answer to an unvoiced prayer, Emily promptly accepted his invitation.

"He can see," she whispered. "Oh, Jared, I was so afraid to take the bandage off, but I'd promised."

"Shhh… Don't cry, Em. He'll be fine now."

Holding on tight, Jared closed his eyes as Emily wept against his shoulder, feeling whole for the first time in months. And this time, when hope sparked, he didn't smother it under denials and recriminations. When a man held an angel, he couldn't help but believe in miracles.

Chapter Nineteen

The following morning, Jared went with Colonel Gardner to the White House. They waited in the East Room while President Lincoln's secretary announced their arrival.

Though most of the North had been spared the ravages of war, the East Room looked battle-weary from use for receptions, levees and, at one time, sleeping quarters for troops. The pale green carpeting, specially woven in Glasgow, had been shredded by muddy, spurred military boots. Curtains of white Swiss lace suffered ragged hems where vandals had cut out delicate floral patterns as souvenirs.

Jared voiced his doubts about John's scheme to take care of Emily's boys. "I don't know, Colonel. This could be a big waste of time."

"It's the best I could come up with, and it needs Lincoln's approval. If he turns us down, we'll think of something else."

Silently Jared followed John up the stairs to the second floor office of the man labeled the Great Emancipator by his admirers and a bumbling buffoon by his antagonists.

Jared hid his horrified reaction as the president looked up from his papers. The burden that Abraham Lincoln carried was deeply carved into his gaunt face. His deep-set, hooded eyes and sunken, lined cheeks belonged to a man much older than fifty-five.

Waving Jared and John into chairs, the president drawled, "Your visit is a surprise, gentlemen, though not unwelcome."

"You may feel differently, sir, when I explain the reason for our visit," John said. "We've come to ask a favor."

Lincoln glanced at the tall stack of mail on the corner of his desk and shrugged eloquently. "Then I shall ask a favor, also. Mother heard of your arrival and wishes an audience when we complete our business. Would you mind, Captain Hunter?"

Jared's smile was genuine when he answered, "It's always an honor to spend a few minutes with your lovely wife, sir."

With a satisfied nod, the president leaned back in his chair. "Your request, Colonel."

Jared watched the president's face for some sign of approval as John requested a special prison assignment for Eric Walters and Seth Jones. Granted, Fort Warren was still a prison, but it was the best run of the lot. Short of sending the boys home, taking them up to Boston offered the best chance of their surviving the war.

"I would like to say yes," the president said after long deliberation. "However, my standing with the press at present is unfavorable. I hesitate to give a reporter the opportunity to misconstrue my motives for showing favor to the enemy this close to the election."

"Mr. President, I anticipated your desire for secrecy," Jared said. "I believe I can escort the prisoners quietly to Boston. All I need is your authorization for General Dimick to accept them."

The president rose from his chair and strode to the window that faced the south lawn. His hands clasped behind his back, Lincoln said wearily, "You will, of course, use the utmost discretion."

"If you wish, sir, I can give you the details for your approval, once I have everything arranged."

"That won't be necessary." Lincoln turned with a meager smile. "If you are successful, I will never hear of your journey or its purpose. Why don't you visit with Mrs. Lincoln while·I compose the order for General Dimick? You will find her in the conservatory.''

Jared excused himself and hurried toward the greenhouse.

Mary Todd Lincoln blended into her surroundings, wearing one of the sweeping, floral gowns she favored. She extended a gloved hand as Jared approached. ''Ah, my dear Hunter. You have been absent from our company much too long, sir.''

''My loss, I assure you, madame,'' Jared said as he bowed elegantly over the first lady's hand, then tucked it into the crook of his arm as they strolled the aisle to admire the potted flowers.

''I had hoped you had come to accept my offer of a post with us, Captain. Mr. Lincoln needs loyal men as guards, now more than ever.''

From the very first, Mary Lincoln had expressed concern for the safety of the president. President-elect Abraham Lincoln, heeding the advice of his Pinkerton guard, had slipped secretly into Washington for his inauguration because of an assassination threat. Furious at her husband's undignified entrance into the White House, Mary had soon hired personal guards, and had been after Jared ever since.

''You've chosen most of the president's security guard,'' Jared reminded the plump, petite brunette. ''You know those men are loyal and efficient.''

''Yes, but Mr. Lincoln insists on milling among crowds and being available to anyone seeking an audience. I know he needs to in order to win reelection, but I worry so.''

Jared couldn't mistake the panic in her voice. ''You really are frightened, aren't you?'' he asked softly.

''More than you can possibly imagine, sir.''

Jared paused, unsure of the wisdom of relenting, then offered, ''Other obligations prevent me from taking a permanent post here. I won't be in Washington for the next week or so, and I must report to General Grant in mid-

January. Would it ease your mind if I spent the days surrounding the election with the President?''

Mary Lincoln's relief was visible. "Oh, yes. Those will be the most dangerous days."

Mrs. Lincoln brightened as they resumed their stroll past the roses, violets and mums that she described with expertise. Jared's concentration wavered, his gaze fixed on a field of gold and white down the aisle.

"Daisies are such expressive flowers," Mrs. Lincoln remarked. "They appear very fragile, yet can withstand fierce spring storms. Do you like daisies?"

Jared pictured Emily, on their wedding day, with daisies entwined in her hair. "I know someone who is very partial toward daisies."

"Your wife?"

Jared nodded.

"You've been remiss, sir, in not presenting her to us."

"Emily has been ill."

"Yes, I've heard, poor dear. As soon as you return from wherever it is you are going, however, you must begin escorting her about town. There has already been gossip, and the sooner you emerge into society together the better."

"What gossip?"

She didn't bother to hide her disdain of Washington's upper echelon of society. "They've thoroughly discussed Mrs. Hunter's Confederate ties, but that is natural, given the circumstances. Of more interest to them is why you live apart from your wife. I've heard speculation that Colonel Gardner doesn't recognize the marriage because of your...mixed blood. Others wonder if a marriage even took place. The worst comment I've heard is that the child she lost may not have been yours and you are planning to seek a divorce on grounds of adultery."

"Good Lord, that's so far from the truth!"

Mary's silence commanded an explanation.

"Our marriage was never meant to be permanent," Jared confessed. "Emily's brother forced us into a situation where getting married was the best solution. We agreed before the ceremony that the marriage was temporary and we would file for an annulment at the soonest opportunity.''

"Annulment is out of the question now that there is evidence you consummated—" Mrs. Lincoln blushed. "This conversation is most unseemly. Forgive me, sir, for speaking so bluntly."

"Please, Mrs. Lincoln, go on. I value your opinion."

"Very well, then. Captain Hunter, do you love your wife?"

"Yes."

"Does Mrs. Hunter care for you?"

"She did, once."

"Then I suggest you forget this foolishness about ending your marriage. If you are to regain her affection, you must start at once. A bouquet of flowers might help."

Regaining Emily's affection and trust would take more than a bouquet of flowers. But it couldn't hurt.

Emily circled the dining room table, plucking wilted flowers from the enormous arrangement delivered several days ago by the White House gardener.

"Beautiful, my dear," Papa commented.

"The blooms stayed fresh longer than I expected."

"I was referring to my daughter. Turn around."

Emily obliged with a graceful pirouette, ending with a deep curtsy that rustled the full silk skirt of delicate peach. The neckline of the gown's snug bodice was low, but not daring. Trimming ruffle extended to top short, puffy off-the-shoulder sleeves. A matching ribbon caught up the long curls that threatened to tumble down her back.

"You'll outshine the bride," Papa said.

"Thank you, Papa, but wait until you see Kate before you pass judgment. She's stunning in her bridal dress."

John pulled out his pocket watch. "Ready to go yet?"

"So early? The Drews' home is only minutes away."

"I would like a chance to speak with Charles Drew before the ceremony."

Emily didn't ask why. Likely Papa wished to discuss

official business with Kate's father, business Emily preferred to know nothing about.

Papa chuckled. "Besides, Frank may need an encouraging word or two. Last I saw him, he was awfully nervous."

Her hand hovered for an instant over a piece of browning fern. Reaching for it, she asked, "Is Jared with Frank?"

"I would imagine. Jared returned to Washington yesterday morning."

Emily remembered walking into Armory Square to find Eric Walters and Seth Jones gone. She hadn't expected Jared to act so swiftly. She hadn't been able to say goodbye to Eric.

To make her day completely awful, on her way home from the hospital she'd slipped a piece of paper to a courier. Kate had assured her the information she was passing was genuine but insignificant. Major Drew's agents had followed the courier, but the man had eluded capture. She would have to pass another note, tomorrow.

Emily gathered the refuse from the table and told her father, "I'll toss this into the trash while you have Sam bring the carriage around."

She went into the kitchen and tossed the bundle into the waste bin. She leaned against Hanna's worktable, her hand resting on her stomach to calm the butterflies fluttering wildly in anticipation.

Tucked away in the top drawer of her bedroom chest was the small card that had accompanied the flowers. They needed to talk when he returned, it said over Jared's signature.

Now Jared was back, would attend the wedding. Was she pinning too much hope on a brief embrace in a hospital ward and a bouquet of flowers? Could she bear it if Jared told her this afternoon that he wanted his freedom?

She heard Papa impatiently pacing in the foyer. Emily took a deep breath, squared her shoulders and pushed open the kitchen door.

They rolled along the streets of Washington and into the

countryside to the Drew home, an old Colonial mansion on the shore of the Potomac. Emily almost expected George Washington and Thomas Jefferson, in white powdered wigs and silver-buckled shoes, to appear amid the tall, white pillars to greet arriving guests.

With her father as escort, Emily entered the mansion. The huge front parlor had been decorated for the ceremony. Several rows of high-backed spindle chairs waited in dignified poise on either side of a short aisle. Streamers of white crepe, draped artfully over windows and the mantel, swayed lightly in the chill breeze from open French doors. Bright ribbons bowed the vases of flowers scattered on tables around the perimeter of the room and engulfed the podium against the far wall.

"Ah, there he is," Papa said, spotting Major Drew. "Why don't you have a seat, dear? I'll join you shortly."

Emily turned to select a seat that would allow a good view of the ceremony—and came face-to-face with Jared.

Her heart leaped.

He cleared his throat. "You look lovely," he said.

"Thank you."

"Did you receive the flowers?"

"They've taken over the dining room table. It's a beautiful arrangement."

Jared managed a smile. "Mrs. Lincoln is generous with her flowers. I'll have to take you to the White House and let her squire you through the greenhouse."

"I would like that."

After a long silence, Jared said, "We should go in. The rest of the guests are taking their seats."

Emily tucked her gloved hand into the crook of his arm. Through layers of fabric she felt his strength, his warmth. Her senses reeled with the aroma of wool and tobacco and a spicy fragrance she couldn't identify.

He walked slowly, and seemed reluctant to leave her after settling her in a chair on the aisle. Then, abruptly, he crossed to the podium to stand next to Frank.

We could be in a cave for all Kate knows, Emily thought

as she watched the bride enter on Major Drew's arm. Kate's emerald eyes sparkled as she lovingly stared up at Frank. Emily remembered the haste and confusion of her own wedding—Terrance scowling, Jared's nonchalance. The vows the chaplain demanded of Frank West and Katherine Drew were nearly identical to those the justice of the peace had asked of Emily Gardner and Jared Hunter.

Then she felt Jared's gaze. He was looking at her left hand, where the gold band still circled her finger, though currently covered by a glove. She saw the question in his eyes before he quickly looked away.

A gay mood prevailed as the guests partook of a light luncheon. At the trill of violins, the crowd moved to the third-floor ballroom. Jared appeared almost immediately, sweeping her out onto the floor. He held her gently and away as they glided through the waltz.

She felt a flush on her cheeks, from the exertion of the dance, and from the elation of following Jared's flawless lead around the ballroom. It would have been perfect if Jared hadn't seemed so far away, distracted.

"Jared?"

He looked down, his expression tight. "This probably isn't the time or place, but there are a few things we need to discuss. Would you mind if we went downstairs? The parlor should be deserted by now."

This was the moment she'd both dreaded and looked forward to since receiving the flowers and the card. Whatever he had to say would determine the course of the rest of her life.

"All right."

He waltzed her out the door, then ushered her down the stairs and into the parlor, which once again looked like a parlor. The wooden chairs had been removed, replaced by sofas and upholstered chairs. Jared closed the door and waved her to the sofa.

"This could take a while. Why don't you sit down?"

Her heart constricted. Tears threatened. Nothing in Jared's demeanor foreshadowed a pleasant conversation, much less the happy ending she'd prayed for.

Jared paced as he related his conversation with Mary Lincoln, repeating the first lady's assessment of the gossip spreading among social circles.

"I'd intended to give you your freedom quietly, but now that's impossible," he finished. "Whatever we decide to do will spread through this city like wildfire. Mrs. Lincoln is right about the absurdity of an annulment. If we file for a divorce, we would end up in a courtroom. One of us would have to prove cruelty or adultery. Of course, the whole thing could be academic. This war isn't over yet. You could end up a widow."

"No!" Emily jumped up, startling Jared into taking a step backward. After several heartbeats, Emily sank back into the sofa.

"I wasn't seriously considering the option," he said.

"I should hope not!"

Emily laid her head back against the cushion, waiting for Jared to outline the plan he'd devised to end their marriage, and do it with the least amount of damage.

When his silence became unbearable, she prodded him. "You have more acceptable options all worked out, I suppose."

"There really is only one, but how well it works depends on you, on whether or not you could accept the situation. I've made a lot of mistakes where you're concerned. I know I should have told you the truth about me, about my mission. I kept putting if off, telling myself there would be a better time, a better place. I hadn't figured out how I was going to cope with your horror when you learned the truth. And then, in Richmond, time ran out."

Jared ran his hand across the back of his neck and lowered his voice. "For weeks I dreamed of bright brown eyes as you told a Confederate lieutenant you loved him. But the loss I felt then couldn't compare to the despair when you had the miscarriage, watching your pale face for a sign that you would live. I vowed then I would stay out of your life, not hurt you anymore. I thought you could file for an annulment and be happy as Emily Gardner again. But the scandal could be disastrous. You would be scorned, and I can't let that happen."

Emily listened with her eyes lowered, inspecting her folded hands where they lay nervously in her lap. The longer Jared spoke, the more fearful Emily grew. Whatever Jared's plan was, it created such inner conflict that he delayed the telling. A flicker of gaslight off his highly polished black boots caught her eye. She glanced up only as far as his outstretched hands, grasped them, and rose as bidden.

Jared clasped her trembling hands to his chest. "I have no right to ask you, but I'm hoping that if you could love a Confederate called Jared Randall, that you could tolerate a Yankee named Jared Hunter. The two men aren't very different."

"Tolerate?"

"Could you abide keeping our marriage intact?"

Her heart pounded and her head spun with joy, until she realized why he offered. He blamed himself for a mission gone awry. He felt accountable and, more than his words, his tone and manner said he thought he'd failed deplorably. Out of misplaced honor, out of duty, Jared was offering to bear responsibility for their present dilemma.

Reluctantly Emily said, "We married because of Terrance's threats. To continue because of outsiders, because you feel responsible for me, would be a mistake. We'll get a divorce. I can live with gossip and scandal. I've done it before."

He squeezed her hands. "If that's what you truly want, we'll find a way to do so without causing a scandal. But before you decide, would you let me correct the biggest mistake I ever made?"

"Which was?"

"We were in a dark, dreary alley in Richmond. You were scared and breathless and disheveled from running. Remember?"

"Yes," she said softly, remembering the shouts of the patrol leader, her anger at Jared for insisting they leave Richmond without talking to the authorities. But mostly she remembered telling a stubborn, protective, buckskin-clad male that she loved him.

"Can you still say the words?" he asked.

Emily wondered at how easy it was to repeat the words, how simple to change the name. "I love you, Jared Hunter."

Jared cupped her face with his hands. "And I love you, Emily Hunter. You're the piece of my soul that makes it complete. We belong together, love. Don't run this time."

Emily flung her arms around Jared's neck. "Oh, Jared..." she whispered through joyous tears.

He sighed, "I've made a mess of things again, haven't I?"

"Oh, no, not this time." She let her kiss tell him how much she liked his latest scheme.

"I feel so wicked!" Emily whispered loudly.

"Wicked?"

"Thoroughly wanton," Emily admitted as she perched on Jared's bed, smoothing the rough woolen blanket that served as his bedspread. "I've never had a man whisk me away to his private domain before."

"Not much of a domain," Jared pointed out. "And you were hardly whisked. We must have taken leave of twenty people before we left the reception."

So they had. One of those people had been Major Charles Drew, who'd slipped a piece of paper into the palm of her hand— the information she would recopy, then pass to a Confederate courier tomorrow. She'd snuck it into her reticule, determined not to give it another thought, at least not tonight.

Jared sat down on the bed and grasped her hand, running his thumb over her wedding band. "Maybe I shouldn't have brought you here. I should court you first with bouquets of flowers and boxes of chocolates, woo you with candlelight dinners and rides in the park."

"I don't need flowers and candy. I need to be with you."

With a fingertip, he traced the gown's neckline, from her shoulder down to her breastbone. With spread fingers he caressed the hollow of her throat, then followed the curve of her collarbone.

"I think I like this gown," he said.

"We should have stopped at Papa's so I could change. This gown has dozens of fastenings down the back."

"I'll savor undoing each one."

Emily smiled. "I was thinking of tomorrow morning, when we have to get me back into it."

"Minx. God, how I've missed you," he whispered harshly, before claiming a kiss that sent months of separation spiraling into oblivion. Jared tasted the sweet honey of her mouth, hungry for the banquet of her body. Without hesitancy, she leaned into the passion, begging for more.

Jared broke the kiss and leaned back, only to fall prey to glazed brown eyes, desire shining in their depths. Jared recognized her need, for it matched his own.

His eyes followed where his hand roved, over the swell of her breast under layers of silk. "I can't tell you how many times I've dreamed of you lying next to me in this bed."

"What did you dream?"

"Do you still have that white nightgown?"

"Not with me."

"We'll skip that part for tonight." Jared got off the bed and pulled Emily up. "Let's get out of these clothes."

Emily pushed Jared's shirt from his shoulders, nuzzling her nose in his chest hair as she uncovered her favorite pillow. Jared blazed a molten trail of kisses down her spine as each button gave way, sending shivers of delight clear down to her toes.

"A corset? These are the damnedest contraptions."

"Civilized ladies wear corsets."

"Mine doesn't. How can you breathe in this thing?" Jared grabbed his bowie knife and cut the lacing.

"It's not the corset that is making me breathless."

Gown and shirt, pants and petticoats, mingled on the floor, discarded by lovers inattentive to their plight.

He took his time unpinning her hair, watching each curl drop softly to her shoulders before his fingers combed the mahogany strands. Emily drew lazy patterns across his lower back, then lowered the design until the muscles in his buttocks constricted.

"It's as if we were back at the farmhouse. Remember?" she whispered, recalling Jared's talent in the bedroom. Only Jared could make her body hum until it shouted.

"How could I forget?" Jared's dizzying kiss said he remembered every minute.

Jared lowered them onto the bed.

She closed her eyes, enjoying the enchanting path his hand wandered. For eons she endured the sweet torture. Patience might be a virtue, but, feeling anything but virtuous, Emily pulled him down, covering his face and neck with wet kisses. Hooking her heel behind his knee, Emily drew his leg between hers, clamping it tightly between her thighs.

"Easy, tigress. We have all night," Jared murmured, his control waning at Emily's insistent gyration.

"Heartless man," she said accusingly. "I'll go insane if you make me wait any longer."

Jared clung to the thin thread of dominance over his body's demand for satisfaction. He eased her legs open, petting her inner thighs before sinking his fingers into her heat. Emily trembled at the contact and hissed his name.

"Stop me if I hurt you," Jared whispered, slowly sliding his swollen member into her hot sheath.

"I'll hurt if you stop," Emily warned, encouraging him with pressing hands and arching hips.

Buried deep within her, Jared sought a moment's respite to master his screaming passion, but Emily gave no quarter. He surrendered to the mating rhythm.

Male to female, mate to mate, they coupled in a flawless cadence, to the beat of healing hearts. Stroke for penetrating stroke, kiss for searing kiss, they matched movement for binding movement. Lustful yearning, charged by loving tenderness, spurred them to swift, exhilarating completion.

Emily cried out her joy. Rivulets of pleasure surged through her centermost being. Jared yielded his control and, with a forward tilt of his hips, kept their joining locked snug to relish each velvet ripple of desire's consequence.

Jared knew he should move, or Emily would suffocate under his weight. Satiated, in harmony with himself and the world after so many months of turmoil, he hated to budge. Such peace, he thought, and all because he'd made love to his wife.

Gently he brushed a clump of sweat-dampened hair from her cheek. "My wife," he said aloud, reverently.

"Who did you expect to find beneath you?" she asked dryly.

"Part of me knew," he answered, thrusting forward the part of his body to which he was referring. "Hell, it's hard to last inside you. I never had that problem with other women."

Emily's eyes narrowed. "Other women?"

"Since I met you, I've barely looked at another woman. You've ruined me for all others, Mrs. Hunter."

"My pleasure, Captain Hunter."

Jared laughed and rolled. Emily automatically snuggled against him. He pulled her in tight. Then her hand drifted from his shoulder to his chest, fingers raking through his hair, until her palm rested over his heart.

There was so much he wanted to tell her, to explain, and to apologize for—but not tonight. Any harsh words—and he was sure there would be several—could wait for daylight. The problems could wait for cooler heads to ponder

Chapter Twenty

"Emily, there isn't one person in that house who doesn't know you didn't sleep in your bed last night."

Her hand poised on the doorknob, Emily slumped a fraction. Jared was right, she admitted, looking down at the shoes dangling from her hand. Sneaking into her father's house was childish, but entering in rumpled evening attire was a brazen announcement that she didn't care to make.

She turned pleading eyes on Jared.

He came to her rescue. "Would you feel better if I checked to see if the hall is clear?" He smiled at her undisguised relief and opened the door. "No one there."

Emily scooted past, the rustle of silk echoing through the vacant hallway.

"Want some help?" Jared whispered loudly when she reached the third stair.

She stopped and turned. "Like you *helped* earlier this morning? Better you should find Hanna and have her make us some breakfast. I'm hungry!"

Jared watched her scamper up the stairs—a flurry of peach silk and drooping mahogany hair—and into her bedroom.

Colonel Gardner appeared in the doorway to the parlor, offering a cup of what Jared hoped was coffee.

"I gather you two have reconciled," John commented.

"More like agreed to reconcile," Jared answered, then took several swallows of hot, strong coffee that jolted his system into false revival. He sat on the edge of a leather chair, shunning the comfort of padded cushions.

"Long night?" John observed wryly.

"Negotiations take time," Jared said, remembering the ferocity and frequency of those sessions—once before midnight, again in the wee hours of the morning, and again as they began dressing this morning.

In between, they had whispered endearments and dozed a bit. Mostly, they'd clung to one another, as if afraid to sleep, afraid to wake and find the other gone.

"Are you moving in here?" John inquired casually.

A niggling sensation of something awry made Jared look at the colonel closely.

"We haven't discussed living arrangements."

"You are more than welcome here. Emily's room isn' large, but there's another at the end of the hallway you might find comfortable."

With sudden insight, Jared saw John Gardner from a new perspective, that of son-in-law. Would the suddenly real, blatantly imposed marriage to Emily affect the friendship he shared with John? Jared hoped not, for Emily's sake, as well as his own.

"Sir, I know we haven't always agreed where Emily is concerned. If you have doubts about my love for your daughter or my ability to take care of her, I'd like to hear them now, before she comes down."

"I don't doubt you love her. My reasons for offering have nothing to do with your finances, either. It's a matter of practicality, and maybe selfishness on my part, because of the timing. I think it would be easier on Emily to live among people who love her while you're gone."

With sobering clarity, Jared understood John's discomfort, and he asked, "Grant approved the mission?"

"I found out yesterday. General Grant feels your proposed mission worthwhile. You should receive formal orders within a week or so."

Jared heard the whisper of rustling silk from the hallway. Emily had come downstairs, he was sure of it, and too quickly to have changed clothing. But she didn't come into the parlor. Was she intentionally eavesdropping, or was she simply too embarrassed to appear before her father in the same gown in which she'd taken leave of him yesterday?

How much had she heard? How much did he want her to hear?

"Does Emily know anything of this mission?" he asked John.

John thought a moment. "I haven't said anything to her directly, but she may have guessed that you'll be taking on an assignment soon, because Kate has been complaining about how little time she and Frank will have together before he has to leave in January. What do you plan to tell Emily?"

The answer came easily, not only because Emily stood beyond the doorway, but because he'd learned his lesson well. He'd deceived her once, and they'd both paid too high a price.

"Everything I'm allowed to." When John seemed about to protest, Jared asked, "Isn't it likely that Frank will tell Kate where he's going and something of what he'll be doing?"

"Well, yes, but... Oh, I see what you mean."

Jared could understand John's wish to shield Emily from further pain or sorrow. To John Gardner, Emily was still his little girl, and, since Terrance's death, his only child. He hadn't yet learned to think of Emily as a grown woman.

Confirming Jared's conclusions, John asked, "Then at least wait until after Christmas to tell her. God knows she's been through enough."

Emily swept through the door, clearly miffed.

Colonel Gardner looked horrified, but Jared couldn't hold back a tight smile.

Shoulders thrust back, hands on her hips, Emily glared at her father and scolded, "Papa, how could you! If you think I'll allow you to treat me as a child, you are very much mistaken.''

John tossed back, ''How long, child, have you been eavesdropping from outside the door?''

Emily flinched, but didn't back down. ''Long enough!''

Sensing the initial moves of a battle, Jared quickly resorted to diversionary tactics. ''I thought you were changing,'' he commented to Emily.

''I was... Well, I tried, but I couldn't reach these impossible buttons down the back and came looking for you.''

''I offered my assistance before, and you turned me down. Changed your mind?''

Emily's anger visibly waned at his purposely suggestive offer. She pursed her lips, withholding whatever retort she wanted to make but had thought better of. After a glance at her father, she nodded and led the way to her bedroom.

''Turn around, and let's get you out of this delightful confection again,'' Jared said.

''Be good,'' she warned, wary of ulterior motives.

''I'm not good,'' Jared said to her stiff back, deftly releasing her from the dress. ''I'm magnificent, wonderful and fabulous, or so my wife told me last night.''

''And conceited, arrogant and vain,'' she countered, but Jared felt her soften. He wrapped his arms around her waist and pulled her against him. There was no resistance.

''I shouldn't have snapped at Papa,'' Emily said just above a whisper. ''I'll have to apologize.''

''You can't blame him for wanting to protect you. Lord knows, I'm guilty of the same feelings. And just how long *were* you standing there, listening?''

Chagrined, she admitted, ''Something else I need to apologize for. I wasn't sure whether or not to interrupt, and then, when I overheard what you were discussing, I just couldn't seem to help myself. Oh, Jared, I just got you back, and now you're leaving. This damn war...''

She sniffed.

Jared tightened his hold. ''We have a little over two months before we even have to think about it.''

"And you'll tell me everything you can?"

"After my final orders arrive. I want to see what's in them first. Grant may have revised my original proposal. Let's just take things a step at a time, all right?"

He felt more than heard her assenting sigh. Then she asked, "Is your mission terribly dangerous?"

"Not unless I get careless, which I have no intention of doing," Jared pledged as he turned her around. "I've managed to come through this war with minor scrapes and bruises. Now that I have someone to come back to, I'll be extra careful."

Emily ran a finger along the puffiness under his eye. "You're tired."

"And hungry."

"We have a great deal of talking to do, don't we?"

"One night of glorious lovemaking does not a marriage make?" he teased.

She managed a small smile. "No, but it was a spectacular beginning."

"How about breakfast and a nap before we undertake this formidable task?"

Emily wrapped her arms around his neck and hugged him hard. "I love you."

"I love you, too," Jared responded, returning the embrace.

Later that morning, using Major Drew's note as a guide, Emily sat at her father's desk and penned a brief message to Colonel Bricker about an upcoming Union troop movement along the Mississippi River.

Having been assured by Kate that the information Emily received to pass on to Bricker was accurate but harmless, Emily pushed her reservations aside.

Maybe today the courier would lead Major Drew's men to Noah, and she would be free of her agreement with Bricker.

Zeke stuck his head into the room. "Sam's waitin' with

the carriage, Missy Emily. You sure you want to go up to the hospital today?''

Today, of all days, she didn't want to go anywhere. And if Zeke thought her actions strange, what would Papa think? What would Jared think?

"I promised one of the soldiers I would help him with a letter today." Which, thank goodness, was true, in case anyone took it into his head to check. "He would be very disappointed if I didn't keep my promise."

"But seein' as how Cap'n Hunter is here and all—"

Emily waved off the observation. "Jared is sound asleep, so he won't miss me for the next hour or so. And Papa will be at the War Department until nearly supper." Emily forced a bright smile. "Which means I'm free to go to the hospital and take my usual walk home."

A wide grin split Zeke's face. "Guess a body can't argue with that. I'll tell Sam you'll be right out."

After Zeke left, Emily folded the message and put it in her pocket. This was the second piece of information she would pass to a courier, and she prayed it was the last.

Kate had urged Emily to tell her father. But there were times when Papa forgot that his little girl had grown up, and, knowing she shared the blame for his attitude, Emily needed time to change his perception. He would demand that she stop meeting Noah's couriers, despite how carefully Major Drew's agents guarded her, or how close they were to capturing Noah.

And Jared? They'd eaten a hearty breakfast and returned to her bedroom. Jared had fallen asleep, but, knowing she had to meet the courier today, she'd slipped out of bed and dressed. Hiding her activities from Jared might be difficult. And she felt guilty keeping a secret, especially since Jared had promised to tell her about his mission.

If she told Jared now, he, too, would interfere. He might not demand that she cease passing messages, but he would certainly insist on becoming involved.

Emily pulled on a lightweight cloak and headed for the

carriage. Maybe today would see an end to the affair, and she wouldn't have to tell either Jared or Papa.

To Emily, the next days felt magical.

They moved into the larger bedroom at the end of the hall. Jared's few personal items fit easily in drawers next to her own. His uniforms hung beside her gowns, his shaving gear rested near her brushes. At night, his gold watch lay atop her jewelry box.

Jared spent mornings at the War Department, afternoons at the White House. Emily continued to visit the soldiers at Armory Square Hospital.

Emily listened to conversations between her husband and father as they discussed their daily activities. Only when their talk centered on battles or military plans did she feel ill at ease.

Kate and Frank West came for supper one night. After the meal, Kate told her the courier had again eluded the agents. Emily decided to keep her secret through at least one more encounter.

Only in the dark, wrapped in the circle of Jared's arms, could she talk about her confinement in Richmond. She was careful not to mention Colonel Bricker's pressure, but she did tell him of Sergeant Taylor's protectiveness and Captain Morgan's one intrusion into her room.

"Sergeant Taylor literally threw Morgan out of the room. It surprised me to see Morgan after all those months."

Jared was quiet for a moment before asking, "You don't know why he was still in Richmond?"

"No. I have no idea."

Jared explained how he and Nathan Wilkins had hidden from patrols until, believing the Confederates were using her only as bait to catch Cougar, they left for Washington.

"I swear, love, if I'd known they would hold you for so long, I would have come in after you."

"There were days when I hated you, and others when I prayed you'd walk through the door and spirit me away. I shouldn't have run from you."

"I shouldn't have let you run."

One afternoon, Emily came home from the hospital to find Jared in the library, writing.

Jared looked up as she entered the room. "The president is giving a campaign speech tonight that I want to attend, so I took the afternoon off. Since you weren't home yet, I decided to write to my parents."

"Your mother will be pleased. There are six sheets here!"

He pulled her down onto his lap. "It's the easiest letter I ever wrote—it's all about you. That's almost our whole history on those pages."

Jared had told her about his parents. She could picture a bear of a man standing before an adobe ranch house. Tucked under Edward Hunter's arm stood a petite raven-haired woman named Anna.

"I think I'm jealous," Emily admitted. "You write beautiful letters, yet I've never received one." At his questioning look, she added, "I saw the letter you wrote to Mrs. Walters."

"That's one letter I wish I hadn't had to write."

"Why did you tell Mrs. Walters you were a Yankee? Why did you take such a risk?"

"I thought if I was brutally honest about my identity, she'd believe I was also telling the truth about the rest."

"Yet you couldn't be honest with me?"

"Not then, love. But I wish with all my heart I'd told you later. Then you wouldn't have run in Richmond, and you might not have lost...lost the baby."

Emily heard his pain, his regret. She wrapped her arms around his neck and held him for a long, long time.

The following afternoon, Jared took her to meet Mary Lincoln and tour the White House conservatory. Exhausted after spending the afternoon with the first lady, Emily said as they left the mansion, "She must have thanked me a dozen times for your agreeing to spend some time by the president's side. It must be awful for her, believing someone wants to harm the man she loves. Do you think some-one will try?''

"The president has numerous enemies. Too, there are always men foolish enough to think that by killing one man they can alter the course of history.''

Jared felt her hand tighten through his heavy coat sleeve and looked down. Emily tried to smile up at him. He tried to ease her fears. "There are several capable men guarding the president, and he rarely leaves the White House. I don't think the danger warrants the degree of Mary's anxiety.''

As the election neared, Jared spent more and more time with Mr. Lincoln. Emily tried not to begrudge the evenings Jared accompanied the president to various functions. When election day came, Abraham Lincoln, much to his surprise, won. As if the victory were a signal for some great machine to operate again, Washington turned its attention once more to the war effort.

The plan was simple and, according to Jared, absolutely necessary. Emily couldn't decide which man was more in-sane, Jared for proposing and volunteering for the mission, or General Grant for approving.

"You're deliberately going into Libby Prison?''

"Yes," Jared confirmed.

She had known Jared was leaving, had accepted that he was a soldier. She now knew which of his highly publicized exploits were true, because Jared had untangled the myriad accounts. Expecting some similar mission, she hadn't been concerned.

"Emily?" He made her return his gaze with a forefinger pressed against her chin. "If you're thinking that I've lost my senses, I haven't. I know the mission is a bit unortho-dox—''

"Unorthodox?" Emily shrieked. "Preposterous is more appropriate, or maybe bizarre! Do you really believe you can help someone escape from Libby Prison? No one has been able to break out for at least a year.''

"Sweetheart, it's not just one man we're concerned about, but all the prisoners."

"Naturally," Emily said caustically. "Why settle for one man, when you can lead a revolt of several hundred unarmed, despondent, hungry men?"

"You're jumping to false conclusions. I'm not going into Libby to help anyone escape, though Lord knows I would relish the chance to try. But I can't, not if the threats and rumors are true."

Jared's splayed fingers raked though his hair; it was a habit of his when he was truly worried. "We don't know if the Rebs have actually done it, but through several channels they've intimated that they've dug a pit in the bowels of Libby, and filled it with enough explosives to demolish the prison. They've threatened to turn Libby into a rubbish heap if any prisoner tries to escape, or if Grant attacks Richmond.

"And Grant *will* attack Richmond, if Lee stays entrenched in the city. The threat to flatten Libby won't stop him. After enduring the hardships of that hellhole, those men deserve to walk out. It's my job to make sure they have the chance."

Too shocked to sympathize, Emily asked, "How do you propose to get into the prison—go up to the door and knock?"

"Stop it! Don't do this, Emily. Don't make me regret telling you."

Emily knew she had gone too far, letting her anger mask her blinding fear—fear that if Jared went into Libby, he would never come out again, not alive, anyway. How could Grant order Jared into a death trap? How could Jared believe that one man could prevent dozens of guards blasting the building to shards if they wished?

General Grant thought Jared capable of averting disaster in Libby Prison. The responsibility was staggering when one considered the hundreds of men involved, all high-ranking Union officers. Emily's concern was for one Union officer, the one whose shirtfront she was crushing in her fists. Resting her brow on his chest, she asked, "If I begged you not to go, would you refuse this assignment?"

"Ah, love. Please don't ask."

She heard his pride and devotion to duty, along with the plea for understanding and sanction. With or without her approval, Jared would obey the official orders delivered by Grant's aide this morning.

"Then I won't ask."

"That's my girl. I knew you would come around."

"I will never come around," Emily stated. "I know I can't change your mind, but I don't have to like what you're doing."

"That makes two of us," Jared said, then shrugged. "Actually, that makes several of us. Nobody likes the idea, but those involved in the operation recognize the need for someone to get in there and find out if they're bluffing."

"Why you?" she asked, punching his chest feebly with her clenched fists.

"Can you imagine them keeping Cougar anywhere other than Libby? The person who goes in must be someone the Confederates won't transfer to another prison."

Given Jared's reputation, the Confederates would want him in Richmond. To finally, though belatedly, have Cougar incarcerated would delight the Rebel leadership. They would keep their renowned prisoner handy for interrogation.

"Listen, love," Jared said soothingly, "there isn't as much physical danger as you may be imagining. I'll tell you the rest, but you must promise not to discuss the details with anyone."

Emily soon learned that Jared had good reason to require her silence. Several lives were at stake. Any leak of information could hang them all.

Disguised as a Rebel patrol, a carefully chosen unit would accompany Jared to Libby's gate. The escort included Frank West, who would command the operation once Jared entered the prison. Lieutenant Thomas Reed, with his ability to mimic a Georgia accent, would knock on Libby's door and relinquish the prisoners— Jared and Lieutenant Robert Atkins.

"Who's Atkins?" Emily asked.

"A member of Grant's staff. Bob could sell snake oil back to the snakes, or, in this case, weasel information from the guards without them knowing what's happening."

"He's only a lieutenant," Emily mused. "Will they keep Atkins in Libby?"

"We're hoping they transfer Atkins, but only after we're sure of the situation. Part of Frank's responsibility will be to watch for Atkins and rescue him if possible. If the Rebs don't transfer him, we'll have to find another way of getting the information out of the prison."

Nathan Wilkins also would go. He would keep a safe distance from Richmond, but could provide invaluable assistance with his knowledge of the city and the government's buildings.

Each would contribute unique talents to the special unit. They would stay in the area, monitor the news, listen and watch for outward signs of trouble. They would be near the prison when Grant attacked Richmond and use the confusion to enter Libby to help Jared if necessary.

Jared tried to make the prison stay sound like a boring interlude in a run-down hotel. Emily couldn't quite accept his calm attitude, but, unable to put into words why she had the awful feeling that something dreadful and terrifying was being overlooked, she said nothing.

Chapter Twenty-One

Emily knew without opening her eyes that Jared wasn't in their bed. She snuggled deeper under the quilt, pretending he had only left for the War Department. The denial worked, until a draft robbed the quilt's warmth.

She opened her eyes. All but one of Jared's uniforms hung in the wardrobe. The saddlebags he'd packed last night no longer sat in the corner.

Emily got out of bed and pulled on the woolen dressing gown Jared had given her for Christmas, a day she would always remember with mixed emotions—as her and Jared's first Christmas together, and as the day General Sherman wired Lincoln with the news of Savannah's surrender. Sherman's devastating march through Georgia had crippled not only the state, but the entire South. General Grant's prediction of Union victory this spring seemed more possible than ever.

She tied the sash. The rough-textured dressing gown pricked against flesh still sensitive from Jared's impassioned lovemaking. She was sore all over from the bittersweet exertion of last night's farewells. Determined to keep her promise to Jared not to succumb to melancholy, Emily counted her blessings.

Her life wouldn't be completely bleak while Jared undertook his mission. She had friends to keep her company.

Kate would come later this morning. They had decided, weeks ago, to spend this awful day together.

During the upcoming weeks, she would play hostess for Papa when he entertained and help Hanna with the cleaning and cooking. The almost daily trips to Armory Square Hospital also would help the days pass quickly. The patients welcomed her visits, and Emily enjoyed the work.

It was a relief, now that winter had come, to ride home from the hospital in the carriage. Union agents had arrested Noah and three of his couriers. There would be a trial, but, considering the wealth of evidence taken in the raid, Major Charles Drew graciously decided Emily needn't testify. Since circumstances had resolved themselves well, she'd seen no reason to inform Papa or Jared.

Emily reached for her brush. The dressertop seemed empty without Jared's shaving gear. She touched the circular indentation in the dresser scarf where his mug and brush normally sat. His humidor, the finely carved wooden box that held Jared's cigars, nestled against her jewelry box.

She opened the humidor—and froze.

Atop the few cigars sat Jared's watch, the gold timepiece he valued so highly. She chided herself for a flash of panic. Naturally, Jared wouldn't take his watch, though he considered it his lucky charm. The guards at Libby would confiscate anything of value from incoming prisoners. Jared wouldn't risk losing the keepsake.

She opened the watch and stared at the picture inside, the portrait Papa had given Jared to help identify a young woman in Adairsville. Jared had cut the picture down to size and placed it inside his watch.

Maybe she should have a new portrait taken while Jared was away, as a surprise for when he returned. The old picture would always be a reminder of the secrecy that had led to so much pain. She vividly remembered Colonel Bricker disclosing Jared's true identity, telling her that Jared was Cougar.

Emily closed the watch. Bricker was in Richmond, no

longer a threat. With his agents incarcerated, and no proof of her involvement in their capture, she was safe. Bricker couldn't harm her or anyone she loved. Or could he?

Libby Prison was in Richmond. Soon Jared would enter the prison and be at the mercy of the Rebs. Emily trembled.

Three times she'd passed messages, in her handwriting, to a courier. Had those messages been forwarded to Bricker? Would Bricker talk to Jared, show him the notes? Presented with damning evidence, would Jared believe she had willingly spied for the Confederates?

"Dear God, what have I done?" she whispered.

It was well past dawn. Jared could be deep into Virginia by now.

She had to find him, or at least send a message to let him know about the notes. Papa. If anyone knew how to get a message to Jared, it was Papa. Still clutching the watch, Emily flew down the stairs.

Two hours later, Emily was pacing the parlor floor. After she'd tearfully blurted out the whole story, Papa had left the house, hoping to catch Jared. She heard the door open and booted feet tread the hallway. She prayed Jared had returned, but Papa entered the parlor.

Papa reached for her hands. "There is an agent in Richmond named Donner who Nathan is supposed to contact. We hope they make contact before Jared enters the prison."

"Only hope? You aren't sure?"

John shook his head. Emily lifted her skirts and dashed for the stairs. She needed food, blankets, a rifle and ammunition, a map of Virginia.

"Emily!"

She spun, halfway up the stairs, at the sharpness in her father's tone. His eyes sympathetic, he said, "Five men's lives depend on the secrecy of this mission. We wouldn't want to do anything that might expose them, now, would we?"

Emily stood statue-still. The gently phrased warning was clear. Torn, she begged, "But, Papa..."

"No, Emily. Jared is a bright lad. Even if he doesn't get

the telegram, he'll figure out what happened. Have a little faith in him, darling.''

Blinking back tears, Emily stared at her father. Papa had the problem backward. Her faith in Jared was unshakable. Jared's faith in her could be ripped asunder. But was keeping Jared's trust worth endangering his life, the other men's?

John smiled wanly. ''Kate should be arriving any moment. Shouldn't you get ready to greet her?''

''Yes, Papa,'' Emily said softly, then turned and slowly climbed the stairs.

Jared preceded the guard into a small room on the prison's first floor. Despite the oddly flattering indignity of having manacles placed on his wrists, Jared had begun looking forward to Colonel Bricker's weekly visits, solely for the luxury of sitting on a chair. The prisoners had long ago fed their furniture into stoves provided for heating and cooking. The guards hadn't stopped the vandals. They were cold, too.

Colonel Bricker sat at the table, riffling through papers. ''Hunter,'' he said by way of greeting.

''Morning, Colonel.''

This was the third interrogation in as many weeks. Bricker always asked questions about Union activities in the South. Jared always gave vague answers.

Bricker slid a piece of paper across the table. Jared studied the list of atrocities committed against the Confederate States of America. Of the dozen charges listed, Jared recognized two of which he was guilty. He could confess to burning the ammunition dump and dynamiting the railroad trestle, if it was warranted. Both were acts of war, not crimes.

Resting his iron-wrapped wrists in his lap, Jared said, ''I'm flattered the Confederacy believes me so capable, Colonel. But even you must realize that no one man is responsible for everything on this list.''

Bricker presented a second sheet. Only three charges

graced this list: the kidnapping of Emily Gardner from Adairsville, the theft of a horse from Terrance Gardner, and impersonating a Confederate officer. Jared hadn't kidnapped Emily. She'd come willingly. And, technically, Emily had stolen Titan. Any witness would have to admit that Emily had led Titan out of Charlotte.

The third charge, impersonating a Confederate officer, was punishable by death—by hanging or firing squad. The Rebs assumed a Union soldier caught wearing a Confederate uniform was a spy. The Union held the same view of Rebs in Union dress. It was the only charge the Confederates could prove with a handy witness, Captain Gilbert Morgan. Jared had seen Morgan in Libby twice, at a distance. For some reason, as soon as Morgan appeared on the floor, the other guards took umbrage at his presence and drove him back down the stairs.

When planning this mission, the unit had thoroughly discussed the probability of Jared facing a trial and what charges could be brought. Nathan claimed the wheels of justice turned as slowly in the South as in the North. For a man of Jared's reputation, the Rebs would want a flashy trial, with multiple charges, and a public execution. The process could take months. By then, they hoped, Grant would have moved on Richmond. Jared had opted to take the risk.

"Maybe I can't prove them all," Bricker admitted. "But these last three, I might."

"It should be interesting to see how you prove I kidnapped my wife."

"Ah, yes, beautiful, darling Emily," Bricker said on a sigh. "A lovely, passionate woman. We grew...close while she was here. I was sorry to hear she lost the baby."

Jared couldn't believe the man's audacity. "You aren't seriously suggesting the baby she lost was yours?"

"Your *wife*—" Bricker emphasized the word "—was quite content to remain here, until I offered her a chance for revenge against the Yankees, against you in particular. Though I hated to let her go, I understood her need to reclaim her honor. Your wife, sir, has worked diligently with an associate in Washington, given us several pieces of valuable information.''

Jared voiced his instant reaction. "I don't believe it."

Bricker produced two small, creased pieces of paper.

Jared couldn't believe his eyes. If that wasn't Emily's handwriting, it was hauntingly similar.

Bricker gloated, "You have a choice, Hunter. We know you're responsible for several of the crimes on the other list. Confess to those, and we'll ignore the charges of kidnapping and horse theft. Otherwise, we'll ask Emily to come to Richmond to testify. I'm sure she'll be most cooperative."

Jared's gut churned. *Retreat and regroup*, his instincts screamed. "You bastard!" he shouted and bolted from his chair.

Bricker quickly motioned to the guard. "Take Captain Hunter back to the second floor, but don't take the chain off."

Jared didn't wait for the guard. He stormed out the door and up the stairs, heading for the thin mattress that marked his private space on the floor.

He ricocheted between belief and disbelief. Had Emily toyed with him all these months, coldly using him to glean bits of information to send back to her lover? His heart screamed, *No*. His head whispered, *Maybe*.

Jared could picture Emily seated at her father's mahogany desk, her slender hand guiding the pen. Why? Bricker said revenge. How? Not difficult, in spy-riddled Washington.

He struggled to push the turmoil aside, to concentrate not on Emily, but on the hard evidence Bricker had presented. The notes. What bits of intelligence had they contained?

He mulled over the note's contents, the dates, how Emily could have learned the details. Trivia, he judged the information, not worth the time or the effort to pass it, not compared with other intelligence he remembered discussing with Colonel Gardner over the supper table, with Emily in attendance.

Bricker had implied there were other notes. What was in them? Jared frowned. If Emily truly wanted revenge, she could have told the Rebs of the purpose of this mission. *Dear God.* His heart sank to his toes. He swallowed hard.

Then a gentle wave of relief washed away the terror.

Emily had known about this mission for months. If Emily wanted revenge, she would have given Bricker the details. And *that* would have been the note Bricker produced and gloated over.

For whatever reason, Emily had passed useless information to the Rebs. But unless Bricker displayed a note concerning this mission, Jared decided, he wouldn't lose sleep over it, or let Bricker goad him into doing something stupid. As for Emily's reasons, well, he would just have to wait a few months, until he got home, to find out why she'd done it—and why she hadn't trusted him enough to tell him if she'd been coerced.

In the meantime, other matters took precedence, like whether or not Bricker would press charges immediately. The thought of a noose around his neck left little room for other concerns.

"The snow melted while you were gone," Lieutenant Robert Atkins said blandly, lowering himself to sit on the plank floor.

Jared opened his eyes, but didn't move. The light hurt his eyes, but he kept them open. Through the stench of unwashed bodies, Jared caught a whiff of warm, fresh air, a definite sign of spring.

For almost two months, he and Atkins had subtly questioned guards and prisoners. But with spring fast approaching, and no definite conclusions, Jared had taken a direct course of action. Knowing the punishment, Jared had slugged a guard. Taken to a cell in the bowels of the prison, where any dynamite pit had to be located, Jared had endured his two-week punishment in solitary along with the rats and slime—and Captain Gilbert Morgan.

Morgan, it turned out, not only blamed Cougar for his fall from grace, but for his present post—assigned to guard the lowest level of Libby among the solitary cells. Not allowed to carry a weapon, given the most menial chores, Morgan was as much a prisoner of the Rebs as Jared.

Jared now knew why Bricker had never pressed charges. Controlling Morgan on the witness stand would prove impossible. The man still ranted about his *report*, the packet of papers that Jared had burned months ago. Morgan might testify that he'd seen Jared in a Confederate uniform, but he wouldn't stop there, and Bricker knew it. Given a platform from which to vent his accusations of ill-treatment by both Cougar and the Confederate army, Morgan would destroy any possibility of Bricker getting a conviction.

Jared turned on his side, ignoring the pain of bruises both old and fresh. Bound at wrist and ankle, he'd been unable to ward off all Morgan's vicious kicks and blows.

"The pit doesn't exist," Jared said quietly.

Atkins nodded. "They tell me I'm leaving in a couple of days. Rumor has it there's renewed fighting around Petersburg. The Rebs figure they'll need space for higher ranking officers. I hate leaving you in here, Hunter."

"I'll survive. Just get word to Frank."

Several days later, Jared found himself in solitary for no perceivable offense. Obviously furious, Colonel Bricker entered the cell.

"They're all dead." Bricker ground out the words. "It was Atkins they were after, wasn't it?"

Jared's stomach churned. Faces flashed through his head. Frank, Tom, Bob, Nathan...dead, all dead. No, they weren't dead. They couldn't be dead.

"I don't know what you're talking about."

Bricker scoffed. "I've been telling you all along that your wife betrayed you, Hunter. She told us if we transferred either you or Atkins, someone would attempt a rescue. We were ready for them, killed them all."

Jared had concluded, though her reasons weren't clear to him, that Emily had worked with someone, possibly Charles Drew, to plant insipid intelligence. Had all Emily's notes been carefully screened, or had she passed along some of her own?

No. Emily loved him. She wouldn't betray him or the others in the company. He couldn't begin to doubt now, not when his sanity depended on her sweet voice calling him back, not when returning to Emily was his only goal.

Then Bricker tossed a silver flask onto the dirt floor. Jared recognized the flask immediately as Frank West's, and knew for certain that Bricker was lying. According to their plan, Frank had purposely left the flask behind. Knowing Jared would likely be questioned if Atkins were rescued, the flask served as a signal to Jared that the mission had succeeded.

"We took this off the leader, a big blond guy," Bricker stated. "Recognize it? Who is he, Cougar?"

"You're wasting your time, Bricker. I don't know why anyone would want to rescue Atkins."

"Captain Morgan," Bricker called out.

Jared snapped to alertness.

"Yes, sir?" Morgan drawled, entering the cell.

"See if you can prod his memory," Bricker ordered, then stomped out of the cell.

Jared glanced from Morgan's evil grin to the open cell door. Futile, he judged the momentary thought to escape. He might get through Morgan, but not the rest of the guards, not without a weapon, not with his ankles manacled.

Morgan laughed hysterically, then pulled a knife.

Jared tensed. "Put it away, Morgan. If I yell, the other guards will come running."

"Ain't no other guards down here. I can do with you what I please, and nobody's gonna know."

"What do you mean, no other guards? There are always at least three assigned to solitary."

"Commandant Turner pulled out half the guards this

morning, sent them to General Lee.'' Before Jared could ponder the significance of the statement, Morgan waved his knife and continued, ''So there's just you and me, Hunter. Your memory getting any better, Yankee? Remember my report, you son of a bitch? You took my report and ruined my career!''

Morgan lunged. Jared jerked to the right and rolled. Morgan crashed into the dirt wall. Jared scrambled to his feet, fighting the restriction of the shackles on his ankles.

''Give it up, Morgan. They'll hang you for murder.''

''No...no.'' Slightly stunned, Morgan leaned against the wall. ''Not murder. Executing a dangerous criminal.''

''We're not in the execution yard. For once in your life, man, think about what you're doing!''

''I have, and I'm gonna carve a piece out of your hide.''

Jared spread his legs as far as the chain allowed and watched the knife as Morgan attacked. Jared sprang to the left, away from the weapon, and hurled both fists into Morgan's stomach. Morgan doubled and fell, but on his way down caught hold of Jared's trousers.

Jared struggled for balance, and lost. He fell backward and kicked. Morgan grabbed the chain between Jared's feet. Jared kicked again, but Morgan held on. A brief glint of light on steel warned Jared. He rolled hard, twisting the chain around Morgan's hand, wrenching the arm.

Morgan yelped and struck out at the nearest piece of his opponent. The knife slashed across Jared's calf. With a strength born of pain, Jared kicked wildly and connected with Morgan's jaw. Morgan moaned, fell back, and dropped the knife.

Jared lunged and grabbed the weapon. He looked down at the stunned guard, tempted to finish the fight with Morgan's death. Reason won over temptation. If he killed Morgan, the Rebs wouldn't hesitate to execute him on the spot.

''Get up, Morgan. Get out of here.''

Morgan groaned and opened his eyes. Anger, then fear contorted his face as he scrambled to leave the cell. He slammed the door behind him. Jared didn't relax until he heard the key turn in the lock.

Jared realized he was panting. Lack of food and exercise had taken a toll on his strength. Jared cut grime-encrusted strips from his ragged trousers and wrapped the bloody gash.

Then he picked up the flask. He looked down at his leg. Blood seeped through the makeshift bandage. Deciding there wasn't enough liquid in the flask to clean the wound, Jared took a swig of the spirits Frank had thoughtfully provided.

"We have to get out of here! Get up," Morgan commanded, tossing Jared's leg irons into a corner.

Jared rolled from his back onto his side and propped himself up on an elbow. His injured leg burned. The slightest movement shot pain streaking through his body. "You'll have to go without me, Morgan. I can't walk on his leg."

"Yes, you can. You're Cougar."

Jared shook his head in disbelief. Morgan had awakened him, mumbling about devils and hellfire. Something had scared Morgan, and he wanted Cougar to protect him from the demons.

Then Jared heard the cannons, muffled but insistent, and understood Morgan's terror. Jared tightened his hold on the knife, wondering if he had the strength to wield it if Morgan attacked.

"General Grant's out there, isn't he?" Jared taunted him. "That's why Commandant Turner pulled guards out the other day, to defend the city. Is General Lee losing, Morgan? Better run, man, while you've got the chance."

Morgan's eyes went wild, like those of an animal caught in a trap. "They're upstairs. There's Yankees swarming all over the prison. But you're going to help me. You're going to help me walk out of here. They won't shoot you."

"You're crazy if you think—"

Morgan's arm swung out, making a grab at Jared's

shoulder. Jared brought the knife up, holding it with both ironbound hands. But his reflexes were slow, dulled by malnourishment and fever. Morgan kicked, and the knife flew from Jared's hands.

Jared rolled toward the weapon. The blinding pain from his leg shot straight to his brain. He fought to stay conscious. He reached the knife just as Morgan grabbed the hilt. Jared felt his grasp slip.

The cell door banged open.

"Morgan!"

Morgan spun at the command in Bob Atkins's voice, careening off balance. Jared jerked at the knife, bringing Morgan down on top of him—and the knife.

Morgan groaned—a gurgling sound from deep in his throat— then went limp. Jared felt blood ooze over his hands, nearly choked on the sickening sweet odor. He used what little strength he had left to push Morgan's body aside. He saw Atkins standing in the doorway, Frank West behind him.

"About time you got here," Jared panted, then passed out.

Consciousness returned slowly, to a rocking motion, like that of a cradle gently controlled by a loving hand. Sounds, clacking rhythms, said he was on a train. He opened his eyes.

"You look like you've been through a war, partner," Frank said, grinning.

On a short burst of laughter, Jared said, "As if I haven't been through enough, you put me on a train, a goddamn train."

"Yeah, well, you weren't awake to protest when we tossed you on the litter. It was either take you to a field hospital or put you on this hospital train. We voted. The decision was unanimous to avoid the field surgeons."

Jared had seen enough field hospitals to understand the decision. Men went in wounded and came out mutilated, alive but missing limbs. Of course, Frank's actions might not make a difference. He knew the infection in his leg was bad, maybe bad enough to warrant amputation.

"I can't feel my leg."

"The doc shot something into the wound, said it would numb the pain. Must be working." Frank cleared his throat. "Ingenious system they've got here."

Jared gladly accepted Frank's abrupt change of subject. He looked around Frank's chest and realized Frank wasn't sitting, but standing. There were no beds in the car. Litters filled with men hung suspended in midair, the handles threaded through thick straps, like giant rubber bands, attached to the ceiling. The unusual, efficient setup was interesting, but not enough to divert Jared completely.

"Morgan?" Jared asked.

"Dead."

"Bricker?"

"Left him in your old solitary cell."

"Find your flask?"

"Even managed to get a refill. Want a swig?"

Frank pulled the flask from a back pocket and unscrewed the cap. He propped up Jared's shoulders as Jared tilted the flask back and drank.

"Oh, by the way, I've got something here you should see," Frank said, trading the flask for a telegram.

Jared squinted at the words, decoding as he read. Emily had tried to warn him. But why had she waited so long?

The train started to slow down. Almost home.

"Look," Frank said, "I'm going to put you into an ambulance, then fetch Emily and—"

"I'd rather you didn't. If the doctors tell me this damn leg has to come off, I don't want Emily there. Let me deal with this first, before I have to face her."

Frank mulled that over, then said, "Yeah, I guess I can understand that, but you know, she might already be at the hospital."

She might, but the odds were against it. But the odds hadn't played out in his favor lately.

He'd told Emily not to worry about him, that he would

return unscathed. The prospect of losing his leg hit him with full force. God, he only knew soldiering and ranching. Could he do either if the doctors amputated?

Jared knew men who'd lost limbs. Most had gone on to lead productive lives; others hadn't been able to cope, a few to the point of blowing their brains out.

Steam hissed. Brakes squealed.

Jared closed his eyes and took a calming breath. He would cope. Just as he'd endured the obstacles inherent with his mixed blood, he would persevere through this new impediment.

But would Emily?

She hadn't trusted him enough to confide her connection to Bricker. He hadn't kept his promise to Emily. If she didn't have faith in him now, would this latest complication shatter an already fractured marriage?

"Frank, if she's home, keep her there," he ordered, before sliding back into blessed oblivion.

Chapter Twenty-Two

Emily raised the tip of the pistol she had aimed at Dr.
Mitchell. "You must have other patients to attend to, Doctor."

"Your husband needs my attention!" the doctor blustered, motioning at Jared, who lay unconscious on the cot
behind her.

"I gather there's a problem," Frank West said softly,
striding down the aisle of the ward.

Emily relaxed on hearing Frank's voice. Frank was Jared's best friend, his partner. Frank would understand.

"The doctor and I are having a disagreement about Jared's treatment," Emily explained.

"Emily, if you shoot the doctor, he won't be able to treat
Jared at all."

"Precisely my point. What's it to be, Dr. Mitchell? Does
my husband stay here, or do I send Captain West for an
ambulance to take Jared home?"

"Mrs. Hunter, I understand your feelings, but take a
good look at your husband's leg," Dr. Mitchell urged.
"He's lucky the necrosis hasn't spread. Amputation is necessary."

"You mean amputation is easy. I won't let you operate.
I think I can save his leg. At least I have to try."

Mitchell finally relented, telling an orderly, "Fetch whatever equipment Mrs. Hunter needs.'' Then he faced her again. ''I wish you luck, Mrs. Hunter, but if the poisoning spreads, I'll amputate, with or without your permission.''

Dr. Mitchell spun on his heel and left the ward.

Her arms shook as she lowered the pistol, a little amazed that she'd won the argument, and none too sure that she should have argued at all.

''Where'd you get this?'' Frank asked, taking the gun.

''The gun is mine, Captain,'' a patient from across the aisle claimed. ''Mrs. Hunter tried to reason with the doctor, but he wouldn't listen. She knew I had this pistol, and when she asked to borrow it, I obliged.''

Frank shook his head, inspecting the weapon. ''This gun isn't loaded. She bluffed her way through.''

''Dr. Mitchell knew the gun wasn't loaded. Hospital rules forbid loaded firearms in the ward. Her actions only proved the lengths she was willing to go to protect her husband. I hope she knows what she's doing.''

The orderly asked, ''What do you need, Mrs. Hunter?

She needed courage, a supply of which the orderly couldn't provide. *Don't think, just do it!*

''I'll need a scalpel, towels, hot water, bandaging, a bottle of whiskey,'' she rattled off. ''I've already sent Sam for a poultice mixture.''

The orderly scurried off.

Frank asked, ''What do you want me to do?''

Emily looked up into Frank's worried face. ''Help me get his clothes off. And you may have to hold him down later.''

''Let's get to it.''

Emily struggled with Jared's shirt. Frank bent to help. Silently, they removed the remnants of Jared's uniform, piling the clothes in a muddied, bloodied heap. Emily drew the sheet over Jared's chest to cover his ribs. His thinness scared her as much as the infection in his leg.

''He promised me, Frank,'' Emily said, a single tear slipping from the corner of her eye. ''He said they wouldn't hurt him, that he would be all right.''

"He didn't lie to you, Emily. We really thought he would be safe, or we wouldn't have let him go into Libby. He was in a solitary cell when we found him. Captain Morgan was—"

"Morgan?" Emily cried.

"Jared didn't tell you Morgan was a guard at Libby?"

"No, he didn't."

"Thanks, Frank," came a weak, scolding voice. Jared's eyes were barely open, but he managed to glare at Frank. "I thought I told you to keep her away from here."

The thread of hope she'd clung to snapped. She'd known Jared would be upset with her, but she hadn't expected rejection.

Frank shot back, "She wasn't home to keep at home. And you're in no position to be giving orders here anyway. Shut up and go back to sleep."

The orderly returned, his arms laden with supplies. No matter what Jared thought of her now, she'd begun this task and she would see it through. She grabbed the whiskey from the orderly's hand and gave it to Frank.

"Get as much into him as you can."

"What the hell's going on?" Jared asked groggily, rising on his elbow.

Frank pushed him down. "Nothing we can't handle."

"What'd the doctor say?"

"He wanted to amputate. Emily wouldn't let him. Now, are you going to drink this, or do I have to pour it down you?"

Jared closed his eyes with a soft sigh, and when he opened them again, the anger had vanished, replaced by apprehension.

"Em? Do you think—?" he questioned softly, his vulnerability tearing at her meager self-confidence. And she had no right to ask for his trust.

"I can't promise, Jared, but I won't let Mitchell operate until we've exhausted all other possibilities."

He relaxed. Frank tilted the bottle to Jared's lips. Emily

slid a towel under Jared's leg and concentrated on washing dirt from the wound.

Sam entered the ward, carrying a covered iron pot.

"He's out," Frank announced, about the same time she finished scrubbing.

Emily slid another towel beneath Jared's leg. The doubts returned, but she quickly brushed them aside. "Hold him down."

Frank pressed against Jared's upper body, and Sam held Jared's foot. With the scalpel point poised, Emily breathed a small prayer, then, with one swift slash, opened the wound. Jared bucked and moaned but remained unconscious.

Emily pressed and squeezed, nearly gagging on the putrid odor of the yellow pus and black gore oozing from the gash. She kneaded the leg until blood flowed instead of muck. After pouring the remaining whiskey over the wound, she sewed it closed with small, neat stitches. If this worked, Jared would have nary a scar. If this worked.

Patients coughed and windows flew open when Emily uncovered the pot. The mixture's pungency made her eyes water. Emily dipped squares of gauze into the potion and applied them to Jared's wound.

"What is that stuff?" Frank choked out.

"Hanna's special recipe to draw out infection. We used it at Rosewood. I've seen it work, hundreds of times."

"On wounds as bad as Jared's?" Frank asked, hope creeping into his question.

Emily finished securing the bandage before admitting, "No, not quite this bad."

Water, Jared thought, as he opened his eyes. Or a beer would be better. Something, anything, to cleanse the rancid taste from his mouth.

He shifted position and was immediately sorry. He clenched his teeth to hold back a groan.

A burly hand clamped down on his shoulder. A gravelly

voice commanded, "Don't move, Jared. Emily should be here shortly to change the bandage, so don't mess it up."

Tom Reed sat in a chair at the head of the cot.

Jared glanced down at his leg, at the white bandaging wound around his calf. It hurt like the devil, but his leg was still attached.

"Why is Emily changing the bandage and not the doctor?"

Tom gave a burst of laughter. "Can that little lady of yours hit what she's shooting at?"

Jared remembered a brace of rabbits dangling from Emily's hand at Rosewood, the hole in the wall mere inches from a drunken lecher's head. "Yeah. Why?"

"Frank says she pulled a gun on Mitchell yesterday and told him to keep his hands off you. Guess he must have figured she would actually shoot him if he pressed the issue. Nobody's allowed near you without her permission."

Jared's memory of yesterday's events was a bit hazy, but he remembered enough. Emily had stopped the doctor from amputating. She'd taken over his care.

He smiled. "Tell Mitchell not to worry unless she threatens to castrate him."

Tom raised an eyebrow.

Laughing hurt, but the pain felt good, reassuring.

"When did you get back?" he asked Tom.

"Yesterday, a few hours after you and Frank. Good thing, too. We've been taking turns playing nursemaid."

"You're one ugly nurse, Reed."

Tom shrugged his hulking shoulders. "Maybe, but I make a hell of a guard. Shoot, every time that Mitchell fella walks by, he eyes up your leg like it's some damn trophy. We're making sure he doesn't get saw-happy. Your wife also wants you to sleep, so get back to it."

Emily put the basket of supplies on the floor at the foot of Jared's cot. "Good morning, Lieutenant Reed," she said absently, staring at Jared's pale, gaunt face. "Any change?"

"He woke up about a half hour ago. His voice is weak, but his spirit's good. He wanted to know why you were taking care of him and not the doctor. He also wanted me to wake him when you got here. Told him that was up to you."

She didn't want Jared awake. She wanted to change the bandage and leave before he could tell her again that he didn't want her around.

"Let's wait."

"Too late," Jared said. "Take a hike, Reed."

His voice might be weak, but the strength of Jared's will rang through in the command. Reed got up, slowly.

"I could use a walk, unless you need me for something, Mrs. Hunter."

"Find Dr. Mitchell. Jared will need pain medication."

"No drugs," Jared stated, his tone firming.

Emily crossed her arms. "This is no time to be obstinate. I can't change that bandage without hurting you."

"Better the pain than feeling nothing at all. And no more whiskey, either. I want to know what's happening."

"All I'm going to do is change the bandage. You needn't be awake for that."

He motioned for her to come closer. She stepped to the side of the cot. He captured her hand and squeezed, a measure of his tenacity emanating from the strength of his grip.

"No drugs."

Emily sat on the edge of the cot. "I know you don't have any reason to trust me right now, and I know you really don't want me here, but—"

He put a finger to her lips. "I would trust you with my life. I asked Frank to keep you away because I wanted to hear what the doctor had to say first, nothing more. I'll always want you with me, love. Believe that, please."

Her voice shook. "You can forgive me?"

"I swear, there were times in the last months when the only thing that kept me sane was the thought of coming home to you. I love you, Em. Nothing you could do has a snowball's chance in hell of stopping me."

"Oh, Jared, I love you, too." She melted into his arms, the anxiety that had plagued her dissipating. If Jared still loved her, everything else could be talked out, maybe even argued over, but righted in the end.

Almost everything.

Emily rose up. Getting Jared on his feet, both feet, might prove impossible. As hard as the words were to say, she had to be the one to tell him.

"Jared, what I did with your leg might not work. I may have only put off the inevitable. You could still lose it."

"I'm not looking for a miracle, only a fighting chance."

Five days later, Emily made her daily trek to Armory Square, to the accompaniment of every church bell in Washington.

The patients wore beaming smiles, including Jared, who was sitting on the edge of his cot, a pair of crutches nearby.

"It's really true? The war is over?" he asked.

She wished she could share his joy, but all she could muster was relief that peace, finally, was at hand.

"Lee surrendered to Grant about an hour ago, at a place called Appomattox. I hear the meeting was congenial and the terms of surrender lenient." Emily put the satchel she carried onto the cot next to Jared. "I brought your clothes. I wish you would reconsider and stay here for a few more days."

"Not a chance. I want out of here, now," he demanded, pulling a pair of underdrawers from the satchel. "Why should I stay? Dr. Mitchell comes by once a day, looks at my leg, and says it's healing beyond his expectations. I think he's still upset that he wasn't allowed to saw it off."

Tiny beads of sweat glistened along Jared's upper lip as, with a little help from Emily, he squirmed into his trousers.

"I still don't think this is a good idea," she protested, buttoning his shirt. "Something could still go wrong."

"And you would take care of me as you've done since I got here. I would think it would be easier on both of us if you didn't have to come to the hospital every day to do what you could easily do at home."

"I don't mind."

"I do." He cupped her cheek, running a thumb over her cheekbone. "Those circles under your eyes get darker every day. I don't want you getting sick because of me."

Her tiredness had little to do with the hours she spent at the hospital. But that piece of news was best delivered in private.

"All right, you win," she relented. "I'll have Sam bring the carriage up to the door. You be careful on those crutches. If you fall and break open the stitches, I'll leave you here."

By the time Zeke and Sam helped settle Jared onto the divan in the parlor, Jared had paled, but his smile was as wide as an open door.

Hanna bustled in with a tall glass of cold lemonade for Jared, and news of Papa's whereabouts. "We're havin' a party tonight, to celebrate the end of the war and the captain comin' home. The colonel's out doin' the invitin', and I got a heap of cookin' to do."

"I'll be in to help in a minute," Emily said.

"You just sit yourself down, Missy. You need your rest as much as the captain does."

As soon as Hanna left, Jared's smile turned smug. "See? I told you it was time for me to come home." He patted the edge of the divan. "So follow orders and come sit."

Emily obeyed. An unsettling quiet descended. Jared picked up her hand and ran his thumb over her wedding ring. "Are you ready to tell me about Bricker?"

They'd skirted this subject for lack of privacy, but, fully prepared for the question, Emily launched into the story from the time she'd first entered Bricker's office to the final encounter with Noah's couriers.

"So, instead of following Taylor's advice and telling either your father or me, you relied on Kate and Major Drew," he commented.

"They seemed the most logical to turn to. I knew Papa

would have a fit and keep me locked in the house. You and I weren't even on speaking terms when the whole thing started.''

"If I'd known—"

"You would have insisted on becoming involved. I didn't want that. It was my problem to solve, and I did so in the best way I knew how.''

"You could have been hurt.''

"I considered the risks before I agreed to meet with Noah's couriers, just as you considered the risks before you went into Libby.'' Emily crossed her arms and said sternly, "Or I thought you had. Someone conveniently forgot to mention that he could get himself hanged, didn't he? Or that Morgan was a guard?''

Jared squirmed slightly, but whether from a twinge of pain or from pangs of guilt, Emily wasn't sure.

"The possibility was so remote that it wasn't worth mentioning. I didn't want you to worry.''

"The editors of the Richmond newspapers thought it rated front-page headlines. How could I not worry?''

"I've made front-page headlines before, and you know how misleading some of those stories were. What bothers me is that you didn't tell me, not even after it was all over.''

"I know I should have,'' she admitted. "But at the time, I didn't see much point. It wasn't until after you'd left for Richmond that I realized how Colonel Bricker could use those notes. Did he show them to you?''

"He showed them to me, all right, saying you'd wanted revenge. But the information you passed wasn't worth the paper it was written on. If you'd wanted revenge, there were other, more damaging pieces of information you could have given him.''

That hurt, a little, hearing that he'd based his judgment on solid evidence, instead of trusting in her. But that was Jared's nature. He had always based his conclusions, decisions, and plan of action on all the facts, and he always would.

"Look,'' he said on a sigh. "You did what you thought

you had to do. I did what I thought was right. Let's just leave it at that and go on from here, strive to be more open with each other in the future.''

"Pretend nothing ever happened?"

"No, but we can put it in the past, where it belongs. The war is over. I'm not going on any more hazardous missions, and you won't be taking any more life-threatening risks."

The time had come to reveal her latest secret. "Jared, life is full of risks. Just because the war is over, that doesn't mean there won't be risks."

Jared's eyes narrowed. "I don't like the way you said that. What's happening, Emily?"

She smiled. "I'm going to have a baby."

"Baby," he whispered. With splayed fingers, Jared's large hand covered her abdomen in a shielding gesture. "When?"

She placed her hand over his. "By mid-October, you won't be able to get your arms around me."

His awe succumbed to concern. "You've seen Doc El-lis?"

"I submitted to a thorough, rather mortifying examination. I'm fine, Jared, and so is our baby."

"You'll be more careful this time," he commanded, then softened it with "After what happened last time... Lord, Em, I couldn't endure losing you."

"Don't you want children?"

"Yes, but only if it's safe for you to have them."

"I'm at no more risk than any other woman who bears a child. It's never safe, but the only way for us to have children is for me to bear them."

Jared took a long time to wrestle with his fears, the same fears she'd put to rest a month ago.

"Well, that settles it, then," he finally said. "Guess I'll have to keep this leg after all. I mean, I can't teach my son or daughter how to ride if I can't get on a horse myself, now, can I?"

"You would manage, somehow. And if you couldn't teach him, I could. There are more important lessons he'll learn from his father, like courage, tenacity, self-confidence."

He touched her cheek. "All lessons he could learn from his mother. You know, we've been together all these months, yet we've led separate lives, each of us making our own way through whatever we've felt needed doing. But this, raising a child, is a two-person assignment. Actually, when we aren't trying so hard not to, we *do* make a pretty good team."

Emily smiled. "You make raising a child sound like one of your missions."

"In a way, I think it is. But for this task, I want—need— a partner. What do you say, Em? You and me? Together, this time?"

Jared wasn't only talking about raising a child, but making a marriage—a good one. Partners. Sounded like a solid plan. And who better to team up with than a man who'd become a legend for completing daring, rigorous missions?

"I love you, Captain Hunter."

"And I love you, Mrs. Hunter, which is the only reason I think the whole thing might work."

Her smile widened. "Where do I go to enlist?"

Gently he pulled her downward. "Right here, love. Right here."

With a long, deep kiss, Emily signed on for life.

* * * * *

Happy Birthday to

**It's party time....
This year is our
40th anniversary!**

Forty years of
bringing you the best
in romance fiction—and
the best just keeps
getting better!

To celebrate, we're planning
three months of fun, and prizes.

Not to mention, of course,
some fabulous books...

The party starts in **April** with:

Betty Neels
Emma Richmond
Kate Denton
Barbara McMahon

Come join the party!